Nich... with
strong heroine...
hell of a ...
and ...
Utah. When she's not writing ...
herself running, rock climbing, practicing ...
snowboarding. She loves hearing from readers through
her website, www.nicholesevern.com, and on Twitter,
@nicholesevern

Justine Davis lives on Puget Sound in Washington State,
watching big ships and the occasional submarine go by
and sharing the neighbourhood with assorted wildlife,
including a pair of bald eagles, deer, a bear or two and a
tailless raccoon. In the few hours when she's not
planning, plotting or writing her next book, her favourite
things are photography, knitting her way through a huge
yarn stash and driving her restored 1967 Corvette
roadster—top down, of course.

Connect with Justine on her website, justinedavis.com,
at Twitter.com/justine_d_davis or on Facebook at
Facebook.com/justinedaredavis

Also by Nichole Severn

Also by Justine Davis

Discover more at millsandboon.co.uk

RULES IN DECEIT

NICHOLE SEVERN

COLTON'S SECRET INVESTIGATION

JUSTINE DAVIS

MILLS & BOON

First Published in Great Britain 2019
by Mills & Boon, an imprint of HarperCollins*Publishers*
1 London Bridge Street, London, SE1 9GF

Rules in Deceit © 2019 Natascha Jaffa
Colton's Secret Investigation © 2019 by Harlequin Books S.A.

Special thanks and acknowledgement are given to Justine Davis for her contribution to the *Coltons of Roaring Springs* series.

ISBN: 978-0-263-27447-9

1119

MIX
Paper from
responsible sources
FSC™ C007454

RULES IN DECEIT

NICHOLE SEVERN

To my Bat Signal group, this book never would've
gotten finished—twice—without you.

Chapter One

"You're not dead." Rage and relief urged Elizabeth Dawson to push away from the conference room table and tackle her former partner to the floor, but she held her control.

"It's good to see you, too, Sprinkles." Braxton Levitt's rich, seductive voice skittered under her skin. The sound of his handpicked nickname for her on his lips— as if they were still friends—tightened the muscles down her spine. That gray gaze pinned her against the back of her chair. A rare occasion. His eyes were normally green, depending on what he wore. She pushed the useless fact to the back of her mind as he planted his elbows on the massive wood table, leaning forward. Thick muscle and tendons flexed beneath his thin T-shirt, and goose bumps prickled down her arms. After all this time, did he honestly think he could walk back into her life after what he'd done?

"Don't call me that." No matter how many times she'd imagined this moment—of confronting him after all these months—there'd always been a small part of grief lodged in her chest. Her fingers curled into the center of her palms beneath the table. She had to stay in control. He wasn't the man she thought he'd been. Her heartbeat pounded loud behind her ears. Something alive—full of fury—clawed its way up her throat, but she couldn't touch him. Not in any way that counted. He'd made damn sure of that when she'd been pulled into countless interrogations after his disappearance. He cost her a career she'd spent a decade building. Now, no one but Blackhawk Security would hire her. Too much of a risk. Elizabeth mirrored his movements, clasping her hands in front of her on top of the table. "You paid my boss for my time, so get on with it. What do you want, Braxton?"

Despite the federal charges stacked against him, Braxton leaned back in his chair as he ran one hand through his dark shoulder-length hair, completely at ease. No longer was he the clean-cut, out-of-shape intelligence analyst she'd known back at the NSA. He'd changed, now something more primal, as though he'd seen things he couldn't possibly forget. New, bulky muscle stretched against the seams in his clothing. Physically different, yet the same man reflected underneath the confidence in his eyes, in his heart-stopping, manipulative smile. Under all those changes, he was still the man who'd walked out on her.

"I missed you." Stubble ran along his jawline, a little fuller than she remembered, deepening the permanent laugh lines around his mouth. She'd once missed the effects of that smile, the gut-clenching delirium he brought to the surface from no more than the upward tilt of his lips. The trust. Scary what that smile could hide.

"Is that why you're here?" she asked. "Because you missed me?"

The blue ball cap pulled low over his head failed to hide the bottom of a scar cut through his left eyebrow he'd gotten during a fight as a teenager. He studied the dark, rainy view of the Chugach mountain range through the floor-to-ceiling windows as if her words hadn't registered then recentered on her. He tapped his fingers against the gleaming conference room table as he sat back in his chair. "No." His shoulders rose on a deep inhale. "Dalton Meyer is dead. Someone tied your old NSA supervisor to a chair and tortured him so they could hijack Oversight and find you. I'm here to make sure that doesn't happen."

Elizabeth's blood iced. "That's not possible."

The facial-recognition program she'd been contracted to build for the NSA had the highest level of security ever coded. She'd designed the system to run autonomously. No human interference. Not even the director of the NSA had access. Its job was to strictly surveil the American population to identify threats to national security using security cameras, traffic cameras, email scanning. Law enforcement, FBI, CIA—they all relied on those feeds. If they'd gone off-line or been hijacked as Braxton suggested…the possibilities were endless.

The threats were endless.

Elizabeth released the breath she'd been holding. There was only one other person in the world who had the ability to override Oversight's programming. And he sat across the table from her. "How did you find me?"

"The fact I'm sitting here says a simple name change isn't working for you, Sprinkles," he said. "If I was able to find you in less than twenty-four hours, how long do you think it'll take someone who's hijacked your program and is gunning for you?"

"Stop calling me that. We're not friends anymore." Her jaw tightened. She followed passing movement outside the conference room through the blinds. Blackhawk Security provided home security, protection and investigative services and handled military contracts. She'd left the NSA behind, left that life behind. She'd moved on. Whatever this was, whatever Braxton wanted from her... No. Protecting her clients was her life now. Sullivan Bishop, Blackhawk Security's founder and CEO, and the rest of the team had taken a chance on her. Trained her without questions about her past. She wasn't about to blow it based on some wild theory the man who'd turned on her had cooked up to come back into her life. If someone had tortured her former project supervisor and was using her own program to hunt her, she had an entire team she could count on now. Former SEALs, Rangers, con men, a profiler. She didn't need him.

"Is that all you thought we were? Friends?" Braxton studied her, staring up at her from below thick, dark eyebrows. "I remember that night, Liz. Hard to believe I was that easy to forget."

"I haven't forgotten anything." She fought against the urge to swipe her hand across her lower abdomen. She'd waited four long months for this moment. Time to get it over with. Time to move on from him. "Since you've brought up that night, you should know I've been trying to find you for a few weeks now to tell you I'm pregnant."

Braxton sat forward in his chair, staring at her from across the table. "H-how?"

Really? That was the question he wanted her to answer? "You want me to explain to you how a woman gets pregnant? Okay. You see, when a woman thinks she's in love with her best friend she's trusted for years—"

"That's not what I meant." He exhaled hard. "We were careful. We used protection."

"Yes, well, obviously that didn't work." The pressure of his full attention tightened her insides. Liquid fire burned through her. She swallowed hard against the sensation. He wasn't supposed to affect her like this. Her crush had ended the night he'd left her to pick up the pieces of his mess. He exuded confidence with his subtle movements. The haze clouding her head dissipated, and she forced everything inside her to go cold as she stood. Digging for her phone, she swiped her thumb across the screen and set the timer. "Now, if you came here for my help, you're out of luck. I don't work for the NSA anymore. So I hope you've got your money's worth. This meeting is over. I'll give you a ten-minute head start before I call the FBI."

"You're being hunted, and you just told me you're pregnant with my baby." Braxton pushed away from the table. Three distinct lines deepened at the bridge of his nose. A day's worth of dark stubble that matched his hair shifted over his strong jaw. "I'm not going anywhere."

"I bet all the girls fall for that line. And, to be fair, I tried to tell you before now, but I couldn't find you." Elizabeth reached for the large oak door. Her instincts screamed for her to put as much space between them as she could. Her muscles had tensed so hard she ached. What did he expect her to do? Take him at his word that he was here to protect her? That he didn't need something from her? Not happening. She flashed her phone's screen at him. "Nine minutes. You're wasting time, Braxton."

He moved fast. Faster than she thought possible. His rough hands pressed into the door, hiking her blood pressure higher as he caged her in the circle of his massive arms. The faint scent of soap and his own masculine scent filled the air, urging her to breathe him in deeper. Two years as coworkers. He'd recruited her for the NSA, helped her land the contract of her career. Taken her to his bed.

"I'm the only one who can protect you, Liz. You know that," he said.

Fury built behind her sternum. A deadly wrath that couldn't be contained anymore.

"How would I know that?" Only the pounding of her heart working overtime filled her ears as she leveled her chin with the floor. She'd been naive to think anything could work between them. Elizabeth fisted her hands at her sides to control the trembling raking through her. She'd trusted him to the end. Denied the allegations the NSA had thrown at her in those interrogations after he vanished.

Braxton Levitt had an entire arsenal of body language, stories and personalities to force his marks into believing he was who he claimed. That was all she was to him. All she had been to him. A mark. "Everything I knew about you turned out to be a lie."

He straightened but kept her caged against the door. "I never lied to you."

"Really? Up until four months ago, I thought we knew everything about each other. You recruited me for the NSA to build Oversight, became the only person I could trust, then took me to your bed, and that same night, you disappeared." The last word hissed from her mouth. She lowered her voice in case the doors weren't soundproofed. "Now you're here, asking me to trust you with my life?" Elizabeth stepped into him, his clean scent surrounding her. It took everything she had—every last reserve of energy—to keep her control in place. "I don't know a damn thing about you, Braxton. I don't think I ever did. Now, let me go before I find a reason to reach for my gun."

His expression fell as he stepped back, taking his body heat with him. "I would never hurt you."

Her heart jolted in her chest from the sincerity in his voice. She studied him with a new mind-set. No emotion. No ties back to the past. Not as a spurned one-night stand but as an operative of Blackhawk Security. The creases around his mouth and the hollow circles under his eyes revealed the exhaustion he'd been dealing with since his disappearance. Worry lines, perhaps? A man on the run certainly became paranoid once stepping back into the spotlight. Every federal organization in the country had searched high and low for him since his disappearance. How had he managed to stay under the radar all this time? Whom had he relied on for help?

Not her. She locked her back teeth together. Didn't matter. This was the last time they'd be in the same room together. He'd slide back under the radar, and she'd go back to doing what she did best: protecting herself—and their baby. She wasn't heartless. She'd just taught herself how to use her heart less. Elizabeth's short black hair slid out from behind her ears as she wrenched the door open. "You already have."

A deep rumble reached her ears, claiming her attention a split second before Braxton shoved her into the hallway, and an eight-foot solid oak door rocketed into her.

BRAXTON LEVITT SLAMMED face-first into the nearest wall. Heat tunneled through his clothing as glass rained down around him. Emergency lighting cast the entire floor into shades of red as alarms kept rhythm with his pulse. He shifted his weight into his hands, flexing his jaw against the pain spreading through his ribs. Something wet slid down his cheek. He swiped at it as a gust of cold Alaskan air and rain rushed through what used to be an entire wall of windows. Blood.

"Liz!" Squinting through the rising smoke, he shoved to his feet. He blinked as a wave of dizziness tipped him into a fern still standing beside the one unhinged door. Yells punctured through the ringing in his ears. The sprinkler system fought to drench the sporadic fires clinging to the walls and the remains of the conference table. He stumbled through what was left of the massive door frame. "You better be alive."

Pain seared through his rib cage. His temples throbbed in rhythm to the alarms. She had to be alive. If he lost her again… No. He couldn't go there. Couldn't think like that. A dull ringing filled his ears. Then a moan. *Her* moan. Braxton's insides burned with an energy he'd learned to contain. A pair of familiar black boots registered in his peripheral vision. "Liz."

Air stalled in his lungs. Not because he'd nearly died in the timed explosion but because for thirty horrible, mind-numbing seconds, he'd lost her all over again. The hollowness of four months and ten days' separation from her vanished as he hauled an oak door and a few other pieces of debris off her with a guttural groan.

Brushing her hair out of her face, he lifted her into him, and the rest of the world fell away. Lean muscle flexed beneath her black leggings and leather jacket as her hand moved to her lower abdomen. Flames crackled around them, sirens already echoing off the surrounding buildings in the street below, but he didn't give a damn. His body's response to Liz had always been off the charts. She'd been the only woman who could make him lose control. Still was. Black smudges highlighted the sharp edges of her cheekbones and jawline. The steady thump at the base of her throat relieved the pressure in his chest, but that relief didn't last long. The bastard who'd hijacked Oversight had set a bomb—for Liz. He was sure of it. That rumbling sound right before the explosion? Had to have been a cell phone on vibrate. A detonator. He should've known the SOB hunting her would've tried to get to her at work. The more casualties, the better chance he had of getting away with murder. More time, more evidence to sift through. Braxton fought the rage spreading rampant beneath his sternum. "Come on, baby, open your eyes. Can you hear me?"

"For once in your life, call me by my actual name." A cough ripped up her throat. She jerked in his arms. Once. Twice. Brown eyes, as dark as chocolate, focused on him. "You do remember what it is, don't you?"

A smile fought for release. He'd missed her fire. Her attitude. Missed her. They'd been a great team back in Fort Meade. Saving the country one line of code at a time. Back before he'd destroyed everything between them to keep her safe. The smile disappeared. None of that mattered now. Keeping her alive—that was all that mattered.

"We've got to go." They had to get out of here before whoever had set that bomb realized he hadn't killed his target. Her lavender-scented shampoo invigorated his senses as she wrapped both arms around him, raising goose bumps on the back of his neck. It'd been a long time since he'd breathed her in. He tightened his hold around her waist. Get her to safety. Find the man using her own program to kill her. Maybe convince her he wasn't the man she believed.

"Liz!" Blackhawk Security's founder and CEO, Sullivan Bishop, shielded his face from the flames as he ran toward them. Braxton had done his homework. He knew the former SEAL had a woman of his own—a JAG Corps prosecutor—but the use of one of his nicknames for her still grated on Braxton's nerves. Liz didn't let anyone give her a nickname. The two had obviously gotten close since she'd relocated to Anchorage, and his gut tightened in response. One of the other operatives followed close on Sullivan's heels. Blackhawk's disgraced NYPD officer, Vincent Kalani, studied the scene, ready for battle. "You all right?"

"I'm fine." Liz wrenched out of Braxton's grasp, struggling to her feet on her own, all contact between them severed. She brushed debris from her clothing and huffed a piece of hair out of her face. From the outside, it was such an innocent movement, but Braxton understood her tells. He always had. Despite her hard exterior, she'd been rattled. And with good reason. Someone had tried to kill her. But she refused to allow anyone to see vulnerability, especially those she worked with. "But I think it's safe to say our conference room is not. Was anybody hurt in the explosion?"

"No fatalities. From what we can tell, most suffered only minor burns and scrapes from the blast." The forensics expert—Vincent—checked a gash on his forearm, swiping the blood away against his long-sleeve shirt. The muscled, tattooed Hawaiian ran a hand through his shoulder-length brown hair. "Was anyone else in the conference room with you?"

Liz shook her head. "No. Just the two of us."

"Good. As much as I'd like to scour through debris for evidence of who attacked us, let's get to the street. Then you tell me who the hell detonated a bomb in my building." Sullivan turned down the long hallway leading past several now-empty offices, a med clinic and the elevators and stairwell.

"Whoever it was targeted Liz," Braxton said.

Liz rounded into his vision. "There's no evidence proving that bomb was meant for me."

Sullivan twisted around, lips thin, hands ready to tear into the person responsible. "You used to work for the NSA, right? Sold classified intel and disappeared?" The CEO closed the distance between them, expression hard, calculating. "How do I know it wasn't you who set a bomb in my conference room? Some sick game to get Elizabeth back in your life."

"I'd kill any one of you before I let something happen to her. Is that a good enough answer for you?" Braxton straightened, surveying Vincent's position in case the ex-cop made a move, then centered on Sullivan again. "The only thing that matters is this guy is going to keep gunning for her. I'm not going to let that happen."

"Let's move out." Sullivan didn't take his attention off Braxton. "I don't trust you, Levitt." Veins pulsed under the skin of the CEO's arms as he pointed a dirt-smudged finger at him. "If anything happens to her, I will find you, understand?"

"I get that a lot." Despite the threat, Braxton didn't take offense. Liz had an entire team watching her back. He couldn't fault the former Navy SEAL for protecting a member in his unit.

Vincent rounded behind him and Liz to take up the rear with silent obedience.

The sirens grew louder. First responders had arrived on the scene.

But Braxton didn't move. The bomber hadn't attacked Blackhawk Security. Not directly. The bastard had had only one target in mind, and he was staring right at her. The bomb was just the beginning. Whoever had set it would try again as soon as they realized Liz had survived. And what better way to ensure a target had been killed than enter the building as an EMT or firefighter for confirmation? Braxton lowered his voice, instincts prickling. There was more at stake now. They had a baby to consider. He shifted closer to her, pain radiating at the base of his skull as they made their way down the hallway, and lowered his voice to prevent the security cameras from picking up their conversation. "Listen to me, Liz. We can't go to the street."

"Wow, you do remember my name." Liz moved to follow her colleagues.

He threaded his fingers around her arm and pulled her to a stop, holding her against him. The small fires burning around them had nothing on her body heat tunneling through his clothing right then. He covered his mouth and nose in the crook of his arm. "The garage. The only way in is with a key card, right? One exit? He'll expect us down on the street with the others. Not exiting the garage."

"What are you talking about?" She wrenched away from him as though his touch had burned her, his fingertips tingling from the friction against her jacket. Those dark brown eyes locked on him. One second. Two. Wisps of her uneven exhales tickled the oversensitized skin along his neck as she turned on him. "You're insane if you think I'm going anywhere with you."

Damn her stubbornness. One day it was going to get her killed. And then where would he be? He couldn't find the bastard hunting her down without her. No matter how many times he'd tried to keep his distance, every road, every move to stay off the Feds' radar had led him to Anchorage…to her. He didn't care that her program might've already recognized him and reported his location to the NSA. He wasn't going to leave her unprotected again.

The floor rumbled underneath his feet. The explosion had most likely damaged the building's structure. They didn't have a whole lot of time.

"We need to get moving." Vincent stepped toward them as Blackhawk Security's CEO disappeared into a cloud of smoke toward the stairwell. Close enough for Braxton to reach out and touch him.

He didn't want to have to do this, but the hard determination in Liz's gaze said he didn't have any other choice. "All right. If you're not going to come with me willingly—" Braxton spun, wrapping his grip around the Sig Sauer in Vincent's shoulder holster, and twisted the weapon out of the cop's reach. With one hard swing of the butt of the gun to the operative's head, Vincent went down. Hard. Braxton hefted the gun up, attention leveled on the shocked woman in front of him.

Liz lunged for the unconscious operative. "What the hell are you doing?"

"I'm kidnapping you. Once the bomber realizes you're not dead, we lose the upper hand." He pointed to her jacket with the barrel of the gun. "Toss your sidearm. Please."

"Do you honestly expect me to leave him here?"

Digging beneath the leather, she tossed her handgun to the floor.

"Of course not. Rescue is already on the way." He kicked the weapon out of her reach and motioned her to her feet. "Head for the garage."

"You should shoot me now, because I'm sure as hell going to shoot you when I get the chance." She rose slowly, expression controlled, voice dropping into dangerous territory. Her almond-shaped eyes narrowed on him. Exhaustion—maybe a bit of pain from the blast— broke through her movements as she stepped around the unconscious forensics expert at her feet.

"Wouldn't expect anything less from you." The muscles in Braxton's arms and neck tensed. In the thousands of times he'd imagined this moment, this wasn't how he'd expected their reunion to turn out. But there was a killer on the loose, and he wasn't about to lose her again. Not Liz. And not their baby. She shifted in front of him. Every second she stayed out in the open notched his blood pressure higher. "I'm trying to save your life, damn it. Trust me."

"Stop asking me to trust you." Liz headed for the stairwell, fire reflecting in her dark gaze. "I'm still trying to get over the last time you betrayed me."

Chapter Two

A wall of cold slammed into Elizabeth as they hit the parking garage. Only a handful of Blackhawk Security vehicles waited in their assigned spaces. There was no mysterious bomber waiting to ambush them as Braxton had suggested upstairs, but the illusion of safety never settled.

Could have had something to do with the fact the man she'd thought she'd loved all those months ago— the man whose child she carried—had a gun pressed against her spine. Smoke still registered on the air, the flashing of emergency lights bouncing off the cement walls from the street. There were only two ways out of the garage, and a bomb had taken out one of them. The other was the gate leading to the street, but she didn't reach for the key card all operatives were required to carry. And she wouldn't. Not until she had some answers. Scanning the SUVs, Elizabeth stopped dead in her tracks. "What's the plan now?"

"Now we get out of here." Braxton pressed his hand into the small of her back, bringing her into his side as he moved them toward one of the SUVs. His natural scent wrapped around her, but she didn't find comfort there like she used to. "Don't suppose you brought a set of car keys?"

"Must've left them in the jacket that doesn't smell like smoke." Pain washed through her. She glanced down at the gun aimed into her rib cage then quickly back to their surroundings as they closed in on the nearest SUV. Safety still on. Interesting. Sweat dripped down her spine as rain struck the cement at the edges of the asphalt. Him coming back here, the explosion… Her pulse throbbed at the base of her skull. This was insane. That bomb could've been meant for any operative on the team. For all she knew, it could've been meant for him. So why come back? Blackhawk Security wasn't in the habit of filling in the authorities on their clients, but her boss should've made an exception for Braxton Levitt. The NSA wouldn't stop looking for him. He'd never be a free man as long as treason charges were on the table. "What makes you think whoever set that bomb is targeting me?"

"Someone tortured your project supervisor and hijacked Oversight." He kept his attention on the prize ahead, occasionally studying their surroundings as they moved. Ten feet until they reached the nearest SUV. His expression tightened beneath the shadows cast from the baseball cap. "Call it instinct."

"Tell me you're joking." Elizabeth ripped away from his touch and shoved him away. He wouldn't use the gun on her. This entire kidnapping was a charade. "That's not enough evidence to insert yourself back into my life. You left, Braxton. You lost the right to pretend you care about anybody other than yourself."

The green-gray eyes she'd been trying to forget for the last four months locked on her, those mountainous shoulders deflating beneath his heavy brown jacket. "Liz—"

The stairwell door slammed closed behind them. Braxton twisted back over his shoulder, hefting the gun up and over toward the imagined threat. He stepped in front of her as though he intended to protect her from harm. But he wasn't a protector. No matter how many times he claimed he'd come back to keep her safe.

Thrusting her knee into the back of his, Elizabeth pushed him forward. The gun dropped to the pavement, metal on asphalt loud in her ears as he fought to balance. Lunging for it, she barely wrapped her fingers around the grip before he pulled her upright, his grip on her wrist cutting off circulation. Damn, he moved fast.

His breath fanned across the sensitive skin along her collarbones. Warmth spread from her neck up into her cheeks as he held her close, his mouth mere centimeters from hers. A mouth meant for spilling lies. "I'm not here to hurt you, Liz. I would never hurt you."

Did she really have to remind him there were more ways to hurt her than the physical? He'd destroyed her career, gotten her pregnant and disappeared. It wasn't until Sullivan Bishop and the Blackhawk Security team had offered her a place as their network security analyst three months ago that she'd started pulling the shattered pieces of her life back together. Without them, who knew where she would be right now.

"Let me go." She fought to free herself, but Braxton only held her tighter. Once upon a time, she would've enjoyed that strong grip around her. Her insides instantly clenched. Now, the only thought running through her head centered on getting as far from him as possible. "What do you want from me?"

Her hand shook around the warm steel of the gun. She couldn't let him get inside her head.

"I want you alive, for starters." He pressed her against him, his fingertips leaving impressions in the small of her back. He studied her from forehead to chin. "If that means I have to knock you unconscious and throw you over my shoulder, I will."

Air rushed from her lungs. The sincerity in his gaze, in his voice… He meant it. A short burst from one of the police sirens tensed the muscles down her spine but brought her back into the moment. "You actually believe someone is trying to kill me?"

"I have the proof." Braxton released his hold on her wrist but let her keep the gun. Offering her a hand, he gave her the space to make the choice for herself. "All you have to do is trust me."

"You make it sound so easy." Every cell in her body urged her to take his hand. The sharp angles to his jaw, the heavy five o'clock shadow, the slight bend in his nose where he'd broken it playing football one summer, even the thin slice of scar across his palm where he'd slipped on ice in elementary school… It was all so familiar. Comforting. But she didn't know this man. The Braxton she'd known never would've deserted her in the first place. She forced her attention to his eyes.

"If I agree to go with you, you will answer every question I have."

"I give you my word." His voice dropped an octave. Sensual, compelling.

Her chest tightened on a deep inhale. She loosened her grip around the gun, the tingling sensation in her fingers subsiding as she leveled her chin with the asphalt. Handing over Vincent's stolen Sig Sauer, Elizabeth drew back when his fingers closed on top of hers. In an almost militaristic manner, he cleared the loaded round, dropped the magazine, slammed it back into place and chambered another. No. Whoever stood in front of her wasn't *her* Braxton. This man was hardened, muscled. Dangerous. She exhaled against the nausea churning inside. "And when this is over, you'll crawl back to the rock you've been hiding under for the last four months. Are we clear?"

The lines etched between his dark eyebrows deepened. He dropped the gun to his side, so casual she'd believe he'd handled a firearm all his life. Which wasn't the case. "Do you remember what I said to you that first day we met?"

The words forced their way forward from the back of her mind. Her throat tightened around the memory of her first day of working for the NSA, the day she'd met him. She swiped her tongue across her dry lips. "I sat down at the desk next to yours with my ice cream from the cafeteria, and you made fun of my choice of topping." Rainbow-colored sprinkles. The nickname he'd called her ever since. A smile pulled at one edge of her mouth. "Then you said, 'One thing you need to understand here, Sprinkles. This place will eat you alive. Stick with me, and no matter what happens, you can count on me to get you out of it.'" A hint of smoke coming off his clothing singed deep into her lungs as she focused on him. "And I believed you."

"Do you still believe me?" he asked.

Yes. No. Her stomach flipped. If someone was trying to kill her, she wouldn't stand around here all day waiting for it to happen. "I don't know what to believe."

Movement registered in her peripheral vision at the automatic gate. A firefighter. He'd presumably been assigned to check the rest of the building for signs of structural damage and flames. Dressed in full protective equipment, including face shield, he stopped just outside the gate and tried to pull it up manually. Wouldn't work. That gate didn't open for anybody unless they worked in the building. He'd have to get the fire code from her boss, Sullivan Bishop. Stiffness drained from the muscles around her spine a split second before the gate lifted on its own. "Everything okay down here?"

Braxton turned, maneuvering the gun behind his back. Out of sight.

"We're fine. How'd you get in? That gate is supposed to be sealed." Warning bells rang loud in her head. That wasn't right. Nobody could access that gate—not even emergency personnel—without a Blackhawk Security operative key card or individualized code. She dropped her voice as the firefighter advanced. Too fast. Alone. "Braxton…"

The firefighter lifted a handgun and took aim. At her.

A strong hand pushed her to the ground as a bullet

ripped past her ear. The garage turned on its axis. Braxton took position in front of her as he returned fire. Pain shot up through her knees, loose asphalt ripping holes in her leggings, but Elizabeth didn't hesitate. Digging in her jacket pocket, she wrapped her hand around the keys to her company SUV near the shooter and hit the panic button.

Headlights flashed; the alarm blared. It'd only distract the shooter for a few seconds, but that was all she needed. The gunfire died. She shoved to her feet and sprinted for Elliot Dunham's SUV. Blackhawk Security's private investigator usually left his keys in the front seat, and she silently prayed he hadn't changed up his routine. "Come on!"

Footsteps echoed close behind her as bullets two and three barely missed their mark. Chunks of cement nicked at her exposed skin, and she raised her arms to protect her face. Wouldn't do a damn bit of good against a bullet, but instinct and adrenaline drove her now. She rounded the tail end of Elliot's SUV and wrenched the door open. No keys. She dived inside, ripping the visor down. The keys dropped into her lap.

Braxton took cover behind the hood, squeezing off another shot. Then a third.

"Get in!" Elizabeth pulled the driver's side door closed and started the engine. Shoving the SUV into Drive, she paused as the shooter positioned himself directly in front of them.

Hiking himself into the back seat, Braxton tapped on her shoulder. "Liz, go!"

The firefighter raised his gun, taking aim. One second. Two. And fired.

She froze as the bulletproof glass held against the shot. Then unfroze as rage coursed through her. The shooter had come for *her*, targeted *her*. Lifting her foot from the brake, she slammed on the accelerator and steered directly into the shooter. The growl of the engine drowned the pounding of her heartbeat in her ears. Pressure built in her lungs. "Hang on back there."

Her leather seat protested against his grip on the headrest. "Liz…"

The shooter pulled the trigger two more times, each bullet caught in the windshield, a split second before he launched himself out of the way of the vehicle.

Elizabeth spun the steering wheel toward the still-open security gate. Bouncing in her seat as they catapulted over the gate's tracks, she fishtailed out of the garage. Blackhawk Security grew distant in the rearview mirror. Two familiar faces stepped into the middle of the road behind them, but she didn't have time to stop and explain everything to her team. Braxton had been telling the truth.

Someone was targeting her, but she wasn't the only one she had to worry about now. She lifted her gaze to the rearview mirror, to the father of her unborn baby. "Fine. You can take me to whatever safe house you've set up until we figure out who you think is trying to kill me. But to be clear, it's not because I trust you." Elizabeth took a deep breath, her ribs aching from the explosion in the conference room, then forced her attention back to the road. "It's because you got me pregnant."

"I STILL CAN'T believe it." Braxton couldn't think. Couldn't breathe. Someone had tried to kill the woman he vowed to protect, but it was more than that. Adrenaline drained from his veins in small increments, but not enough to clear his head.

Wow. Liz was pregnant. And he was the father. She'd told him before the explosion, but he hadn't been able to process that until now. It'd been kind of hard to think when the bullets were flying. Reaction—that was what he was good at. But…he was going to be a father. A smile threatened to overwhelm his features, pure joy exploding through him.

"Someone just tried to kill us. Twice. Can we please focus on that?" The weight of her attention pinned him against his seat from the rearview mirror. "I think we have bigger problems to talk about."

"I think the fact you're pregnant is pretty big." He swayed with the SUV as she wound through neighborhoods, around strip malls and into the edges of the city. Days of staying off the grid, months of grueling physical training, years of working for the NSA…none of it had prepared him for this. A baby. He compressed the safety button on the stolen gun and set it beside him on the seat. They were going to have a baby. "Might as well not have used protection at all."

"Yeah, apparently, latex wasn't strong enough for your swimmers." A hint of a smile played across her mouth, the first softening of her guard since he set sights on her in the conference room. "If you're thinking about asking me whether or not I'm sure the baby is yours, I'll save you the time. Yes, Braxton, she's yours.

No, Braxton, I haven't been with anybody else since the night you took me to bed then disappeared without a word. And, yes, I'm keeping the baby. I plan to raise her on my own without help. Any other questions?"

"It's a girl?" He ran his palms over the baseball cap and interlaced his fingers at the crown of his head. He turned away from her, surveying the curve of the street but not really seeing where they were. The muscles across his back strained under the self-induced pressure. He didn't know what else to say, what to think. They were having a girl?

"I found out the sex a couple days ago." The vulnerability in her voice compelled him to face her again, but she'd turned her gaze back to the road. Snow and ice kicked up along the SUV. She rolled her lips between her teeth. "This wasn't how I wanted you to find out. I tried to find you, but four months is a long time waiting for you to come back. Figured you'd moved on and I could do the same. When I got tired of the NSA interrogating me about your whereabouts, I changed my name in every federal database I could hack and relocated."

He'd known about her search effort but ultimately decided to stay away. It'd been the hardest decision of his life and the only way to keep her safe. Until four days ago when he'd learned about Dalton Meyer's murder and that Oversight's feeds had been hacked. Until he'd uncovered the program's surveillance logs. Someone had put her in their crosshairs.

Intense pressure built behind his sternum as she took a sharp left. The city came into focus for the first time since Braxton had gotten in the vehicle. A familiar line of bare trees surrounding Fairview Lions Park cut off his air. A good foot of snow covered the all-too-familiar horseshoe pit and most of the green and purple playground where he'd spent countless nights as a kid after his father had lost the house to the bank. Right there, under the small rock wall. He forced his attention back to the rearview mirror as a group of homeless made their way down the street, back to her, his anchor. No point in studying the weathered faces as they passed. His old man had most likely died from his addictions a long time ago. Wasn't important. The past was dead, and he sure as hell would make sure it stayed that way. "Did you also figure moving here was enough to keep me from finding you?"

"I'd accepted you weren't coming back." Liz cocked her head. "In retrospect, I guess Anchorage had been on my mind since you told me you'd never step foot in this city again. It'd worked until an hour ago." She glanced at him—almost too fast for him to catch it— then back to the road. "You never told me how you managed to find me."

"You're predictable. I knew you'd never change your first name." Not after what she'd told him about her mother and the long line of Elizabeths in her family. "As for your new last name, I remembered your favorite TV show growing up. Wasn't hard to sift through the short list of Elizabeth Dawsons and track you down from there."

Nothing would've stopped him from finding her.

"I'll keep that in mind next time." Her knuckles tightened over the steering wheel. There wouldn't be a next time. Not if he had anything to say about it. She turned the SUV east, leaving the park and memories he'd worked hard to bury behind. "So are you going to tell me where this safe house of yours is or are we going to drive around all night?"

"Make one more loop around the neighborhood." Braxton studied the cars behind them. They hadn't been followed. Whoever had taken shots at them in the parking garage probably hadn't been able to make it past the wall of police officers and emergency personnel surrounding the building. At least, not in a hurry. On top of that, her team had seen them race from the scene. His pulse hammered at the base of his skull, and he wiped at the dried patches of blood along his forehead. He should've known the bastard would come at her at Blackhawk Security. As far as he'd been able to tell over the last few days, that was where she'd spent most of her time. Day and night. Protecting her clients just as she'd protected millions of lives during her contract work for the NSA. And now with a baby. "Have you told your team?"

"No. Not yet." Her shoulders rose on an audible inhale. Hesitation tightened the cords running down her neck. She made another turn, seemingly refusing to look back at him. "I was thinking of telling Sullivan about the baby today, but then someone blew up the conference room and it sort of slipped to the back of my mind."

A laugh escaped from his control. She always did have a way of downplaying stressful situations with sarcasm. "Understandable."

"I work in network security now." Liz ran a hand through her hair and levered her elbow against the driver's side door. "My clients come to me to assess their firewalls, encrypt the information on their servers, basically make their networks unhackable. I analyze shell corporations and perform background checks for everyone on my team. I can't think of a single person who would want me dead."

"All I know is someone tried to kill you back there." He wouldn't discount the possibility the threat was tied to Blackhawk Security. They had to consider all the angles. Past, present, someone invested in the outcome of the firm's military and private contracts. The list of suspects with the kind of knowledge and training that shooter had to have was endless, but military training was a definite. He needed access to her client files. "And I'm not going to let them succeed."

"Do you think this could be linked to my contract with the NSA?" Her voice wavered. To someone who hadn't memorized every inflection, every emotion, it would've gone unnoticed. But not to him. He knew her inside and out, down to a cellular level. Even with filtered moonlight coming through the SUV's tinted windows, he noted the color draining from her face. Hell. The nightmares. How could he have forgotten about her damn nightmares? Her throat worked to swallow. "Maybe a family member or someone who'd gotten a look at the files?"

Her fear slid through him, and his body reacted automatically. Ready for battle to protect what was his. One breath. Two. "You still have nightmares."

Not a question. He was there during Oversight's trial run. He'd witnessed how it'd affected her.

"Assuming the person who shot at us in the garage is the same person who hacked those feeds, which might not be the case, you should be able to use my backdoor access to narrow down a location." Him? Liz twisted the steering wheel to the right a little too hard. He fell back against the seat and reached out for his gun before it fell to the floor. Okay, so she didn't want to talk about what kept her up at night, but he couldn't find this bastard on his own. He needed her to run the program. "The only problem is the access opens a two-way door. The second you lock on to a location, he has yours."

"Don't you mean he'd have *our* location?" he asked.

"No, Braxton." She set her jaw, chancing a quick glance into the rearview mirror. "I told you the day I terminated my consulting contract with the NSA. I'll never touch that program again. If you want to trace those feeds, you're doing it alone."

Braxton didn't answer.

"Turn right at the next street. Third building from the end of the road." The apartment he'd leased under a fake name off one of those online sites where home owners rented out their homes wasn't much. Two bedrooms, two bathrooms. But it would get the job done while he was back in Anchorage. However long that would be. He studied Liz as she pulled the SUV to the curb then shouldered his way out of the vehicle behind her. She stepped onto the pavement, hand supporting her head where shrapnel had cut into her during the explosion. A groan worked up her throat, and his blood pressure spiked. He stepped into her, her rough exhale skimming across his neck as rain pounded onto his shoulders. "You okay?"

"It's nothing." She dropped her hand and stepped away. Her right hand shook slightly. She tried to hide it by curling her fingers into her palms, but she couldn't hide from him.

She was scared. Rightfully so, but he'd die before he let anything happen to her. Or their baby. "I'm not going to let that bastard lay a finger on you. I promise."

Silence settled between them. Tight, thick and full of distance.

"I only agreed to your help because someone was shooting at us, and I didn't want to die." Liz shook her head. "So I don't need your promises. I need you to keep me alive until I figure out who wants me dead."

Chapter Three

Elizabeth hefted the SUV's gate above her head and lifted the black duffel bag standard for all Blackhawk Security operatives from the dark interior. Mostly supplies. A couple changes of clothes, ammunition, food storage, emergency flares. The basics of her new profession. Never knew what kind of weather or client would come calling. Although they'd borrowed Elliot's SUV, and the clothes weren't going to fit her. "If you're not going to trace Oversight's feeds on your own, fill me in on your plan."

They'd wound a lot of circles through neighborhoods, parks and strip malls, finally ending up at what looked like an apartment complex. The shooter hadn't followed them. She would've spotted him through the maze of routes they'd taken. The SOB who'd taken a shot at her was most likely licking his wounds and devising another way to kill her. If Braxton had been telling the truth about the shooter's target. She paused at the thought. She took care of network security for a start-up security company. Wasn't exactly the kind of job that would

land her in a killer's crosshairs. But if this had anything
to do with her work for the NSA…

No. It couldn't. She'd left that life behind months ago.
Besides, those files were classified. It'd take someone
with much higher security clearance than the director of the NSA to access them. That'd been part of the
deal. She'd signed dozens of nondisclosure agreements
about the program's trial run, and the federal government would hide Oversight's existence at all costs.

"First, I want your forensics guy to analyze those
bullets in the windshield." Braxton leaned against the
back quarter panel mere inches from her, arms crossed
across that broad chest of his. The weight of his attention pressurized the air in her lungs. He watched her
carefully, as though he couldn't miss a single moment.
"Maybe we'll get lucky with an ID on the unsub trying
to kill you, and—"

"And you go back into hiding." That was the deal.
She'd agreed to his protection, and as soon as they had
a viable lead on that shooter, he'd go back to whatever rock he been hiding under for the last four months
and let her move on with her life. Alone. Storm clouds
shifted overhead as the last remnants of rain pelted
against her leather jacket, but the crisp, cleansing atmo-
spheric scent did nothing to clear her head. Unzipping
the duffel, she reached in, wrapped her shaking hand
around her teammate's backup weapon, and loaded a
fresh magazine. Full.

"Right," he said.

Setting the bag back in the trunk, she faced Braxton
with her emotions in check and her guard in place. He

might be the father of her unborn baby, but that didn't mean she had to trust him. Elizabeth lifted her gaze to his. "You think going back to Blackhawk Security to hand over the bullets is a good idea? I seem to remember half of the penthouse floor is missing, and we almost died in the garage."

Braxton moved in close, too close, his clean, masculine scent mixing with the aroma of rain. The combination urged her to lean into him, to forget how much she'd missed him. She'd told herself—hell, told him—she'd moved on, but her body had yet to grasp the idea. "I told you I won't let him touch you. You have my word."

"And I told you your word doesn't mean a damn thing to me." She fought back a quiver. Tightness ran down her neck and back. After countless hours—months—of trying to find him, here he stood less than a foot away. In the flesh. Tightening her grip around the duffel bag, she scrambled for purchase as the past threatened to drag her under. No. She'd been down this path once before. She'd trusted him, and it cost her everything. "We should ditch the vehicle and get inside. If the shooter is the same person who hijacked Oversight's feeds, he'll be able to track us to this area and try to shoot me again."

Ten minutes later, they'd abandoned the SUV, sans bullets in the windshield, and hiked back to the apartment on foot. Braxton led her up two flights of stairs and toward an apartment in the back of the third building, his clothing barely concealing the muscle he'd put on since the last time she'd seen him. And not just in his upper body. His legs flexed beneath denim, powerful and strong. Inserting a key in the lock, he turned the doorknob and shouldered the door open. "Wait here a minute."

He didn't wait for her answer as he disappeared inside.

A breeze shook the trees below, and she stepped to the railing. No shooters waiting in the trees. No bomb ticking off nearby. She smoothed her hand over her lower abdomen as a rush of nausea churned in her stomach. Who would want her dead? And why now?

"Surveillance is clean." Braxton filled the door frame just inside her peripheral vision. "The place isn't much, but it gets the job done. We've got power, water, gas, and I had groceries delivered yesterday."

She followed him inside, the skin along her collarbones prickling with the onslaught of a draft coming from the vents above. "Hiding your how-to-be-a-good-spy magazines before I came inside?"

"No, I keep those locked up all the time." Braxton's laugh replaced the cold-induced goose pimples along her arms with heat, but she couldn't afford to give it much notice. Find out who was trying to kill her and why, then move on with her life. That was it.

He'd been right about the apartment. It wasn't much, but it'd work for what they needed. Large windows took up most of the east wall, providing a jaw-dropping view of the mountains. A large sectional had been positioned in the corner of the living room, only photos of wildlife and scenic Alaska hanging on the white walls. Two bedrooms, two bathrooms from the looks of it. Simple.

Bare. But the setup of surveillance equipment across the dining room table said secure. It suited him. Her, too.

"You can take the back bedroom if you want to clean up. There's a bathroom attached to that one, so we don't have to share." Braxton maneuvered behind her, and she straightened a bit more. "I'll have some food for us by the time you're done."

"Good idea. Give me a few minutes." She checked her wristwatch. Nine at night. They weren't going to get much done at this hour. The investigation would have to start in the morning. Another rush of nausea gripped her tight, and she fought to breathe through her nose to counter it. Didn't work. The target of a shooter, reunited with the man she thought she'd never see again, and suffering from morning sickness all at the same time. Great.

"Take your time." He headed toward the kitchen, tossing his baseball cap onto the counter. His dark hair skimmed his shoulders, and, hell, she'd be lying if she didn't admit the look worked for him.

Elizabeth forced one foot in front of the other. Space. She needed space. Away from him. The lighttan-colored walls passed in a blur as she escaped to the nearest bedroom. She wasn't sure if this was the room he'd meant for her to take, but at the moment, she didn't care. Tossing her duffel onto the floor, she exhaled hard and ran a hand through her hair.

It'd been four months since she'd made the worst mistake of her life by climbing under the sheets with Braxton. That should've been long enough to get control of her physical reactions. Damn it. This wasn't the plan. She'd accepted there would be a bottomless hole in her heart where she'd shove everything she felt for Braxton Levitt in order to raise their daughter on her own. But he'd come back. To protect her. Still, while she might have to stay within physical proximity of him, she wouldn't let him hurt her again. Keeping her emotional distance would have to do. That, and a securely locked bedroom door. "Just a few days, baby girl. We've got this."

The bedroom came into focus. Single queen-size bed, nightstand, dresser with some papers settled on top, same type of photography on the walls as she'd noticed in the living room. And a cardboard box full of phones stashed in the corner. She fished out a phone from the middle of pile and studied the room again. Groceries delivered, a box of phones, surveillance setup. How long had Braxton planned on staying here?

She swiped her thumb across the screen and dialed Vincent Kalani's number from memory. She'd left her phone with the SUV about a mile west of here. Anyone who tried pinging it for a location would only find disappointment. Blackhawk Security training 101. The other line rang three times. Then four. "Come on, Vincent. Pick up the phone." Another ring. If he hadn't made it out of the building alive, she'd never forgive herself for leaving the forensics expert in the middle of a crime scene. "Pick up the damn—"

"Kalani." Vincent's usually smooth voice sounded rough, damaged.

"You're alive." Relief flooded through her. She exhaled hard, closing her eyes with a hand on her forehead. Turning her back to the door, she ignored the burn in her lower lash line. Hormones. Crying came too easy these days. "I was beginning to worry I'd be stuck with your vengeful ghost for the rest of my life."

"No thanks to your new bodyguard there." Muffled static reached through his end of the line. "What number are you calling from?"

"A burner I picked up out of a box full of phones. Consider this my new number for the time being." She chewed on the end of her thumbnail. They shouldn't have left him behind. She could've fought Braxton harder, could've done *something*. "Tell me you're okay."

"I'm good," Vincent said. "Confirm you're safe and give me permission to punch your ex in the face the next time I see him."

"I'm safe. For now. And permission granted." She dropped her hand and rolled her shoulders back. Pain shot through the right side of her rib cage, and she doubled over with a rough exhale. "But you'll have to get in line."

"Liz?" Vincent asked. "You okay?"

"Fine for someone who took an eight-foot oak door to the right side." She breathed through the pain. "Listen, whoever set that bomb tried to finish the job in the garage. I pulled three slugs out of Elliot's windshield, but I'm not sure how to hand them off to you without putting myself back in the open."

"Stay put," Vincent said. "I'll have Anchorage PD's crime scene unit check it out. Maybe we'll get lucky on a stray casing. If that doesn't work, we'll set something up to get me those slugs. You should know, as of right now the Sovereign Army is taking credit for the bombing."

"The privacy activists? Explosives aren't usually their forte." Headlines had taken over national news with the group's intent to sell and publish congressmen and women's browsing histories and darkest secrets, but setting a bomb at a security company? Although if the extremist group discovered she'd helped the federal government create a surveillance system to spy on them for the past year, who knew how far they'd escalate. Still, something about that didn't sit well. A knock at the door pushed her pulse higher. Braxton. She nodded, even though Vincent couldn't possibly see it, and turned as the bedroom door cracked open. "Thanks for the intel. Call me if you find anything else."

She ended the call, nervous energy skittering up her spine.

Green-gray eyes locked on her and, suddenly, the last four months disappeared to the back of her mind. Braxton made his way inside, a white box in one hand and a steaming bowl of something intoxicating in the other. "Your team?"

"Yeah. Hope you don't mind I borrowed one of your phones to make the call." She tossed the burner onto the bed, crossing her arms over her midsection. Grinding her teeth, she fought against the pain ripping through her side. "Looks like Sovereign Army took credit for the bombing. Vincent's sending Anchorage PD to analyze the scene in the garage. He'll call back if he finds something. He's very much looking forward to punching you in the face when he sees you again."

"Fair enough." A smile curled at one edge of his mouth, and his all-too-familiar pull hooked into her. Damn it. When would he stop affecting her like this? Braxton closed the space between them, coming within mere inches of her. Her breath caught in her throat as he maneuvered around her to set the bowl on the nightstand. Straightening, he backed away slowly, that mesmerizing gaze steady on her. "So now that there's nothing more we can do tonight, take off your shirt."

EXPERTS SAID TIME healed old wounds, but what the hell did they know? Braxton popped open the first aid kit beside him on the bed. How many times had he called her over the last month from this very same safe house only to hang up when she answered? Two? Five? Maybe more. She wouldn't have spoken to him if he'd opened his mouth. That was clear now. More than likely, she would've demanded a trace on the call the second she'd realized who was on the other line and sent any resource available his way. His disappearance obviously hadn't torn her apart as much as it had him. But, hell, he deserved it. Even if leaving had been to protect her.

"Excuse me?" Liz cradled her rib cage. Her features contorted but smoothed almost instantly. As though she'd caught herself in a moment of weakness.

Stubborn woman. On a scale from one to ten, he pegged her pain around a seven. Yet she hadn't said a word. He'd noticed the way she favored that side, the small flinches in her expression. She'd been lucky to survive that explosion. If it weren't for the very same oak door that'd possibly cracked her ribs protecting her from most of the shrapnel, she might not be standing here. The ache under his sternum, the one connected with the woman standing mere feet away, refused to subside as he studied the fast tick of her pulse at the base of her throat. "The only way for me to see if your ribs are broken is you taking off your shirt."

"I'm fine. I'm sure it's a rib out of place. It'll either pop back when it's ready, or this girl will kick it back where it belongs in the next few months." She stared up at the ceiling, her fingers prodding into her side. Small lines creased her expression, and his gut clenched. In her next breath, she took back control. "Besides, I'm pretty sure you're just looking for a way back under my shirt. Which isn't going to happen."

A laugh rumbled from deep in his chest. Exhaustion played a wicked game across her expression, but she'd keep going until they identified the unsub responsible for that bomb. That'd been one of the reasons he'd recommended her to Dalton Meyer for the Oversight project at the NSA two years ago. He'd studied her work programming drones for the small start-up company in Washington, DC, and admired her determination to get the job done. Nothing had changed in that respect. But sacrificing her health in the name of the investigation wouldn't get them anywhere. "Can you blame a guy for trying?"

Her burst of laughter filled the room but cut off in her next breath. She doubled over, hiking her hand into her side.

"All right, enough stalling." Braxton tossed the first

aid kit onto the bed and propelled himself to his feet. "I'm taking a look at your ribs whether you like it or not."

"Why?" Liz straightened slowly, pain evident on her features. "Unless you got your medical degree while you were in hiding?"

"Not exactly, but you learn a few things when you're on your own and the government has plastered your face on the front page of the FBI's website." He feathered his fingertips under her shirt and lifted the black silk. Her sharp gasp quickened his pulse, and a rush of satisfaction shot through him. He'd always been able to change her breathing patterns with one touch. Nice to know some things hadn't changed. Smooth skin slid against the rough calluses on his hand. And wasn't that the perfect metaphor for their relationship—rough versus smooth. Bruises had already started darkening around her bottom rib on the right side. He studied her expression in his peripheral vision as he pressed his thumb into the bone. "It's no way to live, though. Strange cities, fake names, avoiding human interaction." Avoiding her. "Gets old real fast."

"Well, now it looks like we have something in common." She hissed as he prodded the third rib from the bottom. "Now I'm being hunted like an animal. Only this predator isn't the federal government and has tried to blow me up and shoot me in the same day."

He locked his jaw to cool the anger churning in his gut. If he hadn't left, none of this would've happened.

"Nothing feels broken." Braxton dropped his hand. Every cell in his body screamed for him to erase the worry lines from her expression, but he couldn't move.

He studied the vulnerability playing across her face. What he wouldn't give to help her forget the nightmare of the last couple hours. "I'll get you a heating pad for the soreness and ice for the inflammation. Should be good as new in a couple days."

A weak smile played across her mouth. "Thanks."

He turned away from her and headed toward the door. If he didn't, the unquenched desire that'd burrowed itself beneath his skin and crackled along his veins when he touched her would take control. Her life—their baby's life—had been put at risk because of him. Anything more between them would only make it that much harder to walk away. That'd been the deal. She agreed to his protection. He'd go back into hiding. Fighting to keep his focus trained, Braxton forced one foot in front of the other.

"Why'd you come back?" she asked. "Why now?"

He froze, his hands curling into fists at his side. Ten seconds. That was all he needed to clear his head, but she couldn't even give him that. "Liz—"

"I'd finally worked out what I would say to our baby the day she asked about her father, but then you walked right into Blackhawk Security. Have to admit—" she fitted her shirt back into place out of the corner of his eye "—I never saw it coming."

Braxton turned. No point in lying. He'd never been able to stay away from her for more than a few days at a time. Even now, he was caught in the undeniable gravitational pull of hers, and he wouldn't be able to fight it much longer. "I always planned on coming back."

"Did you ever think you never should've left in the

first place?" Her expression shifted from genuine curiosity to outright fury. The small muscles along her jaw flexed. Liz took a step back as he approached then brushed right past him. As though his revelation ignited that anger she desperately fought to control. "Maybe then we wouldn't be in this mess."

He wrapped his hand around hers and pulled her into him. Lean muscle flexed along her arm, and he imagined all too easily exploring every inch of the strength under her clothing. Every mole. Every scar. The soft curve of her lower abdominals where their baby thrived. He brushed his thumb over the back of her hand and loosened his grip. Desire surged through him, a mere taste of the chaos capable of rendering him completely useless when she was around. Damn what she thought of him, damn the investigation or the reason he'd stayed away from her for the last sixteen weeks. She had to know the truth. She deserved to know.

Liz stared up at him with that gorgeous fire in her expression—almost daring him to make his next move—but didn't wrench out of his hold.

He forced the words to the tip of his tongue, but no sound left his mouth. Licking his lips, he dropped his hand from hers. No. Now wasn't the time. Because he couldn't lose her again. Every decision he'd made over his career had a price, but he'd never expected her to pay for any of it. And she would once she learned the truth.

"You're right. I never should've left, and I'll spend the rest of my life making it up to you and our baby if that's what you want." He framed her hips between both hands, his thumbs grazing her lower belly. Braxton stepped into her, relishing in the slight widening of her eyes, of her exhale rushing against the skin along his neck. "Starting now."

Reaching past her, he skimmed his hand over the top of the dresser and grabbed the yellow envelope resting on top. He slid it between them and handed it to her. Everything that'd happened today at Blackhawk Security—the bomb, the shooter in the garage—had to do with what was in the envelope. "You asked me why I came back. Why now? This is why."

She took the envelope from him, the furrow between her dark eyebrows deepening. She slid her fingers inside the envelope and pulled out the short stack of surveillance photos he'd collected from Oversight's servers. Photos of her. Confusion deepened the lines across her forehead. "What is this?"

She blinked as realization hit her hard.

He wanted to reach for her. To comfort her. But didn't.

The envelope protested in her hand. Liz shook her head and took a step back. She shuffled through the stack of photos, one after the other. But studying photos wouldn't make the truth any less real. Someone had been hunting her for months. "Wh-how did you get these?"

"I programmed an alert into Oversight's code to notify me when you were the subject before I left the agency." If he hadn't, she—and their baby—wouldn't be standing here right now. "I started getting alerts six days ago. Right after I read about Dalton Meyer's murder and discovered Oversight's feeds were hijacked."

"So many photos. Outside the office, getting into my car." Her voice barely registered. Too soft. Too full of fear. The muscles down his spine responded. She swallowed hard, eyes wide. "This one is from a traffic camera as I drove home." Liz ran a hand through her hair as her mouth parted. "Someone's been watching me? For how long?"

"No, someone has been stalking you." He picked out one particular photo from the back and handed it to her. A photo of her leaving her own home. Whoever had been watching her knew where she lived. "And I'm here to find out why."

Chapter Four

"I don't think the Sovereign Army took these pictures." Elizabeth dropped the photos in her hand to her side. She'd been followed for weeks—maybe months. She'd had no idea, but she couldn't let the fear spreading at the back of her mind take control. What else had her stalker uncovered? Her head spun. Nausea festered. *Focus.* She forced herself to breathe deep. She'd started a new life here, loved her job, was having a baby. Nobody would take that from her. Not some extremist group. Not Braxton. And not whoever had tried to blow her up three hours ago.

She headed for the door. Braxton was a former analyst. Analysts ran secure networks. All she needed was a computer. She trusted her team—trusted Vincent—with her life, but she had to see the Sovereign Army taking credit for planting that bomb at Blackhawk Security herself. The shooter in the garage, the photos Braxton uncovered. Neither of those were part of the group's MO. "An extremist group bent on protecting Americans' privacy wouldn't run illegal surveillance on their target."

"They didn't seem so concerned about protecting privacy when they threatened to leak officials' browsing histories to the public." Braxton cut her off, his mountainous shoulders blocking her view of the door. "I watch the news, too. These guys have been known to do what it takes to get their message across, violently if forced. The best shot we have to uncovering who's coming after you is Oversight's backdoor access."

The breath she'd been holding rushed from her lungs as the past threatened to overrun the present. She fought back the memories, but how could she when all she thought about when she closed her eyes was the last time she'd accessed that code?

"I told you I can't do that." Her voice rose with each word. He should understand that better than anyone. He'd been there. He'd watched how Oversight's trial run had affected her. No. He didn't get to decide how they handled the threat on her life. He'd lost that right the night he'd walked out on her all those months ago. "This is what we're going to do. First, you're going to get out of my way, so I can review the bomb squad's findings for myself. Second, we're going to arrange to get Vincent the slugs we pulled from the windshield. If he gets a hit on ballistics, you get to keep your end of the deal, and we pretend this whole thing never happened. Go our separate ways."

"I'll keep my end of the deal—" Braxton closed in on her "—but if he doesn't come up with our suspect, I expect you to keep yours."

"Agreed." Silence settled between them. It wasn't an empty silence. It was full of anger, of something else

Elizabeth didn't want to identify. "You're pushing me out of the investigation by trying to keep me behind a computer. Why?"

"You know why." Veins fought to burst from beneath his skin. He'd have an embolism if he didn't take a breath. Her guard softened at the concern etched into his features.

"I'm pregnant, Braxton. Not an invalid. I protect my clients, whether it's from behind a desk or strapped in Kevlar, and I'm damn good at my job." Elizabeth shook her head, a disbelieving laugh escaping from between her lips. She tried to swallow around her dry throat. "Just because you're the father of this baby, doesn't give you the right to dictate how I live my…"

Dizziness muddled her vision. She reached out to balance herself, fisting her hand in his T-shirt. She pulled him into her, knees weak. "Whew. If I pass out, don't let it fool you. I'm still going to win this argument when I wake up."

"Liz?" Concern sharpened his voice.

She fought to steady her heart rate. A dull ringing filled her ears as he wrapped his arms around her and led her to the edge of the bed. His clean, masculine scent surrounded her, and she breathed in as much as she could to clear her head. Didn't work. She closed her eyes as the back of her knees hit the mattress. "This conversation is not over."

"Tell me what the hell is happening, or I'm taking you to the hospital right now," he said.

"My blood sugar is low." She'd had it under control the last few days. But running for her life must've forced her body to use up her last meal sooner than she'd expected. She opened her eyes, still clinging to the valleys and ridges of muscle carved into his chest. Nope. Couldn't think about that right now. Food. She needed food. "The baby makes me hypoglycemic. As soon as I eat, I'll be fine."

"Here." Braxton unraveled her fingers from his shirt but refused to let go of her hand completely as he reached for the bowl on the nightstand. Which actually helped anchor her. Steam still escaped from the glossy red ceramic, and the scent of something spicy and warm filled her as she breathed it in. "This should help."

"What is it?" she said.

"Turkey and vegetable soup." He wiped his palms down his jeans. The mattress dipped with his added weight beside her, and she struggled not to lean into him with everything she had. "The protein should bring your glucose back up in a few minutes. I made more if you need it."

"You made this?" Elizabeth heaved a spoonful into her mouth. Vegetables perfectly cooked, ground turkey flavored with spices. No. Not possible. The Braxton she'd known had survived on a diet of cheap cafeteria food and fast food restaurants. Although, studying the lean muscle across his torso, the new bulges in his arms and thighs, he'd obviously made some changes. Living off junk food didn't carve muscle like that. Her mouth watered for more than the soup in that moment, and she fought to concentrate on not dumping the entire bowl in her lap. The pounding of her heart behind her ears faded. "And look at that, not a gummy worm in sight."

Resting his elbows on his knees, he laughed. "Nope. The only sweets you're going to find in this apartment are chocolate ice cream and rainbow-colored sprinkles."

Elizabeth froze, another spoonful of soup halfway to her mouth. "I still can't believe you remember my favorites."

"How could I forget?" His green-gray gaze, grayer now, centered on her. A smile thinned his mouth, and her grip on the bowl weakened. Damn that smile. Damn the soup. Damn the fact he'd saved her life—twice— in the past three hours. "You kept a pint of ice cream in the freezer at the office and a container of rainbow sprinkles hidden in your desk." Braxton straightened. "I still remember the look on one of the other analysts' face when you screamed at him for five minutes for ignoring the 'do not touch' sign on your ice cream. Bad day for that guy."

"Yeah, well, not all women are made of sugar and spice and everything nice. Some are made of ice cream, rainbow sprinkles and a whole lot of swear words." Elizabeth took another bite, talking around a mouthful of soup, then pointed at him with her spoon. "He was an analyst. He was trained to read between the lines, but he flat out ignored my note. He deserved it. Don't touch my ice cream."

Braxton raised his hands in surrender. "I won't. Not after that."

She couldn't help but laugh. Then caught herself. The man in front of her had done something far worse than ignore a note taped to her ice cream in the office freezer. For the past four months, he'd been the epitome of an uncaring, coldhearted, manipulative jerk who'd taken her to bed then run. But now Braxton refused to fit inside the box she'd created for him in her mind. Elizabeth cleared her throat, more to free her head of his clean scent than anything else, and motioned to him with the empty bowl. "Thanks for the soup. I'm feeling better."

"Anything for you." The sincerity in his voice, the way his hand brushed over her knee closest to him, spiked her flight instinct. Taking the bowl from her, he stood and headed for the door. She couldn't stop the flood of warmth rushing through her. And not just from the soup.

No, no, no. She'd been down this road before. She'd trusted him, relied on him when she'd needed someone the most. He'd been the man who would've done anything to protect her, the man who'd had her back when the NSA sought to destroy her career after Oversight's first real-world test run. But the man in front of her wasn't him. Maybe never had been. And falling for him had left her pregnant and alone.

Wouldn't happen again.

Braxton stopped short of the hallway, as though the weight of her attention cemented his feet in place. His dark hair brushed across his shoulder blades as he rested his head back. "You haven't asked me why I left."

The warmth drained from her system. No. She hadn't.

He turned. The scar cut through his eyebrow shifted as he centered his attention on her. The world threatened to pull out from under her feet when he looked at her like that, like she was the only woman in the world for him.

She glanced over the surveillance photos she'd dropped onto the floor—a dozen Elizabeths staring up at her—but didn't really see the details. "I've spent countless hours obsessing over that question, determined to find out the answer, imagining the moment you'd come back into my life. To be clear, none of it involved a bomb under a conference room table or being shot at in the parking garage."

Locking her attention on Braxton, she tightened her grip on the edge of the mattress. Did he realize how much he'd hurt her? How many nights she'd cried over him leaving? Probably not. Stay in control. Survive the investigation. Move on with her life. That was all she had to do. Elizabeth notched her chin parallel with the floor. "But after finding out I was pregnant a few weeks ago, I decided in the end, I don't care."

All that mattered was that he had, and that he would leave again.

That was the deal.

"I'm sorry. I never meant…" The corners of his mouth turned down, those brilliant eyes filled with… guilt? Braxton shifted his weight between his feet, knuckles white around the bowl in his hand. "I never meant for any of this."

"Fortunately for you, you're not responsible for the man trying to kill me or we'd be having a very different conversation." It was nearly ten at night now. Exhaustion pulled at her muscles, but Elizabeth shoved to her feet. No dizziness. No ringing in her ears. His soup had done its job, and she was about to make sure this baby didn't lower her blood sugar for a few more hours. "Now, take me to the ice cream."

LIZ WAS WRONG. He was responsible. He'd left her unprotected.

Lavender filled his lungs as she maneuvered past him toward the kitchen. His heart rate kicked up a notch. Even after all this time, she affected him in ways he couldn't explain, in ways no other woman had. Only her. "I knew you wouldn't be able to resist."

"Which begs the question, why have it on hand at all?" Liz turned toward him, cocking her head to one side as she shifted her weight against the opposite counter. Still reading between the lines. Back facing the wide expanse of windows and the mesmerizing view, she crossed her arms beneath her chest. Clouds clung to the peaks of the Chugach mountain range, rain hitting the glass in rhythmic intervals, but he only had attention for her. "Unless you knew I'd come back here with you."

There'd been no other option when he'd discovered Oversight's feeds had been hijacked to hunt her down. Not for him. He didn't trust anyone but himself to keep her safe. Braxton wrenched open the freezer door and excavated her favorite brand of chocolate ice cream. "I'm damn good at my job, too."

"True," she said.

"I'm almost afraid you would go with anyone who offered you ice cream and sprinkles, though." He grabbed a bowl and a spoon then scooped two huge servings of ice cream and handed it to her. Holding up one finger, he spun the spice turntable around, pulled rainbow-colored sprinkles from the first tier and offered it to her. "Almost forgot the secret ingredient."

Her fingertips overlapped his for a moment, and something resembling an electric shock shot up his arm. A rush of color climbed up her neck, and he fought the urge to close the small bit of distance between them in the tight galley kitchen. Nice to know he wasn't the only one affected by their proximity.

"You seem to forget the more I weigh, the harder I am to kidnap, so ice cream is essentially saving my life in the long run." Liz dumped an unhealthy amount sprinkles onto her ice cream.

"Good point." A laugh reverberated through him. Although he'd kill anyone who tried. Nobody came after her and survived. The pregnancy only made his protective side stronger. "But I only have enough for the next couple of days, so take it easy."

"If you think we're going to be here for a couple days, I'll eat it all tonight, and you won't be able to stop me." Liz spooned a heavy bite into her mouth. She closed her eyes, a moan working up her throat. His gut tightened at the sound, all too eager to bring up memories of their one night together. The stress that'd been etched into her features since the moment she'd set sight on him in that damn conference room melted with one spoonful of her favorite dessert.

"Wouldn't dream of it." Anything to make her happy. Even if that included going back into hiding after the investigation ended. His gaze shifted to her lower abdominals, where their daughter barely made herself known in the soft curve there. Even if it meant never meeting his daughter. He would leave to protect them, to make them happy.

Liz opened her eyes, the chocolate brown surrounding her pupils darker than a few minutes ago. The effect raised the hairs on the back of his neck, his entire body on high alert. Because of her. Her rough exhale skimmed across his neck in the small space. "I never thanked you."

"What for?" The edge of the granite countertop cut into his backside, keeping him in the moment. Rain pounded against the windows, a ripple of thunder shaking the framed photos on the walls. He flexed his fingers into the center of his palms. Reminded him of far too many unprotected nights as a kid under that damn fake rock wall in the park when the shelter was full, something he hadn't thought about in years. Until he'd uncovered Liz's new name and address. Of all the places she could've run, she'd chosen Anchorage. To get away from him.

"I wouldn't be standing here if it weren't for you. We wouldn't be standing here." Liz slid her hand over her belly then set her ice cream, only half eaten, on the counter. The sound of stainless steel on ceramic grated in his ears but didn't distract him enough to take his eyes off her. Nothing could. "You saved our lives."

"Which time are you referring to? The bomb, the shootout in the garage or with the bowl of ice cream?" He notched his chin toward her and crossed his boots at the ankles. "I'm losing count."

"All three. Maybe more for the explosion and the shooter than the food, but it certainly helped me from going into hypoglycemic shock." Her brilliant smile rocketed his heart rate into dangerous territory before it disappeared. Gripping the edge of the counter on either side of her waist, Liz locked her gravity-inducing gaze on his, and he felt a pull. "Maybe we can come at this a different way. Forget about the Sovereign Army as a whole for a minute. The shooter in the garage was alone. It was a single-man assault. Looking for one shooter in the group would narrow down our suspect list." She picked up her spoon and bit down against the steel. "Only problem is, if he is a member, I doubt anyone in the Sovereign Army would roll on him."

They'd already been through this.

"I swore I'd keep you alive." Braxton closed the distance between them, her sharp inhale audible as he reached around her for the discarded bowl. Turning his head slightly, he leveled his attention on her right shoulder. Smooth, flawless skin stood out against the black lace of her cap sleeve, and he wanted nothing more than to taste her again, to see if his memory of her was as good as the real thing. He raised his eyes to meet hers. "And I will do anything to keep that promise."

"Protection is not the same thing as controlling someone's life." She swiped her tongue across her lips, pulling his attention to her mouth and the small purple sprinkle stuck to her bottom lip. "If I was meant to be controlled, I would've come with a remote."

"People don't wake up wanting to be victims." His voice came out too rough, too deep. "They don't ask for bad things to happen. They don't ask for pain they have to live with for the rest of their lives. Every day things destroy someone's life. Attacks like today happen. It doesn't matter how strong they are—anyone can get hurt, but I sure as hell won't let it be you and our baby. Understand?"

Sliding one hand along his face, Liz stared at him. Her mouth parted as though the words were on the tip of her tongue. "Braxton—"

His name on her lips was all it took. In one swift move, he threaded his fingers at the nape of her neck and set his forehead against hers. She tried to escape, but the counter kept her caged against him. Damn, he'd missed her. Missed her scent, the way she fit against him perfectly, her sarcasm, the feel of her skin. Electricity lightninged through him as he slid his body in line with hers, her front pressed against him, her hands reaching for his at the back of her neck. Her fingernails bit into the backs of his hands. Hell, no. His memory hadn't done her justice. She breathed against him, her mouth mere centimeters from his. Dropping his hands to her hips, he lifted her onto the counter and centered himself between her thighs. Her fingers fisted in his hair, locking him against her. Right where he needed to be.

What had he been thinking, leaving her behind? He could've told her the truth. Could've asked her to come with him. He moved his fingers back up to her hair, where her erratic pulse beat against the palm of his hand. He did that to her. He changed her breathing patterns. He expanded her pupils so only a thin ring of brown remained. Braxton swallowed hard. Damn it, no. It wouldn't have been fair to expect her to pick up her life and disappear off the radar. Her life was at risk because of him. Because he'd gotten involved with her in the first place. And there was no telling how far that shooter would go to get to her again. Ten minutes ago, nothing would've stopped him from closing that short distance to her mouth, but he couldn't now. He wouldn't put her in danger again.

Spearmint and lavender exploded across his senses, and he reached between them, swiping his thumb across her lip. The sprinkle fell to the kitchen floor, out of sight. He forced himself to cool things down. "You had a purple sprinkle stuck to your mouth."

Liz planted a hand against his chest, his heart fighting for freedom to reach her, and pushed him back. She cleared her throat, the pink in her cheeks and down her neck fading. "It's getting late. I've had a hell of a day. I'm going to go to bed. We can talk about our next step after we've both gotten some rest."

His backside hit the opposite counter. He'd never been more thankful for the granite than in that moment as cold tunneled through his clothing. He nodded and swiped a hand down his face. Lightning streaked through the front windows as the rest of the world came back into focus. "Yeah. Good idea."

She slipped off the counter. Her gaze glittered at him. "Good night, Braxton."

"Good night." Braxton gripped the edge of the counter hard as she headed into the guest bedroom and closed the door behind her. The lock clicked into place, and he nodded as he stared at the tile. Hell, what was he trying to prove? That he still wanted her? No question about it—he'd never stopped wanting her. Never would. But if he'd learned anything over the last four months, it'd been that emotional ties could and would be used against him. Didn't matter what precautions he took or how long he stayed under the radar. Two attempts on her life in the span of an hour was enough for him. There wouldn't be a third.

Chapter Five

She was supposed to be smarter than this. Stronger.

Muted sunlight filtered around the edges of the thick blackout curtains. They had work to do, but Elizabeth didn't move from the bed. The instant she left this room, reality would set in. Braxton, the shooter, the fact she would most definitely be raising this baby on her own in a few short months. A few more minutes of ignorance. That was all she needed.

Hiking her forearm over her face, she fought to purge the heated moments between her and Braxton from her memory, but her efforts were in vain. The raw desire in his gaze had burned straight through her, marked her. And damn it, she'd almost given in to him. Almost wanted him to kiss her, to make her forget about the fact she'd become a target. A low groan ripped from her throat as she threw the blankets off and hauled herself to her feet. Ice worked through her veins as she padded barefoot across the cold hardwood floor, hand over her lower abdominals. "We're in trouble, baby girl. And I have no idea how to get us out of it."

She'd survived Braxton leaving once. She wasn't so sure she could do it again.

Get ready and come up with a plan. That was all she had to think about right now. Elizabeth froze, arched over her duffel bag, and cocked her head toward the door. Was that…? No. It couldn't be. Straightening, she headed for the bedroom door and opened it slowly, careful to avoid the creak in the floorboard right outside the guest room. The low *plunk* of guitar strings filtered down the hallway, and she set her head against the door for support, just listening. How long had it been since she'd heard him play? A year? More? The muffled sound of strings from down the hall made it hard to recognize the song but pulled her toward the end all the same.

Before she understood exactly when she'd made the decision to push open his cracked bedroom door, there he was. Her insides constricted at the wide expanse of ridges and valleys of muscle flexing across his back as he played, his hair brought back in a loose ponytail to keep it out of his way. Despite the release and contraction of muscles in his broad shoulders, he looked completely at ease, relaxed. And hell if that didn't vault her heart into her throat.

"Did I wake you?" His voice barely registered over the low chord of music, only one side of his features visible from her position at the door.

"No, I can blame that on your daughter at all hours of the night." She shifted her weight into the door frame and crossed her arms. He kept playing, kept pulling at some part of her she thought she'd buried for good when he'd left. The same part that had protected her against wondering where he'd gone, who he'd been with, if he'd ever had feelings for her. "I wasn't sure you'd kept it. When I searched your apartment after…" Elizabeth dropped her attention to his discarded shirt at the edge of the bed and centered her focus. No point in rehashing the past. Wouldn't change anything. "Everything was still there."

Except the guitar she'd bought for him for his birthday last year, the one he held now. That alone had clued her in that something hadn't happened to him. He'd left.

"You are the only person who's ever given me a birthday present. Did I ever tell you that? We never had a lot of money growing up, but after my dad lost his job, then the house, we had nothing. My mom tried. Collected aluminum can tops for me—one for every year—and strung them on a necklace my dad had given her when they were dating. But this…" Braxton paused, sliding his fingers up the guitar's neck, across the engraving she'd had done in the guitar shop. *Everything is better with sprinkles.* They were supposed to be best friends forever. Her fingernails dug into her arm, keeping her in the moment. He finally locked those brilliant green eyes on her as he rocked forward on the edge of the mattress, and a rush of heat flooded through her. "Do you remember the chords I taught you?"

A burst of laughter escaped from between her lips as she shook her head. He'd spent hours trying to teach her to play. Didn't work. She was the least musically inclined person in existence. "Not a single one."

Braxton shifted on the mattress, making room at

the end. With a single nod, he beckoned her forward. "Come here."

Her lungs seized, but the rest of her body refused to follow her brain's orders to fight. They needed to come up with another plan to identify the man trying to kill her. Not mess around on his guitar. Still, she put one foot in front of the other until the backs of her knees hit the mattress, and she sat down beside him. Warmth flooded down her left side as his arm brushed against hers.

Braxton set the instrument across her lap, one hand wrapped around the neck, the other sliding between her arm and her rib cage. A shiver chased down her spine despite the fact she was burning up inside. Goose bumps pimpled down her arms as he set his mouth close to her ear. And the world disintegrated from in front of her, leaving only the two of them and his guitar. He fit his fingers over hers, the calluses rough against her, as she settled against him. Flashing her that gut-wrenching smile, he studied her face from forehead to chin as he forced her fingers to move with his. "You got it."

"It sounds like I'm skinning a cat." His laugh reverberated down her side, and Elizabeth tightened her grip on the guitar. She stilled, heart threatening to beat out of her chest, as she turned her head toward him. She rolled her lips between her teeth. His gaze shot to her mouth as the thick ring of green around his pupils disappeared.

One breath. Two.

"You're doing great." He strengthened his hold on her, almost pressing her into him as he had the night before. He felt so good right now. Her head begged her to run, to not go down this path again, but her body had taken control the second she'd walked into that conference room. After the explosion, the shooter in the garage, she needed this. Needed him.

The shrill ring of her burner phone from the other room brought her back to reality.

She blinked, shook her head. Shifting forward, away from him, she cleared her throat and ran a hand through her hair. Wow. What the hell had she been thinking? Elizabeth shoved to her feet. "That's Vincent. I gave him the number in case he made progress in the investigation."

Setting the guitar up against the wall, Braxton reached for his discarded long-sleeve shirt. "Better answer it then."

She nodded, escaping down the hallway. The problem was she hadn't been thinking. That'd always been the problem when he was around. She shook off the rush of comfort that'd settled into her bones and hurried to answer the phone. "Vincent, hey—"

"Elizabeth Bosch," an unfamiliar voice said. "Or should I call you Elizabeth Dawson now? Remind me, which one of you created Oversight and single-handedly destroyed over a thousand people's lives with one press of a button?"

Her blood froze in her veins. She hit the speaker feature on the screen and dropped the phone away from her ear. Hitting the home button, she raced to record the call and took a deep breath to steady her nerves. "How did you get this number?"

"You're not the only one who can run a trace. I've

got my sources, too." Static reached through the line, making it hard to identify any kind of background noise. But the man from the garage—maybe the same one who tried blowing her up—was a professional. If that same man was on the other side of the line, he'd thought this through, made contingencies. There wouldn't be any mistakes on his end. "I almost had you back at Blackhawk Security. I would have, too, if it hadn't been for your new bodyguard. Have to admit, I hadn't accounted for him."

Confirmation. They were dealing with a professional.

A tingling sensation climbed up her spine, and she turned.

Braxton stood in the doorway, rage and violence carved into his features.

"You set the bomb in the conference room. You knew I had a meeting in there and timed it just right." She needed confirmation, needed to know they were looking for a single suspect in a numberless group of possibilities. She tipped the phone's microphone closer to her mouth and forced herself to focus on the caller, the man who had tried twice now to kill her. "Well, not perfectly. I was halfway out the door when you triggered the explosion. So you had to make sure your target wouldn't get away. That's why you came after me in the garage."

"I'm not going to let you get away with what you've done." Heavy breathing interrupted the static through the line.

Elizabeth swallowed around the dryness in her throat. "What do you want from me?"

"I want you at Town Square Park in one hour. Alone," he said.

Glancing up at Braxton, she licked her lips. The man she'd known—the man she'd loved—had disappeared in the span of a few seconds. All from an unknown voice on the other line. Tension tightened the muscles down her spine as she considered the situation. "And if I don't show?"

"I know who you've been spending your nights with, Elizabeth. I know why your grocery bill has nearly doubled the past few months, why you visit the park so often after work." Another flicker of static from the other line, then muffled words. Then the undeniable sound of a bullet loading into a gun chamber. "Would you really want him caught up in the middle of this?"

No. No, no, no, no. Elizabeth straightened a bit despite the urge to collapse back on to the bed nearly consuming her. "He has nothing to do with any of this."

"One hour," the shooter said. "I'll be waiting."

The call ended.

She stared at the phone. Either she walked straight into what was undoubtedly a trap or she risked losing the only family her daughter might have left once Braxton disappeared.

"Who have you been spending your nights with, Liz?" She almost didn't recognize Braxton's voice. Too distant. Too dangerous. Her stomach flipped at the sight of the violence still burned into his expression, in the tightness of all those new muscles. "Who was he talking about?"

"Okay. I was going to tell you earlier, but the timing

never seemed right." She tossed the phone onto the bed. Braxton wouldn't hurt her. Never her. But the thought of telling him the truth dried her mouth. A wave of nausea threatened to unbalance her, but whether it was from the possibility of revealing what she'd been doing in her spare time or morning sickness, she had no idea. Elizabeth straightened. He deserved to know. No matter how hard the truth would be to get out or how much he'd hate her afterward. "Since I moved to Anchorage, I've been looking after your father."

HIS LUNGS PROTESTED as though he'd been hit in the chest with a two-by-four. She what? "That man literally put us out on the street when I was a kid to support his habit, and you've been visiting him? Bringing him food?"

"He's not the man you remember, Braxton. The drugs…" Liz took a step closer, but where her proximity usually relieved the pressure coursing through him, it now made it stronger. She seemed to realize her effect on him and froze, that full bottom lip dropping open. "Sometimes he recognizes me, asks about you, asks about the baby. Most of the time I'm the only person keeping him alive."

Was that supposed to make him feel better? She'd never met his father when they'd worked together at Fort Meade. Which meant she'd come to Anchorage and tracked the old man down. She'd spent night after night making sure he had a roof over his head when the addict hadn't even had the guts to do the same for his own flesh and blood. "And now whoever is coming after you is using him as leverage."

"I'm sorry," she said. "I didn't know the shooter was watching me—"

"Why?" His head spun. His vision was a blur, a haze of everything but the woman in front of him. A woman who'd betrayed his deepest secret. The old man he'd called Dad for years had never chosen his family over the poison he could buy on the street. Never even bothered to show up to his mother's funeral after she'd caught a cold and died from pneumonia lying in a cardboard box. Because of his father. Because of what he did to their family. Braxton had grown up without the support he'd needed at the time, and he'd vowed never to fall back into that old man's manipulations again. The SOB was selfish. Only looking for a way to score. "I told you about what that man put me and my mother through, what happened to her. Why would you look for him? Why would you try to help him?"

"You weren't here, Braxton. You left." Her lips thinned as she rolled them between her teeth. "And this baby deserves a family."

His blood pressure spiked. Of course she deserved a family. Every baby did. Someone to sing to her at night, to kiss her in the morning, to help her count her fingers and toes. "You don't need him. I can give her that. I'm her father."

"For how long?" she asked.

"What?" What the hell did that mean? She'd told him he was the father.

"How long are you going to be around?" Liz pulled back her shoulders. The oversize T-shirt and baggy sweatpants did nothing to hide her mouthwatering curves underneath as she interlaced her fingers under her lower abdominals. "The NSA interrogated me after your disappearance. They claimed you sold classified intel to an anonymous third party. They're not going to stop looking for you until they've got you in cuffs. So how long are you going to stick around before you choose to go back into hiding?"

He didn't have an answer. The idea of being a distant father—having practically grown up with a shell of one himself—was too much. He couldn't do that to his daughter. And no way would he do that to Liz. Anxiety wound itself through his gut. But serving a possible life sentence behind bars for treason wouldn't do them a damn bit of good, either.

"As much as you might hate that man, he's still your father. He has a lot to answer for, but right now, he needs our help. And I'm going to give it to him." She nodded, her expression resigned, as she strode past him toward the bedroom door. "Now if you'll excuse me, I need to find a hammer to smash this phone to pieces before it gives up anything else today."

He couldn't fight the smile pulling at his mouth as he envisioned her with a hammer in one hand and her burner phone in the other. The shooter shouldn't have been able to get a lock on that number so easily. Braxton had checked that phone personally, along with the others in his stash. No spyware. They were new numbers, too. Which meant her Blackhawk Security teammate Vincent Kalani, the only person to reach Liz at that number, could've been compromised and not even know it. Or if he did... What had he read in the ex-cop's file? Something about taking bribes. The forensics expert had some explaining to do. He called back over his shoulder but didn't follow Liz from the room. "Check under the kitchen sink."

Hell, he couldn't face her yet. Disbelief still coursed through him as he studied the personal belongings she'd left in plain sight from her duffel bag. She'd been taking care of his father these last few months. Every night. And now his old man was being used as leverage against her, and Braxton was expected to risk Liz's life for a man who'd done nothing but disappoint him for years. The meeting was a trap. If he lost her...

No. It wouldn't happen. Without her, there would be no one else. And that wasn't an option. He'd already lost too many people in his life. He wasn't about to lose her, too.

Heavy thumps echoed down the hall, and he worked to shove his own selfish need to keep her in his life to the back of his mind. Sounded like Liz had found the hammer. He spun toward the door to survey the damage but froze as the edge of a photo stuffed into her duffel bag claimed his attention. Not a photo. A black-and-white sonogram. Checking back over his shoulder as another round of hammering reached his ears, he closed in on the bag. His hand shook as he reached for the single piece of thin, glossy paper. Liz's name, the date of the sonogram, the doctor's office and the measurements in centimeters stood out in white lettering around the edge of the dark background. But there, right in the center of the cone-shaped ultrasound, was a baby.

His baby. Sixteen weeks old.

Her perfectly shaped head, her knees drawn up almost to her nose. Braxton couldn't make out much else, but he didn't have to. She was perfect. Sliding his thumb over where he thought her right ear might be, he exhaled hard at a block of letters he hadn't seen before. His heart dropped.

Baby Karina.

Liz had named their daughter after his mother.

He rubbed his free hand over his face and turned toward the door. Five steps. That was all it took before she came into sight. He couldn't breathe—couldn't think—as he closed in on her. Catching her wrist before she swung the hammer down into the debris of what used to be a cell phone, he twisted her into him.

Her eyes widened. "Braxton, what—"

He crushed his mouth against hers. Fire burned through him, raising the hairs on the back of his neck. Sliding one hand around her back, he fought to bring her closer, make her a permanent part of himself. The scent of lavender worked through him, filled him as her pulse beat hard in her wrist beneath his fingertips. Forget the explosion. Forget the shooter. Forget the charges he'd face once the NSA realized he'd stayed in the country. Braxton only had attention for this moment. Only had Liz.

And she kissed him back.

Her grip loosened around the hammer and it fell, barely missing her bare feet. He released his grip on her wrist then held his breath as she planted her palms against his chest. But not to shove him away. Her lips, soft and silky, pressed into his. He licked the edge of her bottom lip then drew it between his teeth.

A gasp escaped her control, and his blood pressure skyrocketed. He thrust his tongue into her mouth, every cell in his body determined to make her his. He set the sonogram on the counter behind her then threaded his fingers into her hair at the base of her skull in a tight grip. Exploring, memorizing, claiming, he consumed her as a dehydrated man consumed water. Damn, she tasted good. How had he been able to live without her all this time? How had he been able to walk away?

Desire blazed inside him as he kicked the hammer out of the way and maneuvered her toward the same countertop he'd caged her against last night. He felt too rough for her, too punishing, but he couldn't stop. Not until he'd claimed every inch or she told him to back off. She tasted too good, and he'd become addicted to that taste a long time ago. What he wouldn't give to kiss her senseless every morning.

The calluses on his fingertips caught against smooth skin along her midsection.

Hell.

Braxton pulled away then set his forehead against hers. His lungs fought to catch up with his racing pulse. As much as he wanted to strip her bare and help her forget the past two days, he couldn't…they couldn't. They'd run out of time. "The meeting."

He couldn't say much else. Not when she was still pressed against him, when her touch seared him down to his core.

"Right. Shooter. Trap." Her short exhales beat against

the underside of his jaw, those brown eyes swirling with confused desire. She blinked then dropped her hands away from him. "I need to change out of my sweats. My shoulder holster doesn't exactly work with this shirt."

"You look good in anything you put on." A laugh rumbled from deep in his chest. His fingertips grazed over the bare column of her throat before he put a good amount of space between them. He had to. Otherwise, they might never leave the safe house. Notching her chin higher, he forced her to meet his gaze. "I won't let him touch you, Sprinkles."

She nodded. "I know."

"Good." He needed her to believe him. "Then let's catch us a bomber."

Chapter Six

When he'd kissed her, she'd lost all restraint.

One second, she'd been working out her frustration at putting an innocent man in danger, at not being able to hold up her emotional guard against Braxton, on the burner phone, and the next his mouth had been on hers. Her heart had thundered so hard, blood pouring through her ears, she'd felt as though she'd been underwater. Couldn't breathe. Couldn't hear. But she hadn't been able to pull away.

Pushing the memory back—a memory she'd never let go—Elizabeth cracked her knuckles as she walked east down the sidewalk toward the Alaska Center for the Performing Arts. She stuffed her shaking hands into her now empty coat pockets and hunkered deeper into the faux-fur folds as a blast of frigid air fought to chase the heat from her skin. They'd handed off the bullets from the SUV's windshield to Vincent as soon as they'd arrived, but she doubted he'd be able to glean anything useful. Whoever had tried to kill her had been planning this from the beginning. He wouldn't slip up unless he meant to slip up. She scanned the rooftops of the surrounding buildings. And the chances of that seemed slight. "No sign of our target yet."

Anchorage's snow-covered Town Center stretched a half acre in front of her. Blue and white Christmas lights had yet to be removed from the branches of pines decorating the grounds, even though the holiday season had ended three weeks ago. Her boots fought for purchase on the icy sidewalk. Or was it the possibility she might be centered in a shooter's crosshairs unbalancing her? Cloud cover made it hard to see into the shadows, and the hairs on the back of her neck stood on end.

"He'll show. You're too good of an opportunity to pass up." Braxton's voice in her ear settled the rush of nervous energy shooting down her spine. Well, that, and the fact he'd taken position thirty yards to her right in case he had to get to her fast. Mostly settled her nerves. There was still the issue of a possible ambush, and the conversation they would have to have after this little operation was over. About him leaving again. The open line between their earpieces crackled as the wind kicked up. A haze of snow danced in front of her. "Remember, I've got a giant bowl of ice cream and rainbow sprinkles waiting for you when this is over. So you better make it out of this alive."

"You always know exactly what to say." Studying the park for a second time, she fought the urge to look in Braxton's direction. The caller had told her to come alone. He should've tried convincing her bodyguard. She slowed her progress as she approached a single snow-covered bench in the middle of the park. With January temperatures dropping by the minute, most visitors had gone inside to warm up. Lower risk of putting innocent bystanders in danger if things went south.

"The cavalry has arrived, and guess what? I brought the big guns." Elliot Dunham's voice penetrated through the stiffness gripping her shoulders and neck, and a smile automatically stretched across her lips. What would they do without Blackhawk Security's con man turned private investigator? Rescued by the CEO and founder of the security firm from an Iraqi prison on fraud charges, the reformed criminal with a genius-level IQ never failed to amuse her. No matter how many times his compulsive sarcasm grated on her nerves, he'd never failed to have her back in the three months they'd worked together. And she'd always have his. "Admit it, Dawson, you missed me."

Gratitude flooded through her. Calling in Blackhawk Security had been her idea, but Braxton had taken point in getting them in place. She buried her mouth in the lining of her coat to hide her response in case the shooter had already arrived and was searching for signs she hadn't come alone. "If by big guns you mean Vincent and Glennon, then yes, I missed you."

"They won't let me touch the sniper rifle without taking a class first." Elliot's lighthearted attitude and the additional backup helped alleviate the nausea building in her stomach. Short exhales said he was still trying to get in position. "Personally, I think they like being the only ones with the heavy-duty weapons."

"Does this guy ever shut up?" Braxton asked.

"No." Vincent Kalani entered the park to her left, head down, barely raising his attention to her before he cut across the open terrain. Hands stuffed into his coat pockets, he moved with lethal grace. The former cop hid his face beneath a mane of wavy dark hair, but the tattoos climbing up his neck stood out. If the shooter had done his research, there was a good chance he'd recognize Blackhawk's forensics expert. "Trust me, we've tried."

"Head in the game, gentlemen." Glennon Chase, the firm's newest recruit and recent wife to their weapons expert, slid into sight at the edge of Elizabeth's peripheral vision. Armed with her own rifle, the former army investigator nodded as Elizabeth took a seat on the bench. Planting her eye against her scope, Glennon shifted out of sight along the rooftop of the building overlooking the park. "I've got movement at the north end of the park."

Elizabeth fought against the urge to look. Instead, she surveyed the area as a whole before redirecting her attention to the man stumbling toward her. Stained jacket, ripped jeans, thick gray hair and beard. Recognition flared, and she pushed off the bench. Wild eyes locked on her as Brolin Levitt reached for her, a prominent limp in his left leg. "Don't shoot. He's not the target." Slowing her approach, she lifted her hands, palms facing him. "Brolin, it's me. Elizabeth. You remember me? I'm friends with your son, Braxton."

Same introduction. Same approach. Every time. Over the past few months, the chances of him recognizing her steered toward sixty-forty. Sixty percent of the time, he didn't remember his own name. He closed in on her faster than she thought possible for a drug-addled old man.

Brolin didn't answer.

"Liz, I've got a bad feeling about this." Braxton's concern echoed through the earpiece, but she didn't pay it any attention. He'd made his feelings for his father perfectly clear, and there wasn't any scenario in which he'd trust the man in front of her. She didn't care. Brolin was innocent in all of this and had obviously been injured.

"I'm wearing Kevlar, I've got a gun and I know how to use it," she said. "I'm only helpless when my nail polish is wet, and even then, I can pull a trigger if I have to."

"While you make valid points, the shooter drew you here using Brolin as leverage. So why let the old man go?" he asked.

"I think I know why." Elizabeth caught a glimpse of two wires coming from the bottom of Brolin's stained old jacket. Her breath caught in her throat. Every cell in her body froze. One second. Two. Too long. "Braxton, your father is wired."

"What?" he asked.

A gunshot echoed off the surrounding buildings.

She spun toward the sound.

Braxton broke away from his position at her left, his ball cap flying off his head as he pumped his arms and legs hard. "Liz, get down!"

Pain splintered across her left arm and she spun, clamping her hand over the graze. She hit the ground hard. Snow and ice worked through her clothing as she scrambled toward Brolin. The shooter had used Brolin and the bomb strapped to his chest as a distraction. Long enough to get her in his sights. Fisting her hands around his jacket, Elizabeth wrenched the old man into her and pushed him forward. Her boots slid against the dusting of snow covering the sidewalks. They had to get moving. They were still out in the open. "Find that damned shooter."

"Got him. Suspect is rabbiting across the roof of the building to the south. There's a car waiting in the alley between buildings. Alaska license plate echo, uniform, sierra, six, eight, seven." Vincent's calm did nothing to ease the adrenaline surging through her veins. "Can't get a clean shot. Glennon?"

Braxton wrapped his hand around her arm and hauled her and Brolin their feet. He shoved them ahead of him as a black GMC pulled up to the curb fifty feet away.

The front passenger window lowered, revealing Elliot Dunham's dumbass smirk. "This never would've happened if they let me have a sniper rifle."

"Now's not the time, Elliot!" They reached the SUV. Elizabeth wrenched the passenger side door open and threw Brolin inside. No time for hellos. There was a shooter on the loose. "Meet your new assignment. His name is Brolin Levitt. He dies, you die. Understand?"

Elliot's deep gray eyes widened. "Is that a bomb?"

"I'm pretty sure it's fake, but you might want to take a look at it just in case." She slammed the door closed, not waiting for an answer.

"I've got a shot." The familiar sound of Glennon

loading a round into the rifle's chamber echoed in Elizabeth's earpiece as Braxton forced her to take cover behind a park bench. The SUV fishtailed away from the curb, shooting down the street. Brolin was safe. "I'm taking it."

The thunderclap of another bullet leaving the barrel of a rifle thudded through her. She held her breath as Braxton wrapped her in a tight hold against his chest. Waited. Silence settled around her. Her pulse throbbed at the base of her throat, the pain in her arm pulling at her attention. The second shot hadn't been meant for her, but a rush of relief escaped from her lungs all the same. Sirens filtered through the pulsing in her head.

"I missed him." Glennon hauled her rifle off the edge of the rooftop above and disappeared from sight. "If anybody tells my husband I missed that shot, you're dead."

"How are you going to kill us when you can't even hit your target?" The growl of the SUV's engine filtered through Elliot's earpiece. Good. Brolin would be safe as long as he stuck with Blackhawk's private investigator. Although getting him to stay might be a challenge, but she was sure Elliot would figure something out.

"I'm starting with you, Elliot," Glennon said.

Squealing tires reached her ears as Elizabeth caught sight of a high-class Mercedes sedan fishtailing out of the alley across the street. The windows were too tinted for her to make an identification, but her instincts said that was their shooter. She dug her nails into Braxton's jacket. "He's getting away."

"No, he's not." Braxton wrapped his hand around

hers, tugging her after him. "You remember that license plate number?"

"Yes." Puffs of her breath crystallized in front of her, freezing air reaching down to the bullet graze on her arm through the new hole in her jacket. The pain slid to the back of her mind as she forced her legs to work harder.

"Good." Braxton pulled her around the south corner of the park, toward another Blackhawk Security SUV. "Get in."

HE WASN'T GOING to let Liz become a victim from circumstances he'd created. If he hadn't tried to keep her in the dark in the first place, she wouldn't be in this situation. And if that bullet hadn't only grazed her arm, he'd have had to live with that the rest of his life. The idea pushed his foot against the accelerator harder. Everyone was created by a defining event. Something that changed them just enough. A loss, a trauma, the end of a relationship. Liz would be his. Always his. "You okay?"

"I'm fine. Focus on the road." She clamped a hand over the wound in her arm, swaying as he forced the SUV around a tight turn. Downtown Anchorage blurred in his peripheral vision as they closed in on the Mercedes's bumper. A minivan pulled out in front of them, and he swerved. She grabbed onto the handle above her head with one hand and the dashboard with the other with a groan of pain. "If I ever need a skilled getaway driver, you are not the person I'm going to call."

Uneven roads lifted them out of their seats. The

shooter barreled through a construction zone ahead of them, taking a sharp right.

Liz tapped her earpiece with bloody fingertips. "Vincent, we need Anchorage PD to set up a roadblock. We can't let this guy get away."

"Copy that," Vincent said.

"Hang on." Braxton made the turn, the SUV's fender barely missing a car pulling out of an underground parking garage. Checking back over his shoulder, he shook his head. "Don't people know how to drive anymore?"

Liz swiped her hand across her face, attention out the windshield. "For crying out loud, it's not this psychopath who's going to kill me. It's your driving."

Those words hit him like a hammer fall. Braxton sobered, knuckles tight around the steering wheel as they cleared downtown, and sped up the ramp onto south Seward Highway. If the bastard thought he'd be able to lose them by disappearing into the trail entrances along the coast, he was wrong. Braxton had had to know them better than anyone else in this city in order to survive on his own. "I'm not going to let anything happen to you."

"You guys realize your coms are still online, right?" Elliot's voice in his head was not what he needed right now. "This seems like a private moment."

"All you need to worry about is keeping Brolin alive, Elliot. Leave the rest to me." Liz shot a quick look in his direction. While putting his old man under Blackhawk Security protection hadn't climbed its way to the top of Braxton's priority list, the drug addict could at least do some good to identify the shooter who'd taken him. "Vincent, we've turned south onto Seward Highway, and this guy isn't showing any signs of stopping. Where are we at with Anchorage PD?"

"There's a pileup downtown, thanks to your driver there." Vincent's disappointment echoed through the earpiece. "And any other available units are closing in on the park due to a wave of calls about shots fired. I'm having the chief send as many as he can your way, but that could be up to an hour."

Braxton picked the device out of his ear and tossed it into the back seat, eyes on the prize ahead. He maneuvered around a fifty-two-foot semitruck, losing sight of the Mercedes for three seconds. Four. Cloud cover made it that much harder to keep their target straight, but he soon had a lock on the shooter again. The bastard wasn't going to get away. Not when they were so close to ending this nightmare. Desperation clawed up his throat. He'd vowed to protect the woman in the seat beside him. He couldn't let her down now. "Guess we're on our own."

"You want to be the one to catch him." Her voice worked to ease the tangle of tension coiling tight at the base of his skull. The Mercedes swerved to maneuver around a group of three cars ahead, but she'd always been able to consume his attention with a single look. A word. "Why?"

The engine growled in protest as he pushed the SUV harder, trying to close the distance between them and the shooter. He had no idea what they were going to do after that, but he'd always been good on his feet. The sun would start going down in the next hour. They'd lose him altogether if they didn't end this.

"You know why. I told you I'd protect you, and I meant it. Catching this guy is the only way to do that." He locked his jaw against the lie, the muscles along his neck and shoulders straining. Chancing a quick glance at her, he read the questions carved into her expression.

"No, that's not it. It's something more than that." The weight of her attention pinned him to the back of the leather seat. She'd never been an analyst, but she could make a damn good career out of reading people. How the hell did he think he could keep secrets from her? "What aren't you telling me?"

The Mercedes disappeared in the midst of four cars ahead of them.

Braxton sat forward in his seat as he sped around a small sedan. Narrowing his gaze, he studied car after car as he backed his foot off the accelerator. "He's gone."

"What?" She turned her attention back to the road then twisted in her seat to inspect the cars behind them. "That's not possible. There aren't any exit ramps in this section of the highway."

Didn't make the shooter's disappearing act any less real. Braxton checked his rearview mirror as a pair of headlights flared to life behind them. "He didn't get off the highway. Get ready—"

Two gunshots broke the soothing sound of tires against asphalt, but the bullets ricocheted off the glass. Bulletproof windows were a nice touch. Braxton swerved into the next lane, narrowly avoiding another sedan, but the maneuver did nothing to distract the shooter. The hood of the Mercedes closed in fast.

"He's going to try to run us off the road." Panic tinted Liz's words, but he couldn't worry about that right now. Keeping her alive. That was all that mattered. She could panic all she wanted as long as she was alive.

The first hit to the bumper thrust them forward. The steering wheel jerked in his hand, but Braxton kept a tight hold. Civilian cars slowly backed off as another collision to their bumper forced them onto the highway's shoulder. The grooves cut into the shoulder to keep drivers awake drowned out another gunshot to the back of the SUV. He fought to keep the SUV on the road, but slowing down, pulling over even, would put Liz directly in the shooter's sights. Not an option. Time to end this, but with the Turnagain Arm waterway on one side and nothing but thick wilderness on the other, he only had a small window to make this work. "Hang on to something."

Her hand shot to the handlebar above her head just before Braxton slammed on the brakes. Tires screeched in his ears, the smell of burned rubber filling the interior of the SUV as momentum thrust them forward in their seats. The Mercedes's headlights disappeared behind the bottom of the back window. His lungs seized half a second before the shooter rammed into the back of their vehicle. The third collision forced the SUV to one side despite how hard Braxton pulled the wheel in the opposite direction.

Tires caught on the road. The world went hazy as the vehicle wrenched to one side then flipped. Every instinct he owned urged him to reach out for Liz. He loosened his grip on the steering wheel, fighting against gravity to touch her, but the highway rushed up to meet the windshield too fast. The terrorizing fear etched into her features vanished as the roof crumpled under the impact. His head snapped forward, glass breaking all around them. Metal protested against asphalt in his ears, but all he could focus on was Liz's scream.

The SUV swung up again, depleting his brain of oxygen, then slammed into the ground. The seat belt cut into his shoulder and across his chest.

Then there was stillness as the vehicle righted itself.

His head throbbed in rhythm to his racing heartbeat. A dull ringing filled his ears, but not loud enough to block out the screech of tires nearby. He blinked against the onslaught of chaos surrounding the SUV, vision hazy, tongue thick in his mouth. "Liz."

No answer.

Braxton strained to look at her. "Liz, baby, can you hear me?"

Footsteps heightened the headache spreading from the crown of his head. Something wet—blood—trickled down the side of his face. He'd hit his head against the driver's side window during the roll. Shadows crossed his vision on Liz's side of the vehicle. Wait, no. Just one. The outline of a man closed in on the SUV.

Black ski mask. Pressed suit. Gun in his hand. Every muscle in his body tensed. Not a civilian.

"Come on, Sprinkles, wake up." The seat belt kept Braxton secured in the seat. He fought to reach for his gun that'd fallen from his shoulder holster. He couldn't move his arms, stomach rocketing into his throat. He leveraged his heels into the floorboards but couldn't move otherwise. "Elizabeth!"

The shooter reached in through the broken passenger side window—too close to Liz—and unlocked the door. Raising the gun in his hand toward Braxton, he wrenched the door open then reached for Liz's seat belt. The SOB wasn't going to take her. Not happening. Dark eyes centered on him. "Well, that went easier than I imagined."

Braxton didn't recognize the voice, the posture, the suit. No accent. Nothing to lead him to an identity of the man taking the most important thing in his life from him.

"I'm going to kill you, you bastard." Braxton ordered his body to move, to reach for his gun, to do anything. No response. A feral scream ripped from his throat. Blood and sweat stung his eyes. He couldn't lose her. Not yet. Not when she'd just come back into his life. "I'm going to hunt you down, and I'm going to end you."

The shooter laughed, dark, merciless, as he compressed the button to Liz's seat belt, wrapped his grip around her delicate wrist and hefted her over one shoulder. All the while keeping the gun aimed on Braxton. "Good luck with that."

Chapter Seven

Pain. Dizziness. A hard pulsing behind her ears that she could only describe as the beginning of her own death.

She felt as though she'd been weighed down by lead. Elizabeth struggled to open her eyes, blinking back the heaviness in her brain. Blackness consumed the edges of her vision. She narrowed in on the movement of patterns in front of her. Blackness and…pinstripes? The subtle lines shifted, and she realized the unbalanced sensation charging through her wasn't dizziness, but movement. The intense pressure in her midsection meant someone had flipped her over their shoulder and was carrying her. She used her remaining strength to raise her head. Tendrils of hair blocked her peripheral vision, but there, straight behind her, was the remains of her destroyed SUV. Sullivan wasn't going to be too happy about another of Blackhawk Security's vehicles being totaled, but she couldn't afford to care. Not with a shooter on their tail. Wait. Confusion gripped her in a tight vise as she sank back against the man carrying her. "Braxton?"

"Not exactly." That voice. She recognized that voice from somewhere.

A whiff of expensive cologne tickled her nose and worked deep into her lungs. No. Not Braxton. He didn't wear cologne. Which meant… Recognition clicked into place. The air rushed from her lungs. The shooter. He'd called her on the burner phone. He'd—

A thread of anxiety unraveled inside her, tangling up with anger, resentment and fear. The edge of her shoulder holster dug into her armpit, but with one look, she discovered she'd been relieved of her weapon. Black asphalt passed beneath her. *Think, think, think.* Rolling her hands into fists, Elizabeth focused all of her attention on the small of the shooter's back and sank her elbow hard in the curve of his spine as hard as she could.

His grip around the back of her knees disappeared, and she toppled backward. The highway rushed up to meet her faster than she expected, and she hit the ground. Loose rocks cut into the side of her head, but she rolled in an effort to get to her feet. Stinging pain spread across the other side of her skull as the shooter fisted a chunk of her hair in his hand and hauled her to her feet.

Six-foot-plus frame, lean, preferred a Windsor knot and a nice suit over Kevlar. It wasn't much to go on, but it was a start. Elizabeth wrapped her grip around his wrist as he wrenched her into him. The black ski mask hid his mouth as he spoke, but those dark eyes would always stick in her memory. Cold. Calculating. Dangerous. "You're going to pay for that, but first, you're going to help me."

"You've tried to kill me three times and put an innocent man's life in danger." Her voice remained steady despite the earthquake exploding inside her. "There's no way I'd do anything to help you."

"We'll see about that." Pulling his weapon, the shooter wrenched her into his side and aimed for the totaled SUV. For Braxton still in the driver's seat. "You should've known changing your last name wouldn't stop me from finding you, Elizabeth. Not when I have Oversight at my disposal." He pressed his mouth against her ear, and a shiver threatened to overrun her. "How about now? Should I pull this trigger, or are you going to get in the damn car?"

Bystanders' screams and panic infiltrated through the pounding of her pulse in her ears. Car doors slammed; tires peeled against the road. Others raised their phones to get the scene on video or capture a photo but didn't move to interfere. She couldn't breathe. Couldn't think.

Braxton's life or her own certain death.

"Liz, run!" His voice punctured through the sensory overload wrapping itself in a tight fist inside. Braxton struggled to free himself from the crumpled SUV, pulling against the seat belt. The sound of liquid hitting the road claimed her attention. She scanned the wreckage until sunlight reflected off a pool of gas beneath the SUV. Any second now the vehicle could catch fire, and Braxton would be gone.

"If you kill him now, you lose your leverage. I'll never help you." Her heart turned over in her chest, her stomach squeezing tight. No. She wasn't going to leave him. He wouldn't leave her. With the shooter's forearm braced against her collarbones, there was only one thing she could do.

"True, but you've made yourself a new life here. Gotten to know quite a few people." His laugh rumbled between her shoulder blades. "I have an entire list of leverage, Elizabeth. And I'm not above ticking them off one at a time until you do as I ask. Elliot Dunham, Vincent Kalani, Sullivan Bishop. And your friend Kate? Hasn't she lost enough?" He moved his finger over the trigger, cocking his head away from her neck. "But today, I think I'll start with your bodyguard there."

She locked her attention on Braxton. "Come find me when this is over."

"Good girl." The shooter dropped his weapon to his side. "Now get in the car."

"No." She took advantage. Inhaling deeply, Elizabeth dropped to her haunches. She rocked back on her heels and sprang back up, shoving her shoulder into his mid-section to knock him off balance. He hit the ground, the gun sliding across the asphalt. They both followed its track. One second, two, and then Elizabeth lunged. The shooter recovered almost instantly. Any physical fight could cost her everything, but she wasn't going to let him hurt anyone else. Not when she could end this now. Her best option was that gun. She wrapped her fingers around the barrel as a shoe stomped on her wrist. Bone crunched, and a scream worked up her throat.

"Elizabeth!" Braxton's yell barely registered over the high-pitched ringing in her ears.

The shooter bent down to claim the weapon from her. "You're not going to win, Elizabeth. I've been waiting for this moment for too long. You're going to help me. Even if I have to kill everyone you've ever cared about to force your compliance."

She hadn't been trained in combat like Blackhawk's weapons expert Anthony Harris, hadn't been trained to fight like a SEAL as Sullivan had. Hell, even Glennon could take down a room full of men on her own if pushed. But Elizabeth wouldn't give up. Her life wasn't the only one that mattered anymore. She was this baby's mother, and she would do everything in her power to keep her safe.

"Go to hell." Elizabeth tossed the gun into her opposite hand and swung up as hard as she could. Metal met flesh and bone of the shooter's left zygomatic, and he stumbled back. The pressure released off her broken wrist, but as long as adrenaline pumped through her veins, she could deal with the pain. She pushed to her feet and pumped her legs hard. Get to Braxton. Bright green eyes widened as she raised the gun. "Move!"

Braxton raised his arms over his head and faced toward the broken driver's side window.

She pulled the trigger, and the lock of his seat belt exploded. "You're welcome."

A strong hand wrenched the gun from her hand, another latching around her throat. Air pressurized in her lungs as the shooter backed her up against the SUV then aimed the gun at her temple. "Move from the vehicle and I kill her now, Levitt."

She couldn't see Braxton, couldn't hear him over the drowning sensation threatening to pull her under, but she didn't have to. He'd promised to protect her, to fight for her, and if there was one thing she couldn't fault him for, it was that he kept his promises.

"Let her go. You and I will end this right now." Fury battered Braxton's words. The SUV door slammed closed, reverberating through her. Then footsteps. Braxton strode into her peripheral vision, hands tense at his sides. Ready for a fight. "You're not going to kill her. You need her. Otherwise you would've already done it."

Calm exhales puffed the ski mask out over the shooter's mouth. Black eyes studied Braxton as a single tear slipped from Elizabeth's left eye. He'd cut off her oxygen. She'd either pass out in a few seconds or die right here. And he knew it. He was buying his time, showing he had control. The shooter lowered the gun from her temple then aimed at Braxton. "Then I'll guess I'll have to put a bullet in you."

He pulled the trigger.

Braxton spun as the bullet made contact and fell to the ground.

The scream didn't make it out as the shooter tightened his hold around her throat. Pulling her into him, he leveled that dark gaze with hers. Sirens and flashing lights closed in on the scene. "One down, Elizabeth. How many more people are you willing to watch die before you give in?"

Her vision blurred, her body growing heavy.

He didn't wait for an answer, wrenching her forward when all she wanted to do was fight back, when all she wanted to do was get to Braxton. But fighting back put her baby at risk.

She fought to stay upright as blackness closed in at

the edges of her vision. Faster than she thought possible, the shooter had shoved her into the trunk of his Mercedes. The engine growled to life as darkness consumed her.

"CALL AN AMBULANCE!" Unfamiliar voices pulled him out of blackness.

Braxton shot up straight with a gasp in his throat, gravel and glass cutting into his palms. The ache in his chest burned through him, and he clamped a hand over the brand-new hole in his T-shirt and Kevlar. A groan escaped as he pushed to his feet and stumbled through the circle of civilians surrounding him. "Where is she?"

He scanned the scene as Anchorage PD and a dark SUV identical to Liz's rolled onto the scene. Vincent Kalani stepped out onto the pavement, and everything inside Braxton froze. While he'd been the one to initially put Liz in the crosshairs by leaving, the call to her burner cell had sealed the deal. None of this—the bullet graze, the crash, her kidnapping—would've happened if she hadn't picked up that call. There was only one number she'd dialed on that phone. Only one way the shooter could've gotten through to her.

Braxton closed in on the forensics expert fast. Rage pushed through him as he fisted his hands in Vincent's cargo jacket and hauled him back against the SUV. "Where is she? You're the only one who called that burner. You're the only one—"

A right hook to the face knocked Braxton off balance. Vincent straightened to his full six-foot-four frame. Violence etched deep lines into the forensic expert's expression. "The next time you come at me, you better be sure to finish the job. Understand?"

A group of Anchorage PD officers stood ready to draw their weapons around him.

"He took her. That bastard took her." Braxton ignored the pulse at the left side of his face, a combination of sweat and blood sticking to his scalp. His heart threatened to explode out of his chest. Every minute he'd been unconscious had been another minute she'd gotten farther away. Damn it. One breath, two… Reason returned in small increments as he forced his blood pressure under control. "He contacted her through her burner phone. You're the only one who had that number."

"I would never put Elizabeth in danger. I trust her with my life, and she trusts me with hers. You see, that's what a team does, Levitt. We trust each other. We risk our lives for each other." Strain tightened the cords running down Vincent's neck as he stepped closer. Thick, dark eyebrows drew together. He extracted his phone from his jacket pocket, swiping his thumb across the screen. Handing the phone off, Vincent nodded. "Take it. If we're going to find her, you've got to trust me."

Braxton took the phone, his attention immediately drawn to the blinking red dot speeding south along a map of Seward Highway. His hand tightened around the device, the back hot to the touch. Elizabeth. "You're tracking her."

"I'm tracking her earpiece. You've got a range of ten miles. I'll take care of things here." Vincent extracted the tiny device from his ear then tossed him a set of keys, pain from the bullet flooding through Braxton as he caught them midair. Setting the earpiece in Braxton's palm, the forensics expert nodded. "Go. Get my teammate back."

Braxton pumped his legs hard and inserted the earpiece as he wrenched open Vincent's SUV door. The engine growled to life as he shoved the vehicle into Drive and jammed his foot into the accelerator. "I'm coming for you, baby, hang on."

No answer.

Seward Highway stretched out in front of him, 125 miles of majestic scenery, trailheads and a hell of a lot of places to take care of a hostage. A groan fought its way up his throat. No. Whoever this guy was, he needed Liz. Otherwise she'd already be dead. Braxton pushed the SUV harder. The shooter would keep her secluded, away from the touristy cabins along the highway. "He's not going to kill her yet."

He glanced down at the phone. Still in range. It'd be another few minutes before he caught up to the Mercedes. Every cell in his body couldn't stand to be apart from her for another second longer, but he couldn't force the SUV faster. His fingers drummed hard against the steering wheel. If her kidnapper hurt her, he'd spend the rest of his life hunting the SOB down. "Come on, come on."

"Braxton?" Her strained voice spread through him like a wildfire.

"Liz." He swallowed hard against the tightening in his throat. She was alive. "Baby, are you hurt?"

"My wrist…" A hard *thunk* registered through the

earpiece. Then another. She hissed. "I think it's broken, but I'm okay. He put me in the trunk. Took the burner phone and my gun. I'm trying to kick out the taillight to see where we are."

"I'm coming for you." He glanced down at the phone's screen. The red dot blinked strong. A few more miles. That was all it'd take to have her back in his arms. He hadn't given much thought to his future. All that'd mattered when he'd come back to Anchorage was keeping her alive then moving on with his life if she decided he needed to leave. But now? There was no life without Elizabeth. And he wasn't going to lose her or their baby now. Brolin might've raised him, but Liz and baby Karina were his family now. And nobody threatened his family. He gritted his teeth, fighting against the rising pressure behind his sternum. "Save your energy. I'm tracking your earpiece. I'm not far behind."

"Braxton," she said. "If I don't make it out of this alive—"

"You will." There was no other option. He was already redlining the RPMs. If he pushed the SUV any harder, the engine would explode. His breath came too fast. His heartbeat shook behind his rib cage. Headlights blinded him from the other side of the highway as he made the last curve. Less than a mile between them. "Just keep talking. Focus on my voice, and we'll get through this. You're not going to be a vic—"

Tendrils of smoke rose from the SUV's engine, the needles in the dashboard falling no matter how hard he pushed the accelerator. Soft ticks from the engine kept rhythm with the headache at the back of his skull as

Braxton jerked at the steering wheel. The vehicle slowed from ninety miles plus per hour to a mere twenty in the span of ten seconds. No, no, no, no, no. "Come on!"

"Braxton? What is it? What's wrong?" Liz's voice dropped into panic.

He pulled the SUV into the shoulder, barely able to see through the thick smoke coming out of the edges of the hood. He wouldn't make it to her—not in time. His feet hit the pavement, and he rounded to the front of the vehicle. After hauling the hood overhead, he braced himself against the white-hot temperatures as he reached for the radiator cap. Pain scalded across his hand, but he got the cap off and looked inside. Empty. Damn it. "Nothing. I'm coming for you."

He tossed the cap on top of the radiator then extracted Vincent's cell phone from the interior of the SUV. He'd trained day in and day out for this. Come hell or high water, he'd get to her. Slamming the driver's side door behind him, he checked his weapon and started running, phone in hand. The shooter might never pull over, but Braxton would never stop looking for her.

"We're slowing down." Rustling filtered through the open line as she shifted inside the trunk. Then stopped. "He's pulling off the highway. I can't tell where we are. I can't see anything."

"That's okay. I know where you are." He confirmed her location on Vincent's phone, air tight in his chest as he tried to keep his voice even. A half mile up ahead, the shooter had pulled into the trailhead for McHugh Trail, a heavily wooded and rocky journey to McHugh Peak. Without snowshoes this time of year, the bastard would have a hard time getting very deep into the wilderness with a hostage, but there were plenty of places to disappear.

Or to hide a body.

Braxton spotted a distant pair of red lights down the highway. Cliffs and trees backed against the highway on one side, Turnagain Arm on the other. Every second he lagged behind, the higher the chance he'd lose them altogether. "Listen to me. I have your location. I'm going to find you. I promised I would protect you, and I will."

A loud thud resembling the slamming of a car door reverberated into his ear.

"He's coming." She lowered her voice to a whisper, a plea on her lips. "Braxton…"

His grip tightened around the phone in his hand. His muscles burned, but he pushed the pain to the back of his mind. "I'm coming, Liz. I'll be there in two minutes. Fight back. Run if you have to. I'll find you."

The high-pitched protest of metal reached his ears. The trunk lid? Muffled static claimed his attention, an all-too-familiar voice growing louder. "You've been holding out on me." Another round of static drowned out Liz's response as though someone was handling a microphone. "Whoever this is, you think you're coming to save her. Well, I've got news for you. You're too late. Elizabeth is mine."

The deafening crunch exploded in his ear.

"Liz?" A quick glance at Vincent's phone said it all: the shooter had destroyed Liz's earpiece. And any chance he had of tracking her location. "Liz!"

Chapter Eight

Her hands shook as the shooter pulled her from the trunk of the Mercedes. He'd found her earpiece almost instantly and crushed it beneath polished shoes. No passing cars. No hikers out as the sun started to lower in the sky.

No one to hear her scream.

Rough hands maneuvered her around the car and toward the trailhead up ahead. Clear skies gave way to a few twinkling stars this far out of the city, but where Elizabeth normally would've taken a few minutes to appreciate the view, now she was being forced deeper into Alaskan wilderness. "You don't have to do this."

She didn't know what else to say as branches from pines scraped across her jacket and the exposed skin of her neck and face. He'd gone out of his way to find her. Tortured her former supervisor, hijacked Oversight's feeds, stalked her for weeks. Something deep in her gut said no matter what she said, he wouldn't listen.

"Walk until I tell you to stop." His voice remained calm, collected. Dangerous.

Her boots scuffed against rocks and downed branches

along the trail. She couldn't see more than five feet in front of her. He hadn't bound her. She'd catch herself if she fell, but she couldn't do much else with her broken wrist. And running into the middle of the wilderness as temperatures dropped for the night in the middle of January would be as lethal as taking a bullet to the head. Braxton had promised he'd find her, but freezing to death out here, where he couldn't track her anymore thanks to the man with the gun pressed into her back, wasn't a chance she was willing to take. Elizabeth checked his position back over her shoulder. "You obviously plan on killing me and leaving me out here for hikers to discover later. Don't I deserve to know why?"

"You don't deserve anything but what's coming to you." He pressed the gun deeper into her back, nearly to her spine despite the padding of her coat.

Freezing air burned her nostrils the higher they climbed up the trail. What did he expect her to do, make it all the way to McHugh Peak with a bullet graze, a head injury and a broken wrist? Her lungs fought against the climb in elevation, her breaths getting shallower with each step. "The Sovereign Army took credit for the bombing at Blackhawk Security, but you've made this personal. This isn't about protecting the American population's privacy, is it? You're using an extremist group as your cover."

She was only guessing, but from his lack of response, Elizabeth bet she had hit the nail on the head harder than she'd estimated. "Somehow you figured out I'd created Oversight for the NSA and changed my name. Then you tracked me down here in Anchorage and started planning my murder." She kept pushing forward. She'd only hiked this particular trail once during one of Sullivan's mandatory wilderness survival trainings, and it was difficult to decipher their location along the trail as shadows crept across the path, but there should be a branch heading off soon. At least a place she could gain the higher ground. She couldn't fight him physically, but she could disorient him long enough to buy herself time to run back toward the trailhead.

Toward Braxton.

"Why go through the trouble?" she asked.

"That's far enough." How the man determined to kill her breathed through the thick ski mask over his face, she had no idea. She chanced another glance behind her. The effect of his pressed suit combined with the mask chased a tremor down her spine. Like Death coming to collect the next soul in his crosshairs. Too bad she'd sold her soul to the father of her unborn child a long time ago.

She stopped in her tracks, about four feet ahead of him. Her pulse beat hard at the base of her throat. The only people who knew about her facial recognition program worked for the NSA or in the Oval Office. Which meant the shooter had either hacked his way into the NSA servers—which was unlikely given she'd set up the latest security—or he'd worked for them. Then again, he'd hijacked Oversight's feeds. Or he had a partner. Her toes tingled, going numb from the dropping temperatures. If he wasn't going to kill her soon, the wilderness would. Elizabeth wiggled her fingers to keep the circulation flowing. She strained to hear footsteps—anything—that indicated someone was coming. A hiker, police. Braxton. The man had a gun aimed at her, and there was nothing Elizabeth could do. "Is this where they're going to find my body?"

Keep him talking. Keep him distracted.

A gloved hand gripped her arm and spun her around, and her breath caught in her throat. Those dark eyes seemed black now with only muted sunlight coming through the trees. His hold on her hurt, bruised. "You're trying to stall, but it won't work. I've been waiting for this day for too long."

Without hesitation, the shooter hauled her off the worn path into shadowed darkness of thick pines and underbrush. Thorns pulled at her jeans and boot laces, but he dragged her along with ease. Dry branches cracked under her boots as they got farther from the trail. Nobody would think to look for her out here. Nobody would find her.

Trees thinned ahead. The muffled sound of passing cars grew louder. He wasn't going to leave her for a hiker—or worse, her team—to find. Elizabeth swallowed hard as they cleared the tree line. The cliff rushed up to meet her before she was ready. Her heel slipped off the edge, her knees buckling as panic spread through her. Loose rocks and dirt cascaded down below onto Seward Highway, but she never saw them land. Too far down. Only the shooter's tight grip on her arm kept her from falling, but she had a feeling that anchor wouldn't last long. Her breath lodged in her chest. She couldn't take her eyes off the black ocean of pavement a few hundred feet below where he intended to let her drown. Gravity pulled at her, but she fought against it.

"Tell me why. You've tried to blow me up, tried to shoot me on more than one occasion now." She didn't dare move, didn't dare face him for fear of taking the wrong step. She wasn't a profiler like Kate, she wasn't trained to read people, but the gunman at her back had certainly made this personal. He wanted her dead, wanted revenge. There was only one reason a man acted so passionately. "There has to be a reason."

"Give me the override password to Oversight's security and I'll make this quick." The slight exhale from behind her barely reached her ears over the sound of passing cars below. Silence settled. His voice became rough, fierce, as her arm tingled from her cut-off circulation. He placed his mouth against her ear. Too close. Intimate. She closed her eyes against the flood of nausea taking hold. "Or I can draw this out until you're begging me to end you."

That was why he hadn't killed her yet. While he might've been able to reroute the feeds, he hadn't been able to get past Oversight's security to operate the program himself. Her insides suddenly felt hollowed out, the rest of her body heavy. Her heartbeat echoed through her. The work she had done for the NSA haunted her every time she closed her eyes at night. She never should've agreed to build that damn program. Never should've let them use it before it was ready. The secrets, the lies, the deaths. Oversight saved lives, but at what cost? Elizabeth licked at dry lips, the dropping temperatures wicking moisture from her mouth. Opening her eyes, she internally braced herself. "It won't do you any good. The password is only the first level to gaining control. You won't be able to hack the second. Not without me."

And not without a retinal scanner.

"Then this is going to be a long night for you." The slightest movement at her back threatened to launch her over the side of the cliff. "You know a person can sustain a three-story fall and live to tell about it. But not much else. You see, your body will be so broken, you'll never be able to do more than blink from your hospital bed until you finally give up on life." He jerked her against him then maneuvered her closer to the edge. "So save us both the time. You have five seconds to give me the password."

The back of her heel slipped off the edge of the cliff, and she held on harder to the man threatening to throw her over the edge. Panic consumed her. Her breath came quick. Her heart rate rocketed into dangerous territory. She didn't want to die. Elizabeth squeezed her eyes tight, fought to keep her balance. One wrong step. That was all it would take and everything would be over. Her stomach pitched as her mind put on a nausea-inducing slideshow of what that meant. She'd never meet her baby girl. Never protect another client. Never take control of the life she wanted.

"Two seconds," he said.

Braxton.

His name slipped between the layers of panic and demanded her attention. Her heart rate dropped, the flush of cold sweats dissipating. She opened her eyes. Fighting to breathe through a rush of dizziness, she shook her head. The shooter wouldn't be able to get past the second level of security. Not without her. So if giving him the password saved her life—saved her baby's life—there wasn't much to think about. "All right!" She licked at dry lips. "The password is 'Inicial Lake,' from my favorite TV show."

His laugh slithered down her spine.

"Your government turned its back on you the same as they did me. Tell me, *Sprinkles*," he said. "How does it feel turning your back on them now?"

"Don't call me that." Something shot down her spine, like an electric shock. Her fingers tightened as fury exploded through her. Elizabeth dug her heels into the dirt and shoved back into his chest. Her momentum knocked him off balance, but his grip still around her arm pulled her down with him. The tree line blurred in her vision as they rolled, locked around one another, in a fight for the gun. A scream worked up her throat as her already broken wrist sandwiched between them, the gun's barrel pointing straight at her forehead. He was stronger, so much stronger, than she was. But she wasn't going to die out here.

She slammed into a nearby pine, bark and dried needles scratching the skin along the back of her neck. A wave of dizziness unbalanced her as she tried to stand. The shooter fought to straighten, the gun missing from his hand.

There. Discarded in a bed of pine needles and leaves, the weapon stood out against the washed-out foliage and ice. Elizabeth lunged, but she wasn't fast enough. A leather-gloved hand wrapped around her ankle, and she hit the ground hard. Clawing at the ground, she fought to reach the gun. Dirt worked under her fingernails, but she didn't care. Without that gun, she was dead.

The shooter pulled her back against him, the weapon farther out of reach than before, and flipped her onto her back. She kicked at him, punched. He was too strong. That same gloved hand wrapped around her throat for a second time and squeezed. She clamped one hand around his wrist as leverage, trying to get oxygen, and reached for his left eye with the other despite her broken wrist.

"Get the hell away from her." Braxton's voice pierced through the darkness. She fought to scream though no sound left her mouth. The few stars above transformed into indistinct balls of light as Braxton raised his own weapon, taking aim. "Or I put a bullet in your head."

"I SAID GET away from her." Braxton widened his stance, pulling his shoulders back to make himself a smaller target. Pure rage filled his lungs, pure fire burning through his veins. Didn't matter the sun had dipped below the trees. He'd rip this SOB apart blind for coming after Liz. Family wasn't who he'd been born with. It was who he'd die for, and he sure as hell was ready to die right here, right now for the mother of his child if that was what fate held for him. But he wouldn't make it easy, either. He motioned the bastard up with the barrel of the gun.

The shooter released his grip around Liz's throat, and she fell back against the dead pine needles and foliage.

Her gasps reached his ears, but Braxton never took his attention off the man standing above her. "You're nothing but a disgraced analyst, Levitt. You might've put on some muscle. Learned some fancy new moves, right? But I've been doing this for years. You can't stop me."

A smile curled at one edge of his mouth. Braxton tossed the gun, his fingers contracting into the center of his palms. Adrenaline dumped into his blood and hiked his pulse higher as he relaxed his stance. "Why don't we find out?"

The shooter took that as his cue, pulling a blade from an ankle holster. Her attacker headed straight for him, that mask still in place.

Braxton met him halfway, the small amount of sun providing enough light for him to make the first strike. The shooter lunged for him blade first. Catching the operative's wrist, he hauled the blade upward and swept the shooter's legs out from under him. They hit the ground hard, the air crushed from his lungs. His elbow made contact with the shooter's sternum, and the knife flipped into the underbrush. Out of the corner of his eye, Liz turned over onto her stomach, struggling to her feet. She searched for something in the grass. Maybe a weapon.

The shooter took advantage of the distraction and wrapped a forearm around Braxton's neck, his back pressed against the bastard's chest, and squeezed. His heartbeat pulsed hard at the base of his throat and grew louder in his ears. He leveraged his fingers between his own neck and his attacker's forearm and took a single deep breath. "Give it up, Levitt. You can't save her. Not this time."

Liz was the one he'd lived for. And he'd fight for her until the end.

A growl resonated through him. Braxton shot his knee directly back into the shooter's face, and the SOB's grip disappeared. He rolled out of range then pushed to his feet, fists up. The shooter closed in on him before he could take his next breath. He blocked the first punch. Blocked the second. But a hard kick to Braxton's sternum sent him sprawling head over heels through the dirt. Dead pine needles and something wet clung to his clothing. He forced himself to his feet as the shooter went for Liz again.

"Braxton!" She threw her hands out behind her as she backed herself toward the tree line, those mesmerizing brown eyes wide and filled with terror.

Braxton closed the distance between them, fisting the shooter's suit in his hand, and shoved a boot to the back of the operative's knee. He followed through with a punch to the face for good measure. His muscles ached, his head pounding hard from the accident. Blood still clung to the side of his face and wouldn't come off with the swipe of the back of his hand. Didn't matter. Getting Liz out of here. Protecting their baby. Ending this sick game. That was all that mattered.

The shooter went down, narrowly missing Braxton's boot to his face as he rolled. A glint of sunlight flashed before the assailant came at him with another blade. Damn it. How many other weapons was the bastard hiding in that suit? They faced off again. Hard exhales and the faint hooting of an owl cut through the groan of dodging the knife. Black eyes locked on him as Braxton sank lower into his stance. "Not just an analyst after all. Where was this fire when you practically begged me to take the intel on Oversight four months ago?"

Braxton straightened a fraction of an inch. Four months ago. The night he'd left his entire future asleep in his bed and walked away. The anonymous transaction had saved Liz's life, but how many others had been destroyed because of his moment of weakness? His attention shot to Liz as she sank to her knees near the tree line, out of hearing range, seemingly out of energy. She couldn't find out the truth. Not yet. Not when they were so close to moving on from the past. Not when the chance of them being a family—a real family—stared back at him through her eyes. "You."

"Me." The shooter rushed forward, knife up. He used the blade as a distraction, hiking a knee into Braxton's rib cage.

Bone crunched under Braxton's fist as he slammed his knuckles into the assailant's face. Once. Twice. A muffled scream escaped from the shooter's mouth underneath the mask as he swung the blade down. Agony washed over Braxton as metal met flesh. Blood dripped onto his shoelaces, the sensation of small taps against the tops of his boots the only indication of how deep the laceration went. He suppressed the scream working up his throat. No telling how fast he was losing blood without being able to take his eyes off the shooter, but the faster his heart beat, the more blood he lost. With a single punch to the shooter's midsection, Braxton used the same distraction technique to reach for the blade. He wrapped his hand around the bastard's wrist and twisted the shooter's arm until the second blade fell to the ground. His opponent dropped to one knee as Braxton forced the arm backward. "You will never lay another finger on her as long as I'm around."

Wide eyes comprehended Braxton's next thought.

"Braxton, no!" Liz's voice fought to penetrate through the haze of violence consuming him. Then her shaking fingers slid over his left shoulder. She tightened her grip on him, her fingernails digging into his flesh, her voice strained. "You can't kill him."

One kick to the sternum. That was all it would take to end this nightmare, to ensure Liz never discovered the truth about the deal he'd made. But…he couldn't do it. Not when she expected him to be the good guy, to take the higher ground. "He's not going to stop."

"He'll pay for what he's done," she said. "The bomb, the shooting in the garage, the shooting in the park and kidnapping me. He's going to spend the rest of his life behind bars. But if you kill him now, you'll be on the run for the rest of your life. And you'll be no better than him."

Braxton let go of the SOB's wrist. The shooter lost his balance, hands desperately seeking something—anything—to grab on to. He came precariously close to toppling over the edge, but Braxton reached out, gripping the bastard's suit jacket, and hauled him away from the edge. He should've felt relief. Should've been able to release the tightness building behind his sternum. But Braxton knew the truth. This wasn't over. Wouldn't be as long as the operative's heart was still beating. "Don't make me regret not killing you."

"He'll never be able to touch me from behind bars. And he's going to have to live with that knowledge until he dies." Liz's grip softened as she raised a gun and took aim. The weapon shook in her hand and, for the first time, Braxton took his attention off the shooter to look at her. Muted sunlight highlighted the sheen of sweat between her brows as she fought to keep her eyes open. She struggled to straighten fully, free hand clutched around her lower abdominals.

"Liz?" Something was wrong. Braxton released his grip on the shooter, panic coursing through every cell in his body as he reached for her. "Liz—"

Her pupils rolled up behind her eyelids as she collapsed. Braxton caught her before she hit the ground, her skin cold and waxy. Pain shredded through his injured arm under the pressure, but he didn't give a damn. Something dark and sticky stained the arm of her coat. Blood. But not enough for her to lose consciousness. Something else was wrong.

A long shadow cast darkness across Liz's features as the shooter straightened. "Looks like my job here is done, after all."

Before Braxton had a chance to stand, the bastard jumped off the edge of the cliff.

Pressure built in his lungs, crystallized puffs forming in front of his lips. What the hell?

Liz. He had to get Liz out of here. Digging his heels into the ground, he tipped her back against his injured arm and used every ounce of strength left to stand. Her thready pulse beat in rhythm to the pounding at the base of his skull. "Hang on, baby. I'm going to get you help."

Pines clawed at him as he ran straight back down the small path he'd used to find her. Another dose of adrenaline flooded through him, but the human body couldn't live off the fight-or-flight response forever. He'd crash soon. But he'd sure as hell get Liz help first. The last remnants of sunset lit the path as he took a sharp left. Rocks and twigs fought to trip him as he descended down to the trailhead. He wasn't going to lose her. Not now. Not ever. He hit the trailhead, nearly sprinting toward the shooter's abandoned Mercedes. The sight of the car alone was enough to push him harder.

He set her down then wrenched the back passenger door open, laying her across the back seat. Framing her jawline between his thumb and first finger, he swept a strand of hair away from her face. "Almost there, Sprinkles. Don't you dare give up now. Fight. Listen to my voice and open your eyes, baby."

No answer.

Braxton climbed from the car, rounding to the driver's side door. And froze, hand on the door handle. The cliff where he'd fought the shooter fifty feet above claimed his attention. He checked the pavement below. That was the same plateau where the shooter had jumped. The hairs on the back of his neck rose on end as he studied the rest of the highway.

So where was the body?

Chapter Nine

"He shouldn't have been able to find me." New name, birth certificate, driver's license, Social Security number, credit cards, established social media accounts. She'd done everything aside from getting plastic surgery. Even with full access to her program, the shooter shouldn't have been able to track her down. At least, not without help. Oversight ran off federal databases, and everything there said she was Elizabeth Dawson. Plain and simple. She'd made sure before terminating her contract with the NSA.

The IV in the top of her hand tugged at her attention, cold fluid working through her veins. Braxton had gotten her to the hospital two days ago, but according to him, the nightmare was far from over. The shooter had jumped off that cliff he'd meant to use as her final resting place, but his body hadn't been recovered. He was still out there. Hunting her. "I changed my name. I relocated."

"Why didn't you tell me?" Sullivan Bishop had taken the seat beside her bed. Protection detail, he'd said. Her boss hadn't taken any of his own cases since taking down one of the most trained stalkers in Anchorage history—his brother. So why was he really here? The former SEAL centered that sea-blue gaze on her, and everything in her heated. Not from attraction—Sullivan had the best damn army prosecutor in the country waiting for him up the road at Joint Base Elmendorf-Richardson—but from embarrassment. "I told you when I hired you, we'd have your back. No matter what, but that comes with conditions, Liz. We're a team. I can't expect my team to function if my operatives are keeping secrets from me."

"I came to Anchorage to start over. I'd left that part of my life behind. I didn't see any reason to fill you in because none of this was supposed to happen." But hadn't she'd always known this day would come? Always looking over her shoulder for those green eyes she hadn't been able to forget. Didn't matter where she'd gone. Braxton would've found her sooner or later. "How is Braxton?"

"The nurses threatened to strap him down if he didn't let them stitch his arm. Knowing what little I do about him, he'll barge through that door any moment to get to you." Sullivan's five o'clock shadow shifted as the small muscles along his jaw flexed. He crossed his arms, massive muscles fighting to free themselves from the signature black T-shirt he always seemed to wear. "He said the shooter jumped off that cliff edge, but neither Vincent nor the crime scene unit have been able to recover a body or any evidence the bastard got up and walked away. Do you trust him?"

Wasn't that the million-dollar question? Elizabeth

pressed the edge of the bedsheet under her fingernail. She had no doubt Braxton would do what it took to protect her. Even if that meant neutralizing the threat after she'd passed out from the cramping in her abdomen. Snapping her gaze to her boss, she pressed her shoulder blades into the pillows behind her. "It's complicated."

"What about the pregnancy? When were you going to tell me about that?" he asked.

Elizabeth swallowed against the bruising around her throat, the rising rhythm of her heartbeat registering on the monitor beside her. The pain she'd experienced on that cliff, the sensation of building pressure... She'd feared the worst as Braxton raced her to the hospital. When the doctor had wheeled in the ultrasound machine, she'd expected for him to tell her the baby was gone. But baby Karina's heart beat strong. Her lower lash line burned as relief still coursed through her. "To be fair, I only told the father three days ago."

"Braxton," he said.

"Yes. What...what happened between us happened before I came to Anchorage, but I only found out about a month ago. I swear I didn't know I was pregnant when you hired me." She focused on a stray thread trying to escape from the white hospital blanket. She licked dry lips as she fought against the memories of Braxton on that cliff, of the shooter's blade cutting through him. He risked his life—yet again—for her. He'd saved her. And she wasn't sure that was something she could ever pay back. Elizabeth moved her hand over the baby. At least, not without letting him back in her life permanently. She forced herself to level her chin with the floor. To prove she could. Her baby wasn't a mistake. She was, however, a surprise Elizabeth hadn't been counting on when she'd taken on her share of clients for the firm. Her work had been the only thing keeping her sane these last few months. But if her withholding information from her boss lost her this job, she wasn't sure what she'd do. Where she'd go. "If you're worried whether or not I'll be able to protect my clients—"

"I'm not." Sullivan leaned back in his chair. "You're one of the best operatives I have. And if you feel you can still do your job while carrying this baby, I trust your judgment to know what you can handle." He ran a hand down his five o'clock shadow, the sound of short whiskers against his fingers louder than she expected. "What I am worried about is the people who blew up my conference room trying to get to you, and what they're going to do next."

"Is that why you're in here and Glennon is standing outside my room?" The Sovereign Army had taken credit for the bomb at Blackhawk Security three days ago, but now she wasn't so sure they were actually responsible. Wasn't sure they were even aware they'd been pulled into the shooter's game. What had he said? A headache pulsed at the base of her skull. The memories had gone fuzzy when she'd lost consciousness.

"I don't know much about your work for the NSA, but I've seen groups like this before, and they're not the kind of people who take government involvement in their lives lightly. For whatever reason, you're their main target." Sullivan sat forward, elbows on his knees, the butt of his favored .40 Smith & Wesson swinging forward from his shoulder holster.

"It's not them." Elizabeth had no doubt in her mind. "The man who shot at me in the parking garage after the explosion was the same one who kidnapped me off Seward Highway. I wouldn't be surprised if he used their cause to throw me off the trail. He's coming after me by himself. It's personal for him."

Elizabeth struggled to sit up without putting pressure on her broken wrist, now in a cast. Her throat tightened. The NSA had run dozens of missions with Oversight after she'd left. Some successes. Some failures. Hundreds of lives had been affected. Every family member, friend and radicalized militant involved could have reason to hunt her down for the program's creation alone. Add losses to that number? There were too many suspects to count. "He's doing this out of revenge."

"Well, that changes things." Sullivan's eyebrows pulled together, deepening three distinct lines in the middle. "Do you know who it is? Did you get a good look at the guy?"

"No. He wore a mask the entire time we were together." Flashes of those dark eyes materialized when she closed her eyes. She shook her head. "But I'm going to find out."

"And we'll be there every step of the way if you need us," Sullivan said. "On one condition."

Her stomach tightened.

Blackhawk Security's CEO shifted forward in his chair, his attention on her. "I want to know who I really hired."

She couldn't keep the truth from him or her team any longer.

"My real name is Elizabeth Bosch. I was born in the smallest town you can imagine in the middle of nowhere, Montana. My parents ran the ski resort there, and that's basically all I can tell you about them." Only the memories of photographs came to mind now. Elizabeth trapped air in her lungs, firming her lips. How long had it been since she'd given up her secret? Four, five months? "They died when I was four. My aunt came to live with me after that, and the minute I graduated high school, I got out of there as fast as I could and haven't looked back."

"And your work with the NSA?" he asked.

"Two years ago, I was working for a start-up company, programming and piloting unmanned drones for their military contracts, when one day…" Elizabeth picked at her chipped nail polish. She was unraveling at the seams, starting with her pathetic chipped, dirt-caked nails. "A man named Dalton Meyer approached me. He said one of his analysts had been keeping an eye on my career and thought I would be the best person for a job they had in mind. The analyst was Braxton. He offered me a contract so I could get the chance to serve my country in a bigger capacity. Turned out, the NSA wanted me to create a facial recognition program called Oversight to identify possible threats across the country. Anything from small-time crime to terrorist plots. And I did. Utilizing surveillance cameras, news coverage, phone cameras, social media, you name it, the program uses that information to predict threats." Her mouth dried. "But I ended up terminating my contract after Oversight's first trial run." She fought to breathe evenly. "Creative differences."

Movement on the other side of the single window to her room raised the hairs on the back of her neck. She didn't have to look at the man trying to force his way past Glennon at the door. Every cell in her body recognized every cell in his. Had since the day she'd met him. Would that ever change?

Door hinges protested loudly. Then he was there. Braxton was there, and she fought back the burn in her eyes from the pure relief rushing through her. "Hey."

"Hey." Goose bumps prickled along her arms. Bruises decorated his face, scratches cutting into his jawline. Proof he'd fought like hell on that cliff. For her. Silence settled between them. Comfortable. Electrically charged.

Sullivan stood and headed toward the door. "I can tell this is going to get awkward real fast, so I'm going to leave, but Liz—" He spun around, pinning her against the hospital bed with that hard sea-blue gaze. "Never withhold intel from your team again. Got it?"

She nodded. "Got it."

"Good. Call if you need something." The former SEAL maneuvered around Braxton without a word then shut the door behind him.

Braxton dropped a black duffel bag and closed the space between them. His bandaged fingers threaded through her hair at the back of her neck then pulled her into him. Right where she belonged. He tilted her head up and kissed her. Slow at first, then with more pressure, harder, as though he thought he'd never get the chance to kiss her again. Which he almost hadn't. If it hadn't been for him... If he hadn't come for her...

A dull ringing filled her ears as she fought to catch up with her shallow breathing. The monitors beeped rapidly a few feet away, and she couldn't help but laugh. Because if she didn't allow herself this small release, she might've shattered completely. Elizabeth pulled back but kept her undamaged hand gripped in his shirt. Meeting those compelling green eyes, she tugged him down onto the bed beside her. "Take me home."

WHEN A PHOENIX rose from the ashes, she was more beautiful and stronger than ever before. And, damn, he couldn't stop stealing glances at Liz as she rested her head against the window. She'd faced death and survived. How many others could say the same?

The stitches in his arm stretched tight beneath the gauze, but he pushed the discomfort aside, attention on the all-too-familiar road. A light dusting of snowflakes fell across the windshield, but it wasn't enough to detract from the intense hollowness setting up residence in his gut. Silent seconds stretched into minutes as Liz closed her eyes.

The baby was okay. Seeing their daughter on the ultrasound, hearing her tiny heartbeat. It was as though a dam had been destroyed and a flood of emotions had washed forward. He'd nearly sank to his knees right there in the middle of the hospital room. And in that moment, he'd allowed himself to imagine things he hadn't before. Meeting his daughter for the first time, celebrating her first birthday, sending her off to kindergarten, walking her down the aisle on her wedding day. The three of them—him, Liz and Karina—together as a real family.

Slush splashed up onto the windshield, bringing him back to the moment. He'd forfeited those fantasies the night he'd walked out on Liz after they'd conceived their baby. Forfeited his right to happiness. His right to ask her for the possibility of a future between them— wouldn't work. Not with the NSA dead set on putting him behind bars for treason. He couldn't ask her to wait, to hope.

Braxton tightened his grip on the steering wheel of another Blackhawk Security SUV, fighting back dark memories of tearing down Seward Highway in pursuit of saving her life in another vehicle exactly like this. He might've forfeited everything that night, but he'd do whatever it took to keep his girls safe. No matter the cost.

Soft snoring filled the interior of the vehicle, and he looked over to see Liz's lips slightly parted, her features slack. As much as he'd been able to research during the last two days of her in the hospital, the first few months of pregnancy were the most exhausting. Keeping up with a growing fetus took a toll he could only imagine. But fending for her life on top of that? Liz deserved to climb under the covers of the nearest bed and never climb out. He could give her that. If only for a few days.

He turned into a long asphalt driveway, and his gut clenched. A gallery of pines lined the property of the forty-year-old, two-story home. Wood-paneled siding and a contemporary design helped the cabin stand out against the others in the area, the nearest a quarter mile away. Typical cabins out here had been designed with winter months in mind, but not this one. The flower boxes still attached under the first-story windows and the long expanse of grass leading to the backyard paid homage to the past best left forgotten, but he didn't know where else to go.

Home sweet home.

The shooter had gotten away. Braxton didn't know how. He only knew that bastard had put Liz in his sights. And Braxton's gut said he wouldn't stop until the job was done. But they would be safe here. Then he'd move them to another safe house. And another. He'd move her around the entire country if it meant keeping her alive until they had a lead on the man hunting her. Braxton turned off the engine, the keys jingling against his leg. Reaching out, he slid his beaten knuckles along her cheekbone and lowered his voice. "We're here."

"Five more minutes." She buried herself deeper in her coat, the one arm still torn from the bullet graze at the park. White gauze lay at the bottom of the hole covering a row of stitches. "Too tired to move."

A laugh escaped through his nose. He dropped the keys into his jacket pocket and shouldered the door open. Rounding to the front of the SUV, he fought the urge to burn the entire cabin to the ground and walk away before she had a chance to step a foot inside. Leave the memories in the ashes. A gust of fresh, chilled breeze cleared his head. Get her inside. Keep her safe. He carefully opened the passenger side door, a smile thinning his mouth as she caught herself tipping out. "I can help with that."

"Haven't you done enough?" She slid her hands up his forearms for balance. Despite the freezing temperatures, he didn't feel the cold. Not with her in his arms. Then again, she'd always made him run hot. Her feet hit the pavement, but Liz didn't make any move to free herself of his hold. "You know, saving my life and all. That one time."

The smile stretching across her face was enough to stop his blood pumping. If it weren't for the thin scratches, the bullet graze at the top of her arm, the broken wrist and the four stitches in her hairline, it would have. But knowing she'd almost died because of him, because he'd left her unprotected all these months, had twisted him into a sick mess. He slid his hand into hers, locking her against him. "Let's get you inside."

She studied the cabin for the first time, it seemed. Took in the wide expanse of windows at the front, the balcony hanging over the covered patio, the line of trees threatening to overtake the roof at any moment. "Another one of your safe houses?"

"No." He took a deep breath, leading her to the sidewalk and toward the front door. He'd told her about his past. Told her about his family, about how Brolin Levitt had lost this same exact cabin to the bank after he decided his addiction was more of a priority than paying the mortgage. Braxton tightened his grip around her hand. It'd taken a lot of negotiation under a fake name with the couple who'd purchased the home after his parents had been foreclosed on, but something inside him hadn't been able to let it go. Now he knew why he'd kept it around for so long. To keep her and their baby safe. "It's the cabin I grew up in."

"You bought it?" She followed him along the sidewalk, past the crack near the front steps where he'd tripped and broken his arm when he was ten. Past the large pile of firewood he'd been chored with stocking most summers before they hit the wooden steps leading to the front door. "Why?"

"For you." Wood protested under their weight as he climbed the nine steps it took to reach the threshold of his childhood. All in all, his family had had happy memories in this place. His parents had bought the cabin right after finding out they were pregnant with their one and only son. Brolin had been manager of a bank then, and Karina had stayed home to raise Braxton. He dug for his keys then inserted the key into the dead bolt and turned. That'd been before Brolin's addiction destroyed everything Braxton had ever known.

A rush of cinnamon-and-apple-scented air slammed into him as he pushed the door open. With Liz's hand still wrapped around his, he led her inside. The crew he'd hired to gut the insides had done a damn fine job. New white tile in the entryway, the perfect color of hardwood flooring off to the left in the living room, peach walls the same exact color as he remembered, only fresher. Windows let in natural light from nearly every angle imaginable, welcoming him home. But Braxton couldn't move. How long had it been since he'd stepped through that door? Twenty years? The house had gone through a lot since then. He'd gone through a lot.

"What do you mean, for me? When did you buy it?" Liz studied the gleaming tile, the sparse furniture, the hallway leading straight back to the renovated kitchen.

"Last year, when I realized I wanted to be more than your friend." When he'd realized he'd fallen in love with the woman who'd sat less than five feet from his cubicle. He didn't dare look at her as he tugged her toward the stairs off to the right and up to three massive bedrooms for her to choose from, two smaller, one master. Beds and bathrooms for each. Braxton slowed down at the top of the stairs but didn't dare drop her hand. Not yet. Not when she was the only thing keeping him anchored in the present. "Have your pick. We're going to be here for a few days."

"Where did you set up your surveillance?" she asked.

"In that one. My old room." He led her to the right, stopping under the door frame as he pushed the door wider. After the renovations, he barely recognized it. No posters from his favorite band, no dartboard, no toys and action figures. Just peach-colored walls, a window with blackout curtains, a king-size bed with new bedding and a desk with his surveillance systems. Braxton leaned his weight into the door frame. "The other

bedrooms won't have the glow from the monitors keeping you up."

"I don't mind." Liz dropped his hand. She moved inside, taking in the room, and sat on the edge of the bed.
Dropping her coat beside her, she looked completely at
ease despite the bruises and scratches marring her perfect skin. Now fully lit from the natural light coming
through the window, he noted the dark circles under
her eyes, the lack of color in her lips, the slight tremor
in her hands. He'd seen her like this before. Only once,
after Oversight's real-world test run in which a CIA
agent had lost his life. She'd tried not to internalize
that guilt, but he'd read it on her face that day, and it'd
taken one night of him finally getting the guts to kiss
her senseless until she forgot. The same night he'd gotten her pregnant. The same night he'd disappeared. "I
want to be able to see him coming."

His gut sank. Damn it. He should've thrown the
SOB who'd taken her off the cliff like he'd planned.
He could've ended this nightmare. Could've brought her
some justice. He pushed off the wall, closing the space
between them. Crouching in front of her, he fought the
urge to use the same tactics he had the night they'd been
together that single time. "Liz—"

"I don't need you to talk." Framing his jawline
with her hands, Liz pulled him closer and crushed
her mouth against his. A burst of her lavender scent
destroyed the wall of care he'd put in place for her.
She swept her tongue past his lips, and his knees hit
the hardwood. No matter how much muscle he'd put

on, no matter how many hours he'd trained, none of it stood against her. Pressing his palms against the small of her back, he took anything he could get from her and more. Then she pulled away. "I need you to stay with me tonight."

Chapter Ten

She didn't want to think about the explosion. Not the shooting in the garage, her kidnapping. The fact she'd very nearly been thrown off a cliff and was still the center of a hit man's plans for revenge. None of it. The only thing Elizabeth focused on now was him. All she wanted in this moment was him. His five o'clock shadow prickled against her palms as she framed his jawline. Seconds passed. A minute?

He backed away from her, those green-gray irises widening as his pupils shrank.

Confusion gripped her hard. "Say something."

"You don't want me to stay with you…not right now." His phone chimed, but Braxton didn't move. He looked over her, her skin burning everywhere his gaze made contact. Raising his hand, he slid his fingertips up her arm and rested his thumb against the hollow at the base of her throat. The tendons along his neck ticked. "I promised to protect you and failed. I should've gotten to you sooner."

"I'm perfectly capable of deciding what I want for myself. I know exactly what I'm asking you to do."

Low-grade pain spread from the bruise around her neck. Elizabeth automatically swallowed against the tightness overtaking her entire body, but instead of flinching, she reached out for him. Fisting her fingers in his long-sleeve T-shirt, she tugged him into her, where he belonged. Tendrils of his hair hid half of his face from her, and she brushed them out of the way with her casted hand, refusing to think of how she'd ended up with the broken wrist in the first place. "I'm alive, Braxton. We survived. And we'll keep surviving as long as we're together. So don't get any bright ideas about pulling away now."

"You should've let me kill him." His voice dropped into dangerous territory, but this had a new edge to it. So sharp it threatened to cut straight through her. The Braxton she remembered vanished as steel hardened his expression. "I could've ended this once and for all."

"Ended this." The words were more for herself than for him. The bullet wound in her arm burned, her muscles wound tight with strain and overuse. But none of that compared to the sinking of her stomach from a combination of the guilt etched into his features and the disappointment consuming her. He blamed himself for the events of the last few days—that was clear—but what he should be worried about was the baby he'd helped conceive. About whether or not he was going to fight to stay in her life. "I know you'd do anything to protect me and this baby, but killing him would've put you back on the NSA's radar. Self-defense or to save me. It wouldn't matter. They would've taken you, and I'd never see you again."

"Wasn't that my end of our deal?" he said.

Silence settled between them as reality closed in. Yes. Back in the garage, before he'd given her a glimpse of how thoughtful he was, how caring, before he'd risked his life to save hers, she'd made him swear to crawl back to the rock he'd been hiding under for the last four months when this was over. Since he'd come back into her life, he'd gone out of his way to prove how much she'd meant to him. The ice cream and sprinkles, the nicknames, the slight lift of his lips when he looked at her, the undeniable physical attraction they shared. Or had it all been an act? A way to force her to accept his protection in order to extinguish his own guilt for leaving? She blinked to clear her head, to build up the wall that'd been in place for so long, and shut down her initial reaction. "You're right. Killing him wouldn't have changed anything."

No response.

She released her grip on his shirt and stepped away from him. She couldn't breathe, couldn't think. Four months ago, he'd taken her to bed, given her everything she'd wanted between them, then disappeared without a word. He was the one who'd tracked her down. He was the one who'd promised to protect her. He was the one who'd kept her alive these last few days. They were having a baby together. But apparently not even the tiny creature in her uterus who'd disrupted absolutely everything could make him want to stay. Damn it, how could she have been so stupid to think this time would be different? The NSA's charges against him hadn't changed. Why would he?

"You should leave when this is over." Elizabeth maneuvered around him toward the attached bathroom. She swiped at the tears in her eyes as the peach walls and surveillance monitors blurred in her peripheral vision.

Cool air rushed against the exposed skin along her arms as she closed the bathroom door behind her. No footsteps on the other side of the door. No knock against the wood. Braxton hadn't followed her. But she wasn't sure if she'd wanted him to. Tapping the crown of her head against the door, Elizabeth steered her attention to the white, brown, tan and teal tile of the soaking tub. What had she been thinking, asking him to stay with her tonight?

That was the problem. She hadn't been thinking. Being the center of a madman's revenge, of nearly dying not once but three times had distorted the single rule she'd set for herself when this whole thing started. Protect herself. Emotionally, physically, mentally. At whatever cost. But for the briefest of moments, he'd slid past her defenses, and she hadn't realized it until right now. For the briefest of moments, she'd let him have control.

Elizabeth forced herself to put one foot in front of the other until she'd reached the tub, and she turned the knob for hot water. To rinse some of the rawness down the drain. She undressed and added a lavender-scented soap beneath the water stream. The same brand she used at home. Wasn't surprising. Seemed Braxton had held on to a lot of things from the past. She studied the rest of the bathroom for the first time. For a while there, it seemed he'd held on to his feelings for her, too, as he'd held on to this house. But now she recognized her own wishful thinking.

He was shutting her out.

And hell, it hurt. She should've been used to that by now. She blinked back the burn in her lower lash line as the truth began to show. Stay in control. Stay strong. Whatever she imagined might happen between them was a fantasy, some twisted desire to have the support system neither of them had had growing up.

She stepped into the bath, flinching from the sting of the water on her fresh cuts, and curled in on herself. Her knees pressed against her cheeks. If the past four days had proven anything, it was that she and Braxton wouldn't work. Not with the NSA's charges over his head. Not with his flight instincts so engraved into his personal arsenal. Not when he tested everything she knew about herself.

She tightened her hold around her shins. The fact she was pregnant, the fact she'd been put in the shooter's crosshairs, was truly as bad as things could get, right? How much more pain did she have to go through before giving up was okay? Elizabeth ran a hand through her hair. No. She wouldn't give up. For the sake of her baby, she had to see this through. Even if her daughter lost a father in the process.

The doorknob clicked a split second before Braxton pushed it open. She lifted her attention toward him but didn't move. Didn't speak. She couldn't. Because the anguish etched across his expression gutted her to the bone. Green-gray eyes locked on her and, suddenly, she was losing the battle against him all over again.

He heel-toed off his boots one at a time then lifted his shirt over his head. The stitches across his arm almost bore resemblance to the bullet graze across hers. He'd been through hell just as much as she had the past three days. She had to remember that. He'd risked his life for her, almost died for her.

Valleys and ridges shifted across his abdomen as he closed the distance between them. Two steps. Three. Her mouth dried as he stared down at her, his dark, fathomless eyes burning straight through her. Climbing into the tub behind her, Braxton sank beneath the water almost fully clothed. Water rushed over the edge of the tub, but she didn't have the energy to care. Traitorous, treacherous need overtook her as he slid callused palms along her shoulders and pulled her back against him. All she wanted was him. Skin against skin, she wanted to feel alive. He wrapped his arms around her and pressed his mouth to her ear. "I've got you, Sprinkles."

A shiver chased down her spine despite the warmth of the water around her and Braxton's heat at her back. The tears came then, so strong she couldn't hold them back anymore. She shook against him, and he only held her tighter. This. This was what she missed about him. Not the promises. Not the offer of ice cream or the nicknames. She'd missed being in his arms, missed knowing she had someone she could count on, if only for a night.

"And I'll never let you go." He swiped her hair out of her face and turned her onto her side. Holding her against him with one arm, he rubbed small circles between her shoulder blades. When the sobs had racked her body and the water dropped in temperature, Braxton lifted her out of the tub. Goose bumps pimpled along her skin as he carefully dried her off with a fresh towel off the rack then led her back into the bedroom without a word.

Droplets of cold water hit her skin from her wet hair as he pulled an oversize shirt and a pair of sweats out of the dresser. He helped her dress, sliding his fingers along the back of her calves and down to her Achilles' heels. Another tremor lightninged through her, one that had nothing to do with the drop in her body temperature. Once she was dressed, Braxton interlaced his fingers with hers, tugging her down onto the bed. Shedding his own clothing, he pulled a pair of sweats from the dresser and shoved his legs into them. His weight on the mattress settled against her, hiking her heart into her throat. The past four days had destroyed her inside and out. And she had nothing left to give. Not to him. Not to the man trying to kill her. Not to her team. "Braxton, I can't—"

"I don't need you to talk." Her own words to him released the anxiety climbing up her throat. He maneuvered under the covers, his heat chasing the chill from her bones, and coiled around her. His fingers encased hers against her collarbones. They hadn't solved anything, but right now, pressed against him, she didn't care. His exhales kept rhythm with hers. "I need you to go to sleep."

Exhaustion pulled her under.

THE SHRILL RING of his burner phone ripped him out of Liz's warm hold.

"What is it?" The grogginess in her voice revealed

she wasn't entirely awake yet, and he smoothed his hand over her shoulder.

"Just my phone. Go back to sleep." Four hours. That was all the peace they'd gotten. Braxton threw the covers off and collected the phone from where he'd left it on the desk with his surveillance equipment. Unknown number. Warning spread through him. He checked the monitors. No movement along the tree lines or around the house. But that didn't mean Liz's stalker hadn't found another way to get to her. Studying the steady, slow rise and fall of her shoulders, he swiped his thumb across the screen then headed for the bedroom door, closing it behind him. If the shooter had somehow gotten ahold of yet another of their burner phone numbers, she didn't need to hear the shooter's voice after what she'd been through. "Talk."

"Hello to you, too, sunshine." Vincent Kalani's voice eased some of the tension climbing up Braxton's spine. He'd handed the operative one of his old preprogrammed burners while Liz had been recovering in the hospital after they discovered cloning tech on Vincent's device, but had pushed the investigation to the bottom of his priorities. New phone. New number. No chance the shooter could listen in on their calls this time. "Guess you didn't get my message."

Memory of his phone chiming earlier—before Liz had walked away from him with tears in her eyes—rushed forward. It hadn't been important then. "Guess not. What do you have?"

"We got a hit on the fingerprints from bullet casings recovered after the shooting at Town Square," Vincent said. "I sent the report to your phone, but looks like you're not checking email right now. Is it safe to assume you two hooked—"

"Say another word and I'll change your name to Veronica Kalani in every federal database I can hack. Which is all of them." Braxton checked over his shoulder. The door to the bedroom was still closed, and he moved farther down the hallway so this conversation wouldn't wake the woman in his bed. What'd happened between them a few short hours ago, her apparent fear of him leaving again, had left him hollowed out. Useless. The dark, raging creature inside him, the one that would do anything to stay with her, even if it put her in more danger, had taken control then. And he'd been lost. Seeing her in the tub, so vulnerable, so lost… It'd broken him. He never wanted to see her that way again. Not Liz. Him leaving had been part of the deal they'd struck before the shooter had tried to take them out in the parking garage. But everything had changed since then. "What does the report say?"

"Can you really change anyone's name?" Vincent asked. "Elliot thinks I don't know he's been stealing my lunch out of the refrigerator here at the office, and I'm currently looking for ways to make him pay."

Braxton took a deep breath, running his hand over his jawline. His normally groomed five o'clock shadow had thickened over the past few days. No time to shave when a shooter had put the woman he'd die to protect in his sights. "As tempting as that sounds, let's go back to the fingerprints."

"Right. Prints match a CIA agent named Justin Valentin," Vincent said. "You heard of him?"

Braxton dropped the phone away from his ear. It wasn't possible. Justin Valentin had been the field operative killed during Oversight's test launch. None of this made sense. Had the NSA identified the wrong corpse? Had Justin survived? The moment Liz heard about the evidence… He didn't know what she'd do. Vincent's voice reached through the haze threatening to suffocate him. Raising the phone to his ear, he pinched the bridge of his nose and closed his eyes. "Are you one hundred percent sure those fingerprints match that name?"

"I ran it twice. Why?" Vincent's confusion reached through the line. "Isn't this good news? You got your man. Liz can put this behind her."

"Not in the least. Did you run a background check after you matched the prints?" If the forensics expert had, they wouldn't be having this conversation. Braxton looked up and froze. Every cell in his body caught fire at the sight of Liz staring back at him from the bedroom door. "I'm going to have to call you back." He lowered the phone again, hitting the end button.

"Vincent found something." Not a question. Liz crossed her arms over her midsection, one of her textbook moves when she slammed her invisible guard into place. Dark circles still haunted her beneath those chocolate-brown eyes, exhaustion evident in her features, but the tears were gone. She'd gotten only a few hours of sleep over the last few days. With the added strain of the baby and the stress of being kidnapped on her body, it was a wonder she was still standing. "Tell me."

"We don't have to do this now." Braxton's bare feet stuck to the cold hardwood floor as he closed in on her. "You can go back to sleep—"

"I'm fine," she said. "Just tell me."

He nodded.

"Vincent recovered bullet casings from the shooting at Town Square. He was able to match the partial fingerprints on them to a CIA agent who died last year." He opened Vincent's email on his phone and handed it to her. "He matched them to Justin Valentin."

"That's not possible." Her exhale swept over his bare neck and chest. Her voice gained strength with each word out of her mouth. "I was there where Dalton Meyer ran the trial run, Braxton. I saw Agent Valentin die on the screen right in front of me. I watched as they lowered his coffin into the ground a week later. Justin Valentin is buried in Rock Creek Cemetery in Washington, DC."

"I was there, too, remember? I know what happened." He remembered every minute. Oversight's first real-world test run would stay ingrained in his memory forever. The program had identified a group of Afghan rebels intent on taking out the US Embassy in Kabul. What the program failed to identify, however, was the CIA agent deeply implanted within the group when the order for neutralization came down from on high. Liz had told them the tech wasn't ready, but her supervisor, Dalton Meyer, hadn't listened, and an American life had been lost on the program's first test run. Liz had never forgiven herself. "Vincent ran the prints twice. Unless you've got another explanation, we need your boss and whatever connections he has to get a court order to exhume whoever is in that coffin."

"No. The shooter…whoever is doing this is trying to mess with my head." She thrust the phone back at him, not bothering to read the ballistics report. Liz ran a hand through her short hair, and she took a step back. The past three days had her spiraling and, hell, he couldn't blame her. But ever since her stalker had tried to kill her with a bomb, they'd been reacting. The explosion, the shootout in the garage, her kidnapping. It wouldn't end until Liz was dead. And that wasn't an option. Not for him. "He must've known about that mission and somehow gotten access to those confidential files. Justin Valentin is dead."

"You think Justin's prints were planted." What was the point of trying to set up a dead man? It didn't make sense.

"In the last three days, there's only been one man I know of who's trying to kill me. He's planned this out for months, if not years." Liz crossed her arms again, accentuating all the mouthwatering curves under his T-shirt. "Do you honestly believe he'd be stupid enough to leave his own fingerprints on those bullet casings where we could find them?"

Not a chance. They were dealing with a professional. No way in hell he'd leave evidence behind without reason. "How do you get a dead man's prints on a bullet casing?"

"That's the million-dollar question," she said.

Braxton checked his phone for the time. "It's too late to have Sullivan get a court order from a judge. But I'm not going to wait around for this guy to take another shot at you. We need to trace Oversight's feeds and attack him head-on."

"That's not a plan." She dropped her arms to her side. "That's a death sentence."

Frustration built. "I don't want you to spend the rest of your life looking over your shoulder, Liz. Especially not with our daughter in tow. She deserves better than that."

Liz stepped back as though she'd taken a direct hit, and his stomach dropped. Waves of pinks and greens filtered through the wide expanse of windows, highlighting the sharp angles of her features. Aurora borealis rippled across the night sky, brighter than he'd ever seen it before. "Are you willing to bet your life on that?"

"I know why you won't touch Oversight's code, but running for the rest of your life is no way to live. I know that better than anyone." Braxton stepped into her range. He couldn't think with her so close. But he was tired of thinking. Tired of running.

"Dalton should've listened to me." Liz shook her head. "Oversight wasn't ready. I told him that the day before the scheduled trial run. I told him the programming kept skipping the background checks because of a broken line of code I hadn't been able to find, but he didn't care. A man died because of my mistake. You really want to take that risk?"

"I'll take my chances on you every day for the rest of my life." He countered her retreat, and his body temperature hiked at least two degrees. "Because of all the variables I bet the shooter calculated before making his move on you in that conference room, I know he didn't account for you fighting back."

Chapter Eleven

She'd stick to her end of the deal. Elizabeth would let him protect her until the threat was neutralized, then he could go back into hiding until the NSA forgot his name.

Her gut tightened at the thought, and she squeezed his hand draped across her hip. He'd convinced her to come back to bed, but she couldn't sleep. The sooner they ended this investigation, the sooner she'd have to watch him walk away. Again. But as much as she wanted to drown in fantasies of Braxton helping her raise this baby—of them becoming the family their daughter deserved—he couldn't stay. And the sooner she realized that, the better. For her and their baby. She trusted him enough to keep her alive. That would have to be good enough.

"You're still awake," he said.

She pressed her shoulder blades against his chest. His body heat tunneled through her borrowed sweats. What'd happened on that trail…she couldn't get that dark gaze out of her mind. "I see him when I close my eyes. I can't get him out of my head."

Braxton hiked her against him, dropping his mouth to her shoulder. "You're not responsible for any of this, Liz. This guy might be doing this out of some sick need for revenge, but I know you. You'd never deliberately put anyone in danger."

"Except I did. On the dozens of missions I let the NSA use my program." She turned her heard toward him, only the glow of the surveillance system highlighting one side of her face. "He used the Sovereign Army to take credit for the bomb, but what if this is about Oversight like we originally thought?"

"If this guy is connected to the work you did for the NSA, we'll find out who he is." He traced his fingers down her arm, coaxing goose bumps in his tracks, and placed his mouth at her ear. He slid his hand beneath the hem of her shirt, right over their growing daughter. "But right now, you and this baby have been through hell. You need to sleep."

"I can't sleep." Not when every time she closed her eyes, fear gripped her throat to the point she couldn't breathe. Elizabeth turned into him, framing one side of his jaw with her palm. His beard prickled against her skin. Images of their one night flashed through her mind. He'd been comforting her then, too, right after Oversight had failed its first test run in the field. A CIA agent had lost his life that day, the same man whose fingerprints Vincent had found on those bullet casings. Justin Valentin. And Braxton had been there for her. How many more mistakes had her program made since she'd told the NSA she'd never work for them again?

How many more lives was she responsible for? She didn't want to think about it.

Four months. Such a long time, yet not long enough for her feelings to disappear as fast as he had. She hadn't expected that. That chaotic tangle of emotions should've left by now. But they hadn't. He'd become part of her a long time ago. And there weren't exactly exorcists for this kind of thing. When it came to Braxton Levitt, she had the feeling he'd never leave her system entirely. But maybe that didn't have to be a bad thing. "Where have you been all this time?"

"Everywhere. Cambodia, Taiwan, Russia. I made it a point to stick to nonextradition countries." A shiver rushed down her spine at his touch, and Braxton flashed her that gut-wrenching grin of his. "But that's not what you want to ask me, is it?"

He could read her so well. Too well. Nervous energy exploded through her. All she'd been able to think about when the shooter had held her at the edge of the cliff had been Braxton's name. She didn't have any right to ask. He'd moved on. So had she. New city, new job, new name. She'd fought to leave her old life behind, a life that had included him up until the end. But the question still nagged at her. Clenching her teeth against the oncoming disappointment, Elizabeth studied the shadows lining his collarbones. "What was…" She swallowed around the growing lump in her throat. "What was I to you?"

He set her chin between his thumb and index finger, urging her to look up. The color of his eyes was lost in the blue light of his surveillance system a few feet away, but she read every change in his expression. Because she'd learned how to read him, too. "Everything."

Her breath came too fast. Her heartbeat seemed to shake behind her rib cage. Everything she'd done to this point—refusing to work with him, laying out the rules, putting up her guard—had been to protect herself, but he'd figured out a way around all of that. He'd buried himself beneath her skin and become part of her. Would it always be like this? When the smoke cleared, could this work? When someone wasn't trying to kill her, when the NSA wasn't trying to put him behind bars for the rest of his life.

"Come here." The lines at the edges of his mouth deepened with his smile. Braxton offered her his hand, sliding off the bed when she took it. Rough calluses caught on her skin, but right now, she only had attention for the slow burn of desire swirling in his gaze.

Her bare feet hit the cold hardwood floor, and he tugged her into him. Right where she needed to be. Without letting go of her hand, Braxton turned toward the desk and pulled open the top drawer. He handed her a small glass bottle with a long neck, the weight of his attention crushing the air in her lungs. "Black fingernail polish?"

"You've been through hell the last few days." He closed the short space between them, crowding her until her knees hit the edge of the bed. Collapsing back, she held her breath as Braxton sank to his knees in front of her. He tugged her sweats up around her calves, his touch somehow hot and cold at the same time. Or had her nerve endings started playing tricks on her again? "Let me take care of you."

"You happen to have black fingernail polish on hand?" Of course he did. Just as he'd put her favorite brand of lavender soap in the bathrooms, how he'd stocked the freezer with chocolate ice cream and the drawers with rainbow-colored sprinkles. He'd gone out of his way to ensure her small comforts came first. At first, she'd thought it'd been to manipulate her, to get her to trust him again. But now? Now a familiar feeling climbed up through her insides. The feeling of falling.

"I've got supplies stashed in this house you can't imagine." He feathered his fingertips down the tight muscles in her left calf then applied pressure. Her grip tightened on the edge of the mattress as she tipped her head back against her shoulders. "We could stay here for weeks without stepping outside this bedroom."

Elizabeth leveled her gaze with his. Her leg jerked beneath his hands as he pressed into one of her more sensitive ticklish spots. A laugh burst from her between her lips. "Sorry. I don't normally let people massage my calves. I'm afraid I'll kick them in the face, I'm so ticklish."

"I'll have to remember that." Half a smile stretched his mouth thin, and her stomach shot into her throat. Setting her foot on top of his thigh, he reached for the glass bottle and twisted off the lid. In the glow of his surveillance system, he touched up the tips of her toenails effortlessly. But what couldn't he do? He'd saved her life from a gunman, tracked her down to the edge of that cliff, fought a professional shooter as though he'd trained to fight all his life, established safe houses to keep them off the grid and learned to cook a turkey and vegetable soup she still couldn't stop tasting at the back of her throat. Blowing on her wet toenails, he sat back on his heels then swung himself up to stand. "Good as new."

Elizabeth couldn't take her attention off him. Something had changed. Some defining moment had altered his life that night he'd disappeared. "The night you left. Something happened, something to make you want to change your appearance, to learn to fight, to handle a gun." Because the man she'd known had never picked up a gun in his life or learned how to throw a punch. He'd been an analyst, glued to his computer screen. "What happened to you?"

His rough exhale reached her ears. The mattress dipped under his weight as he sat beside her, elbows on his knees, the little black bottle of nail polish gripped between his hands. He nodded once. "You happened to me. I couldn't protect you then. That needed to change."

Her lips parted to ask every question running through her mind. Protect her from what? Why hadn't he told her the truth? Did it have something to do with the NSA? But did any of it matter? Not really. This moment, that was all that mattered. "Kiss me."

"Don't start something you can't finish, Sprinkles." He shifted at her side, his dark hair skimming over his shoulders. Braxton moved a strand of hair off her forehead. The past four months living off the federal government's radar had hardened his features, but she still recognized the man beneath the guarded exterior and new muscle. And she wanted him now more than ever. "I have very little control when it comes to you."

"Please. I need this." She rolled her lips between her teeth and bit down. This wasn't an attempt to get him to stay after the investigation ended. It wasn't an attempt to satisfy her own attraction. Pure, unfiltered need coursed through her. The need to be touched, to be cared for, loved, even. If only for a night. Her throat dried. Before she lost him forever. "I need you."

Braxton threaded his fingers through the hair at the back of her neck, pulled her into him and set his mouth over hers. His clean, masculine scent clung to her borrowed clothing, to the sheets, became part of her, and she couldn't get enough. He maneuvered over her, pushing her onto her back, and slid his hand along the outer part of her thigh. He hiked her calf around his hip. Tightening her grip on him, Elizabeth breathed a bit easier despite his added weight. Patience was a virtue, but they didn't have time for that. She cocked her head to one side and opened her mouth wider for him.

Any second now reality would work its way back, but she'd stretch this night to last as long as possible. With a freshly painted set of toenails.

HE'D LIED TO HER.

The changes he'd made over the last four months hadn't been about the realization he couldn't protect her. If he'd known being part of her life would end this way, Braxton never would've recruited her for the NSA. But there was no changing the past. As for the future...

Hell, he needed her as much as he needed oxygen in his lungs. And that was a very dangerous thing.

Braxton buried his nose at the crown of her head, lavender and woman fighting to drown the guilt clawing its way through him. He should've ended it on that cliff side, gotten her free of this nightmare. Gotten her free of him. A murder charge would've kept him out of the country for the rest of his life and put a digital target on Liz's back, but at least then she'd be safe. He'd underestimated the shooter, banked on the SOB taking the intel on Oversight and staying the hell out of her life. Braxton had been wrong.

Wouldn't happen again.

Muted sunlight lit the room enough for him to make out the handle of his Glock across the room. He'd shed his shoulder holster and gun before getting in the tub with her, literally let down his guard for her. But it was time to end this. Maneuvering out from beneath Liz's warm body, trying not to wake her, he crossed the room in three steps and reached for his clothing. He'd track Oversight's feeds himself and finish this today. The bastard had tried to hurt his family, and Braxton would make him pay. He'd make sure the guy never touched her or their baby again.

He dressed fast then fastened his shoulder holster into place and collected a backpack of supplies and a secure laptop he'd stashed in the closet. Liz shifted beneath the sheets, a small moan escaping her throat as she rolled onto her side, and Braxton froze. The backpack in his hand worked to cement him in place. As though it knew the repercussions of leaving her in the middle of the night after taking her to bed yet again. But what choice did he have? Whoever'd kidnapped her would try again. And would keep trying until her pulse stopped beating. Braxton forced himself to breathe evenly through the thought. No. He'd end this now. He'd do what he had to, to keep her safe.

He followed the edge of the bed until he stood over her. Planting a kiss on the top of her head, he memorized the way she smelled, engraved the memories of their night together in his mind. Ran his fingers through the ends of her hair one last time. Dropping his voice, he crouched beside her and whispered more to himself than to her. "It'll always be you, Liz."

Braxton pushed to his feet, out of time, and scanned the surveillance monitors on the other side of the room before making his escape downstairs and toward the front door. He tossed his burner phone onto one of the couches in the living room to his right as he reached for the doorknob. He'd start with the fingerprints recovered from the rooftop shooting. Justin Valentin had been buried back in Washington, DC, but there had to be somebody—a family member, an old partner, a friend—who knew of his work for the CIA and had access to his personal belongings. The only other option was that the agent had faked his own death after Oversight's trial run. He gripped the doorknob hard as metal grew warm beneath his hand. Exhaling hard, he squeezed his eyes shut. Focus. Find the shooter. Keep Liz safe. He'd gone off the grid once, he could do it ag—

"I must be horrible in bed if you have to make a quick getaway in the middle of the night every time you sleep with me." Heat shot through him at the sound of her sleep-ragged voice. Soft footsteps padded down the stairs, but Braxton didn't dare turn around. He dropped his hand from the doorknob as Liz stopped short behind him. "But to be fair, I guess it's morning now, isn't it?"

He turned his head toward her. "Liz—"

"Don't worry, Braxton. I'm not mad." Her voice hollowed. "In order to be mad, you'd have to disappoint me in some way, which implies I had expectations. And I didn't. I knew you'd have to leave." She studied him. "But for the record, you don't have a promising future in clandestine work. You're the noisiest dresser on the planet."

"I can end this." The muscles down his spine tensed, ready for battle. "I can make sure he never comes after you again."

"What happened to us ending this together?" Liz circled into his line of sight. Exhaustion played a wicked game in her expression, but she'd never let it control her. She was determined, strong. Stronger than he was. "Brolin might not have been able to describe the man who'd taken him, but we can trace the fingerprints back to where they originated. We'll find him—"

"I'm not going to lose you again!" The words left his mouth harsher than he'd meant. His ears rang as she flinched. He fought to breathe evenly, rage exploding through him. She wasn't the only one who had nightmares because of what happened on that cliff side. "I almost didn't make it in time when he took you. If I'd been one minute later…"

Braxton wouldn't play the what-if game. He shook

his head to dislodge the memories. Reliving the past would only slow him down, consume him, and he'd lose the war before he had a chance to finish it.

"Do you really think I'd let him touch me again?" Liz locked onto his wrist and, faster than he thought possible, twisted his arm up and back. His childhood home blurred as she spun him head over heels. He hit the ground hard, the air crushed from his lungs. The chandelier above the entryway shook in the middle of the blackness closing in around the edges of his vision. He rolled onto his back, a groan escaping. *What had just happened?* She moved over him as pain radiated up his spine. His head throbbed, shoulders ached. Crouching beside him, she brushed his hair out of his face. "I didn't fight back when he put me in the trunk of his car because I want this baby more than anything, Braxton. I don't want to lose her. But don't mistake my decision for compliance. If he comes after me again, I will do what I have to, to survive."

She offered her hand, and he took it. Shoving to his feet, he ran his fingers through his hair to get it out of his face. "Where the hell did you learn to do that?"

"You're not the only one who's changed." Crossing her arms across her midsection, Liz shifted her weight against the mammoth wood banister lining the stairs. The sweats he'd dressed her in hung off her lean frame, but damn if she wasn't the epitome of everything he wanted. Everything he'd die to protect. "Let me guess. You were going to attempt to trace the feeds yourself from a laptop you stashed in your bag. Public place.

Maybe a coffee shop close to the Anchorage police department that offers free Wi-Fi in case shots were fired."

Braxton slipped the backpack from his shoulder and set it on the floor. Rolling one shoulder back, he ignored the pain of landing on his own arm. "It crossed my mind."

"Except it won't work." She put one foot in front of the other, closing in on him slowly. Her mouth parted slightly, giving him flashbacks to the night they spent together, and his gut tightened in response. Liz dropped her voice. "You can try to convince yourself otherwise, but you need me in order to access Oversight."

Amusement hiked his eyebrows a little higher, his head still pounding from her little move that'd landed him on his back. "Wasn't hard to guess your password."

Just as it hadn't been hard for him to uncover her new name. He'd only had to think like her and home in on what she valued most in her life.

"But even you can't fake a retinal scan," she said.

Retinal scan? "I did not know you'd added that level of security."

"Give me the laptop." She stretched out her hand, a weak smile playing across her mouth. "Vincent already forwarded the ballistics report on those bullets from the SUV. They're clean. So the shooter was sending me a message leaving the casings on the rooftop at the park. He wanted me to know this has to do with Justin Valentin. I'll dig into Agent Valentin's background, see if there's a connection there the NSA might've missed."

It was a start, and her plan wouldn't put her in immediate danger unless the shooter was monitoring Justin Valentin's records. Even then, Braxton's network re-routed his IP addresses all over the globe. The shooter would have a hard time nailing down their location for at least a couple of days. Braxton hefted his backpack up, handing it off to her. "And what am I supposed to do in this plan?"

She shouldered the pack and leveled her chin with the floor. Brilliant beams of light stretched through the wall of windows to his left, highlighting the spots of amber in her eyes. "You'll tell me you're going to stay."

His stomach dropped. Stay? That wasn't part of the deal. "It's not that easy—"

"Say those words, and I will do everything I can to make sure the NSA can't touch you." Stepping into him, she framed the side of his face with one hand. "I'll make sure you can come home. We can raise this baby. Together. We can give her a family, and whether or not that includes your father is up to you."

"You don't know what you're asking, Liz." Air stuck in his throat. Curling his hands into fists, he put a few more inches of space between them. He slipped out of her reach, her eyebrows drawing together in confusion. "You need to know the truth before you ask something like that."

A half-hearted smile stretched across her mouth. "What are you talking about?"

"The reason I left four months ago." He stroked one hand down his beard. Hell, it wasn't supposed to be like this. She wasn't supposed to want him to stay, not when they both knew it couldn't last. Braxton dropped his hand to his side. "I'm the one who sold classified intel on Oversight."

Chapter Twelve

He'd...sold the intel on her program. "To the man trying to kill me and our baby?"

"Yes," he said. "The transaction was anonymous. I had no idea what he was going to do with the intel or that he'd come after you..."

His voice faded in her ears. Her knees shook as she stepped back. Despite the size of his childhood home, the entryway wasn't that big. There was only so far she could go and stay within reach of slapping him as hard as she could. "So all those interrogations the NSA put me through...when I told them you weren't the leak, I was committing treason."

Elizabeth ran a hand through her hair, fisting a tight knot between her fingers. No, no, no, no. None of this made sense.

"Everything that is happening is one hundred percent my fault, and you have my word I will never stop trying to make it up to you." He took a step forward, but she countered almost instantly, and he froze, hands raised.

"You make it sound so easy." Think. Focus. No. Fury exploded from behind her sternum, and all rational thought disappeared. Elizabeth dropped the laptop bag and shoved at him with her unbroken hand as her lower lash line burned. "You put my life in danger." Pushing him again, she fought to keep the tears from falling. "You put our baby's life in danger."

The head wound, the bruised ribs, the broken wrist. She could take the physical injuries. But the emotional? She couldn't put a cast on that. Nausea rolled in her stomach. Oh, hell. Not now.

The three notches between his eyebrows deepened as Braxton dropped his hands to his side. He made another attempt to close in on her. "Sprink—"

"Don't call me that." She forced herself to breathe evenly around the bile working up her throat. Around another wave of betrayal. Around the stabbing pain in her chest. How could she have been so stupid? When Braxton had first informed her the feeds had been hijacked, she'd said it was impossible. Because it was. Less than a dozen government officials had clearance to know about the project. Without chalking it up to luck, a civilian wouldn't have been able to uncover her darkest secret. Unless someone handed them the information. She studied Braxton now and, for the first time, saw him for what he really was. "The intel you sold. It was how to hijack Oversight's feeds, wasn't it? Only in order take control of my program, you knew he needed me. That's why you came back. You realized the second you handed over that intel, he'd hunt me down."

"He already knew about the program. Knew exactly what he wanted and how to get it. I don't know how." Braxton nodded. "But when Dalton Meyer was killed, and the feeds were rerouted, I thought him coming after you next was a possibility."

"Why? Why would you do this to me?" She shook her head. "No. Don't answer that. I think I have a pretty good idea." Her hands shook at her sides. Elizabeth dug her toes into the hardwood to keep her balance, but her entire world had been upended. Slinging the bag over her shoulder once again, she maneuvered around him toward the front door. She didn't care she'd left her clothes and boots upstairs. She'd stop for supplies along the way. Reaching for the door, she turned her head enough to put him in her peripheral vision. "When you realize the mistake you've made, don't try to find me. I don't *ever* want to see you again."

Shattering glass ripped her attention to the living room on her right. Then a hard *thunk* of metal against wood. An M84 grenade rolled toward her. Elizabeth caught only a glimpse of it before a wall of muscle crashed into her and pinned her against the floor. The oxygen knocked from her lungs as she covered her ears and closed her eyes. The thump of detonation reverberated through her. The backpack fell from her arm. Before she could take her next inhale, Braxton ripped her and the pack off the floor.

"Come on!" Smoke filled the room, stung her eyes as he led them toward the back of the house. "Cover your face with your shirt and keep your eyes closed. I won't let you go."

Another grenade broke through the window above the kitchen sink as they rushed through, and she didn't have enough hands to cover both ears without losing

Braxton in the smoke. A white flash, an ear-deafening blast. Her ears rang, a high-pitched keen that worked to unbalance her and overwhelm her senses. Her shoulder hit the wall beside her, and she dropped Braxton's hand.

They were under attack. The shooter had found them. Found her.

His rough grip wrapped around her arms and thrust her forward. She jerked to the right into the downstairs office and dared to crack her eyes open. Smoke worked its way under the door, but not enough to sting.

Braxton pushed the black backpack toward her. She held on to it, heart pounding at the back of her head as he unzipped the bag and removed a gun. His lips moved. Nothing but muffled words reached through the ringing in her ears. He checked the gun's magazine, clicked off the safety and chambered a round. The movements were automatic, something he'd obviously worked at over the last few months.

She shook her head, pointing to her ear.

He took her hand then and mouthed, "I've got you."

A third percussion grenade shattered the office window as though the shooter were following them through the house from outside. She reached for Braxton, spinning them both inside the closet, and closed the door a split second before discharge. They had to get out of the house. Breathing ragged, head pounding, Elizabeth pushed out of the closet and went for the hallway.

Braxton's hand on her shoulder stopped her short of passing the large full bathroom on this level. She poked her head around the door frame from the hall. The bay window around the tub provided a perfect view into the spacious backyard.

And of the single masked man waiting for them outside.

Two taps on her shoulder spun her head around.

Braxton signaled them to the ground.

Getting to her hands and knees, she slipped past the bathroom, safeguarded by both walls that constructed the hallway. The garage was straight ahead, less than ten feet away. The backpack weighed her down and there was a chance they'd slip on the hardwood floors, but they didn't have a choice. They had to run for it.

Sliding against the wall, she sat back and closed her eyes, her hand across her lower abdominals. One breath. Two. They were going to make it out of this. She had to believe that. One tap on her arm brought her back into the moment. A combination of guilt and violence swirled in Braxton's gaze. He traced his fingers down one side of her face, and a shiver shook through her.

Elizabeth ripped away and pushed to her feet. No. He should feel guilty. He was responsible for all of this. She pumped her legs fast, panting through her mouth. The strain at the back of her head increased. Her ribs protested, and her legs felt spongy and untrustworthy. Shattering glass and gunfire exploded from every direction the instant she left the cover of the hallway. She covered her head in a vain attempt to keep a bullet from turning her brain into mush and dropped, sliding into the garage door like an MLB player hitting home plate.

She didn't bother looking back for Braxton—he could take care of himself—and ripped the garage door open. She fell down the six concrete stairs into the garage. The door slammed shut on its own a moment later, Braxton crashing down beside her. Gunfire echoed from behind the thick steel as musty air worked its way into her system, but they couldn't stop now.

Braxton took her free hand again, helped her to her feet and pointed to the only window on the far wall of the garage. Wrenching out of his grip, she exhaled hard. It was their only escape. They wouldn't make it to the SUV parked outside. Not without putting themselves at the end of the shooter's barrel. He maneuvered her ahead of him. She climbed up the steel shelving, pulling off the pack in the process. Elizabeth shoved the bag through the window first as a loud bang erupted from inside the house.

The shooter had breached.

She pushed herself backward through the window, hung onto the ledge for a brief moment then dropped to the ground. The ringing in her ears subsided slightly. Thank heaven her pregnancy wasn't farther along. She might've never gotten through the window had the shooter come after her a few weeks from now. She got her bearings and listened for any sign she'd been seen.

Nothing.

Braxton dropped beside her, studying their new surroundings as she had. Without a fence separating the house from the woods, nothing could stop them from disappearing into the wilderness. Sirens echoed in the distance. Even a quarter mile away, one of the neighbors had most likely called police from the sound of the grenades.

The definitive sound of a chambering round swept a chill down her spine.

They weren't alone.

Her attention diverted to her right, toward the shadow at the corner of the garage, and Elizabeth stepped back. How had he found them? Her stomach dropped. "Braxton…"

"Neither of you seem to understand." The shooter followed their every move as her bodyguard shifted in front of her. Dressed in a nicely pressed suit, ski mask included, the shooter obviously wasn't working for mobility, an advantage if things got physical. The ringing stopped in one of her ears, but the percussion grenade had knocked out her balance. She'd fight through it. Because there was no way in hell she'd let him take her again. The man who'd kidnapped her not forty-eight hours ago approached slowly, those black eyes sizing up Braxton from head to toe. Then raised his gun. "Elizabeth is coming with me."

He fired.

"No!" Liz's scream pierced through the pain-induced haze clouding his head. Blood slipped through his fingers as Braxton gripped his left thigh. The muscles in his leg strained as he kept himself from screaming. The bullet hadn't come out the back of his leg. Which meant there was a good chance it'd hit bone. Didn't matter. Liz mattered. Keeping her safe mattered. He focused on the feel of her fingernails digging into his shoulder to keep him upright, her mouth at his ear as the shooter closed in on his prey. Her. "Come on. Get up, damn it."

He shoved the pain to the back of his mind. The bastard wouldn't touch her. Not again.

"Get out of here, Liz." He shifted his weight onto his uninjured leg and took position in front of her. His jeans clung to him in spots where blood spread, but it wouldn't be enough to slow him down. This ended now. Right here, right now, this was where Liz's new life started. "And whatever happens, don't come back for me."

He didn't give her a chance to respond as he rushed toward the shooter. The bastard fired another shot, barely missing Braxton, and squeezed the trigger a third time. The bullet skimmed across his chest as Braxton turned to avoid the shot. Snow and ice worked into his boots, distracted him from the pain shooting up his leg. He collided with the shooter and tackled him to the ground. The gun disappeared into a snowdrift, out of sight.

The shooter slammed a knee directly into the right side of Braxton's jaw, but Braxton didn't loosen his grip around the operative's perfectly pressed suit. Braxton pulled his elbow back and slammed a fist into the shooter's face. Once. Twice. He pressed his knee into the shooter's sternum to keep him in place as he hit the shooter again and again. His heart threatened to beat out of his chest as the man beneath the ski mask blocked the next hit. With a kick to center mass, Braxton flew backward, his childhood home nothing but a blur as he landed in three inches of snow.

The shooter hauled himself to his feet, brushing snow from that damn suit. "I told you before, Levitt.

You can't stop me. Elizabeth is going to pay for what she's done. One way or another. And you? You're just in my way."

Pain splintered down his sternum. Braxton bit down harder and shook the ice from his hair as he straightened. Blood dripped into the snow, into his boots. If he could still walk, he could still fight. And hell, he'd fight to the death for Elizabeth Dawson. In fact, there was nothing he wouldn't do for her. He'd already lost her once. He wouldn't lose her again. "Even with a bullet in my leg, you won't get to her."

"In my experience, the strongest always fall the hardest." An audible snap broke through the pounding of Braxton's heart behind his ears, and a glint of sunlight reflected off the switchblade in the shooter's hand. The masked man came directly at him.

Wrapping both hands around the shooter's wrist, Braxton twisted to one side to avoid being gutted right on his own front lawn. He hauled the SOB's wrist down over his knee—hard—and forced the shooter to drop the blade. Swinging himself around, he wrapped his forearm around the bastard's neck and squeezed. He locked his arm in place with his free hand, leveraging the shooter's head against his chest. Gloved hands fought to pry off Braxton's hold. In vain. But a swift hit of the shooter's elbow to his rib cage knocked the air from his lungs. The shooter wrenched free, gripped Braxton's throat and forced him to the ground.

The attacker wrenched Braxton's arm behind his back and applied pressure. Pain unlike anything Braxton had experienced exploded from his shoulder joint. "Look at her, Levitt."

Deep in the snow, his body temperature dropped, froze his muscles, anesthetized the bullet wound in his thigh, but he found the strength to lift his head. There, not twenty feet away, Liz searched through the snow. Presumably for the gun the shooter had dropped. Damn it. Why hadn't she listened to him? She should've run as far and as fast as she could. It would've been the only way to keep her safe. She wouldn't find the Glock. Not in time.

"I'm going to kill her after I get what I need from her, but first, I'm going to make her watch you die." Leaning into Braxton, the shooter intensified the pressure in his shoulder until a bone-crunching pop blacked out his vision. "You should've killed me when you had the chance."

A scream ripped from between his clenched teeth. He couldn't stop it. The operative had dislocated his shoulder and possibly torn one of the ligaments. The scream died to a groan after a few seconds, and Braxton fought to breathe through the tremors and the wave of dizziness rocking through him. He crushed his forehead against chunks of ice and snow beneath him to stay in the moment. "Touch her, and I'll kill you."

"Unfortunately for you, you're not going anywhere." The weight against his back disappeared. Snow crunched beneath footsteps, and Braxton shot his hand out to stop the shooter from reaching her and hauled him back. The man in the suit slammed into the ground, and Braxton pushed to his feet with his uninjured arm.

"You're not very good at listening." He circled around the bastard, his injured leg barely holding him up. A wave of dizziness distorted his vision. He was losing too much blood. His body had started going into shock. Soon he wouldn't be able to think. To breathe. His blood pressure would drop, and he wouldn't be able to stand. His words wheezed from his aching throat. He wrapped his free hand around the operative's throat and pulled the man in the mask against his chest for better grip. "I said you're not going to touch her."

Liz scrambled to her feet, empty-handed. Hair in disarray, her eyes red from the percussion grenade smoke, she only stared at him. Waiting.

Braxton could kill the shooter now. End this. But Liz had too many nightmares as it was. She didn't deserve to live with that for the rest of her life. He should incapacitate the SOB, tie him up and wait for Anchorage PD to arrive. Then extract himself from Liz's life once and for all. It was what she wanted. What he should've done in the first place. Snowflakes fell in a thin veil of white between them.

"Braxton, look out!" Liz's warning came too late.

Pure agony washed over him as a second blade buried deep in his gut. The shooter's gloved hand fell away. Braxton dropped his hold on the shooter's throat and stumbled back as the man in the mask rolled out of reach. Hell, he hadn't seen that coming.

Liz rushed forward from across the yard, eyes wide. Too far away. Snow kicked up around her as he collapsed to his knees. His heart pounded even louder behind his ears. He had to slow his pulse. Braxton swallowed to get rid of the muffled ringing in his ears. The faster his blood pumped, the faster he'd pass out. And that wasn't an option. Cold worked through his jeans. He placed his uninjured arm on the ground to keep from falling over. No. He wasn't going to die. Not until she was safe. He fought to stand but fell back as the muscles in his thigh finally gave out.

The shooter maneuvered into his vision. Headed straight for Liz.

"Liz." A growl reverberated through him as he climbed to his feet. His vision blurred again, only the spotting of red dots in the snow clear enough. He forced one foot in front of the other. Move. He had to get to her. Determination propelled him to his feet. No thought. Only her. His Elizabeth.

Sweat dripped into his eyes, but he had enough focus to keep her in sight. A glint of metal caught his attention at his feet. One of the shooter's blades. Sinking into the snow a second time, he wrapped his hand around the handle then used every last bit of strength he had left to stand. Two steps. Three. Pain and exhaustion drained from his muscles as he caught sight of Liz's wide, fearful gaze. She countered the shooter's steps as he closed in on her but wouldn't be able to outrun him. Not unless Braxton slowed him down.

That was all he had to do. Give her the chance to escape.

Police sirens echoed in the distance. Anchorage PD would take him in, the NSA would send an agent to the station claiming him in the interest of national security and he'd never see Liz again. Probably spend the rest of his days locked away inside some black site the government would deny existed if she ever came looking for him. But she would be safe.

And he could never hurt her again.

Reaching out for the shooter, Braxton clamped his hand on the bastard's shoulder, but he was caught off guard when his opponent spun in his grip. Braxton hiked the blade over his shoulder and thrust down with everything he had left. Only the blade never made contact.

Grip tight around Braxton's wrist, the man in the suit wrenched the knife to one side and forced him to drop it. "Don't worry, Levitt. I'm going to take real good care of her for you."

"No." The rush of adrenaline Braxton had been surviving off drained from his veins as blood pooled in his shirt and jeans. Pain flared up his uninjured arm, but he wouldn't back down. And he'd never give up. Not when it came to Liz.

"Let him go." The chambering of a round into a gun barrel claimed his attention. Over the shooter's shoulder, he spotted Liz as she widened her stance, both hands gripped around the shooter's gun. Chocolate-brown eyes shifted to him as the man in the suit dropped his hold. With hands above his head, the shooter turned toward her, and she followed every move. "I stopped Braxton from killing you the first time. I'm not going to make the same mistake twice."

Braxton stumbled back, hand over the stab wound in his side. Blood dripped onto the snow as sirens grew louder. It was over. The nightmare was over.

"Are you going to kill me in cold blood, too, Elizabeth? Just like you killed Justin Valentin or any number of other operatives with your program?" The SOB didn't give her a chance to answer, lunging straight at her.

"No!" Braxton rocketed to his feet. Darkness closed in around the edges of his vision, but he fought back with everything he had.

Liz pulled the trigger. Once. Twice. The gun never fired. Her mouth dropped open. She stumbled backward toward the tree line, caged by a line of pines, reaching for something to use as a weapon as the shooter closed in. "Braxton!"

There was too much distance between them. He couldn't get to her fast enough.

"That gun doesn't work." Wrapping his arms around her, the man in the suit hauled Liz off her feet and spun her around, her back to his chest. The shooter pulled a smaller gun from his ankle holster and aimed directly at Braxton. "But this one does."

Gunfire exploded in Braxton's ears—then pain—right before darkness closed in.

Chapter Thirteen

"Braxton!" Elizabeth couldn't take her eyes off him, off his lifeless body in the middle of ever-darkening red snow. No. He wasn't dead. It wasn't possible. Because the last words she'd spoken to him had been filled with hatred for what he'd done. She'd told him she never wanted to see him again, that he'd never get to meet his daughter. The shooter tightened his grip around her waist, hauling her into him. She pushed against his hands, but he didn't budge. "Get up! Please, get up."

Her throat burned. Eyes stung. He couldn't be dead.

"Save your energy, Elizabeth." The man in the suit pressed the gun's barrel against her temple. Police sirens drew closer, but the shooter barely seemed fazed. "You're going to need it before I'm through with you."

She clenched her teeth to fight the fresh rush of hot tears. No. Something inside her snapped. Adrenaline flooded through her system. Digging her bare heels into the snow, she wrenched out of the shooter's grip and shoved him back. He wouldn't take her again. He wouldn't win. Braxton couldn't protect her anymore. She had to protect herself. And their daughter.

"I don't want to shoot you, but I will." The shooter stalked toward her, gun still in hand.

"That's funny. I really want to shoot you." Elizabeth stepped back toward the pines to keep space between them, hands fanned out to her side. Pain shot through the back of her foot as she stepped on a medium-size tree branch that'd fallen near the tree line. Cold worked through her borrowed sweats as her attention flickered to Braxton, still unconscious twenty feet away. She'd trained to defend herself and she'd do just that. For him. No time to grieve. Time to survive. She wrapped her grip around the dead branch and swung as hard as she could. The wood reverberated through her hand at contact with the side of the shooter's head.

She didn't wait to see if he'd gotten up and pumped her legs hard. The police must be close. They had to be close.

A growl reached her ears, and she pushed herself harder. Puffs of crystallized air formed in front of her lips as she headed for the thick wilderness behind Braxton's childhood home. Tears froze in their tracks down her cheeks, the dropping temperatures working to slow her down. She was a runner, but exhaustion pulled her down. Barreling footsteps echoed from behind.

"Help!" She screamed as loud as she could, branches cutting the skin across her neck and face as she raced into the woods. It was the only place she could lose him. Her mouth dried, her breathing loud in the silent wilderness. Was that an Anchorage PD cruiser she'd just heard from behind?

The trees started to thin, the light brighter here. She

didn't dare stop. Didn't dare look back. *Keep going. Get to the road. Survive.*

A wall of muscle slammed her into the icy dirt.

"You're faster than I gave you credit for." His lips pressed into her ear, his breath hot against her skin. A tremor raked across her chest, intensifying everything around her. The trees. The roots. He wrapped both gloved hands around one of her ankles and pulled. "You know, in a way, I've always admired you. Your determination. Your creative nature when it came to your work. Who else but you could've created a program like Oversight?"

Elizabeth dug her nails into the frozen ground. All too easily, she imagined her boss, Sullivan Bishop, having to come down to the morgue to identify her and Braxton's bodies. Not going to happen. She had to go back. She'd lost Braxton once. She couldn't do it again. He was a part of her. The good and the deceit. He was hers to protect now. He was the family her daughter deserved.

"You've chosen a really awkward time to hand out compliments." Clamping on to the nearest root, she heaved herself closer to the base of the large pine. The root broke away clean, and he dragged her backward. She couldn't think—couldn't breathe—but kicked at him as hard as she could.

A groan filled the clearing, his grip on her ankle loosening, but she sure as hell wouldn't ask her attacker if he was okay. She clawed across the foliage, jaw locked against the pain tearing through her. A *whooshing* sound reached her ears, and she exhaled hard, frozen tears stinging her cheeks. A car. She'd reached the next road over.

Elizabeth embedded her fingernails into the nearest tree and lifted herself to her feet. Run. No looking back. Just run. She stumbled forward, gaining strength with each step before she was finally able to pick up speed. Every muscle in her body screamed for release.

Another car drove past. Louder. Closer. Breathing became easier, but...slower. Something wet and sticky clung to her borrowed clothing. Sap? Taking refuge behind a large tree, she looked back over her shoulder. No movement. He hadn't followed her? Pain registered as she forced her heartbeat to slow. Not sap. She touched the spreading stain on her right side. Blood. When had that happened? She hadn't even felt an injury. She couldn't think about that right now. Braxton was bleeding out from at least two gunshots and a stab would. She'd run out of time. Deep breath. She could do this. Clamping her hand over her wound, she pushed forward. Couldn't stop. The shooter would catch up any minute. She had to flag down a car and circle back to Braxton—

The ground dropped out from under her feet. The world tilted on its axis as she rolled end over end. Branches and bushes scratched at her skin as blackness closed in at the edges of her vision. Sliding down the last few feet before the road, Elizabeth closed her eyes as the oxygen rushed from her lungs, unsure how long she lay there.

"Liz!" a male voice called.

She recognized that voice. A deep rumbling tore

down the road, growing louder, and she forced her eyes open. "Sullivan?"

"I've got tracks!" Her boss's voice grew fainter, but she couldn't respond. Not without giving away her position to the shooter.

No. This wasn't the end. Not today. Another explosion of pain throttled through her as she flipped onto her side. Her team had come. She wasn't alone. They'd recover Braxton, and— She covered her mouth to prevent the scream in her throat from escaping. Save energy. Keep moving. "Any extra calories you can sacrifice would help a lot right now, baby girl."

Thick trees lining the road made it nearly impossible for her to spot movement. If the shooter had followed her, there were countless points where she could be walking straight into another ambush. She wouldn't be able to see him coming. Elizabeth ran a bloodied hand through her hair. She had to risk it. She had to get to Braxton. Had to get to her team.

Briars and weeds sliced into the bottoms of her feet, but she forced herself to keep moving. Anchorage PD wouldn't have been far behind Sullivan and the rest of the team. Somebody was getting Braxton the help he needed. She had to believe that. The alternative would rip her world apart, and she wasn't sure how much more she could take after what they'd been through the last five days. How much more heartache was she supposed to bear.

Swiping a hand beneath her runny nose, Elizabeth held her breath at the sound of a snapping twig. Her head pounded in rhythm to her racing heartbeat. She froze, only redirecting her gaze toward the tree line. He'd found her. Was hunting her. The weight of someone watching her—stalking her—pressurized the air in her lungs. Her fingertips tingled with the need to find a weapon. A shadow shifted to her left, and every ounce of willpower screamed for her to run. The tree line was the only way back to Braxton. If the shooter stood between her and getting to him…

"There's nowhere you can run, Elizabeth. Nowhere you can hide." That voice. She'd never be able to forget it, and she automatically dug her fingernails into the center of her palms. The shooter stepped from the tree line, gun in hand. The black ski mask shifted as he spoke. "Haven't I already proven how far I'm willing to go?"

"You can't get access to Oversight's programming, can you? Even after I gave you the password when you threatened to throw me over a cliff." Elizabeth straightened. He was right. She couldn't run. She couldn't hide. She'd have to finish this herself. She'd have to go through him. It was the only way to save Braxton. "That's why you haven't killed me yet."

Which meant he wouldn't kill her until she gave him the access.

"Seems you've implemented security measures even I can't get past." The man in the mask held the high ground. Any movement and he'd have the advantage. And the longer they stood here talking, the faster Braxton bled out.

"And you never will." Despite the failed mission that cost Agent Valentin his life, Oversight saved thousands of lives every day by predicting violence and threats.

She'd always be proud of that, and she'd do what she had to, to protect it.

Silence stretched between them for the space of two breaths. Three. Time was slipping away too fast. Every beat of Braxton's heart endangered his life. They were wasting time. Wrapping one hand around his opposite wrist, gun pointed toward his toes, the shooter seemed more businessman than professional hit man. Maybe federal agent. "I'll make you a deal, Elizabeth. You give me what I want, and I guarantee your bodyguard lives."

"There's no way I would ever trust you." She wasn't stupid enough to believe he'd ever keep his end of a deal between them. But if she could get close enough to Braxton—ensure he was alive—she could shut down Oversight on her own and end this nightmare.

"Then the alternative is letting him bleed out, and I put a bullet in you now." The shooter raised the gun with one hand. Taking aim, he scrambled down the hill and closed the short distance between them. He fisted the ski mask with his free hand and tugged it over his head. Familiar dark eyes centered on her. "Do we have a deal?"

"You." Her knees shook as she stumbled back from the man in the suit. Shaking her head, she fought to keep her balance. "That's not possible. They said you were—"

"Dead?" Faster than she expected, the shooter slammed the butt of his gun into the side of her face, and Elizabeth dropped hard. Darkness closed in around the edges of her vision, but in the center, a ghost from the past still stared down at her. "Let's just say it didn't stick."

DEATH HAD TO be earned.

But Braxton wasn't willing to pay the price. Not until he recovered Liz.

A migraine pulsed behind his eyes. Three hundred stitches. Two bullet wounds. One stab wound to the rib cage. Two transfusions of blood. Hell of a way to die. But this wasn't over. Liz was missing. Vincent Kalani and Sullivan Bishop had tracked her path through the woods behind his childhood home to the road. As well as the shooter's. Then they'd simply disappeared. Spots of blood had stained the snow in her tracks. She'd been injured. According to the forensics expert, there'd been clear signs of a struggle, but no evidence of where the bastard had taken her.

He forced his legs over the edge of the hospital bed, and another wave of pain shot through him. Braxton gripped the sheets in his hand. He neutralized the groan working up his throat. Didn't matter how many bullets he'd taken or how much blood he'd lost, he was getting Liz back. And he'd kill anyone who tried to stop him.

The hairs on the back of his neck stood on end. Damn, he wasn't alone, and hadn't realized it until right this second. How much anesthesia had the doc given him?

"Look at you sacrificing yourself for others, Levitt." Elliot Dunham, Blackhawk Security's private investigator, propped his feet up on the edge of the bed and laced his fingers behind his head. "From what Liz told me about you, I didn't think you had it in you."

Hell. Of all the people on Liz's team to send, her boss sent this one. "Aren't you supposed to be babysitting?"

"Ah, yeah. About that…" Elliot planted the chair back onto the gleaming white tile and rested his elbows against his knees. Narrowing his gaze, the former con man cocked his head. "I kind of…lost your dad."

A laugh stretched the stitches down his side. Braxton highly doubted that. His old man had a way of disappearing at exactly the right time with exactly the right amount of cash he'd stolen from people's wallets. "You might want to cancel your credit cards. You're about to learn who Brolin Levitt really is."

Elliot patted his back jeans pockets, then his jacket. "Wow, he's good. Didn't feel a thing. I'm going to have to get him to show me some moves."

"Good luck finding him." He'd probably never see his father again. No loss there. Although Liz might have a hard time with the old man's disappearance. She'd kept tabs on the addict, made sure he had a place to sleep at night, food to eat. One day she'd understand how pointless all of that was. Brolin Levitt was a selfish son of a bitch. She'd be better off not knowing the real coward behind the drugs. Shoving off the bed, Braxton dropped onto the floor and shot his hands out for balance. He'd been brought in through the emergency room doors seven hours ago. Liz could be anywhere by now. If that SOB hadn't gotten to her first.

"If you're going after her, you're going to want to see this." Elliot reached for a file folder on the side table and tossed it onto the bed beside Braxton. "Did a little digging into the background of the CIA agent who was killed during the trial run for Liz's program. Justin Valentin."

"You don't have clearance for that intel." Anticipation flooded through him as Braxton reached for the file. A clean-cut photo of the agent had been paper-clipped in front of a military service record, driving record, residency proof and a whole lot more classified documentation Braxton had never seen before. Specific missions, confidential informants Agent Valentin kept. Even as an analyst, he would've had to get clearance or federal warrants for the paperwork in this file. "Where did you get all this?"

"You don't want to know." Elliot leaned in closer from his position in the chair, dropping his voice to a whisper. "It's blackmail. I have files on everyone I investigate. And some people I don't investigate, but that stays between us. Also, I can see straight through your—"

Braxton closed the file and reached for the opening in the back of the hospital gown. If there was another way to make patients more uncomfortable, he didn't know how it'd be possible. He searched the room. Where the hell were his clothes?

"The hospital staff had a hard time getting all the blood out of your clothes. You know, because there was…a lot. So they were incinerated. Good news, though—" Elliot hauled a duffel bag from beside his chair into his lap "—I brought you some of mine. Should fit. Had to guess your shoe size. Don't tell Vincent, but they're his." The private investigator tossed the bag at him, and Braxton was forced to release his clutch on the gown to catch it. Elliot guarded his eyes, chin to chest. "So Liz built a program for the NSA to spy on civilians, huh? I knew I liked her."

Digging into the duffel bag, Braxton pulled jeans, socks, boots and a long-sleeve shirt from the depths. He dressed fast. Every minute he wasted here, the higher the chance he'd never see her again. Hiking his foot to the edge of the bed, he suppressed a groan as he laced his borrowed boots. Pain was temporary. Losing Liz, that would be forever. "The program was designed to identify terrorists and criminals before crimes actually happened. It worked ninety-nine percent of the time, too. Oversight has saved thousands of lives."

"But the one percent got a CIA agent killed last year," Elliot said.

"That mission tore her apart. Valentin had disguised himself as part of the group he'd infiltrated, and Oversight hadn't been able to tell the difference because of a line of broken code. Liz blames herself for the mistake." Braxton studied the photo of Justin Valentin for the second time and narrowed in on the color of the agent's eyes. Ice blue. Not dark enough for the man in the mask. Justin Valentin wasn't their unsub and had only a wife and two young boys left behind. None of whom he considered a threat as he looked over their financials within the file. The shooter could be anyone, doing this for any reason, as far as Braxton knew. His shoulders deflated, the stitches protesting along his rib cage. They were back at square one.

Hell, all of this could've been prevented if he'd just stayed.

"So does someone else. Whoever is trying to kill her

planted Agent Valentin's fingerprints on those casings from the rooftop shooting." Elliot leaned back in the chair. "They wanted her to know they knew she created Oversight and about the failed trial run."

The fingerprints. They were the only piece of evidence left behind in this investigation. He had to look at that report again. "Give me your phone."

The private investigator tossed him the device, and Braxton wasted no time logging in to his own email for the ballistics report Vincent had forwarded him less than twelve hours ago. Scrolling past the diagrams and countless pages of analysis, he focused on the latent fingerprints recovered from the casings. The shading was too light to have been pulled directly from wherever the prints originated. Elliot was right. They'd been planted on those casings and purposefully left at the scene. Which meant the shooter had pulled them from somewhere else using tape or another adhesive. Something Agent Valentin had to have in his possession and the bastard coming after Liz had gotten ahold of.

"What do you got?" Elliot stood, circling the bed.

"These prints are too light to have been taken directly off the source. They were transferred at least once more onto those casings." Braxton zeroed in on a corner of one print and turned the phone on its side to zoom in on the area. A small, clearly defined arrow interrupted the impression at the edge of the print. He'd seen that exact shape, combined with a circle and two more arrows like it, before. On the Trident—Beretta's logo. "The prints were originally lifted off Justin Valentin's service weapon. A Beretta 92 FS, if I had to guess."

Elliot took the phone, studying the impressions on the screen. "The CIA's favored handgun for their field agents. Very nice. Good catch."

"Whoever wants Liz dead got ahold of a CIA agent's service weapon in the middle of Afghanistan. Can't be a long list." The shooter had made this personal by coming after her. He'd obviously been close to Valentin, blamed her for the agent's death. Why else plant those fingerprints? Why else play this mind game? Braxton rolled back his left shoulder where he'd taken the second bullet during the fight. He exhaled hard against the pain but rolled it back again. "Valentin didn't have a partner?"

"Not according to his records." Elliot reached for the file on the bed, thumbing through the pages. "The last time Justin Valentin was assigned a partner was…" The private investigator scoffed. "A year ago. The agency suspected the partner had sold classified information to the Russians, but the agent died in the line of duty before charges could be brought up. That sucks."

Braxton straightened a bit more, his instincts on high alert. "What's the agent's name?"

"Liam Waters." Elliot looked up from the file. "Why? You know him?"

"No." He'd never heard that name before, but it was the only lead they had, and his gut screamed this would get him closer to Liz. Hell, he should've fought harder. He should've been a step ahead of the shooter who'd taken her, but he'd been so caught up in…her, he hadn't been able to think straight for days. And it'd gotten her kidnapped. Again. Braxton stretched the stitches in his shoulder. He'd tear this entire city to pieces to find her. And kill anyone who got in his way. "How fast can you get access to Waters's files?"

"An hour, tops." The private investigator folded his arms across his chest, file still in hand, and leveraged his weight against the edge of the bed. Gray eyes, darker than Braxton's, narrowed on him. "What are you thinking?"

"Make it thirty minutes." He couldn't wait that much longer. Not when Liz's life was at risk. Braxton pulled the shoulder holster, complete with a smuggled handgun, from the duffel bag, and maneuvered into it slowly. Another round of pain lightninged through his injuries, but he pushed it to the back of his mind. Nothing would stop him from recovering Liz. And if the shooter turned out to be a dead man after all, he'd make damn sure the bastard never got up again. "I want to know if former agent Liam Waters is really dead."

Chapter Fourteen

A dull ache at the base of her skull beat through her in rhythm to her heart rate. Elizabeth cracked her eyes then closed them again against the brightness of a wall of active monitors in front of her. Blurry streaks cleared. The wide bay window had been covered with thick blankets. Blue light from the screens highlighted the three walls and large box near a door in her vision but nothing more. No other details. No telling where the shooter had taken her.

Not the shooter. He had a name. Former CIA agent Liam Waters.

And he blamed her for his partner's death.

"You're awake." Footsteps echoed off the worn hardwood flooring, growing closer. "I was beginning to think I'd hit you too hard."

Flashes of the woods, of Braxton facedown in the snow, crossed her mind, and Elizabeth fought to swallow around the tightness closing in. If Anchorage PD or her team hadn't made it to the scene in time... She pulled against the handcuffs behind her back and two more pairs around her ankles and the legs of the chair.

She wasn't going anywhere. A rush of nausea forced bile into her throat. She licked at dry lips. "How long have I been out?"

"About eight hours." Waters maneuvered into her vision and stood in front of her, gun loose in his grip at one side. Lines furrowed between his thick eyebrows, a head of dark hair wilder than she remembered from his files. Before he'd joined the CIA, Liam Waters had been part of the fleet antiterrorism security team, or FAST, where he'd been partnered with Agent Justin Valentin for a number of years then accused of selling classified intel to a Russian contact. After Oversight had misidentified Valentin for an extremist, she'd hacked into the agent's files. Wanted to know the man her program had killed. Agent Liam Waters had been in those files. As were the charges the CIA planned to bring against Agent Valentin's partner before Waters had been killed in action. Bruising shadows shifted in the light of the monitors as he spoke and, suddenly, he seemed so much…older than she remembered from his files. Worn. Desperate. Not dead after all. "Recognize what's on the monitors?"

Elizabeth shifted her focus to the screens. City names from across the country popped up on the bottom of each monitor as it scrolled from image to image. Cars passed beneath cameras, civilians walked down streets, thin white squares homed in on, processed and identified facial features. The weight of Waters's attention settled on her. "You're the one who hijacked Oversight's feeds."

"And you're the one who killed my partner with it."

Cords looped circles behind Waters's feet. Hundreds of them, all connected to the monitors, disappeared behind the door to her left. Not an exit. Most likely a server room, which meant the only way to escape was behind her. Waters crouched in front of her, his knees popping with the movement, gun still in hand. "Justin Valentin had a family. A wife, two boys. I showed up at his house every morning to pick him up for work for four years, and when their youngest was diagnosed with leukemia and they couldn't pay for the treatments, I did what I had to do to make sure they could. Of course, they'd known what I'd done. There was no hiding the fact I'd started selling intelligence to the Russians from my own partner. He was a good agent, but, as it turned out, a father would do anything to save his son. Justin helped me plan my own death. Because you see, they were my family, too." Waters stood, fanning his grip over the gun's handle. The monitors cast his features into shadow from behind. "Now those boys can't look at me without thinking of their dead father. His wife refuses to see me, won't take my calls. You did that. You took my family from me."

"I'm sorry." She forced herself to breathe evenly. Every moment of that failed trial had been burned into her memory. Braxton running to her cubicle with news of the mission go-ahead from her project supervisor, Dalton Meyer, her trying to shut Oversight down remotely. Nothing had worked. In the end, she'd been restrained by security and sealed in an office while the NSA had taken control of her program. She'd only learned of Oversight's mistake after the fact. And had taken the blame for it all. "I tried to stop them. I told them the program wasn't ready, but Meyer wouldn't listen—"

"You think I did all of this for an apology?" A low, dark laugh rumbled from deep in his chest, and a shiver shot across Elizabeth's shoulders. She interlaced her fingers tighter as he closed the short distance between them, her wrists straining against the handcuffs. He leveraged his weight against the back of the chair with one arm. A combination of spicy aftershave and sweat dived into her lungs. "No, Elizabeth. I brought you here so you can watch your creation burn. Then I'm going to kill you."

Shock rocked through her. Her mouth dried. She searched for something—anything—that would get her out of these cuffs. A paper clip. A nail. Maybe if she vaulted herself backward, the wood chair would break enough for her to get free. She was on her own. No matter how many times he'd been there before, Braxton couldn't save her now. "You can't shut the program down. Oversight made a mistake—*I* made a mistake—but it has saved countless lives over the past year. It's protected this country, stopped terrorists. Just as you have."

"And how many more families will be destroyed—families like Justin's—because of your mistakes?" Waters wrapped gloved hands around the back of the chair and shoved her forward until her knees hit the desk. The former agent gripped the back of her neck tight and thrust her over the keyboard. "You built the security for Oversight. You're going to tear it down."

Elizabeth clenched her teeth against the stiffness in her neck. She pushed back, but Waters was so much stronger. And not handcuffed to a chair. A rush of dizziness distorted her vision. No, no, no, no. Not now. The sinking sensation that accompanied her blood sugar crashing pulled her farther into the chair. She fought to breathe through the disorientation. Didn't work. Nothing but food would combat the crash. Closing her eyes against the sudden brightness of the monitors, she dropped her head. And saw blood. The injury from the woods. Her blood pressure spiked. "My side is bleeding. My blood sugar is crashing. I need to eat. I'm no good to you in shock."

He dropped his grip on her neck and instead replaced it by pointing the gun at her left temple. He pressed so hard the steel cut into her skin, but she wouldn't disable the program. Not when the safety of an entire country had been put on the line. "Surprise me."

She bit her lower lip to distract herself from the crushing weight behind her sternum and the pain in her ribs. Nobody was coming to save her. She had to save herself. But she couldn't even do that if she was cuffed to this damn chair. Her senses had started adjusting to the surrounding darkness. There had to be something in this room she could use as a weapon. "If you want me to shut down the program, you're going to have to uncuff me."

"I've read your file, Elizabeth. I've watched you for months." He centered her in front of the nearest monitor. "I know what you can do with your hands. You tell me the second password, and I'll enter it."

He wanted to do this the hard way? Fine. "I told you before when you were threatening to throw me over a cliff. Even if you enter the password, there isn't only one level of security. Oversight doesn't work like that. I made sure no one person could take control of the system. So unless you have a retinal scanner in this dump, you're not getting into my program."

"Then I have no use for you." His rough exhale hit her collarbones as Waters compressed the gun's safety button off. "Blackmailing your bodyguard to get the intel I needed on Oversight was worth less trouble than you are. I'm done with you."

Blackmail?

"You don't have to do this. Justin wouldn't want this. His wife and those boys wouldn't want this." This wasn't how she'd die. Not after everything she'd been through the last five days. Not after losing the only man she'd ever wanted to spend the rest of her life with, the man who'd never get to meet his daughter. Her eyes burned. From the moment Braxton had shaken her hand at their first meeting to the moment he'd sacrificed himself for her to get away in his own front yard, he'd protected her. He'd stood by her side. He'd given her a glimpse of the family she'd always wanted. Needed.

"Guess we'll never know, will we?" he asked.

Elizabeth licked at her lips one more time. She might've already lost Braxton. She wasn't about to lose their baby. "Please, I'm pregnant."

The gun faltered in Waters's hand. "That's not possible. I've been following you for months. I've read your medical records."

"Then you suck at your job. Otherwise you would've noticed me walking into my doctor's office last week." She scanned the room a second time, locking on a blue-and-white pen on the floor to her right. She could do a lot of damage with a pen, but getting her hands on it was a different skill set entirely. Pressing her toes into the floor, she tipped the chair's front legs back a few centimeters at most. She didn't dare look at Waters's face. Any sudden movement on her part could force him to pull the trigger. But if she could walk out of this unscathed, she'd take the risk. "You hijacked the feeds to an all-seeing program. Review the records again. I'm sure they're updated by now."

"You're lying." Keeping the gun aimed at her head, the former agent rounded into her vision. Bruising darkened the shadows beneath his eyes where she'd clocked him with the handle of his gun on Seward Highway, and a small bit of her hoped it hurt like hell. But then those dark eyes centered on her, and everything inside her went cold. "At this point, Elizabeth, I think you'll say anything to stay alive, but you can't get out of this. You're going to die today."

"No, I'm not." She kicked against the floor, every muscle in her body going rigid as the chair tipped backward. The room blurred a split second before she hit the hardwood. Cracking wood claimed her attention, but not for long. Pain stretched up her crushed arms as she rolled from the debris, her wrists still cuffed. She wrapped her fingers around the pen and pushed the sharp end into the keyhole. Slim chance this would work, but she wouldn't go down without a fight. For Braxton. For her baby.

"Clever." Liam Waters stood over her, gun raised. Slipping his finger over the trigger, he widened his stance. "But, tell me, honestly, how far did you think you could run this time?"

"Who said I'd try to run?" The cuff loosened from around her casted wrist, and Elizabeth shot her foot upward. Connecting with Waters's gun, she sent it flying across the room. The gun discharged, the bullet arching wide, forcing her to cover her head with her arms in an empty attempt to avoid being shot.

With her next breath, Waters straddled her midsection and crushed the oxygen from her lungs. He pinned her against the floor. "Why won't you just die?"

The door behind her slammed open. "Get your damn hands off of her."

BRAXTON FLEW OVER LIZ, tackling the former CIA operative to the floor. Monitors on the desk shook from the quake then toppled face-first around them as he pulled his elbow back. Glass and metal hit the hardwood, but nothing would distract him from finishing the job. Not this time.

"How many times do I have to kill you before it sticks?" Waters slammed an elbow into his face and twisted out of Braxton's reach.

Shooting his hand out, Braxton caught the edge of the shooter's suit jacket, but not enough to pull the bastard back. The sound of tearing fabric drowned the pounding of his pulse behind his ears. Waters went for one of the largest monitors, hauling it over his head.

Every stitch in his body protested as Braxton rolled out of the way and shot to his feet. He grabbed Waters by the arm and whirled him into the nearest wall. Adrenaline sang through his veins, blocking out the pain of his injuries. It wouldn't last long, but he'd sure as hell make the most of it. Shifting his weight back as Waters swung a right hook, Braxton kicked out the operative's knee and followed it up with a punch to the gut. "No one hurts my family and gets away with it."

Waters stared up at him. Blood dripped from the former agent's lip. Swiping it off with the back of his hand, the SOB cracked a smile. Then Waters swung up. Flesh met bone and Braxton spun backward, barely catching a glimpse of Liz as she worked to free herself from three different sets of cuffs. He landed face-first against the floor. Footsteps echoed off the hardwood. "Funny. I was thinking the exact same thing."

Liz's gaze shot up, widened at the sight of Waters closing in, then homed in on the gun against the far wall. Braxton could tell from the determination in her eyes she was going to make a run for it.

Waters lunged as Liz pushed off the floor. He got there first, wrapping his hand around the gun and swinging it wide toward her. Braxton launched to his feet, but not before Liz caught Waters's wrist in one hand and pushed her casted hand up under his jaw-line. Shoving him back, she wedged the former agent between herself and the wall, but there was nowhere else to go.

"Liz!" Braxton took a step forward then collapsed to one knee. The stitches in his thigh had torn. Blood seeped through his jeans. Damn it.

She let go of the former agent's throat then slammed her cast against the gun, dislodging Waters's hold on the Glock. And hell if that wasn't the sexiest thing he'd ever seen. But Liz wasn't fast enough. With one blow to the face, she went down. She hit the ground hard, a groan filling his ears, and nothing but rage consumed him.

Braxton closed the space between him and Waters in two steps and lunged feet first. His boots connected with the shooter's sternum, and they collapsed to the floor. Air stuck in his lungs, but he barely had time to stand before Waters came around. Braxton stumbled, shooting his hand out toward the dropped gun. The metal slipped against his palm. He tightened his grip and swung the gun around.

But Waters had the bigger card to play.

With a simple white-and-blue pen.

Crouching over Liz, the operative held the pen to her jugular, waiting for Braxton to make his next move. Waters's shoulders rose and fell in rapid succession in rhythm to his strained breathing. If Braxton had to guess, the operative had broken a rib or two, but he hadn't let it slow him down. It'd take more than a few broken bones to finish this. "I've spent the last year waiting for this moment. You're not going to stop me from getting my partner's family the justice they deserve, Levitt."

Blood spread through his T-shirt, soaking the waistband of his jeans, but Braxton pushed the distraction to the back of his mind. Hell, he'd tear every stitch a hundred times if it meant protecting the woman he loved. Screw the pain. Screw the NSA. He'd left Liz behind once. He wouldn't make the same mistake again. He wasn't going anywhere. Not without her. Lifting the gun, he centered the former CIA operative in his sights. Liz had stopped him from killing the bastard once, and it'd been a mistake. "It's over, Waters. Liz is mine. And I don't share."

Swaying, the former agent dropped his chin but only fanned his fingers around the pen. "I should've killed you four months ago when I had the chance."

"Yeah." Braxton held the gun steady, ready for the last round. Liam Waters wasn't leaving this room alive. Killers like him didn't give up easily. The former CIA agent would keep coming after her. And Liz—and their baby—deserved a life better than one on the run. He could give them that. "You should have. But if you make another move, I'll make damn sure you never get back up."

"Let's see who's faster." Waters raised his hand, ready to plunge the pen into Liz's throat as she lay unconscious, and Braxton pulled the trigger. One bullet ripped through the operative's shoulder but didn't bring Waters down. He fired again, the gun kicking back in his hand. The second shot hit center mass. The shooter held his arm up but dropped the pen. Collapsing to the floor, Liam Waters stared at the peeling yellow ceiling, one hand pressed against the wound beneath his sternum.

"I feel like you should've known not to bring a pen

to a gunfight." Braxton approached slowly, heart threatening to break apart his rib cage. He kicked the pen out of Waters's reach as the shooter dived into unconsciousness, head slumping to the side. The operative's chest stilled, one last exhale reaching Braxton's ears.

Liam Waters was dead.

Dropping to his knees, he framed Liz's face with one hand, sliding the pad of his thumb across her bottom lip. "Liz."

Her resulting groan set every cell in his body on fire. She swung her head toward him and cracked her eyelids. Deep brown eyes locked on him, and his world shattered. Hell, they'd survived. Together. The nightmare was over. And they—relief coursed through him—they could get their lives back. They could start their family. If she'd have him. Brushing her hair behind her ear, he studied her for any other injuries. "Can you move?"

"My blood sugar…" Her hands shook as she wrapped them around the back of his neck. "I haven't eaten."

"Here." He set the Glock on the floor then reached into his back pocket and pulled out two granola bars. Unwrapping both, he dumped the broken pieces into his palm and lifted her against him. "It's not much, but I brought something in case you crashed again."

She closed her eyes, chewing methodically, and sank against him. "You really know the way to a woman's heart."

"Just yours." A smile pulled at one corner of his mouth. He held on to her, resting his cheek against the top of her head. A combination of lavender and chocolate overwhelmed his senses, and he breathed in as much as he could. "I got you. You're safe now."

A gunshot exploded in his left ear.

Liz arched against him, mouth open, eyes wide, but her gasp said it all.

She'd been hit.

Tearing her away from him, Braxton spun. He reached for the gun in Waters's hand. The bastard wasn't dead yet, barely keeping himself upright. Braxton wrapped his fingers around the barrel and wrenched it from the SOB's grip, turning the gun on the shooter. Braxton pulled the trigger. One shot. Waters's head snapped back, a bullet between the eyes. The body dropped hard. And the threat was neutralized.

A sharp inhale brought him back into the present. Braxton lunged. On her stomach, sprawled across the hardwood, Liz didn't move. He reached for her, lifted her upper body into his lap. The bullet hadn't come out her chest. The damn thing was still inside her. No. He would not lose her. Not after everything they'd been through.

"It burns." A tear streaked down the side of her face into her hairline. Her throat worked to swallow as blood rushed over his fingers. She fought to speak, licking her lips, her gaze heavier than he'd ever seen before. Streaks of blood coated her tongue. Hell, the bullet had punctured one of her lungs. Her breath shortened. "Braxton…"

"I've got you, Sprinkles. Stay still. I'm not going to lose you again. I'm never leaving you again." The peeling walls blurred in his vision as Braxton hoisted her into his arms and encased her against him. He carried her out of the room as fast as he could. Footsteps echoed up the second level as Vincent and Elliot raced to intercept. He'd had the private investigator inform the rest of the Blackhawk Security team about this property owned under one of Waters's aliases before Braxton had raced from the hospital. He owed them his life. Stairs jostled their descent, and he tightened his hold on her to keep the slug from shifting deeper. The bullet was too close to her spine. He nodded back toward the room upstairs to direct the team to Waters's body, his focus entirely on the woman in his arms. The love of his life. The mother of his child. Neither Vincent nor Elliot bothered examining the crime scene. Instead, they followed Braxton downstairs to the waiting ambulance. "Stay awake, baby. I have more granola bars where these came from. And there might even be some ice cream and rainbow-colored sprinkles left over for you. But you've got to stay awake, okay?"

"There sure as hell…better be." Liz went slack in his arms as she gave in to unconsciousness.

Chapter Fifteen

Searing heat enveloped her scalp as Elizabeth held herself under the shower spray. Her tailbone had been bruised, if not cracked. The laceration in her ribs from the woods was almost too much to bear. Luckily, surgeons had been able to remove the bullet from her back and patch her lung. But, hell, it felt good to be in her own house. She didn't even want to look at the rest of her body. She washed two-day hospital grunge off, the simple idea of soap helping her muscles relax. As did the gun sitting on the small bathroom sink to her right. Cold air rushed against her as she stepped from the shower and tied a towel around herself.

She didn't have to turn around to know Braxton had let himself in. The weight of his attention from the doorway pimpled goose bumps across her back. "How are you feeling?"

"Still hurts to breathe, but I'm alive." Two days. Two days since he'd charged through that door and shot the man determined to destroy her life. Two days since she'd woken up, facedown on a stretcher getting wheeled into surgery with him by her side. He'd promised never to leave her again, but the situation between them hadn't changed. He'd sold classified intel to an enemy combatant, and the NSA would charge him with treason the second they got their hands on him. So what were they supposed to do now? "Thanks to you."

Liam Waters's body had been recovered by Anchorage PD, as had mountains of evidence proving he'd been stalking her for months. He'd been careful, planned every step and stayed ahead of her the entire time, but even knowing the former agent would never come after her again, she couldn't relax.

"You did a damn good job protecting yourself, Sprinkles." Braxton crossed his arms over his torso, all three hundred stitches securely in place again. "Have you slept?"

"No." The memories running through her head wouldn't let her. It'd take time for her to scrub the slate clean. She reached for the gun on the sink.

Braxton struggled to straighten, the pain in his expression evident. She wasn't the only one who'd been through hell over the last week. "Liz—"

"Waters told me why you did it." She fisted the towel tighter. Waters had blackmailed him. She didn't know all the details, but if Braxton had proven anything over the last week, it was that he'd do anything to protect her. And he'd left thinking the former CIA agent would leave her alone after he'd delivered the intel. But killers rarely kept their end of the deals they struck. She'd learned that the hard way. "He threatened to kill me unless you got him the intel on Oversight, right? Why didn't you tell me?"

"Any reason I gave after you found out would look like a desperate attempt to win you back." The vulnerability and sorrow in his voice raised her body's awareness of him to new heights. "I needed you to find out on your own."

Elizabeth gripped the weapon harder, hot tears in her eyes. "And if he'd never told me, you were willing to walk away from us forever? Never meet your daughter?"

"If it kept you alive, yes." The solemn expression etched onto his face penetrated deep into her soul, as though he'd stolen the very oxygen she needed to live. "I told Waters how to access Oversight's feeds, and people died because of it. Because of me. I'll never be able to forgive myself, and I'll understand if you can't, either. But I made you a promise. I'm not leaving you behind. Not again. I'll avoid arrest as long as I can to stay in Anchorage. For you."

The guilt she'd witnessed inside Braxton consumed his irises. The shock of his admission cut her like a blunt blade, rough and painful. Dalton Meyer and Liam Waters had been killed, an entire country had been put at risk, all because Braxton had tried to protect her.

"You gave up classified intel to a former CIA agent then came back to stop him when you realized that he was going to use it to hunt me down." She could barely believe the words coming from her own mouth.

"He threatened to kill you. I may have lost my temper." He stepped forward, slowly closing the space between them. The steam from the shower penetrated through the thick towel wrapped around her. Or was it her heart racing out of control? He glanced at the gun in her hand. "You don't need the gun, Liz. Not for me."

Silence reigned, perfect silence almost too good to be true.

It took three deep inhales before she could look at him again. Liam Waters would've gotten his hands on Oversight's intel one way or another, maybe tortured and killed dozens more people to do it. She knew that now. There was no reasoning with him, no convincing him killing her wouldn't bring his partner back. And she and Braxton had stopped him. The man standing two feet from her had ensured the world had one less killer to worry about.

Her body ached as Elizabeth set the gun back on the sink. The internal torture he'd put himself through showed in his expression, and she reached for him, framing the side of his jaw with her uninjured hand. His warmth burned a hole through the last bricks of the wall she'd created around her heart, desolating everything she'd held against him.

He'd done it all for her.

"The gun's not for you. I just…need it for a little while longer. What you did, it made me feel protected." She swiped her thumb beneath one bright green eye. Careful to avoid the bandages over his left shoulder, she stepped into the comfort of his arms. How could she ever have thought he'd betray her? The past week alone was proof enough. He'd do anything to protect her and their baby. And she'd do anything to keep him in her life. "Made me feel loved."

"You're safe now. It's over." He ran his fingertips

through her hair. The slight tremble against her scalp mimicked the uneven thump of her pulse. Elizabeth caught the struggle to fill his lungs but couldn't force herself to straighten. Not yet. She hadn't felt so content in months, his skin warm, traces of his clean, masculine scent diving deep into her pores. Her nerves settled the longer she counted his heartbeat. "I won't let anyone hurt you ever again."

"I know," she said.

Physical tension drained from him. Only the sound of their combined heartbeats filled her ears, but her fingers tingled with the urge to touch him. Elizabeth slid her hand across his torso, following the peaks and valleys created just for her. The soul-deep craving she'd always had for him erupted as she craned her head up. The emptiness in those irises had vanished, leaving nothing but her reflection in his gaze.

"I was going to stock your freezer for you." Braxton swiped a strand of hair behind her ear, sending liquid pleasure shooting to her core. His laugh vibrated through her. "Then realized you already have three gallons of chocolate ice cream."

"I stopped at the store right after they released me from the hospital." Something stirred in her lower abdominals. If she was honest with herself, she'd already made her decision, but so much had happened between them. He'd sold classified intel to save her life, had gone as far as putting his own life in danger for her, but the sting of his disappearance hadn't lessened. Four months of wondering, of questions, had nearly driven her to the point of insanity. She couldn't go through that again. "I was hoping we might be able to share a bowl tonight. And every night after that."

Disappointment overwhelmed his features, and her heart shattered from the agony consuming him. She'd experienced the same pain when Braxton had vanished and had completely lost herself inside that betrayal. "I can't. Not without dragging you and the baby into the NSA's manhunt for me. I'll stay in Anchorage, but it'll be at a distance."

Stepping back, Elizabeth ran the pad of her thumb over his left cheekbone. He lifted his gaze to her, staring at her as though she was the center of his entire world. Just as he had when they'd first met. She'd never get used to that. "And if I told you the NSA didn't get to decide our future?"

Those mesmerizing green eyes narrowed on her. "What do you mean?"

"Answer the question." Elizabeth pulled back, eager for his response. This was the defining moment, the chance to risk it all. And if he didn't take it? Her insides churned at the thought. But she'd move on. She'd raise this baby alone. She'd tell her daughter the truth. That her father had to stay in hiding to protect them. "Would you stay here with me—with us—and give us another shot if the manhunt was called off?"

"Damn right I would." Braxton threaded his fingers through the hair at the back of her neck, molding her to him. "Making you mine is the only thing I've wanted since you walked into the office all those years ago."

Her cell phone dinged with an incoming message from the other room. Perfect timing. "Good. I called

Dalton Meyer's replacement when I got home from the hospital and told them I would only help restore Oversight's feeds for the NSA if they cleared the charges against you."

Braxton's expression slackened. He tried to pull away, but she secured him against her. No. No more running. No more lies. From now on, they'd be honest with each other. "Liz, you didn't have to do that. I would've figured something out—"

"Yes, I did. You saved my life more times than I can count. It was time to return the favor." She'd vowed never to work for the NSA or touch Oversight's programming again but ensuring Braxton could help raise their daughter, that he could make them a family, was worth it. "As twisted as it sounds, Waters died for the one person who mattered most to him in the world. His partner. I realized when he had that gun to my head, if I had to, I would do the same thing for my partner." Fisting her fingers in his T-shirt, she pushed against him slightly. "I love you. I never stopped loving you, and I want you here. I want you to help me raise this baby. I want to be a family."

"I love you, too." His breath warmed her neck. Pressing himself against her, he smoothed the tip of his nose along the outside cartilage of her ear. A shudder ran across her collarbones and down her spine, and she closed her eyes to heighten her senses. "What do you say we get out of here? You, me, no more secrets, no guns. Just the open ocean and sandy beaches for a few weeks."

After what they'd been through, she needed it. She

spun in his arms, securing the towel around her once again, and wiped steam from the mirror. She'd have to clear the time off with Sullivan and the rest of the team, but she doubted Blackhawk Security needed her for the next month or so. "I'm bringing my gun."

"You say the sexiest things." Braxton slid one hand along her thigh, below the hem of the towel. The rough patches on his fingertips scraped against her skin, but not uncomfortably. He buried his lips in the crook between her neck and shoulder. He planted a kiss against her skin, tracing the edge of her tendon with his lips. She grew painfully aware of the reaction his lips elicited in her lower abdominals. He slid his hand over their baby from behind, lowered his chin onto her shoulder and held her against him. "Marry me."

Interrupting her next inhale, he guided her head toward him and crushed his mouth against hers, urgent, warm. Her vision wavered as she surrendered herself over to him completely. After almost four months of missing his touch, she couldn't think of anything but the towel and his clothes separating them. Their injuries wouldn't allow them to fulfill all of their physical desires, but having him close was more than enough. Pulling away for a moment, her lips growing cold without his, she reveled in the weight lifting from her chest. He was a free man. He was hers. "Deal."

Hints of that gut-wrenching smile pulled at one corner of his mouth, and her pulse rocketed higher. He swept a stray piece of soaked hair off her face then brought her hips into the circle of his arms. "I only have one condition."

"You realize you're the one who proposed to me,

right? I'm supposed to make the conditions." She melted from the warmth radiating from under his clothing. Something exploded inside, seared her from the inside out and destroyed the horror-filled memories of the last week. Her heart thundered with a renewed possibility of finally having the man she'd wanted from the start, of starting their family together, and she smiled against his lips. "But go ahead. Name your price."

"We get on a plane tomorrow," he said. "And you marry me by sunset."

"What are we supposed to do until then?" Elizabeth had meant the question innocently enough, but the desire burning in Braxton's gaze filled her thoughts with plenty of things they might be able to do despite the near-death injuries they'd sustained.

"I have a few ideas." Braxton pulled her closer, her back pressed to his front, and fit her against him. His pulse was slow and steady between her shoulder blades, and she collapsed her head back against his shoulder. "One of them involves getting this towel off you."

She wrapped her hands around the Glock on the counter and dropped it to her side. Safety on. She might need the extra security for a few more weeks, until the nightmares subsided for good, but at least she'd have Braxton at her side to help her forget. Forever. "Good luck with that."

Five months later...

SCREAMING. BLOOD. ICE CHIPS. More screaming. All for the tiny, perfect human in his arms.

"Karina Dawson-Levitt." He couldn't believe it. Braxton cradled his daughter tighter. Mere hours ago, they'd rushed to the hospital, and before he knew it, here she was. Their baby girl opened her mouth wide in a yawn, and his eyes burned. Hell, he'd never been so happy in his life. A laugh rumbled through him. "Welcome to the world, half-pint."

"Hey, I pushed that watermelon out. I get to hold her, too, you know." Liz slid her fingers across his arm, pulling him back toward her on the bed. The damn thing wasn't wide enough for all three of them, but there was no way he was moving from this spot. Liz pressed against him on his right, baby Karina in his arms. His wife rested her head on his shoulder and set her hand over his heart, right where it belonged. A moan filled his ears as she glanced up at him. "She's so perfect, I want to eat her up. Want to count her fingers and toes again?"

"No, let's let her rest. She's got to save her energy so she can keep us up all night." Planting a kiss in Liz's hair, Braxton caught movement through the small window in the hospital room door. They'd held them off as long as they could, but the team had gotten restless. There was no stopping it, but he was determined to stretch out this moment of peace as long as he could. Stroking his fingers over Karina's baby-soft skin, he braced himself against the oncoming chaos. "They're going to break down the door if we keep them waiting any longer."

"You can let them in in a minute. But only because I'm afraid Elliot will start telling the staff he's a doctor to get in here." Liz leveraged her hands into the mattress and straightened, then ran her hands through her hair. "Hell, he probably has the credentials already made just in case."

"You look beautiful." Braxton brushed a stray piece of hair behind her ear, sliding his thumb across her bottom lip. "You grew a human inside your body. What you did was amazing, and you're more beautiful now than ever."

He still couldn't believe she'd married him on that beach, couldn't believe she'd chosen him after he'd failed to keep her safe. With her work for the NSA behind her, Oversight up and running, and the charges dropped against him, he'd spent the last five months making it up to her every way he knew how. And he'd keep trying for the rest of his life. Without her… No. He wouldn't think of a life without her. There was no life without her. She'd been the one to get him through the darkness. Everything he wanted was right here in this room. And he'd fight like hell to keep it that way.

The CIA had taken possession of Liam Waters's body after the fight in his hideout. The bastard would never hurt her again. Only after receiving confirmation his remains had been incinerated had her nightmares finally subsided. She didn't need to sleep with the gun stashed under her pillow at night. She was safe. And the past was officially dead.

She leaned into his palm, kissing the callused skin there with a wide smile. Her breath brushed lightly over his wrist, and every nerve ending in his body went haywire. For her. "You're just saying that so I'll let you eat the cookies the nurses brought me to get my blood sugar back up."

"I love you." Braxton kissed her with everything he had then handed off the tiny human to her mother. He maneuvered off the bed and crossed the room. Spinning back toward her before he opened the door, he pointed at her. "But I'm getting those cookies one way or another."

He wrenched the heavy metal door toward him, and in three breaths her team flooded the room with congratulations. Sullivan Bishop, Elliot Dunham, Vincent Kalani, Anthony Harris and Glennon Chase all closed in on his wife and daughter. The only operative missing was Kate Monroe, but he was sure the profiler would get to meet the newest member of the Blackhawk Security team soon.

Liz's smile brightened despite the grueling process she'd gone through to deliver their baby, and a rush of joy had him cracking his own smile.

That was his wife. His daughter. His life.

Braxton saw the future in that moment.

And, damn, it looked good.

* * * * *

COLTON'S SECRET INVESTIGATION

JUSTINE DAVIS

Chapter One

She'd only capped off a few rounds, but Deputy Daria Bloom already knew her range score was going to suck. But she kept firing.

Fire.

A new missing girl.

Fire.

Bodies. Too many.

Fire.

Idiot media nicknames for monsters.

Fire.

Blue Eyes.

Fire.

Deputy Gates.

Fire.

Her mother.

Fire.

Stefan.

Fire. Fire. Fire.

She set down the Glock 19, still undecided whether the purchase had been worth it. She preferred her Springfield XD(M) because it fit her hands better. Her boss cut her some slack and let her carry the XD(M), since with it she was the best shot in the department.

But the Glock was the official weapon of the sheriff's office, and so she had to qualify with it, as well.

At the thought of her boss, she would have fired another round if she hadn't already emptied the magazine. What if Trey Colton lost the election that was less than a week away now? She couldn't imagine working for someone else. Not to mention that if he didn't win, it would be so egregiously unfair. He was the best sheriff this county had ever had. But there was a serial killer still on the loose nearly ten months after the first body had been found, and the outcry was mounting. And while it was hardly Trey's fault, he was the public face of the department, so all the blowback hit him.

Daria pushed the button that brought the target silhouette back to her. She studied the pattern of holes. It wasn't as bad as she'd feared, but it wasn't pretty. She'd visited the ten ring a time or two, but otherwise she'd been wide and high. She smothered a sigh.

For a moment she went through the postshooting routine, focusing on every step as if she'd never done it before. She knew she was trying to stop thinking about everything that had crowded into her mind, throwing off her concentration. Her frustration about this case was uppermost, but a certain FBI agent was nearing the top of the list, as well.

And to think she'd been pleased when Trey had selected her to be the local liaison with the Bureau. But that was before she'd laid eyes on Stefan Roberts. In all his tall, broad-shouldered, hard-muscled glory. She'd never really thought of herself as a woman who would go for a younger man, but that guy would give any breathing woman pause. In a twisted sort of way that made her not particularly happy with herself, she was glad his domestic situation was a mess, because it had enabled her to get over the initial shock of this gorgeous creature and put him where he belonged.

In the "not interested in" category.

And yet in the three months they had been collaborating together, the man had turned her carefully controlled life upside down. He was as fiercely dedicated to this case as she was, and that made working with him easier than it could have been. He had also done what she'd been trying unsuccessfully to do for years—he'd unraveled the sad conclusion to her mother's story. She now had the history of Ava Bloom and knew the bravery her mother had shown. Thanks to Stefan.

He had done it as a favor to her. Without hesitation. And she couldn't describe how that had made her feel.

"Well, you qualified, but barely."

"I'm not done yet," Daria told the range master, who had appeared behind her. The man smiled at her. For a rather crusty old guy, Ray Ingersol could be nice sometimes.

"And with those words, wars are won," he said.

She smiled back at that. "I feel as if I'm in a war," she admitted.

"Awful stuff going on. Awful stuff."

She couldn't argue that. With a fresh target and a new magazine, she shut everything else out of her mind and imagined having this ruthless Avalanche Killer in her sights. And this time when the target came back, there were four holes in the ten ring—three small individual holes, and one big ragged one.

Ray gave a low whistle. "Eight through the same hole? That's some fine shooting, Deputy Bloom. I'm guessing you'll be wanting that one turned in as your qualifying score?"

"Turn them both in," she said as she gathered up her brass.

Ray's smile widened, and he gave her an approving nod. "Honesty. I like that. It's in short supply these days."

"Sadly true."

"Any closer on finding that maniac?"

"I think the official phrase is 'the investigation is ongoing.'"

Ray snorted inelegantly.

"My sentiments exactly," she agreed.

And she meant it. This case was beyond frustrating, for so many reasons. The obvious, of course—a deranged serial killer was destroying a town, both emotionally and economically, and here she was nearly a year later with no resolution—but also she felt as if she was letting Trey down. The sheriff had trusted her to get the job done when he'd had to recuse himself because the first suspect's body had been found on his cousin Wyatt's ranch, and there'd been an uproar about the Coltons getting preferential treatment. Which only made the load heavier, given her own personal history—which she had kept secret.

And then there was her gut certainty that Sabrina Gilford had not been a victim of their serial killer, which was just the cherry on top of this swirling mix. It was enough to give her nightmares, and in fact on occasion had.

Straighten up, girl—you didn't get to where you are by quitting. Whoever, wherever this killer is, he's going down, and you're going to do it.

IF HE HADN'T gone for the shaved head look some time ago, Stefan Roberts figured he'd be tearing his hair out about now.

"I won't go! I don't like it here. I don't like *you*!"

He stared at the five-year-old who was his son, standing there glaring at him with his arms crossed firmly across his small chest. He weighed his options. He could spend some more time trying to talk the child into going to school without a fuss. Except he was already running late for work. He could leave it for Mrs. Crane, the sitter he'd hired, to handle. But that seemed…cowardly somehow. He could pick the kid up and carry him out to the car. *And maybe stuff him in the trunk? That'd go over well.*

He sucked in a deep breath and fought for calm. Blowing up at his son would do no good at all, he was sure. He'd snapped at him a few times when he'd hit the end of his patience, and the boy had just closed off further.

"Look, Samuel, I know this wasn't your idea. You didn't want this. But we're here—we're stuck with each other. Can't you make the best of it?"

The glare only intensified. So once more, he'd apparently said the wrong thing. And his already frayed temper lost another thread. When he spoke it was with the rigidness of an anger barely held at bay.

"That's enough. You're going to school, Samuel. How you go is up to you."

Something shifted in the boy's dark eyes, so like his mother's. Something that was there and gone so quickly it was hard to pin a name on it. Had he been at work, he would have immediately registered it as fear, but he didn't want to believe his son was afraid of him. The massive changes in his life, sure. But him? He didn't like that idea at all.

But right now, he just had to get the boy out the door and to school. Mrs. Crane would see to him when school was out. He would have to talk to her, see if she had any ideas on how to deal with the rotten attitude Samuel seemed to have arrived with. But he didn't have time now. He had to get to work. Daria would be wondering where the hell he was. And he didn't want Daria Bloom mad at him.

Might be safer if she was.

He barely acknowledged the wayward thought. He was used to them by now. That day three months ago when he'd first walked into the sheriff's office and seen the deputy assigned to the case, he'd known this wasn't going to be routine. Working every day, in close proximity, to *that*? He'd known the first moment she turned those wide, beautiful, golden-brown eyes on him assessingly that this woman could be trouble. There wasn't a damned thing about her he didn't like, from the way that short, sleek haircut of hers bared the nape of her neck when she bent her head, to the way she moved, like a dancer he'd seen once back in Chicago.

Then again, he'd learned his lesson well; he'd been hot for Leah, too, and look how that had turned out. She hadn't had whatever it took to be married to an FBI agent, if that even existed. She'd been excited at first, but then the reality of long hours away and the stringent dedication that the job necessitated had settled in. When she'd gotten pregnant with Samuel, things had improved a little, but it hadn't lasted. By then she had bigger, grander plans for her future than being married to him.

And then it had fallen apart, and the son he loved so much had become a part-time presence in his life. He hated the fact, but between his work hours, Leah's lack of cooperation, and then his transfer, that's what had happened.

He shook off the thoughts; he needed to focus on the immediate issue, which was getting Samuel to school. In the end it took bribery—the promise of an extra bit of video-game time—but Stefan counted it as a win. At least the kid's favorite game was a fantasy instead of just blowing stuff up or shooting people. And as he finally headed off to work, he found himself smiling wryly that that was the most optimistic thing he could think of just now.

He called the field office to check in. It was a formality, since he'd been allocated to this case full-time until it was resolved. When he got to the sheriff's office and found Daria had not yet arrived, he felt a tiny bit of annoyance mixed with relief.

"She's at the range," the perky secretary they'd been assigned told him. Then, in a tone of confidentiality, she added, "She's the best shot in the department, you know. Some of the guys won't admit that, but she's outscored all of them at one time or another."

"Good to know," Stefan said drolly. "I'll try not to make her shooting mad at me." He was only half kidding. There was something about Daria Bloom that made him think she was not a woman to be crossed.

"Oh, she'd never shoot at *you*. That'd be like shooting at one of the local scenic wonders."

Stefan blinked. Was she flirting with him? She was, what, maybe twenty? He suddenly felt old.

"Now you're a scenic wonder?"

He nearly groaned aloud as the voice came from behind him. A voice he recognized too well, since the husky timbre of it sent the craziest tingle over his skin. But he put on his best unaffected grin as he turned to see the woman in question approaching.

"So's Denver International," he said, referring to the jaw-dropping airport structure voted the ugliest building in the state by half the population, the most beautiful by the other half. And to his inward delight, she laughed. It was rare enough with all the pressure on her right now that she even smiled, so he counted this as a win.

"Sorry I'm late. I needed to clean both weapons, so it took longer."

"Gotta keep the tools clean," he agreed. "I was running behind myself."

"Problem?"

"Only personal," he said with a slight grimace. She let it go without asking, and he appreciated that. He appreciated a *lot* about Daria.

She confirmed with the secretary, who was watching them with a little too much interest, that there were no messages she hadn't already gotten. They were turning to go to the office assigned solely to this case when the door behind them opened and Sheriff Trey Colton stepped through.

Trey was about Stefan's own height and had a no-nonsense air about him that Stefan liked. He was also, as far as Stefan could see, a fine sheriff. By the book and honorable and, up until this Avalanche Killer mess, nothing had happened to mar his stellar record. As the first African American to be elected sheriff, not to mention one of the youngest people ever to hold the office, he was clearly determined to keep it that way. And Stefan was glad to help. He'd had his own dragons to slay on his way to where he was now, so he could relate.

They gave him an update, not that there was much to report. Trey restated his complete faith in them, which made Stefan even more determined, and with a barely concealed grimace the sheriff went off to deal with today's round of media chaos.

Better him than me.

"He's actually much happier lately," Daria murmured as they said goodbye and headed down the hall.

"No thanks to us," Stefan muttered.

"I know. Or the election campaign," she added.

"I registered just so I could vote for him." He'd only been in Colorado for a couple of years, so there hadn't been a major election since his arrival.

"That's good of you," she said, sounding like she meant it.

"He's a good guy. I admire and respect him and the job he's done. And I'm glad if he's happier."

"Thank Aisha for that," Daria confided as they went into what they'd begun to call the Avalanche office. "Now that's a true love match."

"Not something I'd know much about," he grumbled, then regretted letting the words out.

"It's pretty obvious with them, isn't it? Besides, I happen to know she's loved him for years."

"She has?"

"Since they were kids in grade school."

Stefan's brow furrowed. "But they're only getting together now?" The couple had become engaged about the time he and Daria had begun to work together on this case.

"She didn't think he loved her, and she wasn't going to settle for less. So she made him prove he meant it. He had to make the first move."

She said it so approvingly even he couldn't miss it. "Obviously you agree with that."

"Yes. Completely. She had to be sure he felt the same."

He studied her for a moment. Told himself it not only wasn't his business, he didn't want to know. Because knowing more about this woman had so far only drawn him in deeper, and that spelled trouble. But the next thing he knew he was asking, anyway.

"Personal experience?" She gave him a sharp look. He put up his hands and remembered his earlier thought that this was not a woman to be crossed. "You just sounded so…positive."

Her expression changed to something more…he wasn't sure what. Damn, Daria was hard to figure out. "You really want to open those doors, mine and yours?"

Well, that was plain enough; if she talked about her past, she was going to ask about his. Fine with him— the bare bones of his situation were common enough, and he had it down to a sound bite. "Mine's easy. Married, she couldn't handle my job, divorced."

"I notice you left out the most important part."

He grimaced, wishing he'd never started this. "Love? I thought so. Not sure about her."

She studied him for a long moment before she said softly, "I meant your son."

He was glad his skin was dark enough she couldn't see what would be, judging from the heat he felt, a flaming blush. He couldn't remember the last time he'd blushed. Maybe in the academy over a decade ago, when he'd missed a clue so obvious he'd felt humiliated.

"Yeah," he muttered. "Never mind. You're right. Don't open those doors."

Chapter Two

Unlike at the shooting range, there was only one reason Daria was having trouble focusing on the matter at hand right now, and his name was Stefan Roberts. He'd clammed up completely the moment she'd mentioned his son. And that bothered her.

She knew Stefan's son had just recently come to live with him full-time, but other than that he never spoke of young Samuel other than to say they'd had very little contact since the divorce and what there had been hadn't gone well. Most parents she knew were happy to talk endlessly about their kids. Her friend Fiona, with three boys, could go on forever. Yet Stefan never mentioned doing anything with the boy, or his interests, or even his existence. So she sensed things were not going well on that front.

As if this case isn't enough of a distraction, imagine trying to deal with it with a five-year-old at home.

She resolved to cut him some slack as they dived back into the case.

"This room," he said rather sourly as they closed the door on the office, "is starting to look like the lair of a lunatic."

She looked around at the whiteboards they'd wheeled in, covered now with photographs and names and locations and details, with a single, long timeline spanning them all. Those had been Stefan's idea—he said he'd always been able to work better with as much of the case as possible right in front of him all the time. She'd found it worked well for her, too.

"I can't argue that," she agreed. Nor could she argue the fact that his deep, rumbly voice did crazy things to her insides. Which made no sense at all.

"Worked a serial killer case in Rockford once. He had a room in his house that looked a lot like this. Only thing missing is the spiderweb of string he had pinned up, making up his elaborate conspiracy connections."

"Hmm," she said, looking from board to board.

"What?"

"Just wondering if a ball of yarn might help."

He laughed. He really did have a nice laugh to go with that deep, rumbly, sexy voice. And the rare grin that flashed with it was...well, breathtaking. "You got one around?"

"Not here," she said. "I have a stash at home."

He lifted a brow at her. "You hoard yarn?"

She put on her best snooty voice. "It's not hoarding, Agent Roberts. It's therapy."

He gave another chuckle. "What do you do with it?"

"Knit." He blinked. "And before you say anything derogatory, keep in mind knitting involves two very pointy tools."

"I just...never pictured you as the knitting type."

"What you don't want to picture is me without it. Other people count to ten to hold on to their temper. I count stitches."

"Point taken. Er, no pun intended."

"Too bad," she retorted. "It would have been a good one."

And suddenly they were both laughing. And it was the most amazing feeling she'd had in a long time. That they could laugh amid what was going on was probably a bit macabre, but she couldn't deny it felt good.

"Thanks," he said. "I needed that."

"Me, too. So, shall we get back on the merry-go-round?"

As had become habit now, they went through it all again. They'd done it so often they both had every step of the investigation practically committed to memory. But this was her first case anywhere near this magnitude, and Daria was determined to justify Trey's faith in her.

They went over what little they had on the newest missing girl. They knew little except that she was from Denver, had been gone a week longer than expected and resembled the other victims. It wasn't even certain yet that she was a victim of their quarry. But the resemblance was there, so they factored her in, although as of now she was in the category of "possible."

Others were searching for her as an active missing person, and Daria sent up an earnest hope that she was found alive—and not simply because another victim would ratchet up the pressure on them.

"Blue Eyes," Stefan muttered when they finally reached the newest bit of information they had.

"Helpful, huh?" Daria deadpanned.

"More than we had before," he said. He turned to the laptop that was now booted up on the table in the center of the room. He tapped a couple of keys, and the recording she'd heard at least a dozen times played again. She listened to Lucy Reese, aka Bianca Rouge, tell her friend Candace—who had unexpectedly turned out to be the mother of the baby left on Fox Colton's doorstep—that her date had passed out drunk, so she was down in the hotel bar and had connected with an older guy who was "still hot." She had cheerfully referred to him as Blue Eyes and ended with a promise to see Candace later.

A promise she had been unable to keep.

It still gave her chills to listen to that rather ordinary message, given in such normal, even happy tones, by a woman who would soon be dead.

"I don't think I'll ever get used to that," she said.

"Used to what?"

Sighing, she looked at Stefan. "Hearing her sound so happy and chipper. It's still distressing to listen to, knowing what happened to her."

"Don't ever get used to it," Stefan said quietly. "If you ever get to the point where you can hear that, knowing, and not be distressed, it's time to walk away."

She hadn't expected that. Sometimes this man surprised her. There were depths to Stefan Roberts that he kept hidden. It occurred to her to wonder if that might be part of the problem with his son, if he kept his feelings so masked the boy didn't know how he felt, but she quickly pushed the thought away. It was, she reminded herself again, not her business.

An hour later they exchanged a glance, and both sighed at the same moment. He gave a low chuckle. "No sense putting it off any longer."

"Agreed. Frame by frame this time?"

He nodded. He adjusted the settings on the video

player on the laptop while she grabbed the remote and turned on the flat screen. This was going to take hours upon hours, she knew, going through all relevant feeds and angles of the security video from the hotel one frame at a time, but they'd so far been unable to find anything at all, even in slow motion, and this was their last shot.

"What do you want to start with?" he asked.

"The elevator lobby," she said. "We know Bianca at least was upstairs first."

He nodded and called up the video. It was already at the point where they had spotted Bianca coming out of elevator two. The timing coordinated with the message she'd left Candace, which was how they'd located this moment when she had come out of the elevator after leaving her drunken, passed-out client up on the third floor.

It was slow work. By utilizing some facial recognition software Stefan had access to, they had managed to track Bianca from the elevator across the lobby. Daria felt like calling her Lucy, because that's who she really wanted to get justice for, the girl she'd once been who had found her way into this life for reasons they hadn't yet uncovered.

Bianca had been headed in the general direction of the bar off the main lobby, but as far as they had been able to tell, she had not appeared in any video of the bar itself. So they now set themselves to going second by second, looking at every figure in the busy lobby, as far into the background of the video as they could see. They made notes of clothing to compare with other shots, anything that looked even vaguely similar to what Bianca had been wearing.

They studied any exchanges between men and women, taking notes again on clothing and any other distinguishing characteristics, on the theory that any man in the lobby could have been the one she connected with, and that he might have tried to pick up another woman before Bianca. And just because her message to Candace had mentioned the bar didn't necessarily mean she'd met him in there.

She and Stefan had spoken little, but she'd found it interesting. Since they couldn't see eye color on the videos, they'd given up trying to eliminate on that basis. Especially after, when she wearily suggested they just look at blonds for a while, Stefan smiled wryly and said, "I've got a cousin who's darker than I am and has the bluest eyes you've ever seen."

"I was kidding," Daria said. "But I'll bet your cousin is striking."

"She's gorgeous."

Well, that doesn't seem fair. Two of them in the same family? She yanked herself back to the matter at hand, although her next thought grew right out of that.

"That brings up the other issue," she said.

"You mean her description of the guy?"

Daria nodded. Bianca had referred to the man she was meeting as handsome. They'd each pointed out men in videos to look more closely at, but after a couple of startled looks at each other over their selections, they laughed again.

"I defer to your female judgment," Stefan said with a grimace. "Obviously I have no clue."

"Different things are attractive to different women," she replied. "But I'm not sure that applies in Bianca's case. For her…job, she'd be looking for the ones who perhaps couldn't get any woman in the room with a look."

"You mean not the glamour guys, the movie-star types?"

"I mean," she said, risking a grin at him, "guys who don't look like you."

He looked taken aback. She knew it couldn't be at her assessment of his looks—after all, the guy had to look in a mirror now and then. He had to know he was way beyond handsome. Was it that she dared to tease him?

She shrugged. "I figured we'd been working together long enough now I could rib you a little. Sorry if I was out of line."

"I…no. I just didn't think you…thought that."

It was her turn to blink. "What, you didn't think I noticed? I'm not blind, Roberts."

He looked at her for a long, silent moment. Let his gaze slide from her head to her toes. "Neither am I," he said softly.

And that quickly he turned it around on her. Daria's breath jammed up in her throat. She knew she could clean up nice, and when she took the time and trouble in, say, formal wear, she was attractive enough. But on duty she was all business. She'd set her course when she'd first been hired on here four years ago, and any guy who tried to flirt with her on the job was quickly chilled by her lack of response.

She had, with some nudging from Trey, gone out a few times with one of his closest friends, fellow deputy Keith Parker. Dates that were perfectly nice but utterly lacking in chemistry. And they had both quickly agreed they were much better off as friends, especially since they had to work together.

Which did not explain why she'd said what she'd did just now. It couldn't be simply that Stefan was from outside the department. Or that he was quite possibly the most luscious male she'd encountered in a long time, let alone spent any appreciable time with. Could it?

Since she had no answers, and couldn't think of anything to say that wouldn't get her in deeper, she simply went back to work.

On and on they went. Finding nothing. Only when her back began to ache—a rare occurrence for her, since she was determinedly in tip-top shape—did Daria finally glance at the time.

"Whoa," she said, startled.

Stefan, who had been as intent on the task as she, looked up from the screen. She guessed, by the way he blinked, then rubbed at his eyes, that they were as dry and weary as hers were.

"It's after eight," she said.

He blinked again, and apparently as disbelieving as she had been, glanced at his watch.

"Damn. I've got to make a call."

"And I've got to answer a call," she said. "I'll be in the ladies'."

Her way of putting it earned her another brief flash of that grin. But when she came back, there was no sign of the amused man she'd left.

"Problem?" she asked.

"Yeah. Look, I know we've got a long way to go yet on this stuff, but…my sitter has to leave. And I can't leave Samuel alone."

"I should think not," Daria said, imagining all the trouble a five-year-old could get into left to his own devices. "So…you want to call it a night?"

"No, I don't, not when we've got so much more to get through. But…look, I know it's a lot to ask, but I've got a setup like this in my home office. It wouldn't take much to pick up right where we left off there."

Warning bells went off in Daria's head. No way did she want to be in a nice, homey environment with this man. But as she looked at him—once she managed to stop dwelling on his strong jaw, broad shoulders and narrow hips—she realized he was more than a little frazzled. He would likely be so worried about his boy that he wouldn't be thinking about…what she was thinking about. And couldn't seem to stop thinking about.

Just because you think he's the hottest thing that's ever walked these mountains doesn't mean he feels the same about you, idiot. And even if he did, it would not only be inappropriate, it would be downright stupid. For you, anyway.

"Fine," she said abruptly. "I'd like to finish this tonight."

"Thanks," he said, and it sounded so heartfelt she felt even sillier for her own thoughts.

And she shoved them back into that "not interested" box.

Chapter Three

Mrs. Crane couldn't leave fast enough. After a quick report that Samuel had refused to eat dinner or quit playing his video game or go to bed, she was gone. Stefan noticed Daria looking around the house with interest, but he couldn't read her reaction to his place in her expression. He wasn't sure if maybe he should be glad of that.

But right now he shouldn't be thinking about that. He shouldn't be thinking about Daria at all, but about the rebellious kid who had landed on him. He walked over to where the boy was indeed glued to his video controller, his eyes on the screen. He didn't even look up when Stefan came in. And not for the first time, Stefan thought he should never have hooked the system up to the big TV. He'd foolishly thought of it as a peace offering.

He walked over to the couch. "Way past your bedtime."

The boy didn't even look up from his game.

"Come on, Samuel. Shut it down."

Again the boy ignored him.

"He's almost to the big castle. He can't stop now." Stefan turned to stare at Daria. Even Samuel looked up, startled. "Watch out, there's a zombie!" she warned the boy, who quickly went back to the game, and with a couple of button presses, the stiffly walking, sickly-green creature was gone.

"Nicely done," Daria said. "Now, when you get to the castle wall, it's time to come have something to eat before bed. Got it?"

"Yeah," Samuel said, focused on the game but still responding.

And to Stefan's shock, when the game seemed to pause at the foot of a soaring stone wall, Samuel closed it and put down the controller.

"Have you encountered the dragon yet?" Daria asked the boy conversationally as they walked toward the kitchen. Stefan followed, suddenly feeling like a by-stander in his own house.

"Not yet," Samuel said.

"Ohhhh, you wiiill," she said in an over-the-top creepy voice that made Samuel laugh. Stefan was gaping now; he hadn't seen his son laugh since he'd been here.

Then the boy looked at her curiously. "Who are you?"

"My name is Daria. I'm working with your dad for a while."

The boy's expression changed, became something wary. "Oh."

"You don't like that," Daria said. "Why?"

"My mom worked with someone. An' he doesn't like me. So she sent me away. Now I'm stuck here."

Daria glanced at Stefan, and he felt his jaw tighten involuntarily.

"Well, I like you, so no problem," she said to Samuel cheerfully. "What do you want to eat?"

The wariness faded from the boy's expression. And Stefan had the niggling thought that he should be paying attention.

"I don't know," Samuel said. "There's never anything good here."

"Really? Nothing?"

"It's all this fancy stuff."

"Not even a good burger, huh?" Daria sympathized.

"No."

"Maybe we should just look and see if there's anything we can make edible."

"What's edi—ed…what you said?"

"It means you can eat it without gagging," she said in a loud whisper.

And again the boy laughed. Stefan gave a slow, wondering shake of his head. *I should definitely be paying attention here. How does she do that?*

Daria was looking at him questioningly. He realized she was seeking some reaction from him, probably to her taking over. "Don't stop now," he muttered.

And then she was in his kitchen. Looking in the refrigerator. She ignored the leftover Szechuan takeout he'd had last night and figured they would eat later while working, and if she noticed the six-pack of beer—well, five-pack, now—on the top shelf, she ignored it. She poked into the deli drawer, then looked over her shoulder at him.

"Bread?" she asked.

Afraid to say anything for fear of setting Samuel off again, he walked over to the small pantry and got out the half loaf that was in there.

"Good," she said. "Samuel, do you know where a skillet is?"

Stefan blinked, since it was hanging on a rack practically in front of her, opened his mouth to answer, then shut it again.

"Silly, it's right there," Samuel said, grinning and pointing.

"Why, so it is. Good eyes, my friend."

She'd done it on purpose, Stefan realized. She was bringing Samuel into the conversation in a way he never would have thought of. And the boy was responding, right before his eyes.

"Now if only we had some butter, we could have a mega grilled cheese sandwich."

Looking intrigued, Samuel trotted into the kitchen and pointed at a covered dish on the counter. He was tall for his age, but not quite tall enough to reach it. "It's in there."

"Then we're a go." She reached up for the skillet, unhooked it and handed it to the boy, who looked beyond startled. "Go set that on a front burner for me, will you? Don't turn it on yet, though. I have to get the stuff ready."

"'Kay."

With exquisite care, Samuel carried the skillet over and set it down as she'd instructed. Stefan was leaning against the opposite kitchen counter now, watching in complete fascination.

"Good job," Daria said. "But do you see a problem?"

"No."

"Back up a little." The boy did so. "Now walk toward me."

He started to do as she'd said. Then, suddenly, just before his face would have collided with the protruding skillet handle, he yelped, "Oh!" Samuel reached and moved the skillet so the handle wasn't sticking out.

"Wow, you figured that out quick," Daria said. And Stefan felt the strangest sensation somewhere in his chest as his son beamed at her. He'd been wrestling with the boy for a month now, and she had charmed him in fifteen minutes flat.

Not only that, but when she'd finished preparing the thick, melted cheese sandwich, the boy gobbled it down, along with a big glass of the milk Samuel had looked at scornfully when Stefan had offered it to him.

"Now, let's get you to bed, so you can be all rested up to attack tomorrow."

The boy seemed to like the way she put it and happily headed into the bathroom next to his bedroom to brush his teeth. Daria stood in the doorway, saying, "Look at you—you don't even need a step stool, you're so tall. Are you sure you're not six or seven?"

Samuel gave her a toothpaste-laden grin. And just to further emphasize the difference, he jumped into bed happily. Daria pulled the covers up over him as she said, "Kind of a big bed, huh?"

"Too big," Samuel muttered, so low Stefan almost couldn't hear it. He frowned. A bed was a bed, wasn't it? If you fit in it, what did it matter how big it was?

Well, unless you had someone like Daria in it with you.

He could feel the pressure on his teeth telling him just how hard he was clenching his jaw to make sure he didn't say anything even vaguely like what he had just thought.

"I see you've got some fun books there," she said,

sitting on the edge of the bed as she gestured at the two colorful books on the nightstand.

"They're dumb," Samuel pronounced. "For babies. Teacher reads it to us. 'The cat chased the mouse.' What kind of story is that?"

"I see. I guess you'd better learn to read yourself in a hurry so you can get into the good stuff."

For the first time, Samuel glanced at his father. "You mean like the boring stuff he reads?"

Daria didn't look at Stefan. She was fixated on his son as if he were the most interesting person in her life. "Boring, huh? What doesn't it have that it should?"

Samuel thought, his brow furrowed. "Dragons. Maybe spaceships. Or a cool dog, not a silly cat."

"Hmm," Daria said, and she pulled out her phone. "I might just be able to help you there."

Stefan couldn't see what she was doing from here, but he was afraid to move from the doorway and shatter the mood. Plus, he was feeling decidedly extraneous, unnecessary. Add to that the realization that was dawning that he'd never quite thought of his son as a person with opinions and ideas of his own, and he was feeling like a complete failure. *Again.*

He watched as Daria held out her phone for Samuel to see. "Maybe a dog like that?"

"Yeah!"

"Well, I just happen to have his story right here. Want to hear how it starts?" The boy nodded excitedly. "Okay," Daria said. "But you have to listen with your eyes closed, so you can imagine the story in your mind better."

Obediently, Samuel's dark eyes closed.

She swiped a finger across the screen, obviously

opening what was a reading app. And then she began to read in a low, pleasant voice. But when she got to dialogue, her voice took on a different tone for each character, making it come even more alive.

Stefan found even he was caught up in the story of a lost dog looking for home. And when she stopped what seemed like a very short time later, he realized he was waiting for Daria to begin again. But instead she brushed her fingers gently over Samuel's cheek, stood up and stuffed her phone back into her pocket. Only then did Stefan realize his son was fast asleep.

"You're a miracle worker," he said softly when she had crossed the room to the doorway.

"It didn't take that much."

More than I've got, apparently.

He backed out into the hallway and stood there, still a little in shock, as Daria pulled the door closed behind her. Well, almost closed; she left it open about an inch. When he reached for the knob to close it the rest of the way, she looked at him curiously.

"Don't you leave it open a little so you can hear him in the night, if he needs anything?"

In fact, he had not. It had never occurred to him. He had looked upon the closing of that door as a sign they had survived another day, and usually felt a sense of relief that made him also feel guilty.

"I…didn't think of it. We used to, when he was a baby, but I didn't think— Damn, I suck at this," he muttered.

Turning away, he headed down the hall, embarrassed that she'd seen him at his most…ineffective. She followed him into the den, where he powered up the laptop and began to set it up to mirror onto the flat screen that was actually bigger than the one at the office.

"The first time you shot for a score, was it perfect?"

He stopped, wondering where that had come from. Looked over his shoulder at her. "Of course not. I'd never shot at a target before."

"Exactly."

"What?"

"You didn't expect to be a crack shot the first time, so why expect to be dad of the year when you've only just jumped back into the parenting pool?"

He blinked. "I...never thought of it like that. I mean, he's five, and..."

"You said you hadn't had much contact since the divorce?"

"No. And what we had was...strained."

"And you've been on your own for a couple of years now, so in essence, you're starting over. Building from scratch, and that takes time."

Stefan looked at his watch, not realizing why until the thought formed in his head. In the space of less than half an hour, Daria Bloom had both charmed his son and made Stefan himself feel so much better in the process.

"Miracle worker," he said, "doesn't even begin to describe it."

Chapter Four

Daria tried to focus on the screen as they laboriously went through the security video as promised, frame by frame, but her mind kept drifting back down the hall to where a little boy slept. He was a sweet kid who was just feeling helpless right now, ripped out of the life he knew and plunged into another world. A world that clearly hadn't ever had him in mind. No wonder he was snarly. It was self-preservation. Especially if what he'd said was true—that some man in his mother's life didn't like him and so he was discarded. At least her own mother had had no choice. She couldn't imagine what it would have felt like to know she just hadn't wanted her child.

And even more disconcerting, she kept looking up and finding Stefan watching her. Something in his eyes unsettled her.

"Problem?" she finally asked.

"Sorry," he said with a slight shake of his head. "I just can't get over how you handled Sam. Samuel." He said it in the tone of a self-correction. When she gave him a curious look, he shrugged. "His mother insists on Samuel."

"What does *he* want to be called?"

Stefan glanced toward the hallway, then said rather

sheepishly, "I don't know. I never asked him." He gave another, more definite shake of his head. "I never thought to talk to him the way you did."

"I gathered. Talk to him, Stefan, not at him. And more important, listen to what he says. He needs to know he's got your full attention, and not only when you're correcting him. He needs to believe he matters to you."

"Of course he matters." He ran a hand over his head. And let out a long, weary breath. "I remember when he was born. I was going to be the greatest dad ever. I'd had my own father for an example, you know?"

She smiled at him. "Siblings?" she asked.

"Three." His mouth quirked. "All sisters, after me."

"Oh, lucky them," she teased, but also meaning it. "A strapping big brother to look out for them."

He gave her an odd look. "That's exactly what my dad said when I hit about twelve. That it was my job, too, to watch out for them."

"You're close, you and your dad?"

He looked sad again. "We were. But… I couldn't…" Another long breath. "My folks have been married for thirty-five years. And they're still crazy about each other. They live in Florida now. My dad still treats my mom like a queen, and she thinks he hung the moon. But I couldn't even keep that going for five years, let alone thirty-five."

The moment he finished, she could tell he regretted saying all that. Essentially admitting that he felt like a failure for the destruction of his marriage. In the weeks they'd worked together, he'd rarely spoken of anything personal, so this was a switch. She wondered if he shared those feelings with anyone. And if, as she guessed, he didn't, what it must feel like to keep all that bottled up inside.

Asks the woman who has plenty of secrets of her own to keep?

"What about Sam? Does he have any contact with them?"

"Not much." He grimaced. "My ex saw to that."

"Well, I guess you can fix that now, can't you?" He gave her a startled look, as if he hadn't thought of that. "Your mom sounds like the kind of grandmother any boy would love. They'd probably both welcome the chance to help if you sent up a flare."

"I…you're right. Two of my sisters have kids, and they're really close to them."

"So there's some help." She frowned. "Who's the guy who didn't like him?"

Stefan's expression hardened. "His mother's fiancé."

"Oh. Ouch."

"And he doesn't just not like him, he hates him. Gave her an ultimatum. Get rid of him or the wedding's off."

Daria's eyes widened as she looked at him in utter astonishment. "His mother is marrying someone who would make an outrageous demand like that, and who feels that way about her own child?"

"Yeah, well, Leah's always had a…calculating streak."

"What is he, rich?" Daria asked.

"And connected. She's an event organizer, and he moves in all the right circles."

"No wonder your son is angry. He has every right to be."

He stared at her for a moment. And then he closed

his eyes and shook his head. "I never thought of it like that, either. From his point of view."

"You probably haven't had time," she said, trying to be understanding. "Just trying to organize childcare is a pain, with this case ongoing. And you had to get him into school in a rush, so it's no wonder you haven't had a chance to fix up his room or connect with other parents."

He blinked. "What? What's wrong with his room?"

"It's fine…for a grown-up. But a kid needs his own stuff, needs things he likes around him, so he feels at home. And," she added, "a smaller bed."

Something flashed in those striking light brown eyes, something that made her wonder what he was thinking. But he only said, "I heard you say that. What difference does it make?"

"The difference between feeling lost in a place too big for you and safe in your own little shelter."

It was a moment before he leaned back in the desk chair he sat in. She'd noticed early on he had the seat set a good three inches higher than a normal seat, to accommodate his height. Her feet probably wouldn't even touch the floor.

"How do you know all this? You said you'd never had kids."

She felt the old, painful pang. "No. Nor will I ever, biologically. Doctors told me that long ago." She'd had years to get used to the idea, but that didn't stop her from feeling sad about it now and then.

"I'm sorry. You're obviously great with them," he said, and there was a note of genuineness in his voice that she appreciated.

"I have friends with kids," she answered evenly. "In

fact, my best friend has three boys, including twins about Sam's age." She purposely chose the name the boy's mother didn't like, felt a small pleasure in doing it and didn't care at the moment if it was petty. "I've been around them and babysat them since they were born."

"So…tell me what all I need to do. Besides a smaller bed."

"You might not like it."

"I just want *him* to like it."

She heard the undertone of desperation in his voice. He did truly love his son—he just didn't know him. And she doubted she or anyone could have done much better under the circumstances.

"All right," she said. "You want my opinion? There's no place for a kid here, not even a yard, and it's obvious. It looks like the proverbial bachelor pad."

His gaze darted away, and he said uncomfortably, "Yeah, I was kind of going for that, after the divorce."

"Do you still like it?"

"Actually… I never really did. I was kind of reeling, and it was just…"

"A declaration?"

His mouth quirked. "I guess."

"You need furniture a kid can get on, even climb on, without being afraid of hurting it or getting it dirty. He needs books, toys, maybe a stuffed animal to hug at night, although he'd probably deny it. And more playing room—another reason for the smaller bed—and pictures of what he likes."

Again he ran a hand over his head. "I don't even know what he likes."

"He likes that video game. Find some stuff about it—it's everywhere. He likes grilled cheese sandwiches, like most kids, and I'm sure your Szechuan is way too spicy for him. Kids have simple tastes at that age. Peanut butter and jelly isn't just a cliché. And," she added with a grin, "he likes dogs better than cats."

"Well, we're in agreement there," Stefan said with a wry laugh.

"Think about that, then."

"What?"

"A dog."

Stefan blinked. "You mean…get one? I don't even have time to take care of Samuel, and you want to add a dog into the mix?"

"I didn't mean tomorrow," she said with a laugh. "But maybe take a trip over to Max Hollick's place. The K-9 Cadets program. He's got a bunch of puppies there for training. And since they're all already spoken for, you won't be confronted with Sam insisting on taking one home. But you can see how he is with them, see if you think it would be worth it."

"That…makes sense," he admitted. "As long as he knows we can't do it now."

"Maybe when this case is over." She grimaced. "If it *ever* is."

"It will be," he promised. "But not if we don't get back to work."

"Yeah. Right."

They went back to the frame-by-frame analysis of the security videos. They enlarged each frame in quarters to get a closer look at people in the background, looking for even a slight resemblance to Bianca. Daria had begun this by looking for the dress she'd been wearing, but Stefan had pointed out she could have changed at any time. He'd rather offhandedly mentioned a witness he'd once had, also a "working girl," who'd told him she always carried a change of clothes with her in case something happened to what she was wearing. Like an extra-energetic client.

Daria had turned away as heat rose in her cheeks at his words. Unlike Stefan, if she blushed it would show beneath her lighter brown skin. Not, she thought, that he likely ever blushed. He'd probably seen too much, and he'd said that so casually. She didn't want him thinking she was so green that such things embarrassed her, but in fact her county was usually a calm, quiet place, and she'd never encountered a case like this one before. Thank goodness.

It was nearly midnight and Daria's eyes were burning when Stefan finally leaned back and rubbed at his own eyes, then shook his head. "I've had it," he muttered.

"Me, too," she agreed.

"I could be looking right at Bianca or our killer and it wouldn't register."

"Fresh start tomorrow?" she suggested, and he nodded. "I'll mark the spot where we left off."

"Maybe back it up to a half hour ago," he said wryly. "I think that's when my brain checked out."

"Done," Daria replied. She shut down the laptop; it was technically sheriff's department property, so she'd take it with her. As they left the den, she glanced toward the hallway. "You'll work it out with him, Stefan," she said quietly. "Give it time."

"Time? Took you less then half an hour to get more out of him than I have since he got here."

"I have more practice," she said with a smile.

He walked her out to her car, and she guessed from the way her breath made vapor that it was at or below freezing.

"Welcome to November," she muttered. "Why aren't *you* shivering?" He'd come outside in just his long-sleeved shirt, whereas she had on her jacket and was still cold.

"This is nothing. Add a little northeast wind off the lake for some lake-effect snow, and you'd have a mild Chicago winter," he said.

"Humph. I'm from California. I'll never get totally used to this."

"There are ways to stay warm."

She was sure he didn't mean that as a double entendre, so she quashed her instinctive reaction. And he looked as if he regretted saying it anyway, so she turned back to what she knew was his biggest concern.

"Look, I know with work, and especially right now, it's impossible, but Sam's going to need kids to play with. Not to be critical, but Mrs. Crane doesn't seem the type to bend and get down on his level."

"No, she's not," he admitted. "But she was the only one available on such short notice." He grimaced. "Leah called me on a Friday and said he'd be flying in on Sunday."

Daria blinked. "Two days' notice?" He nodded. And her already low opinion of his ex dropped another notch. "I won't ask why on earth you got married in the first place, but…"

"She thought the job was glamorous, I guess. Exciting. Didn't realize it's mostly grunt work. And I…" He frowned. "Let's just say she's gorgeous. And can be quite charming, when it suits her purposes. We eloped after three weeks."

Daria managed not to comment on that. Instead she asked, "Do you have legal custody now?"

He sighed. "No. She just sent him."

Her mouth curled. "I'd want to make it all legal so she can't yank him back if she changes her mind. I can't imagine anything worse for a five-year-old than being tugged in two like that."

"I would, if I was at all sure this was going to work."

At first she winced inwardly. Would he really send the boy back under these circumstances? But he sounded so exhausted she thought she understood; it was all just too much right now.

"Why don't I call my friend Fiona? She lives less than a mile from here. You could set up a playdate with her boys, see how they all get along. And if it works, make it a regular thing."

Stefan stared at her. "I…you'd do that?"

She gave him a puzzled look. "Of course I would. And Fiona is always looking for kids for her boys to hang out with. She's also big on them playing outside whenever they can. They've got a huge backyard with a sandpit and an amazing play set her husband built, with ladders and a slide and a fort up top, and all kinds of things for the boys to wear themselves out on."

"Sounds like five-year-old heaven."

"It is," she said with a laugh. "It's a built-in babysitter and gets them away from screens. She never leaves them alone, mind you, but she can be out there and read or garden or do other things at the same time. Until winter—then she's out there building snow things with them. She and the boys made a dragon once that was amazing. Shall I call her?"

"Please," he said.

"First thing tomorrow," she promised.

"Thank you," he said, with such relief in his voice it made her smile up at him. And in the next instant, before she even realized what was happening, his arms came around her in a fierce hug.

It was a thank-you, she told herself. That's all. Just thank you for help with a situation he was having trouble with. But repeating it didn't help much when her heart was hammering and her skin sizzled at the contact with that broad, strong chest. And there she was, the woman who had been cold enough to shiver mere moments ago, suddenly overheating as if it were midday LA in the summer. All because this man had hugged her? She must be—

Her self-accusatory thoughts broke off suddenly as something else registered.

Hers wasn't the only heart that had suddenly started racing.

Chapter Five

Uh-oh.

Stefan heard the warning in his head quite clearly. Crazily, his first thought was a memory from so long ago he couldn't be sure exactly when it was, except that he'd been a kid, at his grandparents' home, working on one of the endless jigsaw puzzles that were his grandmother's passion. He'd always figured the urge to put the pieces of a crime together had come from her, since often it was the same sort of puzzle, with a ton of tiny pieces that all had to fit together.

It wasn't any of his grandmother's puzzles he was remembering now, however. It was the burst of satisfaction when a piece he'd tried fit. When it turned out to be right. When it slid into place perfectly.

Daria Bloom in his arms felt that way.

And that scared the hell out of him.

So why wasn't he letting go? Why wasn't he backing off? Why was he still standing here, holding her tight against him, letting his body wake up in a way he hadn't felt since…he couldn't remember when?

Because it feels good. Too damned good.

With more effort than it ever should have taken, he released her and stepped back.

"Drive carefully," he said, as if that hug had never gotten out of hand. As if he hadn't been standing there savoring the scent of her, the feel of her luscious curves against him. As if he hadn't barely been able to resist the urge to tilt her head back and claim those lips with his own.

For a moment she just stood there, looking a little stunned.

"I...will," she said, sounding like someone who had momentarily forgotten how to speak.

He watched her drive off. Reminded himself that she was tough, smart, careful and highly trained, so there was no reason for him to feel like he should be seeing her home. Not that he had any choice in the matter. Not with Samuel—Sam—asleep inside.

He realized he was standing out here in near-freezing air, staring after a car that was long out of sight. He went back in the house and made his way down the hall, careful to walk quietly. He peeked in the door of his son's room. Or, rather, the guest room his son was using.

Guest room. And the truth of what Daria had said swept over him. Samuel felt like a guest—in other words, temporary. And that was his fault, for not thinking about this from the boy's point of view.

Stefan eased the door open and went into the room. The light from the hallway cast just enough light to see his way to the bed. He sat down on the edge and looked at the child curled up there. Realized the truth of what Daria had said—he looked tiny and helpless in the big expanse of the king-size bed he'd bought on the chance that someday his folks might come to visit.

He reached out and gently cupped his son's face, taking the time for the first time since he'd arrived to really look at him, to acknowledge that this little boy was the same baby he'd held in such wonder, the same miracle that had filled his heart near to bursting. His, a part of him, yet a unique individual.

When he got up, even though it was late, he settled in with his tablet and started a search for kid's furniture.

DARIA WAS PROUD of herself. She'd gotten up and ready and all the way to the station without letting the memory of that hug last night invade her mind. True, it had been a battle, but by the time she'd settled in with the videos to pick up where they'd left off, she thought she'd beaten it back. Of course, the moment she'd thought that, the man himself arrived, and just looking at him blew up any idea that she'd permanently shelved the memory of what had transpired between them.

He'd stopped in the doorway to the office they were using when Melody Hughes, passing by with an armful of mail, had paused to talk to him.

Or flirt with him.

Daria fought the urge to get up and interrupt that conversation. Melody had a right to flirt with whomever she pleased, and Stefan was far too polite to shut her down.

Assuming he'd want to...

Melody was a cute little blonde whom some of the deputies secretly called Barbie because of her resemblance to the doll. Once one of them had accidentally done it to her face, and to his shock she had laughed. He was, she'd told the deputy, hardly the first person to do so. That reaction had earned her a lot of respect, including from Daria herself.

She watched them for a moment, assessingly. Not so

much gauging their feelings, or lingering on the contrast of Melody's petite blondness and Stefan's tall, dark, powerful presence, but her own response. A response that was sharp, prodding and felt annoyingly like jealousy.

That thought roiled her even more, and she did not like it. She had no time for such nonsense, especially now, and especially with him. Not only was she working this case with him, but he was eight years younger than her, and his personal life was in chaos with Sam's arrival. That was a trifecta of stop signs, and she'd darned well better obey them.

She thought she had managed to quash her unwanted reaction by the time he actually came into the office.

"Morning," he said with that megawatt smile that could light up a room. He hadn't given *that* to Melody. "I see you're set up. I'll just get some coffee and we can dig in."

She gestured at the desk beside the seat he usually took, where a ceramic mug he'd brought in, telling her he hated drinking out of Styrofoam or paper, was already full of steaming coffee. "I poured you a cup when I got mine. Straight, right?" she asked as she sipped her own sugar-and cream-laced brew.

"I…thanks." He picked up the mug and took a sip. Then another. "I may live," he said wryly.

"We were up late." She studied him for a moment, trying not to think about him and Melody in the doorway, or the hug from last night. Truth be told, she was acquiring an annoyingly long list of things she was trying not to think about with this man. "How was Sam this morning?"

"Not bad," Stefan said, sitting down and swiveling

the chair so he was facing her. "And he is Sam, by the way. I asked him. And it's a relief not to have to keep correcting myself."

"Good," she murmured with a nod.

"He asked about you."

She quirked a brow. "Did he?"

"He wanted to know if you were coming back."

"That's sweet. Unless he was hoping I wouldn't," she added.

"Hardly." He took another drink of coffee, bigger this time, then set the mug down. "He liked you. A lot. He asked if you could go with us this afternoon."

She blinked. "Where are you going?"

He held her gaze as he said, "Furniture shopping. For his room."

"I'm glad."

"So am I. He was so wary when I suggested it, it made me feel worse, but so excited when I said he could pick out whatever he wanted that it…it was like… I don't know how to describe it."

"You don't have to," she said softly.

"So will you? He really wanted you to come."

"And you?" The moment the words were out, she regretted saying them.

"I never would have thought of it if not for you, Daria. And this is the first time he's ever actually asked for something. So yeah, please. Unless you've got…a date or something tonight."

She didn't think she'd mistaken that hesitation. Which was odd, since they'd established early on, in that casual, getting-to-know-someone-you-were-work-ing-with kind of way, that neither one of them was see-ing anyone seriously. Or in her case, even nonseriously.

"All right," she said. "It would be a nice break from this for a couple of hours."

There. She'd put a time limit on it. That would make it…easier. Wouldn't it?

"Thanks," Stefan said, and he sounded relieved. "I just hope we can find something local. I'd as soon not drive all the way to Denver for this."

"There's a place over on Pine Peak Drive, where Fiona got some furniture for the twins. Maybe there?"

"Sounds like a good place to start."

They left it at that and started back in on the videos. Unfortunately, they had as little success as last night in finding any sign of Bianca, or any man that could clearly be her Blue Eyes. She'd lost track of how many times they'd watched the woman come out of the elevator, walk across the lobby toward the hotel bar, but never appear in the video from inside the bar. And the only people who visibly left the bar during the next hour they scanned were a group of three giggling women and the bartender who had gotten off duty and who they had verified had gone straight home to his very pregnant wife.

Finally, Daria got up out of the chair; she simply couldn't sit any longer, staring at that screen. "The phrase *beating a dead horse* comes to mind," she muttered. "I think it's time to focus on something else for while. Maybe then something new will bubble up."

"Agreed. Time to back-burner this."

She smiled at the phrase, since it was what she called it as well when she put something out of the forefront of her mind and let it percolate. Often the answer she'd been hunting for popped up after she'd ignored the problem for a while.

*Has ignoring the fact that he makes you twitchy
stopped the feelings?*

"When does Sam get out of school?" she asked
abruptly.

He glanced at his watch. "In about twenty minutes."

"Why don't we go pick him up, feed him lunch and
go shopping early?"

The smile he gave her then was well worth the gamble that a five-year-old boy would serve as a sufficient
distraction—and keep her mind off pathways it most
certainly should not be following.

Chapter Six

Stefan could almost see his son's thought process even from this distance. Sam had come out of class with a small cluster of other boys who looked about the same age, although he was a bit taller than all but one of them. Sam had been talking animatedly with the other tall classmate, gesturing with the hand that wasn't holding what looked like a drawing, but when that boy had apparently spotted a parent and headed that way, Sam's entire body language changed. He slumped slightly and trudged toward the parking lot, where he was apparently used to finding Mrs. Crane waiting.

But then Sam spotted him, and Stefan's jaw tightened a little at the boy's sudden wariness. Things had been better between them this morning, but apparently that had been forgotten. But then Sam spotted Daria and instantly perked up. A smile forming on his face, he picked up speed.

"Hi, Daria," he called out.

"Sam!" She waved at the boy, and a quick glance told Stefan she was smiling widely back at him. Sam broke into a run then and skidded to a stop in front of them. "What have you got there?"

Daria's voice was full of an interest that made the boy practically shine. "We had to draw today."

"Was it fun?"

"Kinda."

"May I see?"

The boy hesitated, then held out the page of rough-textured paper. Stefan looked at it over Daria's shoulder. It was recognizably a person in black, and a brown... creature of some sort, standing atop a long, wobbly green line he presumed was supposed to be grass. In the background was a gray scribble that went up and down across the page.

"Sam," Daria said with a wide smile, "I was expecting stick figures, but this is so much better!"

Again the boy lit up. Was it really that simple? Was genuine praise that important? He tried to remember himself at that age. Remembered the first time he'd brought home a perfect spelling test and his mom had cooed over it and made him cookies. Maybe it *was* that simple.

Daria pointed to the gray scribble. "Are those the mountains?"

"Yes," Sam said, clearly excited that she'd realized this.

"You're not used to those, are you?"

"No. Just buildings."

"Well, you did a good job showing them. And let's see here..." She pointed at the brown creature. "Let me guess. A dog?"

Sam was practically dancing. "Yes! Like the one I want. We watched a movie about a dog."

Stefan looked at the picture again. Okay, mountains he could buy. And the dog. The person...it definitely wasn't completely a stick figure—the person was a long oval with stick arms and legs. And short, straight lines of dark hair applied to the slightly crooked head, almost like a cap.

Hair that resembled, in a five-year-old way, Daria's.

"Well, I think it's wonderful," she said. "It should be on display at home."

"What does that mean?" Sam asked.

"It means put up where everyone can see it."

"Oh."

Sam cast a doubtful eye at Stefan. That doubt stabbed at him, and it was an effort to say casually, "I think the refrigerator is the requisite location? We'll have to pick up some magnets while we're shopping this afternoon."

"Shopping?" Sam asked.

"To find you some new bedroom furniture, remember?"

The boy's eyes widened. "Really? All of us? Today?"

"Right now, if you're ready."

Sam let out an excited yelp. He was even more animated when Daria suggested a local burger joint, and it was a toss-up over whether he talked or ate more. She was so good for him.

And stop thinking she's good for you, too.

And then Stefan found himself somewhere he'd never expected to be—a kids' furnishings store at the south end of the shopping district downtown. They had sections labeled with signs overhead, divided by age, and they headed toward the 5–7 sign.

"Look at everything first," Daria suggested, and Sam nodded eagerly.

The boy darted from piece to piece, first piqued by the bed designed like a race car, then to one painted like an Old West stagecoach. He reached out to touch a comforter printed with famous movie characters, then stood looking up in awe at a wall painted like space, with stars and planets over a bed that looked like a spaceship.

"I had no idea," Stefan muttered.

Daria smiled. "I think it's all about feeding their imagination."

"Kind of feels like I'm trying to buy his affection."

"No," she said quickly. "You're just showing him he has a place in your home. That you're willing to make changes for him. He's a smart kid—it won't take long before he realizes that also means he has a place in your heart."

He stared at her. "How did you get so wise?"

"Comes with age," she said. "You'll catch up."

"You make it sound like you're ancient." He wasn't sure why this bothered him, but it did.

"When I graduated high school, you were ten."

He winced. When she put it that way... "That's different. The maturity difference is bigger then."

She moved then, because Sam had rounded a corner and they couldn't see him. It seemed instinctive to her, and he wondered if it was something in the female DNA. Which brought back to mind what he'd learned from the trace she'd asked him to run on her own DNA. It had explained a lot about her, from her light brown skin to her determination.

"Ah. Here we go." She gestured toward some shelves of bedding. "I'll bet if you dug around in there a bit, you could find some stuff from that video game he loves."

"That might work," he said. He glanced past a couple standing behind Daria, who were discussing when and where to meet up later, and saw a display that looked like it had potential. He had to dig a bit, but he found a bedcover that had the characters he recognized. "We've gone from sleeping with the fishes to sleeping with zombies," he said with a shake of his head.

"Same effect," Daria retorted. "Come on, Sam's over here, and I think he may have found the perfect bed for this."

He glanced that direction and saw his son sitting on a twin bed. It wasn't, Stefan saw to his relief, one of the elaborate things he'd likely have to spend days putting together. It was a bit high, but not so high it made him nervous the boy would fall out and get hurt. There were two steps attached to one end, and the entire thing was painted to look like it was built of stone.

"It's the castle!" Sam was so excited Stefan couldn't help smiling. "From my game!"

"So it is," Stefan said. Then he tossed what he'd found to his son. "Which means this should go with it."

Sam's eyes widened as he recognized his zombies. "Wow!"

"And look who's in the middle," Daria urged. "In the picture on the other side."

The boy turned the plastic-wrapped cover over. "It's the dragon!" He could hardly contain himself now.

"So is this it? What you want?" Stefan asked. "No changing your mind later," he added.

"Well, maybe when he's twenty," Daria said teasingly. The boy laughed, as if the idea of being that old was ludicrous.

Twenty. For a moment Stefan just stared at his son, tried to picture him at that age. *You're still surprised by him at five. Twenty's beyond your imagination.*

Sam shifted his gaze. Gave his father a look that

seemed equal parts hope and doubt. "Did you mean it? I can have this in that room?"

That room. Not *my* room. Daria had been right.

"It's your room now, Sam," he said quietly. "So yes, you can have this in your room."

After a moment, when Sam didn't speak, Daria said, "I'm sure your room would have been ready if your dad had known sooner you were coming." She gave Sam a wide-eyed look. "But who knows what he would have picked out? Maybe something really babyish, because he remembers when you were a baby."

Sam looked horrified. "No! I want this."

They ended up buying the bed, a shelf that could be hung off the end to make a night table, a small dresser and a couple of pictures for the walls. And, when Daria pointed out—tactfully—that as tall as Sam was for his age, he couldn't reach clothes hanging in the closet, they added a clever setup that hung a lower pole from the upper one, right at Sam's height.

Stefan managed not to wince when the clerk rang up the total. But Sam was quite disappointed when he realized they couldn't take it all with them, and that the furniture and some of the other items would have to be delivered in a few days.

"It won't all fit in the car, plus we have to get the other stuff out of there," Stefan explained, "so there's room for your stuff."

"Oh," the boy said. Then, warily again, "Are you mad?"

Stefan blinked. "About what, son?"

"Your stuff."

For a moment Stefan couldn't think of what to say. So he tried to imagine what Daria would say. And running on that impulse, he reached out and ran a hand over the boy's soft, short curls. "You're worth a lot more to me than any amount of stuff."

Sam stared at him as if he wasn't sure whether to believe him or not. They were on their way back to the car when Daria's phone rang. She answered as Stefan got Sam in and situated in the booster seat. The boy didn't like it, and Stefan understood; he was tall enough it seemed extraneous. But it was the law, and so into the booster seat he went.

"That was Fiona," Daria said as she got in and fastened her own belt. "She suggested this Saturday for the playdate. They've got a covered patio with heaters, so the boys can have lunch outside and if the weather holds play on the fort, as they call it."

Stefan turned to look at her. "Just like that?"

"Fiona," Daria said, "is the mother every kid wishes they could have. He'll have fun and be safe. Can't ask for much more than that."

"No," Stefan said gruffly. "I...thank you."

"Thank her. All I did was facilitate."

"Still...if not for you..." He drew in a breath. "If not for you, a lot of things."

And suddenly it was there, in the car with them, the memory of last night and that hug of thanks that had become an entirely different kind of embrace. And he knew, by the way she averted her eyes and became suddenly busy adjusting her purse, that she felt it, too.

Where that left them, he had no idea.

Chapter Seven

"We should probably explain to Sam what's going on, don't you think?" she said as they drove.

"Yeah. Sure."

Something in the way he said it told her his mind had gone exactly where hers had gone—to last night. But that way lay nothing but trouble, and so she quickly turned to Sam and explained about her friend and the invitation.

Sam took the prospect of this new venture Saturday well, even with a little excitement, although he seemed more enthused about his new bed.

It was a few minutes later when Daria said, with no particular intonation, "We're not too far from Max Hollick's place." Stefan gave her a sideways look, and she shrugged. "Just saying. It's early yet."

"You're determined to get me into this, aren't you?"

The corners of his mouth were twitching, and she knew he wasn't upset.

"Not like you'll go home with one," she pointed out. "As I said, they're all spoken for already."

"Safe enough, I guess. Unless somebody starts nagging."

"Make it incentive. For good behavior, I mean."

Stefan surrendered with good grace and made the turn she pointed out.

"Where are we going?" Sam asked.

Daria turned in her seat to look back at the boy. "Do you remember how you felt when you first got here? Like your world had been turned upside down?"

Sam frowned, clearly wondering what this had to do with his question. "Yeah," he said hesitantly, and Daria hoped the hesitation wasn't because he still felt that way.

"Well, sometimes when—" she chose the easier word for the five-year-old to understand "—soldiers come home from where there's been fighting, they feel the same way. Like they don't know how to fit in back home anymore. Does that make sense to you?"

"Yeah," the boy repeated, more certainly this time.

"Well, I met someone a while ago who helps them with that, in the coolest way."

"How?" Sam was clearly intrigued now.

"He finds dogs who have no one to love them, and he matches them up with the soldiers who need them."

"Dogs?" Sam's eyes had gone wide.

"Yep," she said cheerfully. "So the dogs get a home and somebody to love them, and the soldiers get a best friend who will always understand when they're not feeling quite right. Isn't that cool?"

"Yeah." With enthusiasm now, until the boy added sadly, "My mom hates dogs."

"No surprise there," Stefan muttered.

She wondered if Stefan realized his son was testing these particular waters. She went on rather briskly, "Anyway, that's where we're going. To where Mr. Hollick keeps the dogs for the soldiers. He's not there right now, but someone will be."

Sam's eyes went saucer big this time. "Really?"

"They all belong to someone else already," she said carefully, "but it would still be fun to meet them, wouldn't it?"

That Sam could hardly sit still after this gave them the answer to that question. And when they arrived at their destination, and were greeted by an excited cacophony of happy barking, she thought Sam just might lift off, he was so excited.

The fact that within minutes of their arrival Sam was giggling, surrounded by a pack of clearly delighted, gamboling dogs of varying sizes and breed combinations, proved her right better than anything else could have.

The woman who'd greeted them, a grandmotherly sort who said she had become a volunteer at K-9 Cadets after one of Max's dogs had saved her son's life, had been quite happy to oblige when Daria explained.

"It's great for the dogs to encounter all sorts of people, like they will once they're paired with their veteran. It's a wonderful thing Max is doing here."

"Absolutely," Stefan said, but his eyes were on his son, whose joyous laughter as he played with the animals was something Daria was guessing he hadn't heard much of.

When he finally turned to look at her, he caught her watching him. "Convinced?" she asked hastily.

His mouth quirked. "Maybe. Still doesn't give my house any more room for a dog."

"Details," she said rather airily, then added with a

grin, "Of course, details never matter to the person who doesn't have to handle them."

WHEN THEY GOT home and Stefan told Sam to look at his room and decide where he wanted his new bed, the boy scampered off happily, looking for the first time like a normal five-year-old.

"Thank you," Stefan said to Daria again as she prepared to leave. He wanted—oh, how he wanted—to hug her again, but he didn't dare. "I really haven't been thinking in his terms, and I should have been."

"Oh, yes," she answered lightly. "Here, on two days' notice, for the first time in your life, instantly start thinking like a five-year-old."

"You're cutting me a lot of slack," he said, but he couldn't help smiling.

"Somebody has to, since you're certainly not," she returned, smiling back in a way that made him want to hug her even more.

But she left, and he felt a little adrift without her quick, easy and wise support. And when she texted him a couple of hours later, asking if he could take a call, he immediately dialed her cell.

"How's it going with Sam?" was the first thing she asked.

"Better. You really nailed it."

"I'm glad. But listen, I had a thought. About the case."

He was surprised at himself, and the fact that he felt almost disappointed that she hadn't just reached out because she wanted to talk to him.

Business. Colleagues. Serial killer. Hello, Roberts, get with the program.

"Shoot," he said.

"Remember that couple in the furniture store, behind us when Sam was sitting on the bed?"

His brow furrowed. What that had to do with anything escaped him. But he said, "I remember."

"Were you close enough to hear what they were saying?"

"Yeah. They were talking about where to meet up later, after they—" It hit him. "You think Bianca met Blue Eyes before she went upstairs?"

"It's a thought. If she did, then kept her...assigned date, but after he passed out went back downstairs..."

"To wherever they planned to meet up," he finished.

"It's a thought."

"Indeed it is." He let out a breath. "And a better one than we've had yet."

"It also means we need more lobby and bar video, from earlier in the evening."

Which meant more hours spent searching that video. Hours spent alone with Daria.

And somehow he didn't mind.

"ANOTHER DAY OF this and I'm throwing away my cell phone, my tablet and my laptop," Daria muttered, hitting the pause button on the video. "If I never have to stare at another screen again, it would be fine with me."

"I was thinking more along the lines of taking mine back to Illinois and throwing it in Lake Michigan," Stefan said, sounding as weary of this as she felt. "Along with every other screen within reach."

She leaned back in her chair. They had been working backward a half hour at a time from the moment they already knew Bianca had come downstairs for the last time. The security video ran at fifteen frames per second, but they were watching at one-third speed, so an hour took them three times that. Add in that they had to do it twice, once for the lobby video and once for the bar video, and they had only managed to get through two hours of frame-by-frame scrutiny.

Daria's eyes were burning. Stefan was rubbing at his as well, so she guessed they must feel the same. He got up, stretched. Daria tried not to watch, but it was hard to take her eyes off the sheer muscled beauty of him. He moved like...she tried to think of an analogy and couldn't. He was simply, purely male, on such an elemental level it was impossible to ignore. Although when he started to pace to the office door, images of a restless, prowling big cat came to mind.

Then he stopped, apparently to look out the single window that gave them a view out into the rest of the building. But he didn't speak, and so she broke the silence.

"There must be something we can do that doesn't involve—" she waved vaguely toward the flat screen "—that."

Stefan went very still. Then he turned his head to look at her, and for just an instant she saw something in his eyes that reminded her once again of that embrace. Not that she needed reminding; it was never far from her mind. Which was ridiculous, really. It wasn't like they'd shared some long, passionate kiss or something.

And that had been a very poor choice of comparison, she told herself as she had to fight down a jolt of heat at just the thought. She'd simply been closed up in this room alone with him for too long. It was making her mind go crazy places. That was all it was.

"I'm going up to The Lodge," she said abruptly. "I want to see where the places not covered by the cameras are again."

She wasn't sure what she expected to find—they already knew where the few places were—but maybe something would occur to her if she looked again. And if not, at least they would have a break in the eye-straining monotony of going over and over slo-mo video for hours.

"All right," Stefan agreed easily enough, so easily she wondered if he wanted to get out of these close quarters, too. "But," he added, "you might want to be aware that it's snowing."

"What?" she said, startled. He gestured at the door, and she jumped up and went over to look through the window. Sure enough, the white stuff was coming down outside. Rather steadily.

The cold white stuff. Her spoiled California bones shivered.

"They didn't predict this," she said, a bit crankily.

"What a shock. A wrong weather prediction."

Her gaze snapped to his face. He was grinning at her, the smart aleck. She wanted to be mad, but she simply couldn't be in the face of that heart-melting grin. She threw up her hands and laughed instead.

"All right, you found me out, I'm a true cold-weather wuss."

"You've been here how long now?"

"Four years," she said with a grimace. "And my blood shows no signs of thickening up, if that's what you're hinting at."

"I wasn't going to hint, I was going to come right out and say it."

She turned and gave him a mock glare. "Didn't you say your parents moved to Florida?"

"Only three years ago, and after spending their whole lives in Illinois," he pointed out. "And," he added, "Mom says sometimes she misses it. The seasons, I mean."

She gestured toward the falling snow. "Then she should come here to visit you and Sam."

Stefan's teasing demeanor faded. "I've been thinking about that, ever since you mentioned it. And you're right. They would want to be part of Sam's life, now that the major…roadblock is out of the way."

"Then ask them," she said simply. "Surely Sam's happiness and him adjusting to this huge change is the most important thing right now?"

"Yes. Yes, it is."

"You've got the troops, Roberts. Call them in."

A different kind of smile curved his mouth. *That mouth.* But this wasn't that killer grin—this was a softer, maybe hopeful, kind of expression. Then, to her surprise, he reached out and ran the back of his fingers over her cheek.

"I thought I already had," he said quietly.

The shiver she felt this time had nothing to do with the thought of snow.

Chapter Eight

It would help, Stefan thought as he stared out at the falling snow, if she wasn't so damned cute. And funny. And wise. And helpful.

And sexy. *Oh, yeah, Roberts, let's not forget that one.*

If he were going to be honest, and he usually tried to be, he'd admit he'd known he was in trouble the first moment he'd been introduced to the sheriff's deputy who would be the liaison to the FBI on this case. But thanks to her tough-as-nails demeanor and take-no-prisoners attitude, he'd managed to keep it under control and strictly business. Even when he'd done that trace for her on her mother, and found out Ava Bloom's sad, tragic fate, he'd kept it professional. And admired her for how well she'd taken it.

But he was learning that the brusqueness covered a softer side, a gentler side, as she'd shown to Sam. And that his son had clearly fallen for her at first contact had...complicated things. The change in the boy was priceless to him, but at the same time it was harder and harder to be around Daria outside the job. He kept wanting to—

He abruptly cut off his own thoughts. The long list

of what he kept wanting when it came to Daria was not something it was wise to dwell on right now. Besides, given how much help she'd been with Sam, the last thing he wanted to do was drive her away. She'd been pretty clear she wasn't interested. And he couldn't blame her. Who'd want to take on the chaos his life was in right now? Then again, that chaos had calmed considerably since the first moment Sam had met her.

And, of course, that had been before that hug that had become more than a hug.

Maybe it hadn't been more, for her. Maybe he'd misinterpreted her response, and the occasional look in her eyes he saw when he caught her looking at him. Maybe it was just him. He hadn't had time for any kind of relationship, even a hookup, for longer than he cared to remember. Even before Sam, and this case, his job had been all consuming. It had eaten up his marriage, although he was now distanced enough from that to realize that would likely have happened, anyway. Because his wife had not been the woman he'd thought she was.

But regardless of that, it had been so long it was only to be expected he'd…overreact to the first attractive woman he'd spent any real amount of time with. He'd been so wary—and distrustful of his own judgment—since Leah that he'd gone beyond careful and all the way into doing without. For a long time. And Sam had only intensified that; no longer could he be bringing someone back to his…bachelor pad, as Daria had described it.

Well, unless it was her. Because Sam had already made it quite clear he adored her.

Understandably.

"You okay?"

Her quiet question snapped him out of his pointless reverie. "Just thinking about Sam." Which was, to a certain extent, true.

"It will be fine," she assured him. "It will just take time." She put a hand on his arm, clearly intending only to comfort. But all he could think about was all the ways he wanted her hands on him, and he had to suppress a shudder, so strong was the need that swept over him.

"If we're staying here, we might as well get back to it," he said brusquely, as if the merest touch from her hadn't nearly sent him into a tailspin.

"I suppose."

She walked back over to the chairs they'd set up before the flat-screen display and picked up the remote. She pressed a key that turned off the screensaver that had come on and then hit the play button. And they began again.

He wasn't sure how much longer they'd been at it when Daria suddenly hit the Pause button. Only this time she wasn't leaning back, closing tired eyes. This time she was leaning in, staring at the screen. It was stopped at almost exactly an hour before the lobby camera had caught Bianca walking toward the bar.

He looked, but he couldn't see anyone in the frozen image from the hotel bar that even vaguely resembled Bianca. Still, he stayed quiet as she moved the video frame by frame until she reached a spot where she stopped it again. As far as he could tell, she was focusing on a table in the back corner of the bar, mostly hidden in shadow, where Stefan could just tell that a man sat by himself. Then, with a quickly typed command on the laptop keyboard, she zoomed the video in. Definitely a man, and definitely alone.

"Well, well," she murmured.

"Feel like sharing?"

She glanced at him. Her eyes were alight with interest, but the interest of a hunter who had just spotted her prey. "Back at the beginning, I interviewed The Lodge staff. And then when we turned up the body of a Colton cousin, I talked to all of them, including the brass. Including Russ Colton."

Her voice changed a little when she said the Colton name, but that seemed endemic to just about everyone in Roaring Springs. Some spoke it with awe and respect, others with envy, some with downright dislike. Although he'd never had much interaction with them, he'd always been aware of the wealthy, important family. He'd found it fascinating how they were scattered all over the country, each branch holding a unique place wherever they were. One branch had even spawned a president.

And he knew that the discovery of the body of a Colton cousin had kicked the investigation into high gear.

"Russ Colton, the emperor of The Colton Empire?" he said, purposely keeping his tone light.

She grimaced. "That's what he calls it, yes."

"You sound like you don't care for the man much."

"I don't care for anyone who tries to pressure us into rushing through a case to keep the family name clean."

"I'd say that seems typical of a Colton, if I hadn't met Trey."

She gave him an odd look he couldn't put a name to. But then she went back to her original point.

"One of the things he mentioned in passing was that staff and employees were not allowed to frequent the guest areas on their time off."

He caught her meaning and looked back at the screen. "And him?"

"That," she said, gesturing at the enlarged and rather blurry image, "is Curtis Shruggs."

"Rings a bell," he said, but his brow furrowed as he tried to place the name.

"He's the director of personnel at The Lodge."

"Oh?" His brows rose, and he leaned in for a closer look. "And who would know personnel policy better than the personnel director," he said slowly.

"Exactly."

She started the video again. But now she ran it slowly forward, and he quickly guessed she wanted to see exactly how long The Lodge's director of personnel had lingered in the off-limits hotel bar. They watched as the man gradually emptied the glass before him.

Stefan looked at the time stamp at the bottom of the image. They were at ten minutes before Bianca would exit that elevator. In the next moment Shruggs's head moved, as if to look at something on the table. At this magnification the image was very blurry, but there was a small, different-colored shape there.

And then he got up. Picked up the object and slid it into a pocket. Upon closer examination, Stefan would swear it was a cell phone. The entire action was clear, familiar, even if the image wasn't. And then the man headed farther back into the bar and vanished into the shadows where the camera didn't—couldn't—reach. The man he supposed women would think handsome, if they went for the salt-and-pepper-hair look.

Daria paused the video once more. The time glowed at the bottom of the screen. She looked at Stefan.

"That could have been a text coming in. He could have been going to meet her."

"And he went out the back, through the employee door. Where the camera wouldn't catch him if he met someone."

"And he would likely know that. He could have told her to meet him there."

Stefan let out a breath. "That's a lot of hypotheticals."

"I know. We still need to go back and see if there's anything on the lobby video earlier of them connecting."

"That should only take the rest of the night," Stefan muttered. Then the reality of his new life snapped at him, and he was reminded yet again that was no longer an option for him. He had to get home to his son.

"There's more," Daria said, turning her gaze from the video to him. He saw in those lovely, golden-brown eyes a spark of something beyond excitement; she was into this hunt just as much as he was.

"I interviewed him, back when this started. He never said anything about even being in the hotel, let alone the bar, the night Bianca disappeared."

He frowned. "But he had to know we'd be going over the video surveillance. Although, if you hadn't recognized him, I never would have noticed him, back in the shadows like that."

"Maybe that's what he was counting on."

Slowly, Stefan nodded. "There's at least a chance he saw Bianca that night."

"And he didn't even mention that he'd been there. Maybe he's not the killer, but that alone is worth pursuing."

"Indeed it is. Even if he's just one of those people who thinks the rules don't apply to him. Since he's the director of personnel, he could think he's above such things. Or maybe he was checking up on some other employee who might be the exception to the rule."

"Yes. But there's one more thing."

"What?" he asked, knowing from the undertone in her voice that it had to be something important.

"Curtis Shruggs," she said, "has very, very blue eyes."

Chapter Nine

"That was a great catch," Stefan said after they'd gone over it again. "I don't think I would have noticed that anytime soon."

"Thanks. I'm just sorry I didn't see it until now."

They screen grabbed an image from the video, because she wanted proof in case Shruggs tried to deny he'd been there. Of course he could still negate that this was him—it wasn't the clearest image ever—but Stefan had also sent a copy to the Bureau's tech guys, who would clean it up and sharpen the image.

"Back in the corner, in the shadows like that, it's amazing you recognized him at all," Stefan said, still sounding admiring, which warmed her in ways she couldn't afford to think about right now.

"Makes me wonder if he knows perfectly well that table's half-hidden from the cameras."

"It does, doesn't it?" Stefan glanced at his watch and grimaced. "I'm sorry, I have to get home."

Daria glanced at her own watch; she'd gotten so immersed in the time ticking by slowly on the screen's images that she'd lost track of the time in the real world. And when she saw it was nearly ten, she was surprised.

"Of course you do. Sam's probably worried."

Stefan gave her a sideways look. "I don't think we've come quite that far yet, that he'd be worried about me."

She arched a brow at him. "I meant worried you might have changed your mind about his new furniture," she said, making her tone purposely light and teasing.

"Now that," Stefan said with a wry smile, "I could believe."

She studied him for a moment, wondering if it was prudent to say what had just occurred to her. It truly wasn't any of her business. But she decided it was important enough that she should.

"Have you thought any more about legal arrangements for him?"

"You mean getting full custody?" He looked puzzled, no doubt since they'd already talked about that. "I will, now that I have…some hope this will work. Thanks to you."

She smiled at that, but shook her head. And her tone was very serious when she said, "I meant what would happen with him right now, if something happened to you."

It was grim, yes, but in their line of work, a reality they both lived with every day. "It's handled," he said, rather gruffly. "A trust, and guardians."

She merely nodded, ignoring his tone. "I figured it would be. You would see to his welfare, no matter how things are between you."

"Was that a character assessment, or what?"

It had been, she realized. And her certainty of it, that this was a man who saw to his own no matter what, only added to her surprise. "Did you need one?" she countered.

"Sometimes. Lately, anyway."

The gruffness had vanished, and what she heard was a man weary of trying to deal with two of the biggest things the world could have handed him—this case and the full, lone responsibility for his son.

"You'll make it," she assured him. "Both of you. Just remember how long it took you to adjust when he was first born."

"I'm not sure I did," he muttered.

"You're not sure of anything regarding Sam right now. And that can't be easy for a guy who's usually so decisive."

Again the sideways look. "More character assessment?"

"That," she said pointedly, "was from firsthand observation." She grinned at him then, trying to lighten the mood. "Besides, your reputation did precede you, you know."

He went very still, and for a moment he just stared at her. She wondered what she could have said that had apparently hit so hard.

"I'd better get home," he finally muttered. Then, after a sharp shake of his head, as if he were trying to rid himself of something, he added, "The Lodge in the morning?"

She nodded. "I'll go over what we have on Shruggs again tonight. He probably won't even be there on a Saturday, but I want to talk to the staff about his habits. They'd likely know if he violates the order they have to live by, and maybe be miffed enough to say so. But you don't need to come along." At his puzzled look, she added, "Sam has a playdate tomorrow, remember?"

"Oh. Yeah. But that's afternoon. And I have the sitter already set anyway."

"All right, then."

Then he asked, "How far do you have to drive?"

"Home?" She realized it had never yet come up. "I'm just outside town, so not too far."

"So you'll be okay getting there? With the snow?"

"I've learned to deal. Just because I don't like it doesn't mean I don't respect it," she said, surprised anew. And wary of the fact that what had popped into her head at his question was her own earlier thought—that this man would see to his own. No matter what.

"Drive carefully."

"You, too. Get home to your son." His expression changed, tightened slightly, and she added hastily, "Sam would love my place. The backyard, at least. It's huge. He and that dog he wants could play for hours out there."

"Better than my little concrete patio, huh?"

He didn't sound offended, so she answered truthfully. "From a five-year-old boy's point of view? Yes. There's even a little tree house—well, more of a platform, really—in an old mountain mahogany."

He drew back slightly, but was smiling. "You have a tree house?"

"I've even been known to use it on a nice day. Which," she added rather sourly, "would exclude today."

"Better not tell Sam—he'll be showing up."

"He'd be welcome to visit," she said.

"He'd like that."

And you?

Daria groaned inwardly at her instant thought. This man was off-limits for so many reasons, but she seemed to keep forgetting them. Especially when they were working together. It was just proximity, that's all. And when this case was finally over, that would end and so would these crazy feelings.

Her voice a little brisk, she said, "I'll secure everything here. You get going."

"All right."

"Tell Sam hi for me."

"Will do. It'll please him."

She managed a smile but didn't trust herself to say anything more.

When he'd gone, she shut down, considered taking the laptop home and decided she'd had quite enough of watching video for the moment, and locked it up. She stowed away all the paper files, then gathered up her personal things. Flipping out the lights, she turned the lock on the door and stepped out into the hall. As she pulled the door closed, she heard footsteps approaching, looked and saw Keith Parker coming toward her. He was working the night watch this month, so he had to be coming, not going.

"Hey," he said when he spotted her. "How goes it on the case of the century?"

"Too slow, of course," she answered.

"You're keeping some late hours."

"And early," she said wryly.

"I'm glad Trey picked you, not me," he joked.

She laughed. "You're better off, trust me."

He smiled as they parted. That smile that was as warm as ever. She smiled back, even as it struck her that if she'd felt a fraction of the spark she felt around Stefan Roberts with Keith, they'd still be dating. Or more.

She thought about that as she made her way to the door that led out to the employee parking area. She usually tried to avoid thinking about this particular subject, but the only thing that was powerful enough to replace it was this case, and she knew she needed to give that a rest. She had come very close to frying every circuit tonight, with all that video.

But it had paid off, in the end. The Shruggs lead might come to nothing, but at least it was a shot, something they hadn't had in far too long. She had been living and breathing this evil for ten months now. She could barely remember her life before this, before Trey had entrusted her with this case that could likely affect him in a personal and permanent way. Trey, who had been through his own share of crap and yet had still teased her about having to fight even harder than he did; she wasn't just biracial, she was also a woman. But if they didn't break this case soon, Trey might lose the election. She didn't think she could bear that.

And now she was at the third thing occupying so much of her mind, and there was nothing she could do about it except what she was already doing—working as hard as she could on the case.

When you're not having inappropriate feelings about a certain FBI agent...

"Full circle," she muttered to herself as she reached the back door and pushed it open.

For an instant she was startled. She'd almost forgotten about the snow. But it was still coming down, although not as fast as before. There were a couple of inches on the ground, and she could see trails of dark footprints where people had walked to and from their parked vehicles.

She was *not* ready for this. Couldn't it have waited until next month, when it would have at least fit her idea of Christmas weather? She hadn't even worn her sheep-skin-lined boots, so her feet were going to be freezing by the time she got to her car. And it would take a while for anything but cold air to come out the heater vents.

Spoiled California girl. Just get it done.

Taking a deep breath, she stepped outside.

Chapter Ten

The snow had stopped overnight at a lovely three or so inches. Just enough to make everything look white and pristine, Stefan thought, without causing a ton of problems. Much better than the nearly foot and a half most of Illinois had gotten in November a couple of years or so before he'd transferred here.

"Thanks for driving," Daria said as they headed for The Lodge.

"This is nothing," he replied, gesturing at the small, neatly plowed piles by the roadside. They had this snow thing down to a science in Roaring Springs. They probably had to, being that all the great skiing conditions in the world were of no use if people couldn't get there. And the kind of clientele they catered to would likely have little patience with unnecessary delays. "Piece of cake," he added.

"That's why you're driving, because you can say that," Daria said with an arched brow. Which drew his attention to her eyes, of course. They really were an amazing color, the highlights almost like a piece of amber he'd seen in a wealthy man's collection once. And he wondered yet again why some lucky guy hadn't scooped her up yet. What was wrong with these Coloradans, that they let a woman like Daria stay foot-loose? Or was it her choice? That made more sense to him, because he couldn't imagine guys were not lin-ing up at her door.

He forced his attention back to the road ahead; slight or not, it was still snowy, they were climbing Pine Peak and he should be paying more attention. No matter how hard it was with her next to him in the car.

Professional, Roberts. Just keep it professional.

"Was Sam excited about this afternoon?"

"Very excited." *Eventually.*

The boy wasn't, at first. He was back to sulking, glar-ing at Stefan and telling him he didn't want to go. The magic turnaround was when he found out they were friends of Daria's and that she had arranged it.

They're friends of hers?

Yes.

Oh. I guess I'll go, then.

Stefan had added something about not getting into trouble because it would reflect on Daria, but he kind of doubted the five-year-old got it.

And then of course there was the rest…

"I'm glad," Daria said.

"You may not be," he said dryly. "He assumed you were going with us, to introduce us."

"Oh."

She frowned, and for a moment he figured he was going to have to explain to Sam why she wasn't going with them. Then, slowly, she nodded, and when she spoke he realized she'd only been trying to work through Sam's thought process.

"Okay, I get it—strange place, strange family, kids

he doesn't know… I can see that he'd want a familiar face there. At least at first."

As they reached a stoplight and he halted the car, he took the chance to look at her. "Does that mean… you will?"

"What do you think?"

He blinked. *Me? I think you should go with us. I think you should always go with us.*

The shock of that thought rendered him speechless. He stared at her. Afraid to open his mouth for fear he'd look like a landed fish.

"I mean," Daria explained as if he hadn't understood, "I can see it would be easier for him, but would it be better in the long run to have him do it on his own? Or do you think it's too soon for that?"

Sam. She was thinking of what would be best for Sam. That touched him somehow, yet at the same time he was wrestling with the remnants of that unexpected thought. It took him a moment to regroup, but then the light changed and it gave him an excuse to look away.

And he felt like two kinds of coward when he said, "Right now I think easier would be better if you came along."

While that was true, it was so far from the complete truth that he winced inwardly. *Easier for who?*

He'd always thought of himself as a pretty up-front kind of guy personally, with the only subterfuge he did related to his work. But right now he was suddenly holding more back than he was saying, and it was an uncomfortable feeling.

"All right."

Was that all right she understood, all right she agreed

or all right she would come? And why the hell did it matter so much?

Stefan focused more than he needed to as they approached the massive, covered entrance to The Lodge, with its stone pillars and colorful slate surface, free of any snow. He pulled to a halt just under the rough-timbered, beamed roof, out of the way of traffic, then turned to look at Daria again. "Does that mean you'll come?" he asked bluntly.

She looked surprised. "Of course, if you think it's best."

He wasn't sure that shouldn't be the other way around, since she was clearly much better at this than he was. But it didn't really matter—what mattered was that she would be there.

For Sam's sake, of course.

STEFAN SEEMED A bit scattered this morning, but Daria supposed every morning was like that for him now. Working nearly every day, weekend or no, he hadn't had anywhere near the time off he needed to settle in with his son. If he hadn't already been knee-deep in this case by the time Sam had arrived, it would have been reason enough for them to assign someone else. But Stefan had actually been involved indirectly ever since he'd fielded a random call from Detective Kastor at RSPD, asking for the name of a surveillance expert, and had heard the rumblings that they were possibly dealing with multiple murders.

Of course, the avalanche that had uncovered the bodies and given their serial killer his moniker hadn't happened until months later, but Stefan had immediately connected things and so was elected to be the agent to get involved when Trey had made the request. And then his own life had been upended by the unexpected arrival of his son. When it came down to it, Daria was amazed he was as focused as he had managed to be so far.

Stefan cleared the vehicle with the head valet, who either let nothing ruffle him or had grown used to having law enforcement show up over the last ten-plus months. Daria watched as a low-slung Italian sports car pulled up, the driver apparently giving a long string of instructions before he let the valet take the vehicle. One day she'd like to ask the guy what the craziest request he'd ever gotten was, but this was hardly the time.

She noticed Stefan looking up at the rather intricate structure of huge timber beams that held up the portico roof. When he caught her watching him with curiosity, he shrugged.

"My dad's a builder," he explained. "He'd love to see this."

"Then you'll have to bring him here when they visit."

He looked at her then, and smiled. "Yes," he said. "I called them this morning. They never hesitated."

She couldn't help it—she grinned at him. "I knew it. Just from the way you described them."

He looked a tad sheepish. "Dad's finishing up a project, but they'll be here by the end of next week. And stay for Thanksgiving, even."

"Well, if this keeps up, that'll be a shock," she said, gesturing at the snow.

"Illinois," he reminded her, but then he grimaced. "God help me, my dad wants to learn to ski."

Daria's grin widened. "And your mom?"

His mouth twitched. "Knowing her, she'll want to snowboard." She laughed in delight at that. He stopped just inside the big wood-and-glass doors and turned to face her. "Mom even said if Dad couldn't get clear, she'd come. And they never go anywhere without each other."

"Obviously their son and grandson are worth an exception," she said, both amused and touched by the wonder in his voice.

"Yeah," he murmured, still sounding a bit amazed. "I...um...thanks."

"Sometimes it's hard to see the path when you're in the middle of chaos," she told him with a smile as they went in and crossed the lobby, so familiar from the hours of video, and yet so different in person from the ground level.

And different now than it had been even last year; the place was practically empty. Not many clamoring to visit or vacation here when there was a serial killer on the loose. If they didn't wrap this up soon, not only could more women be killed, but the economic base of Roaring Springs might never recover. She had already wondered if the name of the town was going to be forever linked to that Avalanche Killer moniker.

But now she found herself, perhaps because of the fewer people milling about, noticing the building itself more than she usually did. Then, curiously, she asked Stefan, "What does your dad build?"

"Houses, mostly, and the occasional small commercial project. Nothing like this," he said, gesturing around at The Lodge. "He'll love to see it, though."

"It is pretty impressive."

"Yes. And he'll see that. But he'll also think of how many people were employed for how long, how many other businesses got paid along the way." At her quirked brow, he shrugged. "He's a big-picture kind of guy. He likes seeing how a big project like this plays out."

"I like how you sound when you speak of him," she said, meaning it.

"He's my hero," Stefan admitted. "I mean, I went through the usual rebellion stuff when I was in college, figuring I'd learned to be smarter than this guy who had made a solid living and supported a family of six for twenty-five years. Took me until Sam was born to get that completely out of my system and see the real worth of who he was and what he'd done."

By now he was reaching for the door to the hallway that led to the administrative offices of The Lodge. Impulsively Daria reached out and touched his arm. She was startled when he flinched as if burned, but after a moment he only turned to look at her.

"You really want to thank me?" she asked. For an instant something flared in his eyes. She felt a responding flush of warmth and tried not to acknowledge what it was. "Then bring your folks here one night after they arrive. Buy them dinner at the steak house, and tell your father word for word what you just said."

His eyes changed then, to radiating a different kind of heat. "That is a great idea. And I will do it. But how does that thank you?"

"Because I never had that chance," she said softly.

She'd never spoken about her adoptive family for fear she would let something slip about the secret she'd kept since she'd come to Roaring Springs. Being a former president's adopted daughter was complicated, but here amid a ton of other Coltons, it would be even more so. What was it about this family? They couldn't seem to quietly blend into the fabric of any place they landed.

But this somehow seemed too important for her to keep to herself. For Stefan, anyway. And he already knew she didn't know who her biological father was—she'd told him when he'd agreed to try and trace what had happened to her mother. The results hadn't been what she'd hoped for, but they had been what she'd expected. And although she'd thanked him profusely at the time, she had never quite felt as if she'd thanked him enough. But now, maybe she'd at least made a payment.

As she'd expected, Curtis Shruggs was not in his office on this Saturday morning. What she hadn't expected was when his assistant, a middle-aged woman who managed to look both efficient and harried at the same time, told them he usually was around on the weekends, but he'd been out for the last three days with the flu. In the process, Shelly Bates showed herself to be one of those who, with an upward inflection at the end of her sentences, seemed to make every statement a question. Daria knew it was just a vocal tic some people had, but usually it was in people young enough to be uncertain about most things. Before they became positive about everything, she thought, stifling a smile.

"He doesn't answer his phone or texts, which worried me, so I went by his place to check on him, but he wasn't there at all? It's so unlike him?" the woman said, sounding anxious.

"So he's a dedicated-to-his-job sort of guy?" Daria asked.

Shelly nodded. "He never even takes a real vacation, just some long weekends or a few days here and there, you know? Sometimes even just a few hours now and—"

"We'll need those dates," Stefan said.

The woman gave him a rather shy but appreciative look. But she still managed to look surprised. "For Mr. Shruggs?"

"Well, we need to include him, of course, to be thorough," Daria interjected quickly, sounding almost dismissive of the idea of including the man, "But what we really need are those records on The Lodge personnel, staff, management, everyone, dating back to January."

Stefan glanced at her, then gave the barest nod, agreeing that there was no point in doing anything that might give Shruggs a heads-up. Best to keep him thinking they were looking at everyone for as long as they could.

"I thought you had all that?" the woman asked.

"I believe the police department does, but that was before the FBI was called in," Stefan explained with a charming wink Daria had no doubt got him just about anywhere he wanted to go with any breathing woman. "Sorry to put you to work again, but as long as we're here anyway, it would really help."

"Oh, of course!" For the first time it wasn't a question. "Do you want the paper schedules, too?" She sounded apologetic. "We do post them on the bulletin board, so if any of the staff make switches among themselves, there's a record."

"Then yes, we'll need those, too," Daria said.

"It must be tough," Stefan mused sympathetically, smiling at the woman, "working for a guy who ignores his own rules."

Shelly blinked. "I...well, he is the boss? And he can be kind of...intimidating, sometimes, you know?"

"Still," Stefan said. "I had a boss once who demanded no one make personal phone calls, but he went ahead and did it all the time. Kind of like Mr. Shruggs hanging out in the hotel bar when you're not allowed to."

Daria saw a faint tinge of color rise in the woman's cheeks. But Stefan kept giving her that sympathetic look and captivating smile, and after a moment she gave in.

"We do talk about it, sometimes, that he goes in there. But we figured he was just kind of lonely, and maybe didn't want to go home to an empty house, you know?"

"You think he's lonely?" Daria asked.

The woman shrugged. "It's just…a feeling, I guess? He's always nice here at work, very professional, but—"

"Professional except for this?" Stefan asked. She nodded. He gave her an even wider smile. "He's lucky he has you to count on to keep things going when he's gone. So if you could get us those schedules, we'll let you get back to it."

The woman truly blushed this time.

"Well, you flustered her right into hurrying that through," Daria said with a smirk as the woman instantly went to do as he'd asked.

"And you had the presence of mind to not make it look like we were zeroing in on Shruggs." He seemed to be looking at her rather intently when he said, "We make a good team."

They did, investigatively. Together, they were able to bounce ideas off each other without fear that the other would find them without merit or even stupid. He saw things she hadn't, and vice versa. And they were in tune; he was quick to pick up on where she was going, and she often got to what he was thinking before he had to tell her.

They were a good team.

And professionally was all he meant, she told herself sternly.

Chapter Eleven

Stefan saw it immediately, but he didn't say anything. He wanted to be sure, and so he silently let Daria go over the data provided by Ms. Bates as he drove them back to the office. She was interrupted only by a text, which she read and frowned over, before putting her phone away again.

"Still nothing on the newest missing girl," she said. "I asked them to keep us updated."

He nodded. "What's your feel on that? When does she become ours?"

"Hopefully never. But as for a time element, since she'd already been missing a week, I'd say not much longer."

"Agreed."

They were pulling into the secured parking lot behind the sheriff's office when she released a long sigh.

"Do those dates he was away match as closely as I think they do?" he asked quietly.

"Yes." She gave a shake of her head. "And those that don't match are the ones where we aren't sure exactly when those girls vanished."

"Under these circumstances," he said flatly, "that should be enough to buy us a warrant to search his place."

"I'll call Trey. Just for the judge on call's name. I need to update him anyway." She pulled out her phone again, and he saw her notice the time on the lock screen. "We need to go get Sam and head to Fiona's."

"I...yes."

"He'll do fine, Stefan. Her boys are great, and they'll welcome him. And some good rough-and-tumble time might be just what he needs to get some of that anger and uncertainty out of his system."

"If it accomplishes that, it'll be a miracle," he deadpanned.

"If it does, maybe that means you need to keep him too worn-out physically to have the energy to stay mad."

"Maybe I'll start him running marathons."

When Daria's gaze narrowed, he had to suppress a teasing smile. He didn't quite succeed. "Will you be running with him?" she asked, just a shade too innocently.

He went suddenly still, the bit of humor vanishing as the ugly memories connected. "I've run one," he said quietly.

"Oh?"

"Boston, 2014."

He saw the change in her, in her demeanor and in those golden eyes as she understood immediately the significance of the date: the year after the bombing.

"A good choice," she said softly.

He nodded, acknowledging her understanding. "Yes. It was."

For a moment they just looked at each other, not as agent and deputy, not even as man and woman, but as warriors in a battle that never seemed to end. They were part of that wall between the innocent and the ugliness, and he knew instinctively that Daria Bloom would stand, as would he. No matter the insanity from the outside, or even from within, they at least would stand.

She called Trey up on her contact list. And smiled as she said, "He told me he assigned me a unique ring on his phone, but he won't tell me what it is."

He smiled back at that, and her lightening of the mood. He thought of suggesting it was probably something sexy, but that seemed wrong after the moment they'd just shared.

"He said it's so he won't inadvertently dodge me when he's avoiding the media. They're hounding him more and more as the election gets closer. Even the governor's on his case about it, because it makes the whole state look bad."

"Sucks," Stefan said succinctly.

"Yes. I feel so bad for him—he's such a good man."

"Seems he's taking most of the heat for what's happening, even though Roaring Springs itself isn't his responsibility," he said.

"Exactly. But civilians don't care about jurisdiction—they just want this over. Not that I blame them, but still, it doesn't seem fair when the rest of the county that is his responsibility is calm, quiet and peaceful, with the lowest crime rate it's had in years."

"You should do an ad for him," Stefan said. "Except I'm not sure anybody who saw it and didn't know you would believe you were a deputy."

"And why not?" she demanded.

"They'd think you were some actress they hired because of your looks." When she stared at him as if she wasn't sure what he'd meant by the compliment, he tried to save face. "Not their fault. They'd only see the sur-face—they wouldn't know how good a cop you are."

"Oh." He thought he saw a tinge of pink in her cheeks, but he wasn't sure. And then she was making the call, putting it on speakerphone.

Trey Colton answered almost immediately. And was obviously relieved to hear that they had a lead, at least. He didn't ask for anything more; when he'd turned this case over to Daria, he'd meant it. Because he was an honest man, Stefan thought. This was one vote—maybe the only one in recent memory—he would cast with-out qualm.

When Daria asked about the judge for a possible search warrant, Trey answered quickly. "Judge Cruz is on call this weekend. He's been following the case, so he won't slow you down. I can get you his number—"

"No, I'll find it," she told him. "We haven't started on the affidavits yet. Besides, I want to be able to swear all you gave me was a name."

"Copy that," Trey said, sourly enough that even Ste-fan noticed. "And now, lucky me, I have a meeting with Mayor Dylan."

Stefan raised a brow at her when she ended the call. "It's wearing on him. The case, the election…"

"It's amazing he's still upright. Says a lot about him." She sighed. "I'm so glad he has Aisha now. She helps him stay level."

By the time they reached The Lodge gates, she had the judge's number, but there was no point in making the call until they had the paperwork done, or at least their reasoning outlined.

"How fast do we need to move on this, do you think?" he asked.

"My instinct is to jump instantly, because it's the first small break in a long time, but in reality I don't know."

"I don't think we tipped Shruggs—you took care of that nicely. But…"

"But it might be easier to search his premises without him there," she countered.

"True."

"Let's get Sam over to Fiona's," she suggested. "And after we get him settled, we can drive by Shruggs's place for a building description, then we can go to the office and get going on the paperwork while we call the judge."

"Agreed. We can have a plain clothes meet us at Shruggs's place, watch for him and sit on it until we get back with the warrant."

Daria nodded. "Good idea. And have them stay either way, keep an eye on him. And if he is there, we'll want more backup. If he's our guy…"

"He's not going to come quietly," Stefan concurred. "Not with all this hanging over his head."

They made the necessary arrangements, then headed back to Stefan's car. On the way, he made a call to the sitter to tell her they were coming and to make sure Sam was ready.

He grimaced as he ended the call.

"Problem?" Daria asked.

"No. She just said Sam didn't want to get ready."

"I thought he was excited about going," she said.

"He was. Is. She said he didn't want to get ready because he thought we weren't coming. That he holed up in his room after he told her I hated him." He sighed. "I swear, sometimes I think he's actually scared of me."

"Of course he is. You're so much bigger than he is,

and he doesn't really know you. Maybe try getting down on his level a bit more."

Something clicked almost audibly in his brain, a memory of days back in training when they'd covered how to deal with children. He hadn't had to use that often in his career, and so it had never occurred to him to use the techniques—such as what Daria had suggested, crouching down to their level—on his own son. That alone told him how thrown he'd been by this whole thing.

He shook his head, as much at himself as at his son. "Where'd he get the idea we weren't coming?"

"That sounds like a kid who's been let down too often."

"Yeah."

"Well, you'll just have to make sure you don't let him down," she said softly. "And if you ever have to, then you'd better make it up to him."

"And just how do I do that?"

She gave him a sideways look and a teasing smile that did weird things to his pulse. Which was crazy—it was just a smile. "I know someone who has a cabin, out of the reach of cell and internet."

"I'm afraid he'd consider that cruel and unusual punishment."

"To actually have to talk to and get to know his father? Perhaps. But it might be worth it."

She might have a point. Although he had to admit when he thought of retreating to a remote, private cabin with no interruptions, it was Daria who immediately came to mind as a companion. Which in turn made him feel guilty, because he needed to get to know his son as much as the other way around.

Damn, things had gotten deep and murky in a hurry. One day he was cruising along thinking life was pretty good, and the next he was in the middle of dealing with a serial killer and a five-year-old, and he wasn't sure the kid wasn't the worst of it. He knew how to go after a killer, but his son too often had him at an utter loss.

As for Daria, he wasn't at a loss there. He knew exactly what he wanted.

He also knew he couldn't have it.

Chapter Twelve

"Daria!"

Sam's happy cry did things to her insides. And as he ran across Stefan's sleek, rather cold living room, clunking a bit in snow boots, she could see his father in the shape of his face, his nose, even the way he tilted his head to look at her. She was willing to bet that in about ten years, the resemblance would be even more obvious, as Sam proceeded on the journey from boy to man.

"Hey, kiddo, you ready for this?" she asked as he skidded to a stop before her. "It's cold out there."

"Aw, there's not that much snow here."

"Not enough to build a snowman?"

"Maybe a snow head."

She laughed, and he grinned, looking delighted. "Well, you might find a bit more at the Alvarezes'," she said. "They've got a yard almost as big as mine, so you've got a lot more room to gather it from."

Sam gave her another of those head-tilted looks. "You have a big yard?"

"Huge. Too huge sometimes." She leaned down and whispered conspiratorially, "You could get lost out there and have to climb up to my tree house to see your way back."

Sam's eyes widened to huge, dark saucers. "You have a tree house?"

"Sort of. It doesn't have walls or a roof, so it's not the best when it's snowing, but when it's nice you can sit up there."

"You should put walls and a roof on!"

"I'm not sure the tree's big enough for that. But I can guarantee you'll have a full-on fort to play in today. Oh, and I understand there'll be sledding."

Sam lit up. "Really?"

"They've got a little hill in back, just steep enough to really get going. Their dad cleared a nice path for them, too, so no crashes." Sam looked almost disappointed and Daria barely managed not to laugh. "Cool boots, by the way," she added. The boy grinned and stuck a foot out. "Do you have a change of clothes, for when you get all wet in the snow? Especially warm socks?"

Sam's brow furrowed. "I didn't think of that."

"Got something to stuff stuff in?" she asked, and he grinned yet again at her words.

"I've got my backpack," he said and whirled to run and get it.

Stefan had been quiet throughout their exchange, just watching. "What?" she asked, when he just looked at her.

"I didn't think of extra clothes, either," he said. Then, with a shake of his head, "You're amazing with him."

"I just talk to him."

His mouth quirked. "Then maybe it's just that I'm so bad with him."

"You're probably just feeling awkward, still. It hasn't been that long, and you haven't had time with him, with this case."

"Still making excuses for me?" he asked.

"Maybe. You certainly don't seem inclined to."

"My family wasn't big on excuses for not doing what you needed to do."

"And you had to do it right the first time, every time? And fast?"

His brow furrowed. "No. You just had to keep honestly trying."

She said nothing, just looked at him with raised brows. And after a moment he let out a wry chuckle. "All right, all right. Point taken."

"Have you always been good at everything you've ever tried?"

He laughed. "Hardly. You don't ever want to hear me try and play music."

"Sports?"

"Lousy at football, good at baseball, liked tennis."

She leaned back a little, registering again his considerable height. "I'll bet you have a smashing serve."

"Pretty rusty now," he admitted, and she liked that he didn't deny it.

"The Chateau has some good tennis courts. Maybe you should sharpen that up when the weather's better."

He gave her an assessing look. "Know anyone who could help me get that rust off?"

"I might," she said rather airily as Sam ran back, carrying his school backpack by one strap. She could see the sleeve of a shirt hanging out where it wasn't zipped all the way closed.

"Where's your school stuff?" Stefan asked.

"I'll put it back later," Sam said, sounding a bit defensive.

"I wasn't criticizing, son," Stefan said mildly, "just wondering if that big bed was actually helpful for once."

Sam looked surprised. "Yeah, maybe. That's where I dumped it."

"Get your jacket on, then, and let's get this adventure started."

Sam stared at his father. "Adventure?"

"Sure," Stefan said. "What's an adventure except something exciting you've never done before?"

Pleasure dawned on Sam's young face. "Yeah!" The boy ran to grab up the heavy jacket that lay across the back of the tailored gray couch.

"You're getting the hang of it," Daria said softly.

He looked at her. "I've been watching an expert."

They heard a slight thump and looked to see Sam wrestling with trying to get his jacket on without putting down the backpack. Stefan started to take a step toward him, but Daria stopped him.

"Let him figure it out," she whispered. "Aren't you curious to see how he does it?"

He didn't speak but stayed put as they watched Sam stop, appear to be thinking for a moment. Then the boy set down the backpack, untangled his jacket from it, put it on and then picked up the pack again.

"Thanks," Stefan whispered back to her as his son turned around.

"Acknowledgment might be in order," she suggested.

Stefan nodded and shot her an appreciative grin that gave her an entirely new feeling inside. "Nice job," he called out to Sam.

Again the boy look surprised, but he did smile.

"Ready?" Daria asked.

Sam nodded enthusiastically, and they were off. And as the child scrambled into the back seat of the car, Stefan startled her by reaching out to take her hand and squeeze it.

"Thank you," he said again, rather fervently.

"My pleasure," she returned without thinking. Then had to look away to hide the evidence of what had slammed into her mind at the words.

STEFAN WOULD GIVE anything to know what had just gone through Daria's mind, but he didn't dwell on it. He didn't dare; his own mind was already skittering far too often into that dangerous territory.

Besides, for the first time he felt…hopeful that he and Sam would reach some kind of accord. It seemed so simple when Daria did it, so obvious, yet he couldn't deny it worked. He'd even gotten a smile out of the boy with the simple praise she'd suggested.

"So, living here might not be so bad after all, huh?" she said to the boy in back.

"Maybe."

"Not the best way to come here, though."

"You mean 'cause my mom sent me away."

It wasn't a question, and the flat, carefully emotionless tone his son said it in dug at his gut. He was going to have words with Leah one of these days, but not until he thought he had at least a chance of doing it calmly.

"My mother gave me up, too," Daria said softly.

"She did?" Sam sounded astonished. "Why?"

"She was sick and couldn't take care of me."

"Oh. My mom's not sick."

"That," she said rather sourly, "is still up for debate."

Stefan managed not to let out a sharp laugh, but she was right; Leah had to be a certain kind of sick to just kick her son out of her life like this.

"She just doesn't want me." The boy's voice dropped to a pained whisper, but he still heard the words. "He doesn't, either."

In the first moment after Sam said it, Stefan assumed his son had meant Leah's fiancé. But then Daria flicked a glance at him, and he realized with a bit more of that roiling guilt that Sam had meant him.

Daria didn't, as he'd half expected, deny the boy's words. Instead she said quietly, "You know how I felt, after a while, after my mom gave me up?"

"How?"

Sam's voice was so tiny, so scared that Stefan's stomach knotted.

"I felt like nobody would ever want me. And that was the scariest time of my life."

"Yeah." Stefan nearly pulled the car over, so strong was the urge to grab his son and hold him. But Daria, as usual, had gotten the boy talking better than he ever had, so he stifled the urge.

"But Sam," she said, "there's a big difference between having to get used to a big change in your life, especially when it happens without warning, and not wanting that change."

"Huh?"

"I'm saying when things change so much, so fast, it takes time to get used to it. That doesn't mean you don't want the change."

There was a moment of silence before Daria laughed lightly. "Too complex, huh? Okay, it would be like...if you got a dog without knowing you were getting one ahead of time. You'd need dog stuff, a bed, toys, a collar and leash, right?" At his nod, she went on to say, "And then all of a sudden you'd have someone else to worry about, to keep safe and protect, and you'd have to learn what he likes and doesn't like, and he'd have to learn about you the same way."

"Oh. That's a lot."

"Yes. And it would be confusing, but it wouldn't mean you don't want each other."

"Oh," Sam repeated, and now he sounded thoughtful. And a lot less scared.

And once more, Stefan found himself appreciating the amazing woman fate had partnered him with on this case. And denying the other thoughts that word *partner* kicked off in his head. *It's the proximity, that's all. We have to work closely together—can't avoid it. It's natural, but controllable.*

He just wished he was more convinced of that last part.

He wasn't sure what he'd been expecting, but the house they pulled up to wasn't it. Of course, he'd grown up amid tall city buildings and nearby houses built on tiny lots. He should have realized that when Daria said they had lots of room, it meant…well, lots of room.

Stefan also was a bit startled when Fiona Alvarez came to the door. He somehow hadn't envisioned a petite, almost tiny woman with strawberry blonde hair and bright green eyes.

He was also surprised when the first thing she did was cry out in exaggerated happiness, "Sam! My boys are so excited to meet you! Come on in."

Sam looked startled, too, but then shyly pleased. They stepped inside. Daria exchanged a hug with her friend, then introduced him to her.

"We met online years ago," Fiona explained. "And

when Daria was thinking about moving, I pestered her unmercifully to come here."

"For which I will be forever thankful," Daria said with a wide smile.

"And which reminds me, Stefan, we should exchange phone numbers, just in case. That should guarantee we won't need them."

He nodded and resisted even the thought of saying that she could just call or text Daria. Because it wasn't like they were together 24/7. And that made him feel... he didn't even have a word for how that made him feel.

"Might as well keep the jacket on," Fiona said to Sam. "Everybody's already outside." She stepped back and looked at the boy assessingly. "My, but you're tall. It makes you look much older."

The boy looked pleased at that, too.

"Slipper is just going to love you," Fiona told him.

"Slipper?"

"Our dog. He's named that because as a puppy he was always chewing on everyone's slippers."

Sam's eyes widened even more. "You have a dog?"

"Oh, did I forget to mention that?" Daria said with a thoughtfulness exaggerated enough to tell Stefan she'd known exactly what she was doing.

Sam was smiling so widely now Stefan barely recognized him as the same sullen, withdrawn child who had gotten off that airplane, tagged like a piece of luggage. He felt a jab of renewed anger that Leah had done that, hadn't even cared enough to bring him here herself, but he quashed it. It was easier now, he realized, now that he'd seen the boy stirring out of that brittle shell since Daria had stepped in. He knew he hadn't done nearly enough to stay in his son's life, but he would make up for that now.

While Fiona went to put on a jacket and snow boots, Stefan looked around the house. It was nicely furnished, but there were toys scattered about, and the big, cushy-looking sofa simply invited a kid to jump onto it. There was an air of comfort, warmth and...solidity, he thought.

"I see what you mean," he murmured to Daria.

"It's a very welcoming house," she said. "To match the owners."

He nodded. He could see that. It wasn't his taste, exactly, but then when it came down to it, neither was his place. That had been a decorator's taste, or at least their idea of what a newly divorced guy should have. He had this vague memory now of the guy asking him about his son, and he'd brushed it off, saying he'd be going back to Illinois to visit, not the other way around, so not to worry about it.

Talk about tempting fate...

"Come on," Fiona said. "Come see the fort and meet Miguel and the boys. And of course the dog."

Stefan was surprised anew when he stepped outside onto a covered patio with a large table, chairs and a couple of lounges still sitting outside. The explanation came with the heaters built in around the outer perimeter.

"Miguel is always afraid I'm going to get cold, but I like sitting out here when it's raining, even better when it's snowing. My Irish blood is a lot thicker than his," Fiona said.

"Kind of like California and Illinois blood," Daria teased.

He only smiled, because he'd just spotted the rather

impressive structure they were headed for in the large backyard. It was like a two-level tower, open on the bottom and closed in with a roof on top. It had a ladder, knotted ropes for climbing up and down, a slide out of one opening up top, swings and climbing bars on one side, and a large pit that he guessed was filled with sand when not covered with snow on the other side.

Stefan looked down at his son, who was staring wide-eyed at the contraption. The man who was with the boys saw them, spoke to the kids, then headed their way. He was just under six feet, Stefan noted automatically, with black hair and dark eyes.

"Miguel Alvarez," he said, introducing himself as he pulled off a glove to shake hands. "Welcome to the zoo."

"That," Stefan said, gesturing toward the fort, "is amazing."

"They like it, and it keeps them busy and tired," the other man replied with a grin.

"I'll go get Sam started," Fiona said, "while you get acquainted."

The boy went with her unhesitatingly, clearly as excited as Stefan had hoped about this.

"He'll have fun, I promise," Alvarez assured him.

"I'm pretty sure he will indeed," Stefan said. "I sure would have as a kid."

"This is the whole family Saturday, so you picked a good time to call, Daria."

"Whole family?" Stefan asked, confused.

"They have a system," Daria explained. "The twins—who are inseparable, by the way—have Dad to themselves one Saturday a month, Casey gets him the next, and the next the whole family spends together."

"And the last?" Stefan asked.

Alvarez's grin widened. "Oh, that's for the hot red-head and me," he said with an exaggerated leer.

Stefan smiled—there was no way not to—but inside he felt a sudden tug. They had it down, these people. And he realized what he had felt since stepping into their home was the same sort of total connectedness his parents had. They would make it, this couple. No one who stepped into their home could doubt the strength of their bond.

And he wondered what that said about Daria, that these were the friends she valued most.

You know what it says. That she'd want the same thing. And you already failed at it miserably.

And once again he had to shake himself out of his thoughts, wondering why he couldn't stop thinking about the woman who was his partner in this investigation only as an entirely different kind of partner.

Chapter Thirteen

"Are you all right with leaving Sam here?" Daria asked as they got back in the car.

"Fine. They seem like really good people."

"They are. The best. They had to fight to get to where they are now. His family didn't approve."

He blinked. "Of her? What about her family?"

"Welcomed him with open arms. And he used that to shame his own family into coming around, although I think she would have managed that herself, once they saw how much she adored their son."

"People," Stefan said, "are strange."

"And wonderful," she added. "Sometimes both at once."

He smiled at her. "That, too," he agreed.

"As long as there are those at least working toward wonderful, we should make sure they're safe."

For a moment he just looked at her. Then, softly, he said, "Best definition I've ever heard. Wish DC thought that way. It should be in the job description."

It was a quiet moment of accord, something she could only think of as kinship. And an odd sort of quiet reigned in the car as he drove. Not the awkward sort of silence she'd experienced sometimes with him, but a companionable sort, and it was puzzling. She'd felt kinship with people she worked with before, and on difficult cases, but this was different somehow. This was…more.

Because you're attracted to him?

Even as the words ran through her mind, she set her jaw. *Fine, admit it. Who wouldn't be? He is one fine-looking man, smart and with integrity, and that's a powerful combination.* What he also was was a man coping as best he could with a life turned upside down at the moment, a five-year-old son who didn't want to be here, and just to add spice, he was eight years younger than her.

And he has no idea who you really are. There's always that. That would nip whatever this was in the bud.

She'd always thought that if she ever really got involved with someone, she would have to tell them. Being secretive wasn't really in her nature, but she'd learned early in her…other life that sometimes it was a requirement.

As they drove, the silence in the car seemed to change. She knew it was only in her mind, that she was putting this pressure on herself, but suddenly she felt she had to say something, anything.

"I sure hope this is enough for the judge," she said abruptly. "All we have is that Curtis is older than Bianca was, has blue eyes like millions of other people and that he was there that night, in an area he normally shouldn't have been. And regarding the other victims, that he was not at work or his time isn't accounted for at the times of their disappearances."

"Maybe in a normal case it wouldn't be, but this one passed normal a while back. Sure, I'd rather have had a run at Shruggs, see how he reacted, but unless we can find him quickly, I don't think we should wait."

"There is that. And Trey said Judge Cruz is pretty current on the progress—or lack thereof—on this one. But he may really narrow it down," she warned. "Like only things related to his whereabouts on the dates in question."

"Then we'll just have to do our best, won't we?" Stefan said, almost airily. "Who knows what we'll come across in plain sight."

"Spoken like a true fed," she remarked wryly.

His gaze shot to her face. "Problem?"

"Envy," she said.

"That's all right, then," he said with a grin.

She started to roll her eyes but found herself laughing instead. She reached into her bag and pulled out the laptop, figuring she would start working on the forms for the judge. Stefan glanced at her.

"Motion sickness not an issue, I gather?"

She looked up. "Not usually, no. And you're a smooth driver."

He smiled. "Thanks." He hesitated, then said, "People tend to think I push to drive because I'm a control freak. But really it's because passengering makes me queasy."

"And here I thought it was because you're the guy."

He blinked. "Seriously? That's what you thought?" Her straight face failed, and she laughed. And Daria was glad when he joined her. "Are you kidding?" he said. "I've heard about your range scores. You could probably outshoot me with a peashooter."

"I know that's not true—you have to qualify just like we do."

"But there's qualifying and then there's excelling," he said. "Now, you give me a long gun and we'll talk."

"Good to know," she retorted.

They drove toward the address they had for Shruggs. Daria made a call to find out the nature of the neighborhood and any recent activities, suspicious or otherwise. The report she got indicated it was a very quiet subdivision, with only the occasional loud music or kid-generated mischief. Worst incident had been a house fire, but that had been determined to be from a faulty space heater.

The area lived up to the billing. There was little activity, although there were signs of earlier playing in the snow, including a tiny snowman—there hadn't been much accumulation here at this lower elevation— that made her smile, thinking of Sam's snow head. All the houses seemed to be variations on a theme—tract homes trying to look like log cabins.

When they reached Shruggs's street, Stefan drove slowly. "Green roof," he said as they neared the address.

Daria spotted it quickly. "Got it."

They went by slowly, without stopping. As they did, she inputted the detailed description of the building any search warrant request required. She was a little surprised at the cozy-looking, log-style home with the green metal roof, set amid tall cottonwood trees. It was very…picturesque.

"Looks like a freaking postcard," Stefan muttered.

"Exactly what I was thinking," she concurred as she made a note about the mailbox sitting on a stone pillar out at the street, then the large spruce tree in the front yard and the bright red front door that looked a bit Christmassy with the green roof.

"Wonder whose idea the door was?" Stefan mused aloud as he turned the car around and slid it in behind a large truck parked on the street that would hide it from view of the Shruggs house.

"And again," Daria said as he hit upon her thought. "Someone with a Christmas thing?"

"Maybe. It could—"

He stopped suddenly. Daria's head came up. "What? See something? Or someone?"

"I—no. Sorry. Nothing about this. It just hit me that next month I've got a five-year-old's Christmas to deal with."

"Oh, my, lucky you!"

His head turned and he stared at her. "Lucky?"

"Of course. A child's joy in Christmas is a precious thing. I'll bet yours as a kid were special."

"Very. The best," he said, thoughtfully, as if memories were flooding him. "My mom saw to that."

"Ask her then. Tell her you want Sam to feel like she made you feel."

He stared at her for a moment. "Are you sure you've never met my mother? Because you sure know how to get to her."

Daria laughed. "Thank my adoptive mom for that." The moment the words were out she froze. She never, *ever* brought up her adoptive family, and she couldn't believe she'd done it now, with him.

His gaze changed, as if he'd realized she'd never even mentioned them before, except when he'd done her that incredible favor and found out about her biological mother. "You're still close?"

"Yes. She's impossibly busy, but we keep in close touch." She said it rather briskly and went back to her notes.

While she did so, Stefan pulled out his phone and put in a call to Detective Kastor about arranging someone to stake out the house while they pursued the warrant.

"Well, that was easy," he said when he hung up. "Liam was so hyped that we had an actual lead, I think he'll come out and sit here himself if he has to."

"I don't doubt that. He's sharp, too. He put together the resemblance between Bianca and April Thomas before anyone else."

Stefan nodded. "I thought that, too. I think we're safe turning it over to him or whoever he sends." He looked back at the house. "Place sure is quiet."

She nodded. "Wonder if Curtis really is home sick?"

Stefan sat looking at the house they were focused on. "I think a little recon is in order," he murmured.

"I could—"

She stopped when he shook his head. "He knows who you are. I've never met him or been face-to-face with him."

"Good point."

"You have a cell number for him there, don't you?" he asked.

"Yes."

"Good. If all looks quiet, you can call it when I get close enough, see if I can hear it."

"All right," she replied. "Got a story if he's there and catches you?"

"Me?" He gave her a look that was so innocent she almost laughed. "I'm just an accountant, checking out the neighborhood, looking for a house for me and my son where we can have an old-fashioned Christmas."

She blinked. "An accountant?"

He reached into an inner jacket pocket to pull out a

small case, extracted a business card and held it out to her. "Sure hope there's good internet here so I can work from home," he said, still in that tone of utter innocence.

"'Steven Barker, CPA, Barker and Associates,'" she read out loud. Obviously he had this—and quite possibly others for other occupations—on hand for occasions just such as this. She supposed many agents did.

"I do so love numbers," he said with an exaggerated sigh.

She was still laughing when he got out of the car and started toward the house, looking around at the other houses as much as the target house, as if he were truly just checking out the neighborhood. She watched him go and tried to imagine him tied endlessly to spreadsheets and account books. She couldn't.

So instead she just settled in and allowed herself the pleasure of simply watching the way he moved.

And for the moment hushed the inner voice warning that she was edging closer and closer to very big trouble.

Chapter Fourteen

After confirming Shruggs was not at the house, and that the officer Detective Kastor had sent had arrived to keep watch, they headed back to the station to start the process of getting a search warrant.

Stefan looked over the affidavits Daria had prepared while they were on the way. She'd asked him to, to see if she'd missed anything. And as he'd expected, she had not. Deputy Bloom was very thorough, and she had worded things in a way that made it seem a bit more impressive than it was, yet stopped short of blowing smoke, which would likely tick the judge off.

She paced the office while he read. He understood—he was antsy to get going on this, too.

"I'd add a cursory description of the houses on either side, especially the one with the carved bear in front, just to avoid any problems with the houses all resembling each other. Other than that, perfect."

She smiled as she nodded and made the addition. And then she'd picked up the phone and called the judge, going through everything with Cruz after she'd emailed the now-encrypted documents to him.

And as they waited for the call with the judge's decision, they were both pacing.

"Is your gut screaming at you?" she finally asked him.

"Yeah. It is."

"I keep telling myself it's only because this is the first thing that looks like a real break in a long time on this case."

"It has been a long time. But it takes more than that to get my gut going like this."

She looked at him curiously. "I suppose you're more used to cases that take a long time."

"We've had a few," he said. Then, wryly, he added, "Of course, we've had a few that shouldn't have taken as long as they did, too."

She studied him for a moment. "Do you miss the city? That life?"

He smiled, chuckled and shook his head at the same time. "Not one bit."

She smiled back. "Me, either."

The phone rang. Caller ID verified their hopes. "That was fast," Stefan said appreciatively.

With a nod Daria answered, listened, checked for the email that had arrived and said, "Yes, Your Honor," a couple of times, then, "Thank you very much."

Before she'd even hung up, the printer in the corner of the room hummed to life and began to spit out the paper copies they would need to actually serve the warrant, to be handed to Shruggs if he was there, or left openly visible if he was not. Stefan walked over to get the pages.

It wasn't bad, as warrants went. Judge Cruz had narrowed it down more than he'd have liked, limiting them to the Bianca Rouge case. But he'd given them full range on the search itself, for anything connected to that or to Shruggs's whereabouts at the time of her murder.

So who knows what they might turn up, or what they might find in plain sight? And he suspected the judge knew that.

Daria was already back on the phone arranging backup. He took out his own phone and, as they'd discussed on the way here, called the FBI office in Denver to arrange for forensics to respond if necessary. It was a three-hour drive on a good day, so a heads-up was definitely in order.

And Daria hadn't protested at all, as some locals did, not liking the feds getting involved in their cases. *Turn down the FBI lab capabilities on a serial killer case that's been dragging on for over ten months? Gee, let me think about that...*

He smiled at the memory. He did like her sense of humor and her way of putting things. And the way she treated everyone, even the doorman at The Lodge, with the utmost respect. And how she chose good, solid people for her closest friends. And the way she—

He cut off his thoughts, which had somehow turned into a catalog of everything he liked about Daria Bloom.

And you didn't even get to the X-rated section yet.

But he could. Oh boy, could he. But if he started listing all the things about her that fired him up, all the things that woke him up at night in the grips of a dream worthy of some hormone-crazed teenager, not only would it take all day, but he'd end up saying or doing something unforgivably stupid.

"Ready?" Daria asked.

He blinked. He knew she meant the search warrant, but his body still shouted. *Oh yeah. Seriously ready.*

"Let's roll," he said, rather gruffly, hoping she'd take it as impatience to get a move on and not guess he'd just been daydreaming about kissing that luscious mouth and running his hands over her trimly curved body.

It was just as well that she again let him drive. It gave his hands something to do when everything in him wanted them to be doing something else.

IT WAS ONLY, Daria told herself, that they were at last doing something besides going around in circles, combing over the same old information in the futile hope that something new, some fresh approach or angle or thought, would pop out. That was why she was so revved up. Why she was tapping a finger on the armrest of the car, why her pulse was elevated, why she had to work so hard to keep her gaze anywhere except on the man behind the wheel.

She played back all the sound, logical reasons those things were impossible in her head. There were more than three strikes, so it should be enough to outweigh six-plus feet of tall, broad-shouldered, muscled male with those stunning light brown eyes and that gorgeous mahogany skin.

As long as he doesn't smile at me.

Yes, she had to admit, that heart-stopping smile, from the no-nonsense, very by-the-book Agent Roberts, was enough to throw any calculation into chaos.

"If it's there to be found, we'll find it."

His words snapped her out of her reverie. She spared a moment to be grateful he'd assumed it was the case that had been consuming her.

"Yes," she said. "And I think it will be."

"Agreed. It feels...right."

It did. But Daria wished her mind would apply that feeling strictly to the case at hand and not her temporary partner. There were so many concrete reasons why getting involved with him would be wrong, and only one on the other side.

Of course, the fact that that one reason was that she hadn't felt this attracted to someone in a very long time carried a lot of weight.

And then they were there, and she pushed all of it out of her mind. It was her efficient, all-business partner she was with now, and he would expect the same of her. They were on the verge of a huge break, she could just feel it, and no amount of telling herself she'd had her hopes up before on this case could tamp them down this time.

The house, the officer who'd been staked out told them, was still empty. No one had even driven down the street except a minivan full of kids in sports uniforms of some kind. She hoped for their sake it was an indoor sport; the snow was melting and making the ground a soggy mess.

She spared a brief moment to hope Sam was having the time of his life at the Alvarezes', then narrowed her focus strictly to the matter at hand.

They let the tactical team breach; just because there'd been no sign of anyone around didn't mean Shruggs wasn't holed up inside. They didn't think they'd tipped him off, unless his assistant felt inclined to warn him they'd been there, although even then they'd covered all their bases by asking for all the records, not just his, and Stefan had managed to make it sound boringly routine.

Once the house had been declared clear, they gloved up and went in. Daria left a copy of the warrant in plain sight on a bare dining table, then looked around.

"A bit tidy for a guy supposedly living alone," she said.

"Hey," Stefan protested.

"Even your place looked more lived-in than this. I mean, look," she said with a gesture toward a coffee table in the living room where two stacks of magazines were lined up perfectly square, "not even a magazine out of place, no jackets hung by the door, no dishes in the sink." She walked into the kitchen to check, then continued. "Not even in the dishwasher."

"Maybe he's just a neat freak."

"Mmm," Daria said, wondering what percentage of serial killers turned out to be manically tidy in their personal spaces.

"Fridge is pretty sparse," Stefan said, following her and opening the appliance door. "Beer, half a bottle of wine and…leftover something."

"That looks like it should have been tossed days ago."

"Charming. And technically outside the purview of our warrant."

"Not if we need to know if he's actually living here," Daria remarked.

"Point taken," Stefan said with a nod.

She walked around the rest of the kitchen, opening each drawer as she passed. Found utensils, a tray of flatware, some towels and…nothing. She stopped, frowning.

"What?" Stefan asked.

"Just looking for the junk drawer." She glanced at him. "Everyone has a junk drawer, don't they? Where all the appliance manuals, notepads and the like get stuffed?"

"Um…"

She widened her eyes at him. "If you tell me you don't have a junk drawer, I may have to give up hope."

He went still. "And what, exactly, are you hoping for?"

She'd meant him relaxing enough to make Sam feel at home, but something in the way he said it, and in the hot gleam that suddenly came into those eyes, made her want to answer something entirely different. And of all times and places, this was probably the worst.

She had to struggle to get her original answer out. "For Sam to feel he can leave out a glass and not get in trouble."

The gleam faded. "Yeah, right," he muttered.

She turned away, trying to deny to herself that that look in his eyes told her he wanted the same thing.

Chapter Fifteen

They continued the search in silence. Stefan noted that each room matched the living room and kitchen—not just tidy but immaculate. The master bedroom and even the bathrooms were spotless and without a thing out of place.

"Not even a shoe on the floor," Daria murmured as she looked into the master closet.

Even his place looked well lived-in compared to this. "Manic?" he wondered aloud.

"Or overcompensating," Daria murmured as they continued down the hallway.

He saw what she meant. "For the other, messy part of his life?"

She nodded, then looked his way. "Am I letting my suspicions override the evidence?"

"You're just thinking. And as long as you're asking that question, no, you're not."

She smiled at him, although under the circumstances it was fleeting. It still warmed him in ways he doubted he would ever get used to.

They were getting close to breaking this case wide-open. He knew it. He could almost *smell* it. And so, in hindsight, he appreciated her caution. He'd seen other agents act too soon on those gut feelings and end up completely blowing a case. Not that they were wrong, although that happened occasionally, but because they rushed ahead before they had the evidence to justify each step, and the case then fell apart in court, hacked to pieces by viciously clever attorneys who cared about nothing but the win.

So they would proceed methodically, only as fast as the evidence would allow. And they would build this case brick by brick, until the walls were so high and thick this madman would never escape.

He had a sudden vision of the end of this case, of the day when they caught this twisted psychopath. It would be a day of triumph at stopping him, yet sadness that he had killed so many. It would be a day—probably days—of media circus come to town. It would be a day of satisfaction for a tough job finished, but another layer of pained belief in the ugliness possible from humankind.

It would also be the end of their partnership.

No longer would he drive to work every morning looking forward to seeing Daria, to being in the room with her, to looking into those beautiful golden-brown eyes, to watching her move, seeing that smile.

He was surprised—no, make that stunned—at what that realization did to him.

And he didn't want to think about what it would do to Sam. Maybe she would still want to see him. She seemed to genuinely like the boy, so maybe she'd keep in touch, for his sake.

And you can be the side beneficiary?

The realization that he was hoping his five-year-old son could be the reason he would still see Daria after this was over rattled him nearly as much as the realization this would be over soon had in the first place.

He gave himself a fierce mental shake and followed Daria as she walked down the hallway of Curtis Shruggs's house toward the only room they hadn't yet looked at, at the end of that hallway. They stepped inside.

In one corner there was a rather ornate desk, oversized for the space. On the opposite wall was a floor-to-ceiling bookcase about four feet wide. There wasn't room for much else.

"Picked the smallest room for an office," Stefan said.

Daria nodded again, then looked back toward the desk. "And so it continues," she murmured.

"Indeed," Stefan concurred, also looking at the spotless surface of the large desk. The only items on it were an old-fashioned inkwell that looked as if it should have a feather quill sticking out of it and a pristine blotter. Some stationery was tucked into one side, blank except for the name in fancy script across the top. *Curtis Allen Shruggs III.*

Daria blinked. "He's a third? I don't remember…in fact I'm certain that's not in the info we have."

Stefan pulled out his phone and did a quick search. "No. He's not even a second or junior."

"Unless they skipped a generation. His father's name was Charles Ellis Shruggs."

"It's a stuffy-sounding kind of name. Delusions of grandeur, then?" Stefan asked.

"Or perfection. Goes with everything in here," Daria said, gesturing toward the bookcase. "Look at that. Every book a hardcover, no dust jackets, leather- or fake-leather bound, and every last one of them the same height."

"And not a one looking as if it's ever been cracked."

"Then again," she mused as she walked over for a closer look, "given some of these titles, perhaps that's not surprising." She tilted her head to read out loud. "'*Dewey Decimal Classification and Relative Index*.'"

"Seriously?"

"And there's four of them," she said.

"Maybe he wanted to be a librarian."

"Classifying books instead of people? Maybe." She ran her fingers over the row of books. Stefan tried not to think about her running those graceful fingers over every part of him. "Although you'd think if that was true at least one book would have been opened—" She broke off suddenly.

"What?"

"It won't move."

"They are jammed in there pretty tightly. All in that perfect row."

"No, I mean it truly won't move." She tried the next book. Same thing. "It's like he's got them glued down or something."

Stefan stepped over and tried a book farther down, then one on a different shelf. Neither gave even a fraction of an inch. "Boy, they really are just for show, aren't they?"

Daria stepped back, staring at the rows of perfectly matched and lined-up volumes. They weren't only the exact same height, they were each the exact distance, about an inch, back from the edge of the shelf.

"Is that what it is? They simply must always be perfectly in line?"

"I guess it would keep them that way if you bumped the shelf or something," Stefan mused.

Daria's breath caught. "Or…if you moved it."

"Moved—" Stefan started to ask her, then stopped short. He pivoted back to look at the bookcase. Then at her. "How tall is Shruggs?" he asked quietly.

"Shorter than you. Five-ten, five-eleven, maybe."

He raised one arm, easily reaching the top shelf. Then he felt along the row of books, tugging on each, but they all appeared to be as solid as those she'd looked at. Dropping his hand down one shelf, he repeated the action. And when his hand stopped suddenly, Daria's breath jammed up in her throat.

"Well, well," Stefan murmured and shifted his strong fingers over the book he'd stopped at.

It moved.

He pulled the book forward. As it slid off the shelf, the books on either side of it stayed exactly where they were, upright and securely fastened just as all the others had been.

"There's a switch," he said in a very low voice. "Get the breach team back in here."

And she knew he'd reached the same conclusion she had.

It wasn't a bookcase.

It was a door.

Chapter Sixteen

Stefan stood outside in the chill, staring at the back of the house. In his mind's eye, he tried to gauge where the interior walls were, to get an idea of how big the hidden room would be. Not very. If the office had originally been the size of the other bedrooms in the house, then it was missing maybe four feet in width. Which meant that if the secret room ran the length of that room, that would make the space about four feet by ten.

Forty square feet. Not much. But enough for a serial killer to hide...*whatever* he was hiding in there? The possibilities for that were pretty grim. He'd seen some ugly things in his career, and he hoped this wasn't going to be another gruesome scene to add to the memory banks.

He heard the crunch of footsteps on what little snow there was remaining here and looked up to see Daria approaching. She had her heavy coat buttoned up to her throat, the collar pulled up and held by the thick, knitted scarf she had wound around her neck multiple times. It was a deep gold that, wrapped so close to her face, made her eyes look the same impossible shade. Had she made it herself? If so, she was good—the intricate cables looked beyond difficult to his untrained eye. And he smiled inwardly as he remembered her warning about very pointy tools.

Other people count to ten to hold on to their temper. I count stitches.

Point taken. Er, no pun intended.

Too bad. It would have been a good one.

He almost smiled outwardly at that memory. He did like her sense of humor. Besides, with the big scarf and her heavy, fur-lined boots, she looked ready for the Antarctic, which also made him want to smile. He stopped himself, because he didn't really want to explain what he was amused about.

"They're ready," she said as she came to a halt.

And just as she said it, he heard the call of, "Ready team!"

He looked over toward the team leader, who had ordered his crew to suit back up in vests and full tactical gear. Stefan didn't really think Shruggs was in there, but more than one agent had died going on a wrong assumption. He didn't want anyone to be a statistic, so they had left the house and turned it back over to the pros at CQB—close quarters battling without the proper gear was a chance he didn't want to take.

It was a chance he could *no longer* take.

He had a sudden vision of Sam, already lost and scared, having to go through that. He'd arranged for him to go to his parents, but what if Leah had other ideas? She hadn't wanted him now, but she'd never really gotten along well with his parents—they were far too unsophisticated and traditional for her taste. Would she demand to have Sam back to keep him away from them? Unlikely, but he didn't like even thinking about his son having to go back to a mother who hadn't wanted him and a stepfather who actively disliked him.

And for the first time in his career, it had really, truly struck home that he had a responsibility to take care of himself. For Sam's sake. He'd always known his death would devastate his parents, but as long as they had each other, they'd get through it. Sam had no one else. No one who would feel about him as he did. Because he loved his son, even when he wasn't liking him very much.

But he really liked the boy Sam had turned into around Daria. That was the happy child he remembered, the child he wanted back. And he had to stay alive to get there.

Stefan wasn't surprised it only took moments for the team to reappear and declare the small hidden room clear. And to tell them they had, in a macabre sort of way, hit pay dirt.

"We didn't mess it up—it only took a visual sweep from the doorway to be sure it was unoccupied," the team leader said grimly. "You're going to want forensics in there, in a big way."

And so again they waited, he and Daria, as the crime scene unit arrived, and in their own gear to prevent contamination, went into the little room.

Daria started pacing, rubbing at her arms. Gloves, too, he noted. Thick, warm ones. Not knitted like the scarf, though. Could you even do that? With fingers? Clearly his pointy-stick education was lacking.

"You want to go back inside?" he asked as she kept pacing. "It's warmer in there."

"Only temperature-wise," she said with a grimace. "I'll stay out here, thanks."

He nodded in understanding. "Don't blame you." He didn't want to spend any more time in that house than he had to, either. The evilness of it was much, much chillier than the weather outside. "Sometimes I wonder," he said, staring at the house, "if when you see sickness like this…it seeps into you somehow."

"To paraphrase what a wise man once told me, that you ask that means that it's not."

Startled at hearing his own words quoted back to him, his gaze snapped back to her face. Slowly he smiled. "Wise?"

"Definitely," she said.

He had been complimented on a few things in his life—his looks, his brain, his smile, even his height… but nothing had ever pleased him quite like that did. And he was afraid whatever he would answer would come out all wrong, make her think the wrong thing.

Except she wouldn't be wrong.

"I think my son might argue that," he finally managed to say.

"For now, maybe. But he's young."

Finally the forensics team emerged. "I'll get the blood type to you ASAP," the blonde woman said to his rather urgent request, her expression showing she understood quite well what they were dealing with and what was at stake.

The first thing Stefan thought when he stepped inside the small room behind the fake bookcase was that it reminded him of the room he'd told Daria about before. Photographs tacked on the walls, notes beside each one that he sensed were going to be grim and ugly. And… the trophy shelf. This was typical, this kind of collection, something from each victim, so that the man with the twisted mind could joyously relive the thrill of each of his kills.

But what riveted his attention now was the opposite side of the room.

The side with the cage.

It looked like the kind of metal crate used for large dogs. Except those didn't usually have shiny new padlocks on them. Well, it had been shiny, until forensics had blackened it with fingerprint powder, finding nothing but a faint smear that might have once been a print.

But most riveting of all, most *haunting*, was the fact that there was relatively fresh blood on the side of the cage opening.

"I can't believe I sat across an interview table from him and didn't pick up on this." Daria sounded devastated. "If I had, this new victim might not have been taken. If I had—"

"Funny," Stefan said grimly, still staring at the cage, "I don't remember seeing mind reading on your stellar résumé."

He heard her take a deep breath, and when she spoke again, she sounded steadier. He hoped he'd helped with that. He was more…not *inured* to cases like this, because if the day ever came where this kind of thing didn't disturb him, then it would be time to hang it up. But he had seen more of them than she had, probably a lot more, and so was less prone to be shocked at the existence of such human depravity.

Daria moved over to look at the wall of photos. In a sick twist, there appeared to be two of each girl—one alive, one dead. He'd already noted that any image of the new girl, alive or dead, was missing.

"I know her picture's not here, but I still think it has to be the new missing girl," she said.

"My gut agrees," he answered. "Maybe he takes the photos right before he kills them."

"He probably likes to capture the utter terror in their eyes," Daria said, with a loathing in her voice that told him Curtis Shruggs had better be very careful when they finally caught up with him.

"It would fit," he agreed. "I told them to advise us on a match to the blood type ASAP. Not that they wouldn't anyway, but a reminder never hurts." She'd been standing a few feet away at the time, and he wasn't sure she'd been listening.

She was still staring at the wall. "He didn't even want to have to take the time to call the photos up on a computer or phone," she murmured. "He wanted them right here in front of him all the time."

"And in front of them," Stefan added. "That's probably half the reason he brings them in here."

Daria shuddered. "Mental torture. They would know the minute they saw this wall what was going to happen to them."

He felt the strongest urge to put a comforting arm around her. Had they been alone in here, had not a dozen other people been on scene, he might have done it. He remembered his first serial killer scene, remembered the nausea it had caused, being forced to truly confront how evil some people could be.

"But he doesn't kill them here," he said, looking around again. "Maybe he doesn't want the mess."

"A fastidious serial killer?"

"One behavior often comes in conjunction with others."

"Or he thinks he's making up for being evil by being tidy?" she asked, sounding steadier now.

"I've seen stranger thought patterns," he answered. "But the most important thing right now is…we've got him."

He looked at her then and saw the belated realization dawn in those golden-brown eyes of her. She'd been so busy processing all of this, the enormity of it, that she hadn't hit the bottom line yet.

They now knew for sure who the Avalanche Killer was.

Chapter Seventeen

Energized, they spent a few more fruitless hours trying to track down where Curtis Shruggs might be. There was still the sense of urgency, but it had a different cause now. There was a chance, although Daria thought it a very slim one, that the most recent victim might still be alive. That put the entire situation into overdrive, and every police officer and sheriff in the county and beyond now had the bulletin they'd sent out.

A thorough crime-scene processing was not something you could hide from the neighbors. The locals had done a house to house and had reported back that the man seemed to mostly keep to himself—one rather dramatic young man speculated that he was mourning a lost love—but that was no guarantee one of them wasn't friendly enough with Shruggs to warn him about what had been going on.

She and Stefan batted around the possibilities, and she sensed that he was as antsy as she was. Would Shruggs run? Or would he stay on his home turf? More importantly, where was he now? With his victim? Or did he have her stashed away in some secret place, where he could indulge his twisted fantasies? Was part of the torture leaving her there alone, giving her hope she could escape? Or would he be one of those sickos who liked to taunt his victims with what he was going to do to them for hours, even days before he actually took their lives? And when he did it, when he killed them, he did it with his bare hands, up close and personal. That spoke of a particular kind of drive and made it all the uglier.

"I think we need to talk to whoever hired him," Stefan said. "I can't believe the Coltons would employ someone for such a high-level position without vetting him pretty thoroughly first."

"They would," Daria agreed, "but I asked, and the person who actually hired Shruggs over ten years ago was the prior personnel manager."

"The background check must be somewhere."

She nodded. "All of that is in Decker Colton's office, and he's the only one who has access to it."

He gave her a smile then that warmed her. "You don't miss a trick, do you? So where do we find Mr. Decker Colton on a Saturday night?"

"I checked—he's gone until Monday, off the grid with his wife."

"Be nice if serial killers took weekends off," Stefan muttered.

"I know. But it's what we have to work with."

"Hard to feel stalled when there's maybe a still-alive victim out there."

"Tell me about it," Daria muttered.

Stefan gave her a sideways look. "You're still convinced Sabrina Gilford wasn't one of his victims?"

"Yes. And that her murderer knew who the Avalanche Killer was."

"He knew a lot," Stefan agreed, "to make it look like one of his kills."

After the hours spent hashing over it all, dozens of phone calls and several reports from the further door to doors Liam Kastor had set in motion for them, they had a slightly clearer picture. Shruggs had many co-workers and several direct employees, but few friends, which seemed significant to Daria.

Stefan had one of the Bureau's IT people start scouring for signs of his life—open or secret—online. Daria knew that people who had few personal contacts often had many online, and with the illusion of protection that step removed gave some people, they sometimes told those contacts things they would never say to anyone in person.

"If that doesn't net anything," Stefan said as they finally headed out to pick up Sam, "since we didn't find a computer at his house, we'll have to go for his work computer."

She nodded but felt doubtful. "I just can't imagine anyone as careful as he seems to be not keeping his two…lives completely separate."

"Agreed. But people make mistakes. If they didn't, we'd never get anywhere."

"Point taken," she said.

He gave her a sideways look. "Point reminds me to ask, did you make your scarf?"

Surprised but pleased, she smiled at him. "I did."

"You weren't kidding, then. You seriously knit."

"I knit seriously," she corrected with a grin. "Why, you want one?"

He reached out and ran a finger along the line of one of the cables. "Might look a little silly on me."

"I think you could carry it off." *You could carry just about anything off.* "Maybe in a more masculine color."

In the process of pulling back his hand, his fingers brushed her jawline. She gave a start at the little electric shock it gave her. Had he done it intentionally? Of course not, she answered herself. It was just an accidental touch. She almost had herself convinced when something caught her peripheral vision and she realized his hand—the hand that had touched her—was tightened around the steering wheel far more than was necessary.

She didn't dare look at him again and was relieved when they got to Fiona's place. Sam was happily worn-out. But that didn't stop him from chattering away excitedly about his day from the moment they got into the car. And the longer he went on, the wider Stefan's smile at his son became.

"And they said I could come back," Sam crowed. "Mrs. Alvarez said she could get me from school. Then I could come and play."

Stefan glanced at her. "How do you thank people for that?" he asked softly.

"We'll think of something."

This got her the smile. And damn, it was a killer smile.

"C'n Daria fix dinner?" Sam asked innocently.

Stefan gave her another glance, this time wincing, as if he thought the boy was saying she belonged in the kitchen. She nearly laughed.

"Why would you want me to do that?" she asked the boy.

"'Cause you fix stuff that tastes good."

She looked back at his father. "Sometimes," she said with a grin, "it really is that simple."

"How about we hit the burger place?" Stefan suggested. "You can order it however you want."

"Okay," Sam said agreeably.

Apparently a happy day with the Alvarez boys took the angry right out of him, which was what she'd hoped for.

"I mentioned to Fiona that we could be heading into a very demanding phase of the investigation," she said.

Stefan gave her a sideways look as he drove, then lifted one shoulder in a half shrug. "It's not as if she doesn't know what we're working on. The whole town knows."

"Yes. And both she and Miguel instantly said Sam could stay with them whenever necessary."

"Told ya," Sam piped up from the back seat.

"Guess you made a good impression, buddy," Stefan said.

"What's that mean?"

"It means they liked you," Daria said, beaming at the boy, who grinned right back at her.

Dear heaven, he was going to have that same killer charm when he grew up, she thought. She tried to picture it, an adult Sam with an older Stefan. For some reason her mind kept wanting to put herself into that picture, so she veered away quickly.

"They're nice. Really nice," Sam said. He was looking at Daria rather pointedly. "Casey said they come play at your house sometimes."

"They do," she confirmed.

"They said your tree thing was cool."

"They like it because it has other trees all around, and if you're quiet when you're up there, you can see all sorts of birds and animals."

"Really? Like squirrels and stuff?"

She laughed. "More like deer, raccoons, hawks, now and then even an eagle."

Sam's eyes widened. "An eagle?"

"If you're lucky. No wapiti, though."

"What's a—" Sam enunciated carefully "—wapiti?"

"An elk. Like a deer, only way bigger, with *biiiiig* antlers," she answered, drawling out the *big* and spreading her hands as far apart as she could in the car.

"Wow! I've never seen anything that big."

"I saw some down on the golf course just the other day," she told him. "They come down during the winter to eat the grass, because it's hard to find food up in the mountains."

"I wish I could see one."

"I bet you will, kiddo, now that you're here."

"Cool."

They spent a cheerful half an hour eating burgers and fries at the local supplier of Sam's choice. And sitting at the table across from the two of them, listening to Sam tell yet another tale of his exciting day—this one involving a snowball fight that had lasted until they'd run out of snow—she felt something she'd rarely felt in her life. A sense of…something. Wholeness? Completeness? Something she hadn't felt since she'd made the decision to make her way without the weight of her adoptive family name—and the power and prestige of President Joe Colton—behind her.

When she realized it was that sense of family she was feeling, she suddenly found the last of her fries very interesting and stared downward as if she were counting them.

"I can't get over the change in him," Stefan said after he'd gotten the boy back into the car.

"He's already feeling more secure."

"And you did it in a little over three days."

"I didn't do it all," she protested. "So did you. He's starting to believe that you want him here." She hesitated, then went ahead. "You've changed, too, with him. You're not quite as tense, and he senses that."

"Thank you for that, too," he said, and there was so much sincerity in his voice, she couldn't stop the warmth that bubbled up inside her.

When they reached the sheriff's office so she could pick up her car, Sam looked around with interest.

"Is this where you work?" he asked Daria.

"It is. And where your dad works for now."

"On the 'lanche killer," Sam answered knowingly.

She felt rather than saw Stefan tense. Slowly he turned to look at the boy.

"Where'd you hear that?"

"Casey said Daria was going to catch him," Sam said, sounding rather blasé. "Can I go inside and see?"

It took her a moment to get past little Casey Alvarez's complete faith to say, "It would be pretty boring after your exciting day."

"But I wanna see where you work."

She glanced at Stefan then, questioningly. He tilted his head and let out a breath in that "I hate to ask, but…" kind of way.

"I could give him the quick tour," she said.

"Please, Dad?"

Something changed in Stefan's expression then, and she wondered if he had ever heard such a normal, wheedling request from his son.

"All right," Stefan said, "but only because you asked nicely."

Surprise then thoughtfulness flickered across the boy's face, and when they got out of the car, before he opened the back door for his son, Daria looked at Stefan across the roof of the car. "Speaking of nicely, nicely done," she said. "That registered."

"Even as a brand-new shooter, I hit the target now and then," he said with a wry smile, clearly referring to her earlier reassurances.

"In six months it will be like he's been here forever, and you'll have a happy, well-adjusted kid on your hands."

"Can I get that in writing?"

She grinned back at him, but as he opened the door to lean in and unstrap Sam from the booster seat, it faded away. Because now that they knew who they were after, she had every confidence they would wrap up this case in short order.

And once they did that, Stefan—and Sam—would be gone.

Chapter Eighteen

Not for the first time in his career, Stefan felt a jab of impatience on Sunday. He felt as if they were treading water, when he wanted to be powering full speed ahead. Especially now that there was another potential victim, who might—however tiny the chance was—still be alive.

They knew who the Avalanche Killer was now, and it was just a matter of finding him. They knew Curtis Shruggs had been at work at The Lodge as recently as Wednesday—the three days since were mostly a mystery. The blood at the house, in that obscene little room with the cage, was fresh enough for them to say it was likely he'd been there with the girl sometime in those three days. Yet none of the neighbors had seen or heard him. Or her.

But then, they universally said, they rarely did see Shruggs. They'd all tended to think of him as a hard worker, because he left for The Lodge early and came home late. He was more likely to be seen by the garbagemen, one woman had joked, clearly unaware of what all the fuss was about. But Stefan had made a mental note to check with the waste-management company and whoever handled this route. Who knows what they might have glimpsed in the man's trash? At least they wouldn't need a warrant for that.

It all came back to not knowing enough about their quarry to even begin to predict what he might do. And so far, no one they talked to had been much help.

Feeling restless, he began pacing his living room. He stopped a couple of times to look at the room, mentally comparing it to the warm, welcoming feeling of the Alvarez place. Realized that not only did it not feel kid-friendly, it didn't feel particularly friendly to him. And suddenly he wanted to clear it all out and start over.

He heard the clump-clump of Sam running down the hallway. He turned, and the boy skidded to a halt and looked at him warily. He tried to think, to imagine of what Daria would say.

Talk to him, Stefan, not at him. And more important, listen to what he says.

"Hey, you're just in time. I need your help," he said.

Sam looked startled. "Me?"

"Yeah." He gestured around the room. "I'm thinking all this stuff—well, most of it, not the TV—needs to go away."

Sam looked around rather cautiously. "Go where?"

"Anywhere but here. I'm thinking we need some stuff like the Alvarezes have, where a guy can put his feet up and watch TV or play a video game without worrying about it."

He wasn't sure if it was the video game mention or the *we* that did it, but the wariness vanished. And in its place came a small smile that bolstered Stefan's hope for a future with his son.

"Or maybe even a different place," he said. "Someplace with a bigger yard to play in."

Sam's eyes widened. Then he looked thoughtful. "Daria said her house has a big yard. We could move there."

If the boy had kicked him in the gut, he couldn't have driven the breath out of him any more completely. The easily spoken *we*—had it really only taken him saying it?—was enough, but the innocent suggestion that they simply move in with Daria not only stole his breath but made it hard to remember how to get it back.

He struggled for something, *anything* to say. The best he could do, after a gasping moment, was, "You haven't even seen her place."

"But it sounds cool. And Daria wouldn't lie," Sam added with a childlike certainty Stefan envied.

"No," he agreed quietly. "No, she wouldn't."

He was still pondering his son's more-than-accurate assessment of his temporary partner when his phone chimed, alerting him to a text coming in. He walked over to the kitchen counter where it was, swiped the screen and for a moment just stood staring at the name. Because, as if conjured up by Sam's cogent assessment, it was Daria.

But then he read it and found himself smiling.

"Hey, Sam?"

"What?"

"Daria says the wapiti are on the golf course right now."

The boy ran over, instantly excited. "They are?"

He held the phone out to his son, who stared at the photo Daria had sent. "Wow!"

Driven by a few impulses at once, he said, "You want to go see them?"

Sam's eyes got even wider. "For real?"

"If you can get your shoes and your heavy jacket on in the next three minutes. I don't know how long they'll stick around."

The boy didn't even answer but ran for his room. Stefan was smiling as he texted Daria back and she answered. Because even if the elk headed back to the hills, Daria would wait for them there.

As it turned out, the majestic animals stayed, seemingly unconcerned—or unimpressed—by the humans who were gawking at them mere yards away. By the time they arrived, there were ten or so people in various spots along the golf course, pointing and taking pictures.

"Do you suppose they know there won't be golfers out because of the snow?" Daria asked Sam as he excitedly exclaimed at the size of the animals.

The boy took her question very seriously. And after a moment of thought, he nodded. "Prob'ly. 'Cause they live here."

"I'll bet you're right," Daria said, and Sam gave her that beaming smile. Then he looked back at the small herd, brow furrowed as he made some gestures with his fingers.

"Thanks for thinking to text us," Stefan told her. "I've been here for a while, and I've never seen them like this."

She smiled at him, nearly as widely as Sam had grinned at her, and Stefan had that same breathless feeling he'd had before. Damn, this woman got to him, in ways he didn't fully understand. They'd been working side by side for months now, and he'd been fighting it from the first moment he'd laid eyes on her. And sometimes, despite all his best efforts, he wanted nothing more than to grab her, whisk her off somewhere private and find out if the chemistry between them was truly as explosive as he thought it would be.

"There's 'leven of them!" Sam exclaimed, and Stefan suddenly understood what the boy's hand motions had been.

"Good counting," Daria said. "Now, can you find the leader of the herd?"

"The leader?"

"The boss. He looks different than the others."

"Oh!" Sam exalted. "The one with the…the…" Failing to find the word he wanted, the boy put his hands to his head in a descriptive gesture.

"Antlers," Stefan told him. "And he is a big one, isn't he?"

"Yeah," the boy said.

"Where were you off to this morning, that you ended up here?" he asked Daria as Sam went back to watching the herd.

"Nowhere in particular," she said. "I just wanted to get out of the house. Quit pacing, actually."

"I know the feeling," he muttered.

"It's so hard to be so close and yet be able to only tread water because we don't know enough."

"Maybe the new door to door will turn something up," he stated. "Somebody who wasn't home before might know something."

"Maybe."

He noticed Sam had moved a little closer to the elk. Which put him on the edge of the rather steep slope that led from the pavement down to the course itself.

"Hey, buddy," he called out. "Watch the edge."

Sam looked down, as if he hadn't noticed how close

he was or how far the drop was. He swayed, and Stefan moved so quickly Sam looked startled. He wobbled just before Stefan got there and grabbed his hand.

"Don't want to scare them off," Daria said to Sam as she got to them. "They're calm now, but if we get too close, that boss elk will show you why he's the boss."

Sam laughed at the way she said it, and the startled look vanished.

And when they walked back toward the pavement, the boy reached up and took Daria's hand with his.

It was such a simple, natural thing, walking along with his son between them, hanging on to both their hands. But Stefan had that same sense of breathlessness for the third time this morning. And when he finally worked up the courage to look over at Daria, the soft expression on her face and the warm glow in her golden eyes made him feel something he didn't even have a name for.

Sam was chattering away about the elk, but Stefan barely registered what he was saying. At least, until the boy interrupted himself.

"And—hey! Look!"

Stefan turned to see the Alvarez family piling out of a large SUV that had pulled up a few yards away from where he and Daria were parked.

"I texted them, too," she explained. "They like having the boys see the local wildlife."

"Hey, you three," Fiona called out cheerfully, waving toward the herd of elk. "Beautiful, aren't they?"

They chatted while the boys greeted each other and excitedly watched the big animals. Since he and Daria couldn't talk about their work, they chatted about other things, and he learned that she and Fiona had both once tried skiing and had quickly decided it wasn't for them, but that Daria had somewhat of a knack for ice-skating. Now that he would like to see someday. He could just imagine her, graceful and beautiful, sliding across the ice.

"We're off to go sledding at the big hill," Fiona said when the boys finally started to get restless with just standing and watching the grazing animals.

Sam's head came around. "Sledding?"

"Yeah," Casey, the oldest boy, said excitedly. "There's this really cool place we go, at the bottom of the mountain. It's a lot bigger than our little hill at home, so you can go really fast. Dad found it."

As he started to tell Sam all about it, Miguel stepped up to say to Stefan, "Sam's welcome to join us, if that would be all right. This will probably be the last chance with this snow, it's melting so fast."

"That's very kind of you."

"The boys would love it. They really liked him."

Stefan smiled at that. "I'm glad. More than you know."

"We would have called and suggested it, but we know you're so busy with this awful case," Fiona said.

He didn't want to admit they were not at a dead end but helplessly immobilized temporarily, so instead he looked at his son.

"Sam? The Alvarezes have very nicely asked if you'd like to go sledding with them."

The boy's dark eyes widened. "Really? Can I?"

Stefan couldn't stop himself from smiling at the boy's hopeful expression. "I think it would be all right."

"And he can stay and have dinner with us, too,"

Miguel said. "We're having spaghetti, and Fiona always makes a ton."

"Because my boys eat a ton," Fiona said with a teasing grin at her husband. "You can have him back about seven, since it's a school night."

There were a few more minutes of scrambling and making arrangements, and then they were gone, Sam so enthused he was practically dancing.

"It's good to see him so happy, isn't it?" Daria asked.

It was way better than good. It was something he'd been afraid he would never see. And in less than a week, Daria had accomplished this.

Miracle worker was the only description that came to mind.

Chapter Nineteen

"They're amazing people," Stefan said, watching the Alvarezes drive off.

"They are. They live for those boys."

"That's like my folks were. I never really appreciated it until Sam was born, how their lives revolved around us kids."

Daria was silent, and when he looked at her, she was gazing out over the golf course again, but not toward the elk. In fact, she looked as if she were a million miles away. "Good parents," she murmured.

It hit him then. Her mother. He instinctively reached out, took her arm and turned her to face him. "You know she did what she thought would be best for you," he said quietly. "She knew she couldn't take care of you the way she wanted you to be taken care of."

Surprise flickered in her eyes for an instant. But then she smiled, a soft, gentle curve of those lips that sent heat rocketing through him.

"You're a perceptive man, Stefan Roberts."

"I…thank you." He didn't know what else to say.

"No, thank *you*. If not for your help, I would have never known. I wouldn't even have known what she looked like."

He knew Daria meant the old driver's license for Ava Bloom he'd gotten for her, which showed a young woman with lovely features, whose daughter was nearly a carbon copy of her—only Daria's skin tone was lighter.

He heard her let out an audible breath before she said what he'd guessed had to have been the most crucial question to her. "I would have always wondered why she gave me up."

"I'm sorry she had to," he said. "I wish…"

She looked at him as he trailed off awkwardly. "You wish what?"

"That everybody could have had my parents."

She smiled at him again, brighter this time. "I don't even have to meet them to bet the world would be a better place if everybody could have."

He had a sudden vision of that meeting happening, of introducing Daria to his parents. Speaking of bets, he'd make a sizable one that they'd like her. There was no snobbery about her, even though she had as much reason as some of the snootier sorts they'd encountered on this case.

Perhaps that's why she never mentioned the connection she had to the Coltons; it wouldn't surprise him at all that she purposely avoided it. Daria was a woman who had made it on her own. That's why his parents would both like and appreciate her. He'd kind of skipped that step with Leah—they hadn't met her until after their whirlwind courtship and elopement, and when they had, they'd been welcoming but reserved.

Because they knew what you'd gotten yourself into. That's what you get for not letting them vet her first.

But Daria… Daria was what his mother called good

to the bone. He was certain of it, in a way he'd never even thought about with Leah. And he knew his parents would see that. He truly could picture it—

He gave himself a sharp mental shake. What the hell was with him? Imagining taking her home to Mom and Dad? When they hadn't done…anything more than that single impulsive hug?

They hadn't even really discussed this powerful pull between them.

Or maybe it's only you that feels it, Roberts. Ever think of that?

He didn't want to believe that. Which sounded childish to him even as he thought it.

"Stefan?"

He snapped back to the present. And was immediately irritated with himself. He wasn't usually given to mental meandering. "Sorry," he muttered. "I was thinking about…my parents."

"They'll be here soon," she said.

"Yeah."

"Is Sam excited? Does he even remember them?"

"I…don't know." He'd almost forgotten about that. In fact, in the midst of the case and everything else that had been changing so rapidly, he'd overlooked a few things. Including telling his son they were going to have company. "I've been a bit consumed."

"I know the feeling," Daria said. "I feel guilty every minute I'm not working on the case."

"So do I."

"But I was going crazy, spinning my wheels. I was hoping getting outside for a bit would help."

"Did it?" he asked.

"I don't know."

"I suppose," Stefan said slowly, "the only way to find out is to try, but the thought of going back to the office makes me cringe."

"Me, too," she agreed. Then, rather hesitantly, she said, "I have most of the stuff on my laptop at home. That's where I was working before the walls closed in on me. We could…go there instead, if you think it would be better."

He was smiling at her correct assumption they would both rather be working than pretending there was such a thing as time off during a case like this one. And then it registered what she'd suggested. She was inviting him to her home?

To work, idiot.

But he couldn't deny he was curious.

Daria said her house has a big yard. We could move there.

Sam's words echoed in his head. He could only wish life was as simple as a five-year-old could make it sound.

And he caught himself again. His mind was careening out of control. How could he be wishing it were that simple, with a woman who was not only a work colleague, but one he'd never even kissed, and who had made it pretty clear she considered him off-limits?

"Okay, obviously that was a bad idea."

Daria's words snapped him out of his reverie yet again. "I…no. No, it wasn't. I was just…thinking about something Sam said this morning. About…your yard."

God, he sounded like a complete idiot. He was usually reasonably articulate, but when it came to anything outside of work with this woman, he seemed to trip all over himself.

He tried to recover. "He'll be jealous I got to see it."

"Well, he'll have to come another time, then."

And so he ended up following her, since he'd need his car to go pick up Sam later. She'd mentioned she lived just outside the city limits, so he wasn't surprised when they left the density of town behind and headed into the foothills. But he was when she turned into a long, curving driveway that led up to a ranch-style house with a touch of The Lodge's log finish, a prow sort of front with huge windows, sitting on a slight rise. The way it was situated, he figured it would have a great view down over the hills, and that if you didn't know, you'd never guess there were other, similar houses on the way up to here.

And she hadn't exaggerated if that entire clearing behind the house was the yard she'd talked about.

A garage door rolled up as they neared, and she pulled into the shelter of it. He pulled up behind her in the driveway, stopped and got out.

"Wow," he said, looking back the way they had come. He couldn't see any sign of the neighbors he knew were there, except for a glimpse of a roofline off to the left. "Nice."

"It's bigger than I need, but it was a great deal, and my dream location." She walked over to him. "I like it. It's so…peaceful."

"You don't feel… I don't know, isolated up here?"

"There are neighbors closer than you might think. Besides, I've had enough of living with a lot of people around all the time." Her expression shifted, as if she were remembering something specific. "I find it a nice change."

"I've always thought of myself as a city guy, but this could change my mind."

"At night, if it's clear, I get a bit of the sparkle of lights in town," she said. "And if I look the other way, I get the mountains. Seems perfect to me."

"Best of both," he agreed.

"And don't forget the backyard," she said, grinning now. Damn, it lit up her face, and those golden-brown eyes. "Come on, I'll show you, and you can decide if you think Sam would like it."

He was almost sure he already knew the answer to that, but he went along anyway. And the moment they rounded the corner of the house, the "almost" vanished. What kid wouldn't love this, a vast expanse of open meadow with occasional trees, intriguing paths and a small stream that wound its way down past the house? He saw a small, arched bridge that crossed it farther out, along a path that disappeared on the other side into thick trees. The whole area was groomed enough to be in control, but with enough wildness left to look natural.

"The stream is just a trickle in summer, but the rest of the year it flows pretty steadily," she said. "And the path that leads over the bridge continues on to the tree platform."

"Definitely five-year-old heaven," he murmured. "Or any other age, for that matter."

"I like it."

"How long have you been here?" Stefan asked.

"Three years now. I lived in town when I first started with the sheriff, but I always wanted a place with more room."

He studied the yard, then her. "Who does your gardening?"

She laughed. "And that quickly he spots the problem."

"It just looks…intensive."

"It is. Usually I do most of the day to day, and I have a crew come in every month to handle the bigger stuff. But since this case… I hired a service some of the neighbors use. And I confess, it's been a relief."

"Might be worth it to keep them, then. Be more fun to enjoy than to worry about."

"I'll have to look at the budget," she said.

His gaze snapped from the bridge he'd been admiring to her face. Surely money wasn't an issue for her? With her connections?

And you think she'd use those connections?

He realized with a sudden shock that he not only liked this woman, he admired her. Not just for her smarts and work ethic, which was a match for his own, but for the fact that she'd carved out a spot for herself in a job that wasn't always welcoming to women.

Add that to the fact that he was, plain and simple, hot for her, and he suddenly felt like he was in way over his head, in a very different way than he'd felt since Sam had arrived.

Maybe this hadn't been the best idea, coming here where they would be alone. Secluded. Unnoticed. And following her into the house seemed like an even worse idea. But follow her he did, when she walked back around the corner of the house and into the double garage. Which was tidy, although somewhat full, with boxes stacked along one wall and metal shelving filled with various things on the other.

She stopped. "I'm sorry, I didn't think. If we're going to be working for a while, do you want to pull your car inside?"

He could think of a lot of other things he'd like to share with her besides garage space. Before he could descend into crudity—but not before a few images had flashed through his mind that made him very aware just how close to being out of control he was—he thanked her and went to move the car.

At least it would be warmer when he went to get Sam, he thought as he got out and she closed the garage door behind them. And as if she'd sensed where his thoughts had gone, which he wouldn't put past her at this point, she said, "When it's time to get Sam, there's a shortcut over the hill to the Alvarezes' place. You can be there in less than ten minutes."

"Thanks," he rasped, his voice sounding oddly tight, even to him.

The garage entrance put them in the kitchen. Where his was sleek, modern and rather cold, hers was… homey, he guessed was the word. The appliances were modern, yes, but the butcher-block countertops gave it a warmer feel, as did the artful arrangement of branches with dried fall leaves that graced the large island.

Beyond that island was the great room, a wide-open space boasting a big river-rock fireplace, which, judging by the stack of logs beside it, was not just for show. There was a large, cushy chair at an angle to the hearth, and beside it a large basket of yarn, with something half-knitted lying on top. He could see the needles with their indeed pointy ends. He found himself smiling again at the memory.

The rest of the room looked just as homey. There were two comfortable-looking couches, one arranged to take advantage of the view out the front, which was as spectacular as he'd envisioned, the other facing the fireplace, where he guessed it would be warm and cozy on a cold winter night. Maybe with snow falling outside, reducing the world to a soft quiet.

He yanked his thoughts off that path when he realized he was picturing them together on a night like that, on that couch before a roaring fire, wrapped in each other as the snow fell.

As if reading his mind, she went to that fireplace and quickly, efficiently built a fire. She had obviously learned what worked, for the paper and kindling she'd laid out neatly were almost immediately aflame, and when she added a couple of bigger logs, they caught quickly.

The fire completed the image. And he faced the simple fact. Her home was everything his wasn't. Warm. Welcoming. Just as Daria herself was.

He wondered just how much trouble he'd gotten himself into by coming here.

Chapter Twenty

Daria had a moment to be grateful she'd instigated what she called her full-schedule protocol: when things were normal, she tended to get a bit lax about keeping things picked up, but when things got crazy she was a lot more strict, knowing she had no time to deal with looking for things she might have left here or there.

And things hadn't been normal for months now.

"Coffee?" she suggested. "Hot chocolate, maybe?" She gave him a sideways glance. "Or, if you're insane enough to want it, something cold?"

"Let's keep it warm," he said, and there was a rough note in his voice, slight yet enough to have her thinking of other contexts in which that comment could be meant. "Coffee's fine," he added quickly.

She only nodded, because she didn't quite trust herself to speak, and went to the kitchen to set up the coffee maker. While it was running, she got out two coffee mugs from the cupboard. Her glance fell on the mug that Keith Parker had given her as a joke, before they'd ever gone out, with a scene of a California beach and the caption "If I was here, I wouldn't need hot coffee." He'd known she was from California, but nothing else.

No one here knew the full truth of her California roots except Trey.

Stefan took the mug of coffee she offered him, and then she led the way to her home office. She booted up the computer, sent the display to her larger, separate monitor, and a few minutes later they were looking at the data they had on Curtis Shruggs. Not that it did any good, because after going through it all yet again, and then again, after nearly three hours spent retreading worn, unproductive territory, they had nothing more than they'd started with.

They went for refills on the coffee then walked into the living room. It was warm, that special kind of warmth that only came from a wood fire. She added another log, aware as she did so that Stefan was pacing the room. She stayed in front of the fire, both for the warmth and the distance from this man who so unsettled her.

Finally he said, "I know we didn't turn up any registered weapons, but I was thinking we should check for a fishing or hunting license in his name tomorrow. It might give us a clue if he frequents wilderness areas or lakes."

"Good idea. Parks and Wildlife would have the records." She grimaced. "Although a fishing license is for the entire state, all fresh water, so it wouldn't narrow it down. I'm almost hoping there's nothing, because the range that would open up would be huge."

"Too bad they're not like a passport, with entry stamps."

She nodded, thinking. "But if he has a hunting license, the stamps might tell us something. There are places that are prime for waterfowl, others for elk, whatever stamps he might have. It's more than we have now, anyway."

"Of course," Stefan said rather wryly, "we're assuming a serial killer gives a damn about permits to hunt or fish or anything else."

"Our lives would be easier if it worked that way, wouldn't it?" she agreed, feeling a bit morose about it at the moment.

"They call 'em outlaws for a reason," Stefan quipped.

She had to laugh at that one, even though it was a rather grim laugh. "We sure don't have much else."

"I know," Stefan said, starting to pace the room again as he ran through what they'd gleaned so far. "To his assistant's knowledge, he doesn't play golf, or tennis, or ski. The most she had on his leisure time was that he's used The Chateau spa for a massage now and then."

Daria suppressed a shudder. "Can you imagine being one of the staff who did that? Especially if you were a woman?"

"Frightening," he agreed. He shook his head, slowly. "I've been thinking his assistant is lucky she doesn't fit the victim profile."

Another shudder, and Daria began pacing, as well. "Is it making you as crazy as it is me that we know who he is, but have no idea where?"

"Well, at least it's a fairly narrow search area, since he's likely still in Colorado," Stefan said. "I mean, he hasn't bought a plane, train or bus ticket, and we've got a watch on his credit cards and there's been no activity, no gas purchases, or food."

Daria stopped pacing to look at him. And then she chuckled.

"I said something funny?" he asked, clearly puzzled.

"No. It's just sometimes I forget. That to you, the entire state of Colorado is a small search area."

"Well…yes." He smiled back at her. "But we've got a lot more resources, don't forget."

"Lucky for us," she said. Then she looked at him curiously. "Did you always want to be an FBI agent?"

He laughed. "No. I wanted to be a baseball star."

"Understandable." She tried picturing him in a baseball uniform. The image came quite easily. "So how'd you end up where you are?"

He hesitated, then shrugged. "They sort of recruited me."

"The FBI?"

He nodded. "Something…brought me to their attention, and they came calling and told me to come see them as soon as I finished college."

"'Something'?"

"An incident when I was nineteen. A shooter, at a restaurant."

Her eyes widened. "What happened?"

He gave her a rather sheepish look. "In reality? I got mad. I figured if he was going to kill me, he was going to have to work for it."

"And?" she prodded. "What did you do?"

"It was a pizza place. I had just gotten mine, so I offered him a slice. It kind of took him off his stride, and he instinctively reached out to take it." Another shrug. "I grabbed his weapon and threw it across the room and shoved him back out the front door."

"That was you!" she exclaimed. "I remember that incident. You were a hero across the country."

And, she realized with a little jolt, he'd visited the White House. If the timing had been different…

He grimaced rather ruefully. "I kept telling them I was just saving my own ass, but people needed a hero, I guess."

And that, she thought, was what made a true hero. One who didn't see what they did as heroic, but just as what had to be done. "I can't believe I didn't remember your name."

"Not the rarest name around," he said with equanimity.

"You really were unimpressed with yourself." She flashed him a smile. "Which impressed me."

"My folks saw to that. My dad said he was proud of what I'd done, but if I let it go to my head he'd take me down a peg." He grinned suddenly. "I've got about four inches and thirty pounds on him, but I have no doubt he could take me out even now."

"Because you'd let him," she said softly.

The grin faded, changed to a slow, loving smile. "Yeah. Yeah, I would."

And Daria was seized with a strong, very real desire to someday meet the father who had raised this man to become who he was, from pizza-parlor hero to honest, tough, smart FBI agent.

And an even stronger desire to have that kind of loving smile from this man turned on her.

She turned away before he read the longing in her eyes. Then headed back for the warmth of the hearth and the fire, since she was denying herself a different kind of warmth.

But an instant later she knew she'd been too late, because he came up behind her and said huskily, "Are we going to just keep ignoring this?"

She opened her mouth to say, in her best innocent

tone, "Ignoring what?" Knew she couldn't manage it. She thought about simply saying, "Yes, we are." Couldn't manage that, either.

In the end, what she said came out a little desperately. "We have to."

"Why?"

"So many reasons."

"Such as?"

"You need to settle in with Sam. I'm older than you." She swallowed tightly. "And there are things you don't know."

"You're secretly a video-game addict?"

She blinked. "What? No, I—"

"As for Sam? Yes, it's been a struggle, but we've made great strides, thanks to you. He adores you, and I think you like him. So there's that argument shot down. Older?" He made a dismissive sound. "Big deal. If it was the other way around, it wouldn't even occur to anyone to think about it. So strike a blow for equality. As for not knowing everything about each other, well, that's half the fun, isn't it? Discovering all that?"

She turned and stared up at him. He was so close. So big. Couldn't he be less gorgeous? She could feel his heat. She could feel an answering heat building in her, no matter how she tried to fight it. It made the warmth from the fire seem a mere flicker. She couldn't even imagine what it would be like if he actually touched her.

And she couldn't think of a thing else to say.

"You told me Aisha made Trey make the first move, and you approved."

"That's different."

"Is it?" Something in his expression changed then, and when he spoke, his voice was softer. "So, when this case is over, we just go back to our regular jobs, our regular lives? Forget about…this?"

He leaned in then. Slowly, giving her a chance to pull away, to dodge.

She did neither.

And when his mouth—that mouth that could create that smile that melted her—came down on hers, the heat that had been building in her exploded, sending fire along every nerve.

She felt a moment of stunned shock. She'd lived forty-two years, some of them hard, some of them wonderful, but she had never in her life felt anything like this. Faint echoes of it, yes, and she'd thought that's all there was to it. But this…this was as if those prior feelings had been tiny candles leading to this impossibly deep, impossibly rich explosion of sensation.

And it was just a kiss.

Even as she thought it she dismissed the idea jubilantly. This was no mere kiss—this was fire as surely as the one going in her fireplace. No, not just fire, because it was hotter, more insistent than mere warming fire. This was…inferno. Conflagration.

And she, who had ever and always been cautious, flung herself into it without hesitation.

An awareness of how solid and strong he was came to her. She'd known it before just by looking, but now she knew, because she was touching. Sliding her hands over him so eagerly it would have embarrassed her had she been capable of such an emotion just now. But she wasn't. There was no room for anything except this blazing heat and the sensations the feel of him erupted in her.

He deepened the kiss, stole her breath. It didn't matter, because he was touching her in turn now, and having those big, strong hands stroking her so gently was more fuel to the blaze. He cupped her breasts, and she instinctively arched toward him, a tiny moan escaping her. His thumbs rubbed over nipples already achingly taut, and this time his name broke from her on a gasping breath.

He broke the kiss, and she felt a shudder go through him.

"If you're going to say stop, say it now," he said, his voice sounding hoarse and strained.

"No." It was all she could manage. Another shudder, and he started to pull away. She realized what he thought she'd meant. She grabbed at him, tried to hold him close. "I meant…no, not saying stop."

She looked up at him, and what she saw in those gorgeous eyes had her breathing even more quickly. "Daria by firelight," he whispered. "I can't think of anything more beautiful."

And she knew it was going to happen, right here, right now. And it felt so right, so good that her heart began to hammer in her chest, her body rising to the promise in those eyes.

She didn't know or care who undressed who—all she knew for sure was that she wanted to see him, *all* of him, wanted to run her hands over every inch of him, wanted to claim him in whatever way she could. And when they'd untangled themselves from their clothes, something seemed to snap inside her. Triggered by the simple fact that he was power and strength made visible, that he was even more magnificent than she'd imagined, need rocketed through her.

Once unleashed, her hunger overwhelmed her and

she was stroking, kissing, even nipping at him, everywhere she could reach. She'd become some wild thing that astonished her. She was glad he'd thought of a condom, because she certainly hadn't.

She heard him swear, low and deep and heartfelt, that gruff, rumbling male voice kicking her pulse up a notch higher. And then he'd scooped her up and taken them both to the soft rug on the floor in a smooth flow that spoke of the power in that big body. The beautifully sculpted body that, for now at least, was hers to touch, to caress, to ravish.

The body that moments later was surging into her, the ease of his passage telling her the truth of how much she wanted this man. And then he was in her, stretching her until she would have sworn she couldn't take any more. But he kept on, until the exquisite sensation made her cry out at the joy of having that empty place inside her filled.

He said her name, low and harsh, and she knew she would carry the sound of it in some sacred part of her mind forever. She felt a shudder go through him, felt his entire body go rigid.

"Can't go slow," he ground out. "This has been building too long."

"I know," she whispered and lifted her hips to him.

And then he was moving, stroking, caressing as he withdrew and plunged deeper, until she was crying out with every thrust. He drove her higher and higher, his hands seemingly everywhere, his mouth on her lips, her cheek, her neck, all while the rhythm he set nearly drove her mad.

And then he reached between them, to where they were joined. He stroked with a single finger once, twice, and she reached that peak of madness. Every nerve in her body seemed suddenly to lead to that place, and they all fired at once. Her body clenched, then exploded, so fiercely all she could do was wrap herself around him and hang on.

Chapter Twenty-One

Well, having your first wild, crazy sex in the middle of the day was one way to avoid the dreaded morning after, Stefan thought.

He kept his eyes closed. He was full of so many sensations he was having trouble sorting them out. Uppermost was the feel of Daria draped over him, her skin as silken as he'd known it would be. She felt good. More than good. He thought he might just lie here forever with her delicious weight on him. Well, maybe eventually move to a bed. Her bed. His bed. He didn't care, he just wanted more. Much, much more.

He'd gone a little crazy with her. Or maybe she'd made him a little crazy. He wasn't sure which, wasn't sure it mattered. All he knew for certain was that he'd never felt anything in his life like sex with this woman. And he had the feeling it was just as much because of who she was—smart, determined, quick, kind—as it was because she was so damned intoxicating. But whichever it was, she'd fried every nerve in his body.

And in that moment when he'd exploded inside her, he hadn't been a hundred percent sure he'd survive it. Nor did he care, because that would be a hell of a way to go.

He realized abruptly he was almost falling asleep. A warning bell went off in the back of his mind, that this was not a good thing to do the first time with a woman. Especially one you genuinely cared about. But he hadn't been sleeping much lately, and she felt so damned good, naked against him. So good that even now, even just moments later, other parts of him were declaring rather fervently that sleep was not on the agenda.

He wasn't surprised at that. What he was surprised at was himself. Because he was lying here thinking a guy could face almost anything if he had this waiting for him every night. Or afternoon, he amended with an inward smile. But the image conjured by those two words, *every night*, lingered in his mind. And the thought of a never-ending stretch of moments like this filled a place inside him that he'd never even known existed, let alone that it was empty.

Maybe it hadn't existed, until he'd met her.

"Why did we wait so long?"

He hadn't really realized he'd spoken it aloud until her head came up. "Because it complicates things," she said, and the husky note in her voice completed what the feel of her skin had begun—his body started clamoring for a replay.

"Regrets?" he asked, carefully keeping his tone neutral as he thought maybe he hadn't avoided the morning-after minefield after all.

But a slow, pleased-looking smile curved that mouth that had driven him to that crazy state. "No. It does complicate things, but no."

Belatedly it struck him that it wouldn't complicate things unless she expected it to continue, would it? So she wasn't going to pull away, change her mind? Relief at that flooded him, because he couldn't understand how anybody could not want more and more of this.

It did complicate things, but only logistically. Between this case and Sam, free time was at a premium. But relegating what they'd just discovered together to only that minimum of free time seemed...impossible.

"I want more," he declared.

"I noticed," she said with a grin that made him feel oddly light even as she left a fiery trail along his body when she slipped her hand downward to curl around flesh already eager for a repeat. "Hard not to."

"Hard's the word all right," he growled, and he had to fight not to roll her under him right now. "But I meant more than just today. And more than just until the end of this case."

"Stefan—"

"Don't even try, unless you've got better excuses than before."

"But—"

He stopped her with a feverish kiss, giving in to the demands of a body that had nearly begun to shout, "What are you waiting for?" She was the one with the excuses, so if he had to show her again why they didn't matter, he would. Happily.

He forced himself to take it slower this time, vowing to himself he'd make her crazy for it before he slid into her welcoming heat. He wanted to hear her cry out his name again, wanted her legs wrapped around him, wanted her fingers digging into his back, wanted to feel the incredible clasping of her body as she climaxed around him.

He blazed paths with his hands, traced every luscious curve, then followed with his mouth until she was moaning, twisting under his touch, his kisses, his tongue. She was the most delicious thing he'd ever tasted, and on some gut-deep level he knew he would never, ever get enough of her. That should have rattled him, but it didn't; it only filled him with a joy he'd never known and a soaring feeling that he finally, finally understood.

And in the end, she didn't cry out his name—she screamed it as her body bucked beneath him, and the feel of her sent him hurtling over the edge right after her. And he thought he must have shouted her name as he went.

It was much later, in the dancing light of the fire, that she gave him a shyly wondering look. "I've…never been like that. I'm not sure what got into me."

"I'll refrain from making the obvious joke," he said, grinning at her.

She blushed slightly, just enough for him to see beneath the color of her skin. He found the fact that she was blushing beautiful. In fact, he couldn't think of a damn thing about her he didn't find beautiful.

And he didn't feel the slightest urge to back off, the way he always had with any other woman since his hideously faulty judgment about Leah. He'd worked beside this woman for three months; he'd seen her smarts, her dedication and her integrity. If he was wrong about Daria, then he should just give up altogether. And he wasn't going to give up. Wasn't going to give *her* up. He wanted it all, no matter what they had to do, how they had to arrange things.

"I was serious," she said after a moment when she'd regained her composure. Which, considering they were sprawled naked on her great room floor, was saying something. "I have never, ever been like this."

"I'm glad. Because you blew circuits I didn't even know I had." When she gave him a fleeting look that was almost bashful, he shook his head. "No inhibitions. Not with us. We blew right past that."

"Apparently," she said, with just a touch of wryness that told him she was regaining her humor, too.

When his cell phone chimed an alarm, he was startled. Because he only had one for today—the one he'd set when he'd sent Sam off with the Alvarezes. He scrambled over to the spot on the floor where their clothes lay as entangled as they had been, and tugged it out of a pocket. He'd been half convinced he'd set the time wrong, because it couldn't possibly be—

It was.

"Time to go get Sam?" she asked, getting to her feet and, sadly, reaching for her own clothes.

"Unbelievably, yes. Although I've got a little margin, because when I set this I assumed I'd be coming from…my place."

"Lucky you're here, then."

He covered the short distance between them in one stride, grabbed her shoulders. When she was looking up at him, he said solemnly, "I have never, ever been luckier."

Again she blushed slightly, and he wondered what the hell was wrong with whatever men had been in her life that such a simple compliment got to her so.

"And here I was thinking I was the lucky one."

"Remember that," he said, rather fiercely, "the next time those excuses float through your mind."

Chapter Twenty-Two

Daria watched as Trey Colton drummed his fingers on his desk. That was the only outward sign of tension, despite the fact that tomorrow was the day that would determine the course of the rest of his life. Election day.

"I read your reports," he said, looking across at her and Stefan. "Great work, both of you."

"It's finally going to be over," Daria murmured.

"We have to find him first, but yes, it is," Stefan agreed. His gaze shifted from her to Trey. "And maybe just in time. You could put word out that we know who the Avalanche Killer is now. Before tomorrow."

Trey's brows rose. "The election, you mean."

Stefan nodded. "It would be big, favorable news."

Trey looked affronted. "And could well spook Shruggs into running, lose us the chance to nail this guy, put him away for good. That's more important than any damn election."

Stefan smiled as if this was the answer he'd expected. "And that, Sheriff, is why I'll be voting for you tomorrow."

Daria saw a slight smile play across her boss's lips. "Just go find this miserable excuse for a human being, all right?"

"Yes, sir," they both said.

"Thank you for that," Daria whispered as they left Trey's office.

"Just confirming I was voting for who I thought I was voting for," Stefan said easily.

"What if he'd gone the other way? He never would, but what if?"

"Then I'd be voting for the lesser of two evils, which I hate, so I'm very glad he didn't."

And that little scene, Daria thought, told her a great deal about both of these men.

As they walked to the back of the station, toward the parking area, she said, "I meant to ask, how's Sam?"

"Remarkably compliant," Stefan answered as they got into his car for the ride to The Lodge. "Obviously the answer is keep him exhausted."

She laughed. "I talked to Fiona last night—she said he did marvelously. Even Casey likes him, which from his vastly superior position of two years older is saying something."

That wasn't all Fiona had said, of course. A great deal of the conversation had been taken up with the fact that apparently Sam had chattered even more about her than his father. And, Fiona being Fiona, with teasingly probing questions about how on earth Daria managed to resist the tall, dark and gorgeous Stefan.

And now that she'd stopped resisting, she wasn't sure how to answer that. Except that she couldn't be unhappy about it. How could she possibly be unhappy about anything that made her feel so darn good?

She warned herself against making incredible sex into something more, something it wasn't. Warned herself against hoping this was the start of something bigger, longer lasting. Because once this case was over—and thank God it appeared it might actually be, finally—there would be no reason for them to spend so much time together, unless that itself was the purpose. And she was afraid to even hope for that.

I meant more than just today. And more than just until the end of this case.

His words played back in her head, and she felt a tiny shiver inside. He couldn't have been much clearer, so why did she doubt him? Why did she assume he didn't mean it?

You know why. Because you haven't told him the truth, haven't told him who you really are, and it could change everything.

She thought back to their conversation about the pressure of the Coltons being involved in this case, and his rather pragmatic assumption that Colton pressure was why Trey had asked the FBI to step in.

Contrary to what some think, we don't always go around butting into local affairs if we're not asked.

When he'd said it, she'd merely observed that a lot of people made a lot of assumptions, and there was a good chance half of them were wrong. He'd laughed, commented her estimate might be a little low, and they'd moved on. At least, *he* had; the truth of what he'd said, and the secret she was keeping, had been nagging at her ever since.

But it had to wait. Because right now they were close, *so close* to ending this nightmare that she barely wanted to stop to breathe, let alone have what would likely be a long and possibly devastating conversation. At least, as far as her relationship with this man went.

A relationship she very much wanted but had doubts would survive.

The trip to The Lodge was silent, although Stefan kept giving her sideways glances as he drove.

"Problem?" she finally asked.

"Not unless you have one," he said. "It's just, you're… quiet."

"Antsy," she clarified. "We're so close, and yet…"

"I'm glad it's the case you're thinking about."

And not…us? Did they qualify as an *us* now? He was certainly acting like it. And on some level, she knew it was her own guilty conscience that had her thinking anything other than that he'd meant what he'd said. He wanted more, and he wanted it beyond the end of this case.

But he doesn't know…and given who he works for, it could matter.

"When this is over," she began, but she had no idea where to go from there and so the words hung in the air unfinished.

"Then we'll work out the details," he said, as if the big decision was already made. She felt a tiny spark of…something. Speaking of assumptions, he seemed to be making a big one, since all she'd agreed to was that she didn't regret what they'd done. And she wasn't quite sure how she felt about that. All the reasons against it still existed—they just didn't seem to matter anymore.

When they arrived at The Lodge, they parked the car themselves in the lot rather than leave it under the portico, because this time they were going to be here as long as it took to get something, anything, that would tell them where Curtis Shruggs might be. And if that entailed talking to every one of the hundreds on staff, so be it.

"Great tennis weather," Stefan remarked as they got a glimpse of the courts and saw two people out playing. There was still a bit of snow lingering around the edges and in shady spots, so it did look a bit odd.

"Helps when the courts are heated," she said.

He turned his head to look at her. "Seriously?"

"Of course. This is the crown jewel of The Colton Empire. Unless you're talking to Mara Colton, of course, then The Chateau is the crown jewel and The Lodge merely the adjunct."

"No wonder she and her husband are having problems," Stefan muttered.

"Not to mention that little affair of the nephew who's really his son," Daria said dryly.

Stefan had facilitated the DNA testing that had revealed that bit of news that shocked the Coltons. And he'd done the same for her, although instead of finding out that she had a living parent, as Fox Colton had, she'd found out what she'd suspected was true—her mother had died years ago, after giving her up when she became so seriously ill. But she owed this man for the closure.

And a few other things.

"And speak of the devil," Daria said, suddenly realizing who was coming out of The Lodge's front doors.

Stefan looked. She heard him make a sound and knew he'd spotted Russ Colton approaching. A tall, broad-shouldered man, with once dark brown hair now mostly gray, the head of The Colton Empire had clearly passed his good looks on to his sons. He thankfully hadn't passed on his rather overbearing manner to any of them she'd spoken to.

"Wonder what he's doing here?" Stefan asked.

"Down from the Manor?" she said rather dryly, using the grand name for the building in the mountains that looked like what it was—some very wealthy family's home base. She knew it had been built ten years ago, and that before they had lived down by The Chateau. She had always had a suspicion the Manor existed so the Coltons didn't have to mingle quite so much with the regular folks. "He's pretty hands-on. He must work about twenty hours a day."

"I have no problem with people who work hard to get to where they are," Stefan replied. "But speaking of the Colton home, he's got a bit of that lord-of-the-manor thing going on, and that I find annoying."

"The business is his baby. More than his children ever were, I think. It's amazing most of them came out pretty decent people."

Stefan murmured as Russ spotted them and headed their way, "I wonder how he's going to feel about someone so high up in his company being a serial killer?"

"I vote we don't find out just yet," she whispered back.

"You win."

"Deputy Bloom!"

"Mr. Colton," she said. "You remember Agent Roberts?"

"Yes, yes, of course. What are you doing back here? Shouldn't you be out hunting down this maniac?"

"We have bloodhounds for that," Stefan said smoothly. Daria shot him a look, both appreciative of the joke and startled that he'd risk it with the powerful tycoon.

Russ looked a bit taken aback. But he recovered

quickly. "This just has everyone so on edge. It's very difficult to do business, which is in a horrible state with all this going on."

"Nothing like a serial killer to shake things up," Stefan said. Again Daria blinked. She supposed being an FBI agent gave Stefan the freedom to say things she only thought, since she was a lot more likely to encounter the Coltons on a regular basis.

"Yes, yes, it's awful, but I'm very tired of my family being blamed for any part of this when we're victims. Accusing us of getting special treatment when we've only tried to help. You have no idea what it's like, having people judge you for something as simple as your name!"

Daria and Stefan exchanged a pointed glance.

"Oh, really?" Stefan drawled.

They had no idea? She, even with her skin tone being lighter than Stefan's rich, deep brown, had had her share of being judged by something even simpler than a name.

"You know what I mean," Russ said, a little defensively.

"Yes," Daria said; this was not the time or place. "Now if you'll excuse us, we have work to do."

"Chasing after that maniac," Stefan added with a too-charming smile.

After Russ had hurried away, they continued inside. "He really does rub you wrong, doesn't he?" she asked.

Stefan shrugged dismissively. And then, with a slow smile, he said in a voice rich with the husky undertone she'd heard when she'd been in his arms and he'd been murmuring her name, "You, on the other hand, rub me very, very right."

She felt a frisson of sensation shoot down her spine,

as if he'd touched her. And she wondered yet again what would happen between them when this case that had seemed endless just two days ago finally did wrap up.

Chapter Twenty-Three

They started at the top.

The office of the director of operations of The Lodge quite suited the rest of the place, elegant yet fitting the majestic mountain setting. Since Daria had dealt with this side of things practically from the beginning, Stefan let her explain what they wanted.

Perhaps because they'd just encountered the senior Colton, Stefan thought he could tolerate Decker Colton a lot better. He'd not interacted with him much on this case, but when he had, he'd noted the guy had the air of someone who had learned there was more to life than business, a lesson it appeared his father had never learned—and likely would never learn.

He'd mentioned that once to Daria.

And he learned it by falling in love. With a whip-smart woman.

She'd said it with a wide smile. Obviously she approved of the idea, he thought now. So why was she so wary with him?

He suddenly went still as he realized the path of his own thoughts. Falling in love? Was that what he'd done? What he wanted her to do? Was that why it bothered him that she seemed so…cautious?

A tangle of emotions jammed up in him. Didn't he have enough on his plate with Sam and a serial killer? Shouldn't he resolve at least one of those before he added something new and all consuming? Did he even want to add the complication a serious relationship would bring?

But it was only because of Daria that he was where he was with Sam. If not for her, they'd likely still be at each other, with him searching for patience and constantly reminding himself his son was only five, and Sam giving him those angry looks and throwing out those hateful words. She had changed that, had set them on a path that he hoped would lead to a genuine bond with his son.

Not to mention he was not about to give up what they'd discovered together yesterday. That had been no casual encounter, no simple onetime hookup. He'd had enough of that to know the difference.

He wondered if he and Daria gave off the same sizzle Decker Colton and his wife, Kendall, did. The pretty blonde had been leaving just as they arrived and had stopped to greet Daria enthusiastically—Daria's boss had been instrumental in finding the kidnapper who had grabbed her, and in discovering it had been orchestrated by someone her family owed money—and Stefan more decorously. But her face glowed with happiness, along with that sizzle.

Of course, she and Decker were newly married. That put them in a different category. Didn't it?

The smile Kendall had left on Decker's face faded when he realized why they were here. Since Shruggs again hadn't shown up at work today, they'd decided there was little to gain by trying to hide that he was a suspect, although they refrained from confirming he was the only suspect. Decker looked shocked but thoughtful. Shruggs had been here since before Decker had taken over, and since they had relatively few personnel problems, he'd never had reason to question his effectiveness or look into his methods.

It was Daria who quietly made the suggestion that Shruggs might have used his office to hunt for victims among the job applicants. Decker went pale, but Stefan could sense the change as he went from shock to anger that a Colton executive would use his position in such a hideous way. He offered them his full assistance before they had to ask and quickly set them up in his spacious meeting room and began to personally send employees in to them.

From there it became an extensive string of interviews, some short, some longer. They began with all the people who worked in Shruggs's department. Including his assistant, whom they had now concluded Shruggs had chosen because she was the most uncurious being he could find. The only thing this interview with her accomplished was to have Daria say sourly, after Shelly Bates had left, "If I ever start uptalking like that, shut me up, fast."

"Well, now you've got me hoping you do," Stefan said, thinking of the ways he'd like to quiet her in that very unlikely event, most of which involved keeping her mouth otherwise occupied.

And for a moment it was there in the room, alive between them, what they'd discovered together. The power of it took his breath away, and that rattled him. He'd never felt this way, and he wasn't quite sure what to do with the roiling emotions she caused in him. All he knew for sure was that if she asked him for a re-play, he'd do it, right here, right now on this expensive Colton table.

Sex is the easy part, son.

His father's words from long ago echoed in his head even as he had the arousing thought. And they were fol-lowed by the rest of what his father had said, which sur-prised him a little, because he would have sworn back then he hadn't been paying much attention.

When you find yourself wanting to make her life easier, even if you have to go out of your way to do it, when you put what you want on hold for something she wants, not begrudgingly but happily—and when she does the same for you—well, then you've got something.

He'd ignored that wise, fatherly advice with Leah, who had never put anything she wanted on hold. And look where it had gotten him.

But it did get him Sam. And for the first time, he had hope that it would work out, that he could do for his son what his father had done for him. And that truly was thanks to Daria. And somehow no amount of men-tal orders not to get ahead of himself seemed to stop his mind from racing wildly in the direction of forever with this woman.

Forever.

He had a sudden image flash through his mind, of them years—hell, decades—from now, still together, as solid and unbreakable as his parents. He'd spent so long thinking he wasn't capable of that kind of bond that it was beyond startling to realize that he was think-ing about it now, easily, with Daria. And he felt both thrilled and scared about it.

He wasn't sure if he wanted to know how Daria felt. Because if she hadn't had the same kind of thoughts...

He made an effort to yank his wandering mind back, which in itself was a warning. He never had trouble focusing on a case. That alone told him how much deeper Daria had dug into him, and without even trying.

If she ever did try...

This time he slammed the door on his thoughts and issued a stern order to his unruly mind to focus. He didn't want to be the reason they missed some hint or clue, not now that the end was nearly in sight.

They moved on to the managers at Shruggs's level, people he would have felt were worth his time, if they were judging his character correctly. Most of them recalled the man attending various social functions, but always alone. A couple of the women even admitted to offering to set Shruggs up with a friend, but he had always declined. They'd finally written him off as a confirmed bachelor who didn't want any change to that status.

And when they realized what this interview meant, that Shruggs was suspected of being the Avalanche Killer, even the most composed of them were completely shaken.

But once they got over that, every one of them made an obvious effort to remember anything about the man that could offer a clue to where he might be now. And as they'd expected, once they realized what was up, everybody seemed to have a memory of some creepy thing Shruggs had done or said. Stefan and Daria were both familiar with this Monday-morning-quarterbacking aspect of an investigation, so they dismissed the more general observations, but made note of everything anyway and highlighted the ones that seemed more solid.

But one stuck out to them, from the head of housekeeping, who had mentioned how, whenever she encountered the personnel director on a Monday, she would politely asked him how his weekend had been.

"He always said something like 'Beautiful,' or 'Wondrous,' but he said it with the creepiest expression I've ever seen. A hundred times worse than my ex-husband when he thought I didn't know he was cheating again." She'd paused then before adding, "He did say something once about there being lots of fish in the pond. I remember that because my mother used to say that, but it was fish in the sea, not pond."

Her words had made Stefan think of their discovery this morning, just before their meeting with Trey, that Shruggs had once had a fishing license but it had not been renewed in the last decade.

"Which proves nothing, really," Daria had said, sounding frustrated.

"Except that he might know some remote places to hide."

She'd brightened slightly. "True. And it's not likely a killer's going to worry about something as mundane as keeping his fishing license up to date."

"You might be surprised, some of the things serial killers obsess about. They can go either way."

"But still twisted."

He nodded in agreement.

They plowed on now. Swearing they'd talk to every employee if they had to had sounded good enough back at the office, but they hadn't really factored in the time the interviewees' shock would eat up, and they weren't moving as fast as they wanted, not when the chances of Shruggs's latest victim still being alive were shrinking rapidly.

They were down to the last couple of managers on the list when the door to Decker's conference room flew open. A woman burst in without knocking, making them both tense. Stefan rose out of his chair, but took no action as he recognized her as the director of guest services here at The Lodge.

"Is it true?" the woman demanded. "You know who the monster who killed my sister is?"

"I think," Daria said quietly, also getting to her feet, "you'd better sit down, Molly."

Chapter Twenty-Four

"It's…really Curtis? The Avalanche Killer is Curtis Shruggs?"

Molly Gilford trembled slightly as she sat across the table from them. Daria saw the tremor in her fingers as she brushed a strand of blond hair back from blue eyes that were suspiciously bright. She could only imagine how she must be feeling right now.

And Daria quickly decided that this woman had been through enough—the murder of her sister, that terrifying incident on the gondola and then being kidnapped herself by her half-crazed sister-in-law who wanted her then unborn baby. True, she was now married to the baby's father—Max Hollick of K-9 Cadets—apparently happily, but nothing could change the fact that she had been terrorized and her sister had been viciously murdered. And she deserved every bit of the truth Daria was able to give to her.

"I'm afraid it's true," Daria said gently. "We found definitive evidence in his house." She left it at that—no need for the woman to know about the hidden, sound-proofed room, the cage where he apparently tormented his victims before he killed them.

"But… I've worked with him for years. And he's always been…very vocally pro-women. Supportive. In his hiring, too. I never…he never…"

She stopped, took a deep breath.

"I know it's hard, feels impossible to believe," Daria murmured.

Molly took another breath, then looked Daria in the eye. "My sister and I weren't as close as some, because of the seven years' difference between us. I used to wish she would—" Her voice broke, but after a moment she went on. "I used to wish she would hurry and grow up, get through the partying stage. And now…"

She never will.

The words echoed in the room as clearly as if she'd spoken them. And Daria had no idea what to say, because deep down she knew nothing she said could adequately ease what the woman was feeling.

Even as Daria thought it, Molly drew herself up and said with remarkable steadiness, "But she was my sister and I loved her. I named my baby after her." She looked at both of them. "I want the truth."

Daria knew the woman meant it, but since she had little but a gut feeling to go on that Sabrina Gilford hadn't been one of the Avalanche Killer victims, she kept her own theories to herself. Right now she needed to focus on the facts at hand, the evidence they had and the man they knew had a woman in his clutches right now. And if Molly could help them with that, they had to push to find out anything she might know. If it turned out that she'd been right about Sabrina, they'd deal with it then.

"How closely did you deal with him?" Stefan interjected, his tone very gentle, and Daria knew he, too, realized what this woman had been through in the past few months.

"Sometimes very, sometimes not," she answered, her voice hanging on to that new steadiness. "I always check with guests during their stay to make sure everything's to their satisfaction. If I came across an employee who handled a guest's problem or a request well enough that the guest mentioned it to me, I made sure he knew."

"And complaints?" Daria asked, genuinely curious.

Molly gave her a fleeting smile. "If it was a first complaint on an employee, I let it go. We have some… very particular guests."

Daria presumed that was her tactful way of saying some of their guests were a pain. She could imagine, having lived both sides of that divide. "The type no one can please?"

"Exactly. So unless it became a pattern, I let it go. If there was a second time, I'd talk to the employee, but if it came to a third—unless it was all from the same guest who clearly just didn't like the employee—then I'd let Curtis know." She gave a shake of her head. "And he always handled it well enough, I thought. Fairly, anyway. I just can't believe this. Curtis, a…a serial killer?"

"I understand the shock you must be feeling," Daria said. "But we need you to just set that aside for the moment, because right now we have to focus on finding him."

Molly nodded, although her expression made her feelings clear. Daria didn't blame her in the least; finding out someone you'd known and worked alongside for years was truly that monster she'd mentioned was enough to rattle anyone to the core.

Daria thought about speaking some platitude that it might turn out Curtis was innocent, but they had to find him to prove that, so she didn't. This woman had asked for the truth, and if she was this solid after all she had been through, she had earned it.

"Think back, Molly," Stefan urged. "Did you ever hear Curtis say anything that might be a clue to where he would go to be...alone? Anyplace that was a favorite haunt, maybe someplace he went on vacation or something?"

"I don't think he ever really took vacations. Not like other people, you know, for a week or two. Just extra days here and there."

Stefan nodded; that tallied with what his assistant had told them. But Molly went on and instantly had Daria's complete attention.

"But he did mention once that a friend of his had a place near here that he'd gone to."

"A place?" Stefan was just as on alert as she was.

"A fishing cabin. I remember it because Curtis never seemed like a fisherman type to me."

Not for fish, anyway. Daria tried to rein in the inner kick of excitement that hit her. "Do you have any idea where, exactly?"

Molly shook her head. "I don't think he ever told me exactly, just that it was up above the biggest of the springs, at the west end. Except..."

"What?" Stefan encouraged her, and Daria heard the change in his voice, sensed the same wiredrawn tension in him that she was feeling. This was something, she was *certain* of it.

"He mentioned how...isolated it was. He said you could scream at the top of your lungs and no one would hear you." Daria felt a shiver go down her spine at the description of the perfect serial killer hideaway. Molly swallowed visibly. "I thought it was an odd thing to say, but that was all. I never… I should have…"

She stopped, gulping now. Daria reached out and put a hand on her arm. "You had absolutely no way to know, Molly. He's obviously very, very good or he wouldn't have gotten away with it for this long."

"Did he ever mention this buddy's name?" Stefan asked.

Molly shook her head. "He only said something about him being pretty nice for a…well, he used some nasty slang for someone who's Japanese."

Stefan was already on the phone, probably to his office, as Daria tried to soothe the understandably upset woman.

"You promise you'll find him?"

"I promise I will not give up until I do, one way or another," Daria said fiercely.

And she meant it. If it took years—which, God help her, it had better not—she would take down the man who had slaughtered those innocent women for no better reason than they matched his "type." She didn't care what justification for murder his twisted brain might come up with. All she cared about was stopping him at all costs.

"I believe you," Molly said. "It's why I'll vote for your boss tomorrow. And I don't care what the Colton haters say about having a Colton for sheriff."

Tomorrow. One more thing to deal with, Daria thought as the grief-stricken woman left. And Molly had no idea that what she'd said had a double meaning for Daria. That Trey wasn't the only Colton connection in the department.

Stefan was ending the call as she turned back. "They're on it, cross-referencing property owners around the springs with any Japanese names. It shouldn't take too long."

"Assuming he could even be identified by last name," Daria said, thinking he could have divided parentage like her own.

"All we have to go on," Stefan reminded her. "And," he added with a gentle rub at her shoulder, "a heck of a lot more than we had when we started."

"Yes." She turned to look at him then. "Let's start that way."

Stefan blinked. "I called for a team, but it'll be a while before they can get rolling, especially since we don't have a location yet."

"But we can be in the area, check it out first."

"Get the lay of the land, you mean?"

She nodded, so antsy to do something, *anything*, that she thought she might go on her own if he refused.

"I'm not sure that's a good idea," he said.

"I've got to do something," she insisted, feeling as if she were about to jump out of her skin. "I can't just stand around and wait, not when we finally have him!"

"I've had that feeling," he said cautiously, "but a lot of times that's when mistakes get made."

"Look, all I want to do is look around, see what we'll be dealing with. If he's even there. And if he's not, we can search the place for any evidence."

"All right," he finally agreed. "But that's all we're doing. We're not going after a guy with this many kills to his name without backup."

Daria knew better than to think it was his own safety Stefan was concerned about. He was just worried about Shruggs getting away. And he had a point, she admitted. It just wasn't enough to tamp down her impatience.

"And," Stefan added, "I take the lead." She pursed her lips. Waited for an explanation of what had sounded rather peremptory. Because she knew this man now, and knew he usually had a good reason for such decisions. When it came, it made perfect sense. "Just like at his house. He's seen you, but I've never been face-to-face with him."

"All right."

It wasn't until they were gathering up gear—Kevlar vests, tear gas, the Remington 700 rifle Daria hoped never to have to fire in a real-life sniper situation, and for good measure a couple of flash-bang grenades— that it occurred to her to wonder if maybe, just maybe, it wasn't just Shruggs escaping that Stefan was thinking about.

Maybe it was her.

Chapter Twenty-Five

As he drove the department SUV, Stefan's instincts, honed by intensive training, warned him this was not what he wanted to do. Not what the Bureau would do. Barring interference from above, thankfully rare this far from the halls of power, they would wait until they had all the pieces in place, all possibilities they could think of covered. But Daria was so determined he knew there was no stopping her. And if he let her go alone, it could all too quickly devolve into disaster. Because he knew she'd risk herself, if it came down to it, to take this beast out. She was too damned fearless for her own good.

And for his peace of mind.

And that simple realization—that he was worried as much about her as this case—was a screaming warning that he was in way over his head with this woman. Never before had his emotions interfered with an investigation, and most especially a case like this, particularly when they were this close.

He tried to focus on the fact that she did have a point, about scouting the area. They needed to know the surrounding terrain, scope out possible escape routes, and if they could get that done before the backup team arrived, they'd be that much further ahead. And if they came across the target alone, he would just have to keep Deputy Bloom reined in until help arrived. No way in hell was he letting her go in after Shruggs without a full team, including a sniper—maybe two—in place and ready.

The old nightmare rose in his mind, and full daylight made no difference. That horrendous night, back in the killing fields of Chicago, when bodies had been strewn in the street, among them two agents who had moved too fast, without backup. True, they had done it because they had to—the suspect and his gang were shooting random citizens—but the aftermath had looked like a battlefield.

And two of their own had been among the dead.

This isn't the city. And we're going after one man, not a mob.

Not, of course, that one well-armed psychopath couldn't do a great deal of damage. And just because Shruggs had no concealed carry permit meant nothing. Less than nothing. Expecting a serial killer to abide by the law was a fool's game.

But he didn't do his kills with a weapon—he killed with his hands, up close and personal. Stefan had seen interviews, and done one himself, where the killer professed his delight in seeing life fading out of his victim's eyes.

He gave himself an inward shake; this was accomplishing nothing. Right now he needed to focus on keeping Daria out of trouble while they gathered the intel they could pass on to the backup team. At least she had realized he was right about him taking the lead, just in case the worst happened.

"Thank you," she said suddenly.

. "For?"

There was a half second of silence, enough to make him glance at her. The slight smile that barely curved her lips warmed him inside in a way such a minute expression shouldn't have been able to. And the warning bells sounded again.

"Many things," she answered just as he had to turn back to driving, "but right now, for agreeing to this. I know you didn't want to."

"No, I didn't. I'm more of a get-your-ducks-in-a-row-first kind of guy."

"And what if while you're lining up those ducks, the vulture escapes?"

He glanced at her. "I wouldn't have thought of you as…impulsive."

Before he had to look back at the road ahead, he saw her expression change slightly as the word registered. "I'm not," she said. "I make very sure I know what I'm doing before taking a big step." He had time to wonder if that applied to what had happened between them yesterday as she hesitated for a moment. But then she said, very quietly, "I have a feeling my mother acted on impulse, and look where it got her."

He thought of what else the DNA testing he'd arranged had shown, but this was hardly the time for that discussion. He'd never pushed her about her parentage, and he wasn't about to now—not when they were heading into a situation that required them to be completely focused.

"She did what she had to. To give you both the best chance."

"I know." His next glance at her caught a very speculative look in her eye, but all she said was, "And it probably did work out for the best."

"You were adopted."

"Yes. And they were…wonderful to me." Again that speculative look, but it was the last time he was able to notice her expression, because they'd reached the area above the west end of the springs the town was named for, which also meant they'd reached the end of paved roads. Hence the SUV. Daria had known the roads up here were gravel at best, more often dirt and too often mud. He could already see she'd been right.

He paused the vehicle once, to get oriented in his mind. They'd called up the satellite imagery and he'd studied it until it was set in his mind, a knack he'd often put to good use. He was looking at a thick stand of trees off to the left when she spoke again.

"Isolated," she said, "could mean different things to different people. Did he mean out all alone with no neighbors close enough to hear, or just secluded among trees, so no one can see, either?"

"Could go either way," he replied. "But…"

"You're thinking trees?"

"Just a gut feeling." He knew she'd get this. Most cops of any persuasion did.

"Me, too. Something about his house, the log cabin look…"

"So…north-facing?"

"A good place to start," she murmured.

"Then that narrows down the escape routes, unless he's got a plan to get out on foot if he has to."

"He struck me as even less of a hiker than a fisherman," she said.

"All right. We'll go with that."

It took Daria a moment to realize what had caused the oddly emotional reaction she had to what should have been a strictly businesslike, even grim decision-making process—to hunt for a serial killer was hardly a heartwarming subject.

But what was heartwarming was Stefan's easy acceptance of her assessment of Shruggs. He'd always been respectful of her and her skills, but this, so close to what she hoped and prayed was the end, was bigger, and if he'd ever been going to take over it would be now. But instead he respected her instincts, her training, trusted her judgment as a cop, and she was a little taken aback at how much that meant to her. That he took her word as an equal, not just as a woman to a man, but a small-county sheriff's deputy to a federal agent.

But then she realized she must have already known it on some level. Because if she wasn't certain, even subconsciously, that she had that respect from him, yesterday afternoon never would have happened. And the very thought of having missed what she had found in his arms, the sheer joy his hands, his mouth, his body had given her, was chilling. She was old enough to know such perfect matches came along rarely in life. What she didn't know was where they went from here. He'd said—

A bounce that jarred her teeth interrupted her thoughts.

"Sorry," Stefan muttered. "That was more of a pot fissure than a pothole."

She found herself grinning at that, and given the circumstances, she took it as a sign of how far gone she truly was for this man.

The road got even rougher, and Daria saw some

patches of lingering snow as they entered the shade of the evergreen trees standing amid the deciduous ones.

"At least the leaves are mostly gone from the cottonwoods, or we'd probably have some branches down," she said.

"And it means we can see farther," Stefan added, not looking at her as he negotiated another rut in the rural road.

"It's nice out here, and I'll bet the view of the mountains is spectacular, but..."

"I like your place better."

She turned her head to look at him. "You do?"

"I like your place a lot."

"I'll...keep that in mind." The emphasis he'd put on that last word sent her mind racing in a direction she couldn't deal with right now. She needed to focus. How would she feel if they lost Shruggs because she was mooning around planning a rosy future she wasn't even sure he wanted?

But Stefan had said he wanted more.

With great effort, she tamped down thoughts of forging the kind of future that she'd almost given up even hoping for. Because if this failed and Shruggs got away because she wasn't focused, Stefan would find that hard to forgive.

And if this failed and it was her fault, she would never, ever forgive herself.

Chapter Twenty-Six

When the steering wheel jerked yet again as they went over a rough spot in the dirt road, Stefan realized he missed that aspect of the city. It startled him, because he hadn't missed anything about the city for quite a while.

Spoiled. You want the whole planet paved? Even beautiful places like this?

Of course, that beauty was tainted at the moment by the presence of the human scum that was Curtis Shruggs. This place—and the planet—would be a lot better off once he was put away.

He glanced over and saw Daria studying something on her phone. It gave him a chance to see her in profile, to appreciate the delicate line of her jaw, the way her hair caressed her neck, the place in her throat where her pulse beat, where he had nuzzled and licked and kissed her…

He snapped his eyes back to the rough road. He was going to drive them into a tree at this rate. But the combination of her strength of will and body, her quick mind, and her unassuming beauty was intoxicating. And unlike this place, nothing could ever taint that beauty.

He had a sudden vision of her a quarter century from

now, her hair perhaps gray, or even his mother's almost glowing silver. She would still be stunning, probably regal, an elder who demanded and got respect. And him? He'd be pushing sixty then, maybe thinking about retiring. Or flying a desk, something that seemed anathema now, but if he had her to go home to…

Damn.

Rattled, he stared at the road ahead. But he still saw that picture, of his future life, so full and complete in his mind, as if it were a given. Complete with the woman at his side now still at his side then.

Then again, why not? He admired her. Respected her. He'd thought her beautiful from the first moment he'd turned to see her coming into Trey Colton's office. He'd already known she was sharp, smart, or the equally sharp and smart sheriff wouldn't have signed this case over to her. But he hadn't expected the lithe, graceful knockout that had walked in, hadn't been— could he have ever been?—prepared for those gorgeous gold-flecked brown eyes.

And now you know you're hotter than hell together.

Well, yeah, that, too. They'd damned near set her hillside on fire.

And he was about to drive off this one. He scrambled to regain control of his thoughts. This was not the time to be lost in envisioning a future like he'd never even dared hope for before.

He hit upon the one thing powerful enough to match his flooding thoughts of Daria. *Sam.* But even he was no longer the distraction he'd once been, and that, too, was thanks to Daria. They were tentatively finding their way to the kind of relationship he wanted with his son. And as for Daria, Sam adored her, and she clearly liked him.

Enough to want both of us?

And suddenly that future image in his mind shifted, altered. Sam would be...damn, he'd be thirty then. And what kind of thirty he'd be would depend on what kind of father Stefan was now. Just as the man he was now was because of his own father.

Tell your father word for word what you just said.

Daria's words echoed in his mind, as they so often did. And he added the thought he'd just had to the list of things he was saving up to do exactly as she'd suggested. Tell the man who deserved to hear it.

And suddenly he was looking forward even more than before to his parents' trip out here. Not only for the help they'd be, but...he wanted them to meet Daria. He was as certain as he could be of anything in this life that they would see her for the amazing woman she was. He could even picture his father taking him aside, as he never had with Leah, and telling him to hang on to this one. And—

"You want me to drive?"

His head snapped around, and he stared at her. "What?"

"You look a bit white-knuckled. I've driven on roads like these quite a bit, if you'd rather not."

"Oh. No. I'm fine."

"We're going to get him, Stefan."

Of course she thought that was what had him all wound up. Why wouldn't she? It was probably the only thing she was thinking about. She certainly wasn't sitting there fantasizing about them growing old together.

And he was coward enough to seize on the out she'd unknowingly given him. "I know we are."

"I wish we'd gotten to him sooner, but—"

"We've got him now. It's just a matter of reeling him in." His cell rang, and on this road he pulled over before he tugged it out.

"At least the call got through," Daria murmured. "Service is particularly spotty up here."

"It's my office," he said as he answered. "Lisa? What do you have?"

"Two names and locations," the woman replied. Stefan saw Daria was already prepared with her own phone to take notes. "Go."

He quoted back the names and addresses Lisa gave him, and Daria keyed them into her notes app.

"I'd tell them to text as backup," she suggested. "Sometimes texts get through up here when calls won't." He relayed that info, all the while watching her as she switched to a map and did two quick searches. "One's on the left fork we'll hit another half mile or so ahead. The other's that gray house we passed on the way up."

"Gray one seems too close to civilization," he said.

"Agreed."

He drove on as she did something else with the image on her screen. The track that branched off to the left from the one they were on looked little more than something a mountain goat would use. He wasn't even sure the SUV would make it. Yet if Shruggs was up there, he had to have gotten there somehow. So he kept going, at a pace that would lose to the proverbial snail.

The track veered slightly more left, and the surface was even rougher.

"Maybe we should stop here." Daria indicated a very small space to her right where they could pull over at least halfway. "And go in on foot."

"Maybe," Stefan said neutrally, "we should wait for the troops to go in at all."

"I don't mean go up and knock on the door," she retorted. "Just to get a closer look."

He smothered a sigh. He supposed there wasn't any harm in that, if they were careful to stay under cover. "Let me get some gear out of the back. We'll need binoculars and communications at least."

She nodded, back to looking at her phone. "I'll enlarge the satellite view, see if we can tell anything from that."

His brow furrowed. He pulled out his own phone, to see the "No Service" warning. She glanced at him, and he turned it toward her.

"I know," she said. "I figured that would happen, so I took a screenshot of it back there where we had a signal."

He stared at her. "You never miss a trick, do ya?"

She gave him a smile then that nearly sent his pulse into overdrive. And suddenly he wanted that future he'd imagined, growing old with her by his side, more than he'd wanted anything. Ever.

"Here," she murmured, holding her phone out to him. "It looks like there's a footpath here that goes up around the back."

He silently questioned what she considered a footpath. Decided he was definitely still too much of a city boy and said only, "The house looks smaller than the gray one, but it's bigger than what I'd call a fishing cabin."

"True. So maybe it's not the one. Maybe when we get closer, we'll see a family with the traditional two-point-three kids and a dog, and we'll know."

He'd never thought himself that bound by tradition, but somehow that sounded...wonderful. Even the dog. Sam would love a dog—she'd obviously been right about that. And maybe more, later. Adoption was fine with him, although he would have liked to have seen what kind of child he and Daria would have produced.

And the realization he was thinking in those terms barely rattled him anymore. But they had to get through this first.

They slipped their earpieces on and verified they were working and that they could hear each other clearly. Then he let her take the lead, staying close enough behind her to grab her if she slipped, which looked uncomfortably possible on this very narrow path. Branches brushed him as they passed, and once a bird chattered at him crankily as they disturbed him.

"So much for stealth," he muttered.

"I don't think it matters," Daria said. She'd come to a stop, the binoculars to her eyes. He came up behind her, and she handed them to him.

He looked. It wasn't the two-point-three kids—more like four, with three adults, all bundled against the chill, a Japanese couple and a single Caucasian female. The adults were watching the four kids, an equal mix of the same races, playing in what was left of the snow. All smiling happily. As they watched, another male exited the house, carrying a tray with cups of something steaming that made Stefan suddenly crave that hot chocolate Daria had once mentioned.

"If I have to believe that group knowingly has anything to do with the likes of Shruggs, I'm going to quit and become a hermit," she whispered.

"You won't be a hermit, because I'll be right there with you," he said.

"Promise?"

She said it teasingly, but he got the feeling there was more behind it. He put a hand on her shoulder, and she looked back at him.

"Yes," he replied quietly.

Something flashed between them, something vivid and alive, and he knew she'd understood. And when she looked away, he didn't feel slighted, because he realized the intensity was too much right now, when they had no choice but to be focused on the matter at hand. The details—for in his mind that was all that was left—could wait.

Had to wait. Because they were close, he could feel it.

Although he agreed with her completely about the innocence of this group, he watched them for a moment longer. The biggest child had raced off toward a small outbuilding, a shed of some sort, likely to gather the snow that lingered on the side still in shade.

And Daria went suddenly still. She pulled out her phone and swiped it on. He could see from where he stood behind her that the satellite image was still there. She enlarged it, then moved it slightly.

"See it?" she asked softly.

He frowned, scanning the screen. It took him a moment to orient himself, to place the edge of the clearing they stood a few yards away from now, but then he had it. In a thick stand of trees, east of where they were, was another roof. He looked that direction and saw nothing but trees. So hidden. Then he glanced back at the screen, the nearly hidden roof in the image. Definitely smaller than this house.

Just about the right size to be called a cabin.

Chapter Twenty-Seven

"It's a bit far, but it could still be on the same property if they have acreage," Daria said as she studied the phone, glad she'd thought to screenshot the image. They'd moved away from the happy group at the big house; the last thing she wanted was such obviously innocent bystanders getting caught up in anything. When the backup teams got here, they'd either corral them safely in the house or evacuate them, depending on how the situation looked.

"And thus be under the same name in the records," Stefan agreed. "It looks pretty basic—just a rectangle with a simple roofline."

She nodded. "I don't see any path from here to there," she said, enlarging the area around that second roof.

"Trees are thick enough over there it might not be visible on that," he told her. "We might have to—" He stopped as her phone signaled a text. "I see what you mean," he said as she switched over to read the message that had gotten through.

Her breath caught as she read. And when she looked up at him, she knew the triumph had to be glowing in her eyes.

"I had my office call Molly Gilford." Daria gestured

back toward the house they'd just left. "I thought the owner of that place might have tried the area out first, to see if he liked it enough to buy. She just called back. Mr. Nakamura was a guest at The Lodge several times before he bought this place."

Stefan's eyes widened. "And thus had multiple chances to encounter Shruggs."

"Yes."

He looked back the way they had come, although they could no longer see the house with the families. "That place looked fairly new."

She nodded. "Maybe when they bought the property, the cabin was the only thing on it. Then they built the house and let people rent or borrow the cabin. I know it's guesswork—"

"But it's good guesswork," Stefan said. "It makes sense, and it fits with everything we know."

"We could go back and ask him," she suggested. "Assuming he's the guy who's there now."

Stefan thought for a moment. "Let's not risk it yet. Just in case Shruggs is here and watching." He checked his own phone for texts. "Nothing," he muttered. "I want an ETA on backup."

"They'll get here when they do," she said, far too antsy to think about how long that might be. She knew she didn't have to remind him Shruggs had a new captive, who just might still have a fighting chance. "In the meantime, let's see if we can get the lay of the land around the cabin, and any sign that he's been here."

"We should wait. If he's there now—"

"We should at least be where we can see if he leaves."

She saw him take in a deep breath, then he nodded. "Point taken."

She thought she saw a flicker in his eyes, as if he were remembering what had become a private joke between them. She'd knit him that scarf, she thought, when this was over.

They made their way with as much stealth as they could manage in the general direction of the small cabin. And he'd been right—there were paths, of a sort. Just narrow tracks that meant walking single file, one foot directly in front of the other, and brushing branches both bare and evergreen as they passed.

"Animal paths," she murmured as they left the big house with the happy gathering behind them.

"And the city guy in me is a bit edgy about that," Stefan, who was ahead of her, muttered.

"I'll take these animals over city animals any day," Daria said.

It was a moment before she heard him say rather wryly, "Once again, point taken."

They fell into silence then as they got closer to where they were guessing the hidden cabin was. Stefan stopped in the same moment she spotted a straight, man-made angle through the trees, although the color was nearly the same brown as the winter-bare trees.

"Not quite as isolated as I expected," she said.

Stefan looked back toward the house where the families were playing. "No. I'd think someone down there could easily hear someone scream from here."

The possibility that they were completely wrong about this place shook her, threatened her with a burst of despair.

"It's still the best lead we've got," Stefan uttered firmly. "Let's go."

She nodded and they went forward even more carefully, until Stefan stopped again. Although this time he was looking down.

"The animal-track path dies out," he whispered.

"Odd," she murmured back. "I wonder why."

"Maybe they know."

If he'd been facing her, he would have seen her practically gaping at him. That was such a fanciful, if very dark, thing for this man in particular to say. He seemed utterly grounded in reality to her, and she wouldn't have guessed him capable of it. But were the circumstances different, she thought it would have charmed her. Not that he needed any help in that arena.

But the idea was now vivid in her mind—that even the wild creatures knew there was something abnormal here. Something to avoid. Something dangerous.

"They don't call us the apex predator for nothing," Stefan muttered, as if he felt the need to explain away what he'd said. Later, she thought, she would tell him how unnecessary that was.

"And we're the ones who take out the predators."

He looked back at her then. Gave her a quick, flashing smile that took her breath away and nearly blasted all sense of focus out of her.

"Yes, we are," he said.

And in that moment Daria knew he was as determined as she was, that they shared this goal, that it was why they were who—and where—they were. A sudden, crazy image shot through her mind, of her and Stefan sitting in her living room some unknown amount of time from now, discussing their respective current cases as Sam played his favorite game on the floor in front of the fire. And she was seized with a fierce ache inside to make that come true, to have that, for all three of them. Because they all needed it. And each other.

She felt the sudden need to say so, to say yes to the question he hadn't yet asked but had hinted at when he said he wanted more. And it seemed important to say it now, despite her common sense telling her this was hardly the place or the time. Then again, maybe that was what made it seem so important right now. Maybe it was the same sort of instinct that had stopped the animals from getting closer than they were now. She didn't know what might happen next, and—

Before she could even begin to find any words, a sound from the direction of the cabin snapped both their heads around. In an instant Stefan had the binoculars up to his eyes. Daria held her breath, waiting.

"Nothing moving," he whispered after a few tense moments. "Except there's a squirrel or something by that trash can out to the left from the building."

She leaned forward and spotted the large metal can. Even as she looked, the small creature vanished into the trees. She wondered if it had given up the task of trying to loosen the lid or if something had scared it off. Perhaps it had belatedly sensed whatever the other creatures who had gone no farther had sensed.

"I think we could get there," she said softly, gesturing through a gap in the trees.

"Want to go trash picking?"

"No, but yes."

That smile again. They should make him get a permit for that, because it was more lethal than any firearm.

"I suppose it wouldn't hurt," he said. "As long as we can do it without getting spotted."

It took them a little longer to get there than she'd

expected, because of the effort to hold down the noise. Luckily for their purpose, the trash can was set against a row of trees that marked the end of the small clearing behind the cabin, masking anything—or anyone—behind them. Unluckily, the trees were so close together that it would be nearly impossible to get to the can without either making noise or visibly moving the branches. If no one happened to be looking this way at that moment they'd be fine, but...

"I'll try," she whispered. "I'm smaller." *And then some.*

Another of those flashes hit her, of just how much bigger and stronger he was. Cliché though it might be, it was true in his case. But then she veered into how he used that size and strength, that amazing body, when he'd been driving her mad with a sexual heat she'd never felt before—

Stop it!

He was looking at her, and she knew by the set of his jaw he wanted to say no. Was probably weighing what would happen if he did. His protection elsewhere might be needed, even welcomed, but if she couldn't do her job, there was no point in having it.

"Not on the job," she said to him, very quietly.

For an instant he looked surprised, but then rueful, as if he'd realized how well she'd read him. "Just—"

"Be careful. Got it."

"And if I touch you, freeze."

Not likely.

"Not a sound or a move," he went on.

"Copy," she said.

She got down on her hands and knees and crawled ever so slowly through the lower branches of the trees.

Using the large trash can itself for cover, she reached up and released one of the latches that held the lid on, a frequently seen protection against bears and other animals that might be scavenging around. She fleetingly wondered if Shruggs was even aware of such things as she edged the lid partially off. Half afraid of what she'd find, she raised the lid slightly and straightened just enough to look into the can.

She had to move the lid a bit more to let in more light, for the contents were in the shadowy bottom of the can. But it only took her a quick look and a reading of a single torn wrapping to have her closing it back up and working her way backward. When she was clear of the low branches, and they had slipped back into place, masking them from the cabin, she rose into a crouch. Stefan came down to her level quickly, with that easy grace of his.

He didn't speak, just waited. She appreciated that, because the surge of adrenaline had her breathing quickly and it took her a moment.

"This is it," she whispered, letting her gut-deep certainty into her voice. "This is the place."

He didn't argue, just led the way back the same way they'd come, until they were safely far enough it was unlikely they'd be spotted or heard from the cabin. Then he glanced back toward where the trash can was. "What?"

"Wrappers." He looked back at her then. "From packages labeled…soundproofing."

She saw Stefan's jaw tighten. "That son of a bitch. He built himself another torture room."

"So the one in his house was just a…holding pen."

She couldn't disguise the shudder in her voice. "Stefan, if that girl is still alive…"

"She might not be for long," he said grimly.

Chapter Twenty-Eight

"No texts?" Daria asked. Stefan shook his head. "So we don't know how far away they are."

"We need to know if he's here. We can't assume he's not just because it's so quiet."

"Agreed," she said. "But the girl…she could be in there, dying, right now." Tension echoed in her voice; she could hear it herself. But she went on. "If he's not there, this could be our only chance to save her."

"Daria, we have to wait for the breach team."

"I know, I know," she said. "I just hate this."

"So do I," Stefan told her. "But there are protocols for a reason."

"I know," she repeated. "Just tell that to my gut."

He gave her a commiserating grimace, and she knew he did understand. That underneath that cool, calm exterior he was probably as roiled as she was. But he was a professional to the core and wouldn't let it sway him.

"I didn't see a garage, or even a carport," Stefan said.

"Maybe it's down the hill, hidden on the other side of the cabin. For that matter, we might not be able to see a car out in the open from here, if it's on that side."

"It would help to know if his vehicle is there. Assuming he uses his. That bright yellow Italian sports job is pretty noticeable."

"Making up for his other shortcomings, no doubt," she quipped.

Stefan blinked. Then he grinned at her. As she had intended.

"Not," she said airily, "a problem you'd understand."

The shared moment of intimacy, achieved without even a touch, warmed her. But it was immediately back to business. They needed to know about a car, and there was only one way to do that.

"Up or down?" he asked, checking both directions in turn from where they stood.

"We could each take one way. Up means more cover but tougher terrain—it's pretty steep," she said, looking that way. "Down's easier, probably quicker, but more chance of getting spotted if he is in there."

"Kind of decides it, then."

She nodded. Then, decisively, he said, "Get back to where you can see the cabin, and I'll see how far I can get up there." She pondered that for a moment, wondering if he was pulling the protector card again. Before she could speak, he said quietly, "You're the sharpshooter—you need to be stationary."

He had a point. And his easy acknowledgment of her skill took any sting out of staying here while he risked the climb.

She heard him go, but once he was a dozen feet away from her, she heard nothing except the faintest brush of branches that could have been from any light breeze. It was amazing that a man his size could move so quietly. That was, it would be amazing if you didn't know him, if you hadn't seen that tight-knit grace up close and personal. As she had.

She had to suppress a shiver, which was odd given the heat that had shot through her at the memories of that up close and personal. She almost gave herself an order to stop thinking about sex with him. Aloud. Which would have been picked up by Stefan's earpiece.

Now that would have been seriously embarrassing. Then again...

Daria snapped out of it when something from the cabin caught the corner of her eye. She shifted the binoculars that direction, but nothing had changed. All she could discern was that a shaft of sunlight had broken through the November gloom, and it caught the upper corner of a window and sent back a flare of light. Yeah, that must be what she'd seen. She settled in to watch and wait. And listen. Most of all listen to that tiny unit in her ear.

It was several minutes before she heard anything, and then she couldn't be sure if it had been Stefan or some creature he'd disturbed.

"Okay?" she asked quietly; they'd decided on plain English because ten-codes varied between agencies.

"Proceeding," he said back, just as quietly. "And there's a pond in view on this side."

Lots of fish in the pond...

It seemed an endless stretch of time after that. She wondered idly how snipers did it, how they simply waited, ready, sometimes for hours. Sometimes even longer. Then she wondered about how some people were great shots with long guns, some with sidearms, a rare few with both, and what it was that made that difference.

Her mind kept racing in an endless loop. But it was

the distraction she needed to keep from thinking about what could be going on in there, what that evil, repulsive psychopath could be doing to an innocent woman. Because if she started thinking about that, she wasn't sure she could just wait this out.

She'd thought, occasionally, about the hazards of the job. Known that the day could easily come when she'd be one of those uniforms that went down in the line of duty. But she'd set that fear aside most of the time. Besides, she had memories others didn't, memories of the biggest and best bodyguard service in the world, watching over her adoptive father like the predators they could become at the slightest hint of a threat. The people who could and did tell the president of the United States what to do, and he listened. Joe Colton had, anyway.

After all that, the peace of these mountains seemed endless.

Except you're sitting here waiting for a serial killer to stick his head out like a pumpkin in a shooting gallery. And praying his latest victim is still alive.

She told herself the girl must be, or Shruggs would be back home, his twisted, insane needs assuaged for the moment. Until they built and he struck again.

You will not!

Her mind nearly shouted it, as if he could hear her thoughts if he was indeed in the small cabin.

Stefan's voice came over her earpiece. "I've got movement—"

Crack!

Shot. Handgun. Large caliber. Probably a .45.

Daria's mind raced through the cataloging in a split second as she scanned the cabin again, but over it all hung one simple fact. Stefan carried the standard FBI-issue Glock 23 in .40 caliber. That was not what she'd heard fire.

Someone else had taken a shot.

"Stefan!"

When no answer came, her pulse kicked up another notch.

Daria started moving, trying to balance her haste with care, but as a second shot came, she abandoned any pretense at secrecy since it was obviously blown already. She simply ran, scrambling, glancing at the cabin when there was a break in the trees but otherwise focused only on getting to him.

"Window to the east of the back door."

Her breath came out in a rush at the sound of Stefan's voice in her ear. He sounded strained to her. But who wouldn't be with somebody capping off .45 rounds at you?

"Almost there. Status?" She allowed herself the question.

"Just get him. I'll keep his attention here."

His dodging the question in effect answered it, and her tension ratcheted up yet again. But he was conscious and coherent, at least. She kept moving. She had to veer right to go around a large rock, but as she did, she realized the spot had a clear view down to the cabin. To the back door, and the half-open window beside it.

And she could see Shruggs.

Even as she looked, another sunbeam broke through. It lit up this window as it had the other one, only this time it also caught the hand holding the large 1911-model pistol.

Again her mind raced through the calculations in a split second.

Right hand. Puts body mass to center or your right. Fifteen-degree downhill slope. Distance twelve yards. No wind.

Easy peasy.

Daria heard Stefan's shots from farther up the hill—he wasn't hurt badly if he was capable of shooting. But she stayed focused on the window. She saw the weapon fire, saw the recoil kicking that hand back as he tried to do it with one hand. Using the big rock for cover, she let out her breath slowly as she sighted in. Put everything, even Stefan, out of her mind. Her vision narrowed to her front sight, the window and her target, out of focus but there.

Three rounds as fast as she could pull. The hand and weapon in the window jerked upward.

Two more, one lower, one to the side, covering if he went down or dodged instinctively toward the solid door.

It was only then she hesitated. Their presence could drive Shruggs to kill his victim right now if he hadn't already. But if Stefan was hurt…

"Solid hits. He's down."

"Copy."

He sounded okay. Maybe she'd been wrong—maybe he hadn't been hit. But she couldn't let herself think about it now. She had a job to do, a life, please God, to save.

"What if he runs?" she whispered. His answer came back in her ear without hesitation.

"Let him. He's hurt—we'll find him. Let's get to her."

She felt a tug of some deep, heartfelt emotion as he put the victim over a capture.

Daria came out of the tree line, aware she was exposing herself completely. She dived, rolled, making herself as tough a target as she could. But Stefan fired again from up the hill. And she fired, too, only at the trash can, and her round made a loud, echoing pinging sound as it hit the metal.

Nothing.

She felt her tension ease when she saw Stefan emerge from the trees above, on his feet and moving fast. He was all right. They came at the cabin from opposite sides, reached the wall and started edging toward that back door.

Still nothing. She got closer, then close enough to get a darting glance through the half-open window.

Shruggs wasn't just down, he was out. She couldn't tell if he was still alive, didn't care. She reached through the window to the back door, had to flip a dead bolt but got it open. It jammed up against Shruggs, but she kept shoving. And then Stefan was there, adding his weight, and they were through.

She checked, found a faint pulse. "He's alive. Barely."

"There's a landline. I'll call it in—you find her. She'll trust a woman."

She nodded, shouted out an ID, hoping the victim would realize the good guys were here, and began a methodical search. She'd barely taken three steps when she heard a muffled cry from the right. Her gaze shot that direction, and she saw a closed door. She made her way over there, half listening to Stefan calling in the troops and medical help.

At the door she hesitated, then called out. "Are you alone?" There was no indication Shruggs ever let anyone else in on his ugly games, but…

Again the muffled sound, definitely female. Daria turned the doorknob, shoved it open and jumped back out of a potential line of fire.

Silence.

She risked a look.

And saw a pair of terrified eyes, looking at her out of the badly bruised face of a naked young woman bound and gagged in the corner of the small, soundproofed closet.

"It's all right. It's over."

She knelt beside the woman, pulled out her pocket-knife and quickly cut her free. The woman's sobbing was broken, and she sagged against Daria. On instinct she pulled off her own coat and slipped it around the woman, who pulled it tight with trembling fingers.

Daria drew in a deep breath and turned to give Stefan a smile. It died on her lips.

He'd slid down the wall next to the landline phone and was sitting on the floor, one hand pressed to his side.

A side that was bleeding. Profusely.

Her heart skipped a beat as her mind screamed a protest.

No. No!

Even as she looked, his eyes closed and there was a slight thump as his head went back against the wall.

"Stefan!"

She wanted to run to him, but the victim beside her had to be her priority, her job. But—

"He's yours?"

The tiny, tremulous question took her aback. She looked at the young woman, who was looking at Stefan. Who had been shot coming to her rescue.

"Yes. He's mine." Never had she meant those words as she did now.

Even as she said them, she heard something in her earpiece, realized belatedly that the breach team would be on that same system.

"More help is here," she said to the woman, then gave the people outside the all clear and ordered up medical personnel.

Full of dread when she finally was able to get to Stefan, she knelt beside him. The moment she touched his cheek, his eyes opened. They were a little glassy, and she could see he was in some pain, but he still smiled at her.

"Nice shooting," he said softly.

She smiled back at him, realizing only when she felt the trickle down her cheek that she was crying.

It really was finally over.

Chapter Twenty-Nine

If one more person asked how she was doing, Daria thought she might just erupt. How did they think she was doing?

The ones that congratulated her were the worst. *Nice work, Bloom! Save the victim and take down the killer—can't ask for better!*

Well, yes, she could. She could ask that Stefan not be lying in the other room, hooked up to a blood bag as they replaced what he'd lost. Especially knowing if he'd stayed put after he'd been hit, if he hadn't run down to back her up, he wouldn't have lost nearly as much.

She sat in the waiting area clinging to the other, much more important words, from the young woman in the blue scrubs, that he would be all right. That in fact he'd been very lucky—the wound had done little damage as gunshots go, and it was the blood loss that had weakened him. Daria had thanked her even as she wondered what on earth the woman had seen that she could say any gunshot wound had done little damage. Especially after she'd peeked into the room and seen Stefan lying there, his beautiful mahogany skin a stark contrast to the sheets.

"Daria."

She looked up at her name being spoken softly. Trey. She rose quickly, even after he waved at her to stay seated. He was simply looking at her, and she couldn't read his expression. Her boss could be as inscrutable as he needed to be when it was called for.

"I won't say nice work, because I know you think anything that resulted in an injury to one of us didn't go well, but…you got him, Daria. I read both your preliminary statements, and that was some fine shooting."

She liked that he referred to Stefan as one of them. Some local and county officials got huffy over fed involvement, even when they'd asked for the help. But not Trey. The capture of the Avalanche Killer had always been his top priority.

"Thank you," she said, not certain what else to say.

"They're prepping Shruggs for surgery now. He's in bad shape but conscious. I thought you might want to see if you can get a statement out of him."

"You could do that," she said, thinking it might be that last bit to nail down a victory in the election tomorrow.

"You did the work," he told her. "You earned it."

Daria gave him the best smile she could manage just then. "As long as you talk to the media," she said and smiled at his grimace.

She walked in the direction he'd indicated, her thoughts practically glowing in neon in her head. This was why the people of this county had darn well better reelect this man. They'd never find a more honest, trustworthy and fair person to stand for them.

Shruggs was in much worse shape than Stefan; his skin looked like the underbelly of a dead fish. She felt no pity for him, not even hatred, for he was not worth so much emotion. She coolly opened the record function on her phone, just in case, although there were three other witnesses in the medical staff standing there, and none of them looked particularly sympathetic toward their patient.

When he looked at her as she stood by the gurney he was lying on, even the blue of his eyes—*Blue Eyes*—was faded.

She made her voice purposely nonchalant. "Anything you want to say now, in case you don't make it out of surgery?"

Even as weak as he was, his gaze narrowed. "What the hell are you doing here?"

"Me?" Daria gave him a dazzling smile then. "I'm the *woman* who shot you."

That one hit home, as she'd hoped. She thought he would have snarled if he'd had the strength. She pushed a little harder.

"And if you die in there, no one will ever know or care. You'll be forgotten as nothing but a sicko who got stupid and got caught." She saw something shift in his gaze at a particular word, so she repeated it. "You're nothing. Less than nothing."

"I'm the one who's gotten away with this under cops' noses for over a decade," he snapped.

"Not *this* cop," she said. "How does it feel to know a woman took you down? A woman just like April Thomas, Lucy Reese, aka Bianca, Sabrina Gilford—"

"She wasn't one of mine."

Daria sucked in a breath. Feigned surprise. "What?"

"That Gilford woman. She wasn't one of mine. She's not my type. Not my type at all—looked nothing like her."

They took him away then, leaving Daria staring at the swinging doors as they closed.

She'd been right.

HER MIND WAS still spinning as she sat at Stefan's bedside. He looked much better already, and she silently thanked whoever the blood donors were. She knew his FBI brethren had lined up to donate when word had gotten out he'd been shot, and she was pleased when they'd told her several of her own department had been there for him, as well. And those who weren't a match for him would help others. A lot of others, it seemed, since his wound wasn't nearly as bad as she'd feared.

He appeared to be asleep, and she completely understood. She felt exhausted herself. They had both been running on adrenaline for so long that the crash couldn't help but be long and ugly. That was the one good thing that had come out of him being shot; he was resting whether he wanted to or not.

Now, if she could just turn off her own brain for a while…

She had told Trey what Shruggs had said about Sabrina Gilford and her not being his type. He'd told her not to worry about it right now, that she and Stefan had both earned a break and he expected them to take it. But she couldn't quite let go of it. Had Shruggs been telling the truth? It wasn't quite a deathbed confession—and almost sadly, it hadn't been his deathbed, he'd survived the surgery. But still, was he likely to lie knowing it could be the last chance he'd have? So many serial killers were proud of their work and almost gloried in bragging about it once they were caught. Was Shruggs one of those? She knew some of them were scrupulous about their kills, wanted credit for those they'd done and wouldn't take it for those they hadn't.

Problem was she didn't know enough about a serial killer's mind-set. She'd never expected to be entangled in a case like this, not here in Roaring Springs, where an out-of-control party or thefts from some upscale store were usually about the worst things they encountered. This was why Trey, no fool who refused to admit when something was outside his experience, had called in the FBI.

And Stefan.

She looked at him again, so relieved he was going to be all right. The depth and power of her relief was undeniable, and that in turn told her a great deal about what she'd come to feel about this man. He was—

"He's responding very well." Her head snapped around, and she saw the same doctor who had examined him initially, a petite brunette with a scattering of small freckles over her nose, standing there smiling. She rose to her feet as the woman finished with, "He won't be here long."

Daria smiled. "Thank you. So much."

"Thank him," the doctor said with a grin. "He's a very strong guy."

"Yes. He is."

"Taken?" she asked with an arched brow.

"Oh yes," Daria said fervently. "Very."

"I thought so. He was worried that you would worry," the doctor murmured, and winked at Daria as she added, "Hang on to that one, girl."

Daria was smiling as she turned to sit back down. And saw Stefan awake and looking at her. He was smiling, too.

"Very taken, huh?"

"Yes," she replied firmly. "And don't you forget it."

"Not likely," he said, and what she saw in his eyes warmed her down to her very soul.

"How do you feel?"

"Not sure," he admitted. "They give me something to put me out?"

"I'd think the last three months would have done that. And in case you forgot, you were shot."

He scoffed. "Barely more than a gouge. Only missed being a graze by a half inch."

She rolled her eyes. He grinned. And her world seemed to right itself. She gave him a quick update on things, purposely lowering her voice when she saw his eyelids start to close. He drifted off again soon after that, but Daria clung to what the doctor had said, that he wouldn't be here long. Of course what was long to the doc might not be what was long to Daria, which would be anything longer than him getting out right now. She wanted him out of here and where she could look after him. And Sam, he'd be worried—

Sam.

Her eyes widened as she looked at her watch.

Sam would be getting out of school in half an hour. Mrs. Crane would be there to pick him up as usual, but... Trey had gone to deal with the media. So it was already out there, no doubt.

She grabbed her phone and checked a couple of news feeds. Oh, it was out there, all right. Not that she was surprised. In a place as on edge as Roaring Springs had been, you didn't roll out vans and SUVs full of agents and deputies—and three ambulances—without it spreading like wildfire. And these days the theories were running amok on social media even before the people on scene had a full handle on what was happening.

She looked a little further, and there it was—the rumor that an agent had been shot at the scene. Would Mrs. Crane be aware enough to keep that from Sam until the boy knew his father was all right? She found Trey's initial brief statement, which said only that the victim had been rescued alive and an agent had been injured in the process but his injuries were not life-threatening. The suspect, he had ended with no small satisfaction, had been shot but was alive and in custody.

It hit her suddenly, really for the first time. Past tense. She'd been so worried about Stefan, and grimly focused on making sure Shruggs was wrapped up tight, she hadn't really let her mind run to the bigger picture. That the Avalanche Killer case was over. Oh, there was a quagmire of things yet to come—reports and eventually a huge, public trial—but the twisted, psychotic man who was Curtis Shruggs was finished.

With a burst of energy she stood, found a piece of paper in her bag and scribbled a quick note, and tucked it into Stefan's fingers. To make sure, she found the floor nurse and asked her to tell him, if he woke again before she got back, where she'd gone.

And then she left to pick up the child who had come to mean almost as much to her as his father.

Chapter Thirty

Stefan heard the nurse's quiet voice from just outside the room he was already tired of looking at. He glanced toward the door, glad he had convinced that nurse to raise the head of the bed so he could see. Okay, maybe he'd demanded. A *little*. But she had remained calm, only smiling and saying she was always glad to see fighting spirit in her patients. Especially those who had taken down a monster in their midst.

"That was Dar—Deputy Bloom," he'd said. "She did it."

That had earned him an even larger smile. "And I like even more those scrupulous enough to give credit where it's due."

The door was pulled back, and he smiled himself the instant he saw it was Daria. But it froze when he saw she wasn't alone.

Sam.

What the hell? Why had she brought him here? He didn't want his son, his little boy, seeing him like this, wounded and in a hospital bed.

Sam was staring at him, wide-eyed. "See?" Daria bent to whisper to him. "I told you he was all right."

To his shock, Sam ran across the room toward him.

Setting aside his anger, he held out a hand to the child. "Some people said you were dead."

He went very still, focused only on the feel of his son's small hand in his. Daria had been right. He hadn't thought that even at his age, Sam would have heard what had to be huge news all over town. "They were wrong."

"Daria told me they were. So I didn't worry anymore."

Sam had been worried? About him?

He lifted his gaze to her then. "I understand," she said softly. "But he needed to know. To see for himself." And as if she'd also understood his thoughts, she added, "He was very worried."

He wondered if the boy was actually worried about him or about what would happen to Sam himself if the worst had been true. Decided at the moment it didn't matter. Especially when Daria picked Sam up and sat him on the edge of the hospital bed, and the boy plopped down beside him. As if he felt that was where he should be, beside his father.

"You can't protect him from everything," Daria said. "However much you want to. He needs to know this kind of thing might happen."

Something in her voice made his brow furrow. "You say that as if from experience."

She nodded. "I—" She hesitated, then went ahead. "Yes. My father, my adoptive father, was a big believer in knowing what you were facing. He made sure we all did, and I think we were the better for it."

As he had before, when he helped her discover the sad fate of Ava Bloom, he wondered what it would be like not to know. His parents had been the rock of his life, the reason he was where he was instead of in trouble somewhere. He knew she loved her adoptive family, but it still had to make her wonder who the man was who had abandoned both her and her mother to their fates.

"They didn't give you any trouble at the school, did they?" he asked, glancing at Sam, who was now studying the IV pump with interest. "Picking him up, I mean?"

"No." Her expression was half smile, half grimace. "My face is apparently more known than I would prefer."

"You are…memorable."

"Only because I've had to talk to the media so much."

"No. Not only that. It's also because you're so beautiful."

He felt an inward burst of pleasure at the faint color he could see rising in her cheeks. Liked that he could see it, for it helped him know what she was thinking.

He looked back at his son, who was leaning over to look at where the tubes came out of the pump. "Wondering how it works?"

Sam nodded. "It puts blood in, right?"

"How'd you know that?" he asked.

"I saw it in a video. Only, it was about a hurt cat."

"Same principle."

Sam looked up then. "What's that mean?"

"It means it's the same idea as the cat one, just for people."

"Oh." Sam went back to studying the piece of equipment, leaving Stefan marveling at how much their relationship had changed. He shifted his gaze to the big reason for that change. Daria. "They told me just now you might get out of here tomorrow," she said.

"Yes."

"And how hard did you push to get them to say that?"

She, apparently, needed no help at all in knowing what he was thinking. "Maybe a little," he grudgingly admitted.

"If they do let you…escape, you'll need some help for a few days. At least until your folks get here."

He grimaced. Glanced at his boy. Knew she was right.

Suddenly Sam smiled at him. "Daria says we could go home with her tomorrow. Can we, Dad?"

His breath caught. "You'd like that?"

Sam nodded energetically. "I wanna see her house an' her yard an' her tree house."

His gaze shot to her face. She smiled. "It might be easier. And Sam would have…more room to run and play."

And get tired. He read it as clearly as if she'd said it. And he had to admit she had a point. And he also had to admit, the idea of being under the same roof as Daria was immensely appealing.

Unless, of course, she was looking at him as an invalid. His side might be hurting a bit more than he'd let on, but he wasn't about to let it slow him down. Much.

"You're not going to fuss over me, are you?" he asked warily.

She reached out and touched his cheek with the back of her fingers. And for that moment, he didn't feel anything except that jolt of warmth.

"Maybe just a little," she said softly.

And suddenly his entire outlook about it changed. Because, to his astonishment, he found himself *liking* the idea of Daria fussing over him. Taking care of him. Worrying about him. As his son had been worried, something he'd not dared hope for.

Once you've had that, son, that feeling of knowing you have someone who loves you enough to worry about you, to want to take care of you, and you her, then you'll know just how important it is.

His father's words, dismissed lightly in his know-it-all years, as his mother had called them, came back to him now with the fierce smack of truth. Because were it Daria who had been hurt, he would want to do exactly that. And how strongly pain and fear bubbled in him at the very thought of her hurt was like a flashing light in his mind. At one time, he might have wondered if that light was flashing green or red, but now he had no doubts. For him, it was full speed ahead.

"YOU'RE HERE FOR our star patient?" At Daria's nod, the nurse gave an amused rolling-eyes glance at the ceiling. "Good. He's been up pacing all morning. Night shift said he was up and down all night, too."

"He must be feeling better, then."

"He needs to get out of here."

Daria smiled. If Stefan was feeling as well as he had said he was when she spoke to him this morning, he was pretty restless. He was not a man to be kept caged for long.

"Driving you crazy?"

"Himself, mostly," the man admitted. "I'll check on the paperwork. Should be almost done. He is a VIP, after all."

With a grin she returned, he turned on his heel and headed toward the nursing station.

She turned to head for Stefan's room with the small

bag she'd brought. He'd given her his keys—apparently without a second thought—and she'd gone to his place to pack some things for him and Sam. The boy had, excitedly, given her a list, which she had fulfilled, but for Stefan she hadn't asked; she simply made sure she'd brought things he'd be comfortable in, since she had every intention of keeping him inside for the duration. And had to remind herself he would be recuperating to quash the images that thought brought on.

She had felt a little qualm as she'd decided how much to pack for him, and ended up calculating the days until his parents arrived. She supposed his mother would want to take over—he'd called them last night, he'd told her, so they wouldn't see one of the more fallacious news reports and assume the worst—and she could hardly protest. Especially when she hadn't even met them.

Yet.

Maybe she wouldn't. Maybe by then Stefan would be back home, and her life would go back to normal. Normal being full of work, reading, knitting and gardening come spring. What had once been a much-longed-for peace and quiet suddenly seemed empty and endless.

She shook off the image of a rather dull future and headed for his room. She'd brought him the shaving items Sam had pointed out that he used every day, and clean clothes. Including a pair of knit boxers that she had to stuff hurriedly in the bag before her pulse kicked up too much as an image of him clad in them—and her peeling them off him—shot through her mind.

It was a new experience for her. She'd had relationships but too often she'd found out the man knew of her connection to the most famous Coltons and was after a connection of his own—but never, ever had she had to fight so hard to keep from thinking about a man every minute of the day. And while common sense might tell her that was because they'd been together so much and that it would change now, her heart—and apparently her body—felt differently.

When she stepped into Stefan's room, she saw he was already up and pacing. She'd told him she would bring fresh clothes, since his shirt was unsalvageable, and in her opinion the rest—except his shoes—was, too; she wanted none of those bloodstained items around as reminders that it could have been so much worse.

Normally the sight of someone in the usual floppy hospital gown was either sad or amusing. She was neither sad nor amused now, though, because nothing could detract from the sheer masculinity and power of this man.

Suddenly nervous, she set the bag down on the bed. "I brought your clothes and shaving gear if you want it."

"I might." He was looking at her intently.

"Sam told me what you used in the mornings, so that's what I brought."

That seemed to startle him. "Sam told you?"

She nodded. "I think he's watching you much more than you think. And that's good. He wants to know about his father, even if he hasn't realized it yet."

He looked a bit disconcerted at that, and her nerves eased a little. Doing something as personal as packing underwear for him had unsettled her, which was silly, considering.

"I'll just wait outside so you can get dressed," she said, groaning inwardly when she realized she sounded flustered.

He'd picked up the jeans she'd brought, but his gaze snapped back to her face.

"A bit late for modesty, wouldn't you say?"

She grabbed at the remnants of her poise. "Maybe I'm just afraid I won't be able to resist your gorgeousness," she managed to say in a teasing tone.

That grin, that killer grin that had been so rare in the beginning that she'd savored every instance, flashed at her.

"Oh, I hope not," he rasped.

She felt heat flood her cheeks. "You're going to be convalescing."

"So you'll have to do all the work."

He was still grinning, damn him. The heat that had begun to recede rose anew. And flared when he nonchalantly dropped the hospital gown to get dressed. When he caught her watching him, that grin flashed yet again.

"Want to help me…tuck things in?"

"Not if you want to get out of here in time to pick Sam up from school," she managed, although the images his teasing brought on nearly derailed her self-control.

"Oh, well," he said in exaggerated disappointment. "I'd rather you untuck them anyway."

By the time he was dressed—without needing help, she noted, his innate strength and fitness helping him rebound more quickly than she would have ever guessed—she was grateful for the arrival of the nurse to tell them his discharge papers were ready.

"One thing I want to do on the way," he said as they headed out to deal with the paperwork.

"What?"

"Stop and vote for your boss."

She smiled widely. "I'll be more than happy to get you there."

She meant it. If there was any sense at all in this county, it would be a landslide.

Chapter Thirty-One

"Hard to believe this case is actually over except for the paperwork," Daria said as she slowed to go over the last speed bump in the hospital parking lot.

"Little matter of a trial," Stefan pointed out, stifling a wince as the bump, even as slowly as she was going, caused a tug on his wounded side. He knew they'd only let him out because he'd told them he was leaving today whether they discharged him or not. He had a small stack of papers stuffed into a pocket of the bag Daria had brought, including detailed instructions on how to care for the wound. He'd read them. Eventually. As soon as he could stop thinking about Daria truly wanting him—and his son—to come home with her.

"That, too," she agreed, "but that'll take a while."

"But Shruggs confessed to you. Not quite a death-bed confession, but still."

"Only because he survived." She halted at the driveway, scanning traffic. "But he couldn't resist the need to brag, just in case. Which reminds me…"

She checked her rearview mirror, he noticed, to make sure they weren't blocking anyone in the driveway. Then she pulled out her phone and called up what she wanted, explaining as she did, "Trey called me this morning.

He said he mentioned what Shruggs said about Sabrina Gilford not being his type to his fiancée, Aisha—you met her, didn't you?"

"Yes. The clinical psychologist"

Daria nodded. "She's wicked smart. And an ace kick-boxer, I might add."

He blinked; he hadn't expected that. "Kickboxer?"

"Yep. She's going to teach me."

He studied her for a moment, remembering with vivid clarity how her trim, strong body had felt in his arms, beneath him, atop him. "That," he said fervently, "I want to see. You'll be brilliant."

Daria flashed him a smile that told him he'd said exactly the right thing.

"Thank you," she said warmly. "Anyway, Aisha's the one who figured out his election opponent's brother was behind that attempt on his life."

"The one we thought was a hate crime at first?"

She nodded. "Anyway, she did a little research of her own and came up with this."

She held out her phone to him. He looked at the image on the screen. His brow furrowed. The woman looked familiar somehow, yet he was fairly sure he'd never seen her before. He'd seen a string of photos that resembled her, though, tacked to a crime board.

"Someone else missing?" he asked grimly. "Shruggs has another victim buried somewhere we haven't found yet?"

Daria looked oddly satisfied at his question. "It's his mother."

Stefan looked up to meet her gaze. He nearly rolled his eyes. "So he's not only a vicious killer, he's a walking cliché?"

"So it seems."

"I guess things become clichés for a reason," he muttered, handing back her phone.

They found his polling place, and the voting itself didn't take too long, but he was still glad when he got back in the car. He had the niggling thought that maybe he'd pushed a little too hard too soon, but once he was sitting down again, he felt better.

"Lots of talk going on in there," he told her. "Most of it good, about your boss. Word that we got Shruggs spread fast."

"Good," she said. "Although they should have voted for him anyway."

"You're very...loyal."

"He's earned it."

He studied her as she pulled back out onto the street and they headed for Sam's school. Realized with a bone-deep certainty that Daria would be that loyal to anyone who earned it. Had he? If he hadn't, what did he need to do now to make sure? Maybe he'd ask his father, when they arrived. Winning the trust, loyalty and above all the love of a woman like his mother couldn't have been an easy thing. His mother was a force of nature, by turns as fierce as she was gentle. In fact, Daria reminded him a lot of her in many ways.

He found himself mulling over men and their mothers, the thoughts about his own coming so soon on the heels of the discovery about their serial killer's seeming a bit ironic. But if nothing else, it reminded him how fortunate he'd been to have his mother, with her steady, unwavering devotion to her family. Daria would be like that, he was certain. Once she decided, she would never falter.

They reached Sam's school, and she pulled into the parking lot and to a stop where there were other vehicles with people waiting for children. She parked neatly, glanced at the clock—they were nearly half an hour early—then looked at him. Caught him avidly soaking in her presence. "I was wrong," he said softly.

"Wrong?"

"You're not just memorable. You're unforgettable."

She lowered her gaze almost shyly. He leaned toward her, wanting a kiss from that luscious mouth more than anything just now. He felt the sharp twinge from his side but hid it. A little pain was a small price to pay for this. And the moment he touched her lips, the pain seemed to vanish, swept aside by the heat he'd only ever felt with her. He deepened the kiss, tasted her, knowing with a strange sense of utter certainty that it would ever and always be like this, with her.

The honk of a car horn broke the moment. He straightened a little too quickly and winced.

"You shouldn't move like that."

"The day I can't lean over and kiss my woman," he began but stopped when he saw her eyes. She had that look that told him that mind he admired was working. Well, admired most of the time; at her expression he was a bit wary.

"There's something you need to know. And I should have told you before we…"

She gave a vague wave of her hand that irritated him.

"Spontaneously combusted?" he suggested, his own voice a little tight.

She nodded, and he saw the faint color in her cheeks again. "But more importantly, before I invited you both to stay at my place now."

"Retracting the invitation?" He didn't want to think about how that would hurt Sam. He didn't want to think about how it would hurt *him*.

"No!" She said it so fervently it soothed his annoyance. "I just mean…there's something you should know before we go any further."

He kept his tone mild. "I don't recall that the invitation was to move in permanently." That he almost wished it had been was something he kept to himself just now.

She lowered her gaze again, and something about the way her lips tightened slightly made him wonder if she did, too. But he knew full well he was no expert in reading the female mind, so he kept his mouth shut. Another wise lesson from his father.

After a long enough moment that he wondered if she'd changed her mind about telling him whatever it was, she said, "It's about…who I am. Really am, I mean."

His puzzlement cleared, and the annoyance vanished. In fact, he felt a jolt of relief that this was all it was. "A Colton, you mean?"

Her head snapped up and she stared at him. "You knew?"

"Well…yeah."

"Have you always known?"

He frowned. "Only since I ran the DNA for Fox and Kelsey."

Now she looked utterly flummoxed. "What?"

"You know, for the baby. You came up as a possible relative."

She was gaping at him now. "I…*what*?"

Puzzlement returned. "You're in the system, as law enforcement, right?"

"Of course. To be eliminated in case of evidence contamination."

"So that's why you came up when we did the genetic markers for the baby." She still looked bewildered, and he hastened to assure her, "It's confidential information, and since I knew you weren't the baby's mother, it was irrelevant to the case. I'd never say anything."

"I wasn't… I didn't think you…"

She seemed way too baffled for what was a fairly simple thing. He knew how smart she was, how together she was, so this made no sense.

"Daria?"

He saw a slight shudder go through her, had the feeling she'd given herself a sharp mental shake. When she spoke, she was enunciating so carefully it made his focus zero in on her like a case about to break open.

"Are you saying," she said, each word spoken with careful precision, "that I am a *biological* Colton?"

"Not me, the DNA," he said. "And not closely related to the baby, but…"

Her expression practically screamed the truth.

She hadn't known. She hadn't known she was genetically connected to the Coltons. But she'd been going to tell him she was a Colton? Now he was confused.

"Daria…"

The moment he said her name out loud, it belatedly hit him. Daria. *Daria Colton.*

He swore, low and harsh. He felt as if the entire world had tilted on its axis. Her words came back to him vividly. *I've had enough of living with a lot of people around all the time*. He'd just bet she had, because she'd once lived in the biggest goldfish bowl in the world.

No wonder she had seemed familiar from the first time he'd seen her. Because she was. He'd even seen her photograph years ago, in FBI informational reports put out when the Secret Service was in town, although she was always in the background.

Daria Bloom…or was it Colton?

Of the California Coltons. Headed up by Joe Colton. The former president of the United States.

Chapter Thirty-Two

Stefan was on his phone. She had no idea to whom—
she couldn't focus on a single thing beyond the internal
turmoil that had erupted the instant she'd realized what
he'd meant. That the DNA tests he'd pushed through
for Fox Colton had turned up an unexpected connection. A possible relative to that tiny baby that he and
Kelsey were adopting.

Her.

She was a biological Colton.

She felt a hand on her arm. Slowly, as if moving underwater, she looked over at Stefan. "Maybe there was
a mistake," he said quietly. "Maybe because of…of your
adoptive name something got crossed."

"My adoptive name," she said, very slowly. And for
the first time thought of a very unpleasant possibility.
"Did they know?" she asked, barely aware of saying it
out loud. "Dear God, did they know and never tell me?
Did my father—the freaking president—lie to me all
these years?"

"Whoa, now, don't jump the gun here. Let's make
sure of this. I'm no expert on reading DNA reports, and
there could have been a glitch somewhere."

She thought, as if from a distance, that it was nice

he was so worried. And that he'd set aside what she'd told him—or rather, what she'd meant to tell him—in favor of addressing her more pressing concern, touched her to the core.

"Here's the plan," he said briskly. "We head for the Crooked C. Now, because Fox and Kelsey are both there, but they have to leave soon. They've got the reports. Can you access yours?"

She nodded, rather vaguely. She'd filed a copy in a cloud storage service, just in case, during her long search for her mother.

"Sam," she said, not even sure why.

"We'll pick him up first. He'll have fun—he's never been to anything like a working ranch. He'll have plenty of distraction while we find out what we need. I don't think he's ever even seen a cow up close."

"Duck pond…there's a duck pond behind the main house." Somewhere in the back of her mind, a faint alarm bell was ringing. It took her a moment to find the words for it. "Can he swim?"

She heard an odd sound, as if Stefan's breath had caught in his throat. Then she felt his big, warm hand over hers, which was cold for reasons that had nothing to do with the temperature outside.

"I can't tell you what it means to me that you're worried about that now, in the middle of what you just learned."

"Of course I am. He doesn't need any more trauma in his life."

"You've just had a bit in yours."

She tried a smile, managed only a brief, slightly lopsided one. "Here I thought I'd be shocking you."

"Oh, you did." He gave her a rather wondering look. "I can't believe I didn't recognize you."

"That was years ago." *I'm older now. Too old for you.*

She tried to quash the thought, because he was right; if it were reversed, no one would think a thing of it. She had the feeling that would be one of the last inequities to fall in this world. If it ever did.

"I saw you once. When President Colton made a stop at the capitol in Springfield. I remember thinking how amazing it was that someone who looked like you lived in the White House."

"You mean because I'm Black?"

"No. Because even then I thought you were beautiful. I thought you should be modeling, or maybe out in Hollywood."

She made a face. "Please," she muttered.

"But now I know better. You wouldn't settle for doing anything you didn't think was important."

"I got that from Dad," she said. "He told me he didn't care what I did as long as it was something that made me eager to get up and get at it every morning."

"Sounds like my dad."

She realized suddenly that she was calmer. Much calmer. She'd even managed to speak of her adoptive father with the admiration she'd always felt for him. And on the heels of that, she realized that had been Stefan's intention all along, he who rarely indulged in small talk but just had. To get her through the sudden chaos of this unexpected discovery.

She met his gaze, held it. "Thank you," she said softly.

He lifted a brow at her as if he had no idea what she meant. But she knew better.

"IS THIS THE way to Daria's house?"

"No," Stefan said. "We have to make a stop first."

"Oh."

His son sounded so downcast it almost made Daria smile. Or rather, smile again, because she had smiled broadly and happily when Sam had first emerged from the school and worriedly asked his father if he was all right now.

"I'll be okay, buddy, but I have to take it easy for a while," Stefan had said. "Rest a lot."

"You mean stay in bed?" Sam asked innocently.

Daria had had to look away then, and she felt her cheeks heat yet again when Stefan said with all seriousness, "I think that's an excellent, excellent prescription, Dr. Roberts."

She had had the feeling Sam had no idea what a prescription was, but being addressed as Dr. Roberts set off a gale of laughter. The boy had come a very long way in a short time. And if she'd had some little bit to do with that, she was both happy and proud.

"We're going someplace very cool, though," she said as she made a turn.

"Where?" Sam asked, wide-eyed.

"It's a ranch," Stefan answered.

"You mean with horses and cows and stuff?"

"Exactly that."

"Cool!" the boy exclaimed.

She knew too well where the Crooked C was, because it was where all this had started for her, when Wyatt Colton had found the first body. It had also been the first direct experience she'd had with the kind of pressure the Colton name could bring to bear.

The Colton name.

She felt a little stab of the guilt she'd been carrying since Trey had turned this case over to her. He'd done it to avoid any appearance of favoritism, given he was a Colton himself. She'd rationalized it with the fact— she'd thought—that she wasn't really a Colton, it was only by adoption.

But now…

She was going to have to tell him. And she had no idea how he would react. She had no idea how she herself would react, once she knew exactly what the connection was.

She made herself focus on her driving. She noticed the last bits of snow were disappearing, with the occasional trickle of water from the melt crossing the roadway. It was a near-balmy sixty-one degrees today, and Sam had already shed his jacket. She hoped the good weather made people get out and vote. And hoped the news of Shruggs's capture reassured any who had doubts about their current sheriff.

The Crooked C was a sprawling ranch of hundreds of acres, and Daria smiled anew as Stefan pointed out to Sam the weather vane on the roof of the main house, which was a rearing horse made of copper. But they kept going, past the promised duck pond, southward until they reached a large red barn that looked a bit weather-beaten on the outside. But when she'd first been here—when they'd found the first body—Daria had noticed there were several features that didn't fit, including glass windows that looked fairly new and double paned, both on the upper level and below.

"Fox is really dedicated to breeding healthy, long-lived horses. So he took this barn over and converted it to living quarters upstairs, with his office and work space below. Guess which is bigger," Stefan added to Sam with a grin.

Daria smiled. She liked seeing anyone with a passion following it.

Sam was looking around wide-eyed. He immediately fixated on the corral beside the barn, where a couple of horses that looked young to her inexperienced eye were watching them in turn.

"Can I go see 'em?" Sam asked, practically dancing with eagerness.

Fox Colton and his new wife, Kelsey, a petite woman with lively hazel eyes and strawberry blond hair, had come out the door in time to hear this.

"I'll get somebody to show him around while we talk, if that's okay with you," the tall, lean man with bright blue eyes and rather shaggy brown hair said.

"Please, Dad?" The boy was practically dancing with excitement.

"That would be great," Stefan said. "If it's not too much trouble."

"After what you did for us?" Kelsey said. "Not a chance."

Once Sam was set up, they went inside. The newlywed couple's first words were congratulations—and thanks—that they'd cracked the Avalanche Killer case.

"Word gets around fast," Stefan mused.

"For all the glamour, underneath Roaring Springs is still a small town," Fox said with a smile.

"And that *is* huge news," Kelsey added, with a wide smile.

Daria had been a little surprised at first, at the wom-

an's immediate and enthusiastic offer of any and all
help, but then she recalled Stefan had used his connections at the FBI to rush through the DNA testing
that had proven the paternity of the baby that had been
abandoned literally on Fox's doorstep.

Besides, Fox had gone through a shock of his own
recently, discovering his dead father had not really been
his father after all. So he understood how she was feeling and was thoroughly empathetic to her plight.

As it turned out, Kelsey, who was an equine genet-
icist, was of the most help. She was much more used
to deciphering genetic reports, had gotten out the one
that had proven who Fox's real father was, and had already started sorting through what they had and begun
comparing it to the report Daria had accessed for her.

"Things settle down for you at all?" Stefan asked
Fox.

The man shrugged. "My parents—or rather, my father and my aunt—said this morning that they've sep-
arated. I think… Dad needs some processing time."

The correction, and the way he'd hesitated over the
word *Dad* told Daria he was still adjusting to the idea
that his father wasn't just alive, but was Russ Colton…
the man who'd actually raised him. She wondered how
long it would take her. She supposed it would depend
on what she learned in the next few minutes. Assuming there was enough here to tell her that.

She didn't pace while Kelsey continued to pore over
the papers spread out on what she guessed was Fox's
desk, but it was an effort. When she finally straightened up, she gave her a sympathetic look.

"It's there," she said. "The number of markers is undeniable."

"So," Fox said, turning to look at her. "It's official. You're a Colton."

Chapter Thirty-Three

"How close?" Stefan asked since Daria couldn't seem to find her voice.

"I can't be sure. I can only extrapolate from what I've got here," Kelsey said. She glanced at her husband. "This looks close to Russ, but she's not your half sister. That much I can say."

Fox let out a relieved breath, then looked rather guiltily at Daria. "Not that I'd mind if you were, I mean, but—"

"It would mean your father made it a habit," Stefan said gently.

"Exactly."

"Maybe your uncle Whit?" Kelsey asked.

"He's got the track record for it," Fox agreed. "But could it be?" he asked, gesturing at the reports.

"I don't know. If there was one more marker either way… I'd need a genetic test from him to be sure. And one from Earl wouldn't hurt."

"At this point, I want everybody in the damned family tested," Fox muttered. "As if life as a Colton wasn't already complicated enough."

Stefan was quite aware Daria still hadn't uttered a

word. He turned to face her, reached out and gently grasped her shoulders. "What do *you* want?"

She looked up at him. He saw the rapid-fire emotions in her expression, guessed she was feeling pretty tangled up right now. Probably even wishing, with some part of her, that she'd never found this out. But he also knew what was at the core of her and knew what her answer would be. And after a long, silent moment, it came.

"I want the truth."

He'd known she would. And the fact that he'd known, that he'd been so certain she would want exactly that, proved to him that this woman was exactly who he thought she was. That he knew who she was to the core.

"Then we'll find it," he said softly, in that moment meaning it more than he had ever meant any vow in his life.

Fox looked back at Stefan and Daria. "We were already set to make a trip to the Manor. I think we should go now, and you'd better come with us."

Stefan blinked, felt Daria draw back slightly. "The Colton Manor?" she asked.

"Yes. Speaking of my uncle Whit, his son Remy's half brother, Seth, called a meeting. He's got some sort of announcement to make. We should make it just in time."

Daria's brow furrowed. "Seth Harris? I've talked to him. He works at The Lodge, right?"

Fox nodded. "He manages the whole guest operation. He's really good with the high-end clients."

Stefan remembered the slim, sandy-haired man who looked like he'd be more at home in New York City than the slopes of the Colorado mountains. He could see where the guy would make those high-profile sorts feel at home. Personally, he'd found him a bit over-the-top unctuous, while Daria's conclusion had been a bit more forgiving, given the rough start he'd apparently had in life before his half brother had stepped in.

"Why don't you round up your boy and we'll get ready to go," Kelsey suggested. "There's a playroom at the Manor with every video game known to man. Will that keep him occupied while we deal with all this?"

"He'll be in heaven," Stefan replied.

"What, exactly," Daria said, rather carefully, "is the plan?"

"Beard the lions in their den, as it were," Fox told them cheerfully, and headed upstairs after his wife.

Daria seemed to hesitate when Stefan turned to do as Kelsey had suggested and find Sam.

"Second thoughts?" he asked.

"They're the power around here. Anybody would have second thoughts."

"This, from the woman who calls a former president Dad?"

She looked startled, as if she hadn't thought of it in just that way. "Point taken."

"And I see now why you like your place so much—partly, anyway. Got pretty tired of all the fuss and bother of the White House and a protection detail?"

"I declined the detail, but it was still…a lot of pressure."

"Then this should be nothing. Besides," Stefan added, "you're returning the victor. The one who probably salvaged their entire year's business by taking out the Avalanche Killer. They should bow down."

As he'd hoped, that got a low chuckle from her. "Right. Their savior."

He grinned at her. "Exactly."

She reached up and brushed her fingers over his jaw. His pulse kicked up instantly. "Thank you. For being here for me, through this. And making me feel so much better."

He leaned over and kissed her, then whispered a rather potent suggestion for how he could make her feel even better.

"You're supposed to be taking it easy, remember?" she said, but she was smiling now. Widely.

"Yeah. In bed, like Sam said."

She laughed then and shook her head. "I'll deal with you later."

"Promise?" he said archly.

"Fervently," she said, with a smile that sent a shiver of anticipation through him. "But now, let's go find Sam."

COLTON MANOR WAS as huge and sprawling as one might expect from this rich and influential family. Although from what Daria had gathered, the Colton children didn't have much connection to it. She could understand that; the place wasn't exactly a warm, cozy home.

Essentially it was a massive, eighteen-thousand-square-foot showplace for the senior Coltons, including the now rarely seen patriarch, and a staff she couldn't even guess at the size of. She supposed the size of it had a benefit, however; Russ and Mara Colton could live completely separate lives under the same roof until they decided what their future would or wouldn't be.

"Ten bathrooms, I heard," Stefan muttered as they went inside.

"Eleven," Fox corrected with a grin.

"Obnoxious, isn't it?" Kelsey said, also grinning.

And Daria realized she quite liked both of them.

The gathering was in the living room—one of them, anyway—with its high, vaulted ceiling and the view of the gondolas going upslope out the expansive windows.

"Ever been on that thing?" Stefan whispered.

She shook her head. "And after Molly Gilford's experience, not likely to."

"Copy that," Stefan said rather fervently.

Thinking of the sweet, good-natured woman reminded her rather forcefully that while Roaring Springs no longer had a serial killer haunting its environs, there was still a murderer on the loose—the one who had killed Molly's sister. She had made a brief call to the woman, who had just had the baby now named after that sister, and in view of that had broken the news as gently as possible that Shruggs had not killed Sabrina Gilford. Molly had been understandably upset, but at Daria's vow it was not over and Sabrina would not be forgotten in the hubbub about Shruggs, she had calmed a little.

Daria had suggested to Fox that they wait with Sam in the game room, since whatever Seth's announcement was, it appeared to be a family affair, but Russ Colton spotted them first. His voice boomed out in the room, congratulating them for finally catching the killer. The buzz through the gathered group, many of whom she recognized, but some she did not, was loud and exuberant. Mara was there, Daria noted, but carefully on the opposite side of the room from her husband.

Daria was more interested in observing the rather intense look shared by Fox and the man who'd raised him and who had turned out to also be his biological father. And she was honest enough to admit that she was watching because she was wondering how she would feel if somehow this new discovery led her to her own father.

"He looks a bit miffed," Stefan whispered again.

She looked up, realized he meant the man who'd called this gathering. Seth was indeed frowning a bit, as if they'd stolen his thunder. But when he saw them looking at him, he managed a creditable smile. And proceeded with his announcement, which turned out to be his engagement to Vanessa Fisher, the tall, dark-haired woman who stood rather shyly beside him. She noticed the woman was slouching slightly, wondered if it was because she was taller than the man beside her. Daria knew Vanessa was the daughter of a wealthy investment banker, but not much more.

Some of the people gathered looked surprised, some not, but the most loudly congratulatory was Russ Colton himself.

"A great match," he exclaimed. "Just wonderful. A wonderful addition to the Colton family," he added, smiling widely at Vanessa, who looked as if she were a bit uncomfortable in the spotlight. Then he turned to Seth. "I see a very bright future for you with The Colton Empire."

Seth fairly beamed, while Daria was inwardly rolling her eyes at the grandiose name, although she supposed it fit what the man had built here.

"I wonder where Remy is?" Fox muttered. Daria knew he meant Remy Colton, the director of PR at The Chateau.

"Maybe getting his first sleep in months," Kelsey suggested. "He's had his hands more than full trying to cope with the ton of bad press from the Avalanche Killer."

"Or working, glad to not be spinning for a change," Daria said.

Stefan nodded in agreement. "I'd guess now's the time to trumpet the return to normalcy, and get reservations back up."

Fox smiled at them. "You two ever want to change jobs…" His smile faded. "I still can hardly believe Shruggs pulled this off right under our noses. All those women…it's horrific."

Daria liked him even more for that. The Lodge.

Kelsey said something quietly to Fox, who then looked at Daria. "I'll go get… Russ," he said, clearly still having trouble adjusting to the change in their connection. "I think we're going to need his cooperation on this."

"Will you get it?" Stefan asked.

Fox's mouth twisted into a wry smile. "He wants a relationship with me, so yeah, we'll get it."

When he'd headed across the room toward Russ Colton, Daria looked at Kelsey. "Your husband is quite a guy," she said quietly. "Going to this length to help someone who's practically a stranger."

"Yes," Kelsey agreed as she watched him go, the love clear in her expression. "Yes, he is." Then she looked back at Daria. "But I hope you don't stay practically a stranger, whatever we find out. All of you," she added with a glance at Stefan. "Especially that adorable kid of yours."

Stefan smiled. "Speaking of kids, how's little John doing?"

That sent Kelsey off into new parental joy, and she

happily told them about the baby who would be theirs as soon as the paperwork was done with Fox's cousin Mason.

And then Fox was back with his father. Russ Colton was still an impressive figure and an obvious power broker.

"So what's this all about?" he asked briskly.

"Not something I think you want to discuss out here," Fox said.

Russ looked at the young man he'd raised but had never known he'd fathered and quickly stated, "All right, let's go up to my study."

They started up the curved staircase, and Daria saw the edge of what appeared to be an indoor pool on the level below. She wondered what other extravagance the place held and guessed it could be just about anything. Even the hallways were spacious, with niches here and there where artworks worth probably more than she made in a year were hung and seen only by those invited to the inner sanctum.

Russ stopped at a set of carved wooden double doors and reached for the door handle. There was a sound a few feet farther down the hall—a set of footsteps and an odd sort of whooshing noise. Daria's reaction was automatic; she turned to look. She saw a very elderly man in a wheelchair, pushed by a woman in a nurse's uniform.

Earl Colton, she thought. Even now, fragile and frail, he resembled the pictures she'd seen from the days when as a dynamic and clever young man he'd built what was now The Colton Empire, thanks to his penchant for slapping his name on everything he bought. She had heard he suffered from dementia now, and often talked to the wife who had been dead for fifteen years. She herself found that understandable; if he took comfort in that, he'd earned it, if only by surviving this long. Although she had to say he looked quite alert and aware now, and she heard him call the nurse by the name on her name tag, so he appeared to be coherent at the moment.

He'd noticed them now, and his rather shaggy white eyebrows lowered as he stared at them.

No, her. He was staring at *her*.

His eyes widened, and his jaw went a little slack. And then, in a tone of shock, the old man spoke.

"Ava."

Chapter Thirty-Four

He had pushed, Stefan had to admit, nearly as far as he could. He could feel collapse hovering, much as he hated to admit it. And no amount of telling himself his wound was minor was helping.

But Daria had just received the shock of her life, and she needed support. And he wasn't going to do her much good if he passed out on his feet. So he summoned up what reserves he had left and kept going.

It was at that moment he realized just how far he would go for this woman he'd come to so admire. To respect.

To love.

He hadn't really admitted it before, had shied away from the possibility even to himself, but now that he had, the truth of it rang like a clarion bell. He had to resist the urge to tell her, right then. Even if she had recovered enough from the earlier shock, he doubted she would want to hear it just now, in front of this handful of strangers who she had just discovered were actually family.

His brain was too weary at the moment to figure out the intricacies of her connection to each one, but only one really mattered. And that was that the old man in the wheelchair, Earl Colton, was her father. Because once the obvious shock in his lined face and weary eyes had faded, everything had come pouring out as the old man faced the woman he obviously thought was Ava Bloom.

He swore he hadn't known she was ill, and for a Colton fairly groveled for abandoning her and their child when he'd found out she was pregnant. He should have manned up, Earl had said brokenly. Alice would have understood. Stefan had his doubts about that, but there was no doubt that the Colton patriarch meant what he said.

Lot of good that does Daria now.

He was silently grateful when they finally made it into Russ Colton's office and sat down to begin to sort it all out. It took some time for the chaos to settle, but in the end cautious welcomes were extended from some, happy and amazed welcomes from others. Russ Colton, Stefan suspected rather strongly, was calculating the worth of having the deputy who had broken the Avalanche Killer case in the family. Although, to his credit, he seemed as concerned as the rest of the Coltons that their cousin Sabrina's case was still unsolved, and her murderer still out there.

But most of them seemed cordial enough to the idea of Daria being one of them, and he got the feeling she would have a place here if she wanted it. For some reason Sam's angry face flashed through his mind. An anger he hadn't seen…well, practically since the boy had met Daria. He wondered idly how much of a difference it made to be an adult and have your whole world shift on you. It belatedly occurred to him that she might want some time alone with her newfound family, and he stood up, feeling stronger now that he'd been off his feet for a bit.

"I need to go see my son," he said when everyone looked at him. Nobody seemed to question that, and Daria smiled when he looked at her and added, "Take your time."

It had been a rather tight smile, however, and he knew she was still processing. Driven by an urge he didn't even try to resist, and despite the twinge in his side, he bent down and rather blatantly planted a kiss on her cheek. In front of all of them. As if he were staking his claim in front of the family she had just gained. As, perhaps, he was.

He lingered there for a moment and whispered, "I'll stay if you need me, but some alone time might be good."

"Go to Sam," she whispered back. "I won't be long."

So she wasn't going to linger, let them throw a party for her since everyone was already here. No, his Daria would want time to process this revelation, and he would see to it that she got it.

Even if he had to enlist the help of someone who knew quite well what it was like to have your entire life turned upside down.

He found the game room, and Sam engrossed in driving a race car over some very unlikely terrain. Having learned by now, he waited until the inevitable crash, then sat down beside the boy.

"Can you pause for a minute? I need your help. For Daria."

That startled Sam enough that he immediately put down the controller. "What?" he asked, sounding anxious. "Is she all right?"

"She will be, I think. But do you remember how you felt when your whole life got blasted apart and you had to come here?"

"Yeah," Sam said, watching him warily. Then, with a frown, he added, "You're not sending me back now, are you?"

He reached out and gripped the boy's shoulder. "Not a chance. You're mine for good, buddy, and even if your mother wanted you back, I'd fight her."

The shy smile that curved his son's mouth made the dull ache in his side recede.

"What about Daria?" Sam asked, sounding anxious.

"Well, her whole life just got upended, like yours did. So we need to take extra-special care of her for a while. Can you help me with that?"

"We're still gonna stay with her while you get better?"

"Yes. It's just now…she and I both need to heal a bit. So we'll need your help."

This seemed to intrigue the boy, and he drew himself up straight. "I can do it," he announced.

For a moment Stefan felt a surge of wonder that Leah hadn't managed to cripple the boy's generous heart. And a bigger surge of gratitude that Daria had come into their lives and shone a light on the path to where they were now. That his relationship with Sam had improved so much so fast was, he knew, entirely due to her.

"I know you can," he said softly, this time running a hand over Sam's close-cropped curls. The boy ducked his head but didn't pull away.

It was approaching dark by the time the three of them left the Manor. Stefan had offered to drive, but Daria said the distraction of having to focus on driving would help her. She didn't talk, so Stefan instead sat and savored the image of Sam immediately going to her and taking her hand and assuring her everything would be all right. He didn't think he'd mistaken the sheen of moisture in her eyes. That those eyes had stayed calm and assessing while her entire life changed before them, yet teared up at soft words from his son, made him ache inside in a way he could barely fathom.

When they got to her place, there was just enough light for Sam to excitedly explore a little bit. And it had been all Stefan could do not to laugh when his son had solemnly broached the idea that maybe he should skip school tomorrow. "To take care of you and Daria."

And he wondered how bad a father it made him when he gave in and agreed the boy could stay home. And if he was crazy for, when he said the word *home*, thinking of this place, not his own.

"They won't be surprised when he doesn't come to school," Daria said as Sam ran off to unpack the bag she'd brought for him in the bedroom she'd shown him to, the one with the view of the backyard and tree platform, which Stefan knew he wanted to climb up to the first chance he got. "I'm sure it's all over the news that we broke the case."

"And that I managed to get myself shot in the process?" he suggested dryly.

Her brow furrowed. "If I could only have gotten him—"

"Stop. Right there." He'd been about to sit down but instead turned and grabbed her before she could finish the sentence. "You did great. Spectacular, in fact. I'm the one who pushed my luck and risked being spotted for a glimpse inside the place."

He was glad when her arms came around him, didn't even care when she brushed his wound and he felt a twinge. They'd done it, at last. Solved that damned case. The relief was staggering.

Then a small gasp escaped her. "Your parents! What if they heard? It's probably national headlines by now."

"I called them on my way to get Sam."

"Oh. Good."

Her worry about them nearly sent his emotions spiraling out of control; she'd hadn't even met them yet, but they were connected to him and so she cared. The enormity of what he'd found with her was truly beginning to sink in.

"Daria."

She tilted her head back. And for a moment, as those stunning golden-brown eyes looked up at him, he completely lost the power of speech. So he kissed her instead, trying to put the words he couldn't find into it. He poured everything he was feeling into that lip-lock and ended up setting them both on fire.

"Wow," she said, sounding a bit wobbly when at last he broke the kiss. "That was…"

"That," he said carefully, "was because for a moment I couldn't find the words."

"I'm not sure mere words could match that. But what words?"

"I love you."

Her eyes widened. "Stefan," she began.

He shook his head. "I don't expect it back, not now, not when your whole life's been upended. But… I needed you to know."

She said his name again, softly, and hugged him. Hung on as if he were the only thing holding her in place.

"Do you really know somebody with that cabin with no cell or internet?" he asked after a moment.

"Yes."

"Does it have a bed?"

He heard the smile in her voice as she again said, "Yes."

"Can we borrow it?"

"I'm sure we could." But then she pulled back sharply. Looked down at his side. "You're bleeding!"

He'd been vaguely aware of the dampness for a bit now but hadn't let it stop him, since that's all it was. "Seeping, I think. They said it would happen."

"We need to clean that up right now. And get you into something more comfortable."

"Naked's comfortable," he said in mock thoughtfulness.

She gave him an arch look. "You're in no condition—"

He pulled her back close. "I'd have to be dead not to want you."

This time she stayed there, and he thought in that moment, with her in his arms and his son down the hall, life was as close to perfect as it had ever been.

Chapter Thirty-Five

Three days. They'd had three days of peace and perfection, and Daria couldn't seem to stop smiling. The house that she had at first hesitated to buy because it was bigger than she alone needed was suddenly the perfect size. The weather outside was perfect, chilly but crystal clear. The warmth inside was perfect, with Stefan and Sam sitting at her table on this Saturday morning, the boy chattering excitedly about going outside as soon as he finished the French toast she'd fixed especially for him, because he'd once told her it was his favorite.

Even the ache inside her was perfect, because it was only there because of how full her heart was.

The day after Stefan had been released from the hospital had been a marvel of being together for all three of them. Sam had delighted in his explorations of her vast yard while she and Stefan, still taking it easy, had watched, arm in arm, both smiling so broadly it almost hurt. Waking up to the news that not only had Trey won his election, he'd won it handily, had been the icing on the cake.

"Thank you," her boss had said in a call just after the seasonally late sunrise. "It could easily have gone the other way if you hadn't wrapped up Shruggs when you did."

Daria had laughed. "I think you underestimate the respect you've built. But you're welcome anyway, if it did help."

"You always have had great timing," Trey had joked, and it had done her heart good to hear the lightness in his voice. "Now take a few days for yourself. You've earned it."

Normally she would have declined the offer, preferring to work. But not now. Now, she wanted to savor every second of together with the two men in her life.

"I will," she told him. "And when I come back, I'll need a few minutes with you for…something else."

"You can have my whole day," Trey had said, and she could almost see him grinning.

And when she'd hung up, it was to find Stefan grinning at her. "Gonna tell him you're his aunt?"

She rolled her eyes at him, then sighed. She had realized that particular connection somewhat belatedly, and while she had felt very strange about it, Stefan had only laughed.

"I hope that doesn't overly complicate things," she said.

"You broke the Avalanche Killer case. I think nobody's going to care."

"We."

His grin had widened at that. And he'd kissed her rather urgently; he'd clearly been feeling much better already.

Sam had only very reluctantly gone back to school the next day, although the excitement of his grandparents arriving this weekend was a distraction. And she decided she would sort out the tangle of actually being a Colton by blood—albeit a very different branch than her adoptive one—eventually. She didn't need or want the rich connections, but maybe she would take the name back. Eventually.

And come Sunday—God help her, tomorrow—she would meet the parents. Stefan's mother and father had already assumed epic proportions in her mind, and she was having to make an effort not to be intimidated.

Chastising herself for her nerves, given that it had to be a lot more momentous for Sam, she put that aside and tried to savor the day. She had hours of peace and quiet coming to her, and she was going to take them. She had the two people she had come to treasure under her roof, and she was going to enjoy that. She wanted to savor this perfection and didn't want anything to change the way she felt at this moment in time.

All brought on by three little words. *I love you.*

That night Stefan steamrollered her protests about his injury as if intent on proving the truth of those words—and that he was physically fine, more than fine—driving her body to new heights with a fierce intensity that she supposed was born of having escaped an injury that could have been much worse. If this was what getting shot and surviving did to you, no wonder some people became danger junkies.

And in the quiet aftermath she returned the words, although she had to work up to it.

"I hope your parents like me," she said quietly into the dark.

"They will."

"That's good. Because otherwise it's going to be awkward when I tell them how much I love their son."

Stefan went very still beside her. She heard him swallow, as if his throat was tight. "You think maybe you could tell him first?"

She lifted up on one elbow. Reached out to cup his cheek. "I suppose I could. I love you, Stefan Roberts. For so many, many reasons."

"Even as a...package deal?"

He sounded slightly hesitant, and it took her a moment to understand. "You mean Sam?" He nodded. "I wouldn't have it any other way," she assured him. "I'm quite enamored of the little charmer he's become."

"That's good, since it's thanks to you. He's crazy about you, too."

She smiled, widely, at the admission in that *too*. But she answered the just now more important part. "Don't discount yourself in that process. You've made great strides together."

"Only because you showed me the path," he insisted gruffly.

That night, when they both went to tuck Sam in, it was clear the boy was nervous about the imminent arrival of the grandparents he'd never met.

"They're going to spoil you rotten," Stefan told his son.

"What's that mean?"

"It means that, unlike me, they'll find you very hard to say no to. Use that power carefully."

Sam blinked. "You're funny, Dad."

Daria saw Stefan blink a couple of times, rapidly. It hadn't been so long ago that Sam never called him Dad—now he always did.

"He is," Daria confirmed, saving him from trying to speak just then.

But then the boy had sighed sadly.

"I thought you were looking forward to meeting them," Stefan said, his voice steady enough now.

"I am. I just… I don't wanna go back to the other house." He gave Daria a sideways, shy look. "I wish we could stay here. F'rever."

Daria thought her heart would melt at the longing in the boy's deep brown eyes. "Me, too, Sam," she whispered.

She sensed rather than saw Stefan go very still beside her. But he waited until they were back in the living room before he spoke.

"Did you mean that?" His voice sounded oddly strained, as if he were having to try and keep his emotions in check.

She didn't pretend not to understand; they were way past that. She had been happy here, in the nest she'd built. But it had begun to seem much too empty. Until now. "Yes," she said simply.

"Daria—" He stopped, swallowed. "Are you sure?"

"Very. I could give you a string of reasons why it only makes sense," she said. "I have more room, especially outside for Sam to play. He wouldn't have to change schools, and you would actually be closer to your office."

"All true." He said it, then stopped, as if he knew there was more. There was, and she said it.

"But the most important reason is I love both of you, in a way I was afraid I never could. Until now this place has been a…cozy nest for me, but it's been an empty one. Now it finally feels right."

For a moment he just stared at her. But then she was in his arms, and he kissed her until her blood was singing in her ears and her pulse was hammering with all the swirling emotions only this man had ever roused in her.

"Can I take that as a yes?" she asked when she could breathe again.

"Daria." He said her name as if it were the only thing he could get out.

"I know there'll be details, and changes—I was thinking we could turn the den into a game room, and I've been thinking about moving my office into the sunroom in the back, so if you need an office of your own—"

He put a finger to her lips to hush her. "I'll share. I just want to be with you."

"Your parents—"

"Will be fine with it. Once they see us together, they'll know."

"Know?"

He gave her a slightly crooked smile that made her stomach do a little flip. "That I finally figured it out. And found what they have." His expression changed slightly. "Fair warning, they're very traditional. They're going to ask when we're getting married."

"And what will your answer be?"

He reached out and ran the back of his fingers lightly over her cheek, as if she were some precious, fragile thing. "I'll tell them as soon as I can convince you."

"I can hardly wait. You do some pretty impressive convincing."

He laughed. Daria let the sound wash over her. There was still much to do professionally, first and foremost the still-unsolved murder of Sabrina Gilford. But her personal life had never looked better. And she knew with Stefan's solid, clearheaded help, she would find her way through the complications of the changes in her self-identity.

With this man beside her, and with Sam to bring her the kind of delight she'd never dreamed possible, her future was suddenly as bright as the sun on new snow.

* * * * *

COMING SOON!

We really hope you enjoyed reading this book. If you're looking for more romance, be sure to head to the shops when new books are available on

Thursday 14th November

To see which titles are coming soon, please visit
millsandboon.co.uk/nextmonth

MILLS & BOON
Desire

Indulge in secrets and scandal, intense
drama and plenty of sizzling hot action
with powerful and passionate heroes who
have it all: wealth, status, good looks…
everything but the right woman.

Six Desire stories published every month, find them all a

millsandboon.co.uk/Desire

LET'S TALK
Romance

For exclusive extracts, competitions
and special offers, find us online:

f facebook.com/millsandboon

🐦 @MillsandBoon

📷 @MillsandBoonUK

Get in touch on 01413 063232

For all the latest titles coming soon, visit
millsandboon.co.uk/nextmonth

MILLS & BOON

THE HEART OF ROMANCE

A ROMANCE FOR EVERY KIND OF READER

MODERN

Prepare to be swept off your feet by sophisticated, sexy and seductive heroes, in some of the world's most glamourous and romantic locations, where power and passion collide.
8 stories per month.

HISTORICAL

Escape with historical heroes from time gone by. Whether your passion is for wicked Regency Rakes, muscled Vikings or rugged Highlanders, awaken the romance of the past.
6 stories per month.

MEDICAL

Set your pulse racing with dedicated, delectable doctors in the high-pressure world of medicine, where emotions run high and passion, comfort and love are the best medicine.
6 stories per month.

True Love

Celebrate true love with tender stories of heartfelt romance, the rush of falling in love to the joy a new baby can bring, and focus on the emotional heart of a relationship.
8 stories per month.

Desire

Indulge in secrets and scandal, intense drama and plenty of sizzling hot action with powerful and passionate heroes who have it all: wealth, status, good looks…everything but the right woman.
6 stories per month.

HEROES

Experience all the excitement of a gripping thriller, with an intense romance at its heart. Resourceful, true-to-life women and strong, fearless men face danger and desire - a killer combination!
8 stories per month.

DARE

Sensual love stories featuring smart, sassy heroines you'd want as a best friend, and compelling intense heroes who are worthy of them.
4 stories per month.

To see which titles are coming soon, please visit

millsandboon.co.uk/nextmonth

JOIN US ON SOCIAL MEDIA!

Stay up to date with our latest releases, author
news and gossip, special offers and discounts, and
all the behind-the-scenes action
from Mills & Boon...

 millsandboon

 millsandboonuk

 millsandboon

might just be true love...

MILLS & BOON

MODERN

Power and Passion

Prepare to be swept off your feet by sophisticated, sexy and seductive heroes, in some of the world's most glamourous and romantic locations, where power and passion collide.

Julia James
Heiress's
PREGNANCY SCANDAL

Jennie Lucas
Chosen as the
SHEIKH'S ROYAL BRIDE

Kim Lawrence
A WEDDING *at the* **ITALIAN'S DEMAND**

Sharon Kendrick
The
SHEIKH'S SECRET BABY

MILLS & BOON
True Love
Romance from the Heart

Celebrate true love with tender stories of
heartfelt romance, from the rush of falling
in love to the joy a new baby can bring,
and a focus on the emotional
heart of a relationship.